W9-BLC-804

# Big Girl Small

**Center Point
Large Print**

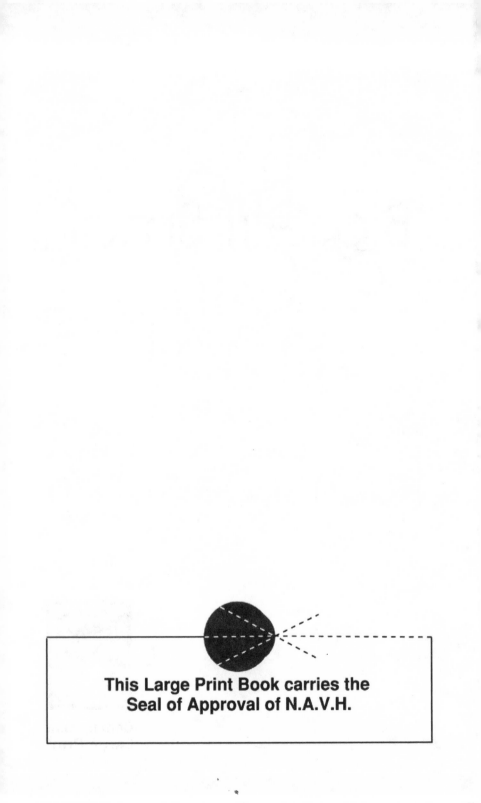

**This Large Print Book carries the
Seal of Approval of N.A.V.H.**

# Big
# Girl
# Small

## Rachel DeWoskin

South Country Library
22 Station Road
Bellport, NY 11713

CENTER POINT LARGE PRINT
THORNDIKE, MAINE

JUL 2 8 2011

This Center Point Large Print edition is published in the year 2011 by arrangement with Farrar, Straus and Giroux.

Copyright © 2011 by Rachel DeWoskin.

All rights reserved.

Grateful acknowledgment is made for permission to reprint excerpts from the following: "We Belong Together" by Rickie Lee Jones. Copyright © 1981 by Rickie Lee Jones. Reprinted by permission of Rickie Lee Jones. *Runaways* by Elizabeth Swados. Reprinted by permission of Samuel French, Inc.

The text of this Large Print edition is unabridged. In other aspects, this book may vary from the original edition. Printed in the United States of America. Set in 16-point Times New Roman type.

ISBN: 978-1-61173-113-2

Library of Congress Cataloging-in-Publication Data

DeWoskin, Rachel.
  Big girl small / Rachel DeWoskin.
     p. cm.
  ISBN 978-1-61173-113-2 (library binding : alk. paper)
  1. Teenage girls—Fiction. 2. Dwarfs—Fiction.
     3. High school students—Fiction. 4. Adolescence—Fiction.
     5. Large type books. I. Title.
  PS3604.E927B54 2011b
  813′.6—dc22
                                                    2011007263

For my spectacular daughters,
Dalin and Light

1 When people make you feel small, it means they shrink you down close to nothing, diminish you, make you feel like shit. In fact, *small* and *shit* are like equivalent words in English. It makes sense, in a way. Not that small and shit are the same, I mean, but that Americans might think that. Take *The Wizard of Oz*, for example, an American classic everyone loves more than anything even though there's a whole "Munchkinland" of embarrassed people, half of them dressed in pink rompers and licking lollipops even though they're thirty years old. They don't even have names in the credits; it just says at the end, "Munchkins played by 'The Singer Midgets.'" Judy Garland apparently loved gay people, was even something of an activist, but she spread rumors about how the "midgets" were so raucous, fucking each other all the time and drinking bourbon on the set. People love those stories because it's so much fun to think of tiny people having sex. There was even an urban myth about how one of the dwarfs hanged himself—everyone said you could see him swinging in the back of the shot—but it turns out it was actually an emu. Right. A bird they got to make the forest look "magical." And what with the five-inch TVs everyone had in those

days, the two-pixel bird spreading its dirty wings apparently called to mind a dead dwarf. In other words, people wanted it bad enough to believe that's what it was. Magical, my ass. I know that small and shit are the same because I'm sixteen years old and three feet nine inches tall.

Judy Garland was sixteen too, when she made *Wizard of Oz*, but I'm betting she must have felt like she was nine feet tall, getting to be a movie star and all. I should have known better than to try for stardom myself, because even though my mom sang me "Thumbelina" every night of my life, she also took me to *Saturday Night Live* once when we were in New York on a family vacation, and it happened that the night I was there they had dozens of little people falling off choral risers as one of their skits. My mom almost died of horror, weeping in the audience. Everyone around us thought she was touched, that all those idiots on stage must have been, like, her other kids. Like they were my beautiful Munchkin brothers or something, even though my mom's average-size and so are my two brothers. They'd even have average lives, if only they didn't have me. My mother's idea has always been to try to make me feel close to perfect, but how close can that be, considering I look like she snatched me from some dollhouse.

Nothing on *Saturday Night Live* is ever funny, but the night we went was especially bad. One of the little people even got hurt falling off those risers, but no one thought anything of it, except my mom, who made a point of waiting for an hour after the show was done, to ask was he okay. I was furious, because everyone who walked by us kept saying "Good show" to me.

I would never be in anything of the sort, by the way, because my parents don't believe in circus humiliation. That's what my college essay was going to be on, freak shows and the Hottentot Venus. Most people don't know that much about her, except that she was famous for having a butt so big the Victorians couldn't believe it. So they made her into an attraction people could pay money to stare at and grope. I bet you didn't know, for example, that her name was Saartjie, or "Little Sarah," or that she even had a name. The "Little" in her name is the cute, endearing version of the word, not the literal *little*. Or even worse, *belittle,* which, by com-bining *be* and *little,* means "to make fun of." I think I would have included that definition as, like, the denouement of my essay, after the climax, where I planned to mention that after her nightmare carnival life, Little Sarah died at twenty-six and they preserved her ass on display in a Paris museum. She was orphaned in a commando raid in South Africa; otherwise maybe none of those terrible things would have happened to her.

I have parents, thankfully. And they always tried to keep me private. I don't mean they hid me in a closet or anything, but they also didn't let people take pictures of me when we traveled or touch me for money. And when people stared, even kids, my parents stared back, unblinking, but friendly-like. The thing is, you can't blame kids for staring. Not only because I'm miniature, but also because I'm a little bit "disproportionate." That's what they call it when the fit of your parts is in any way off the mainstream chart: "disproportionate." Maybe your arms or legs are too stumpy or your torso is small and your head is huge. Or maybe you're just you, like Saartjie Hottentot, and it's only relative to everyone else that you're disproportionate. Maybe someday they'll think *disproportionate dwarf* is a rude expression and they'll come up with a nicer way to put it. I think most people know now that *Hottentot* is considered a rude word. Maybe not, though. Most people are stupid as hell when it comes to things like which words are rude. And a lot of people, even once they find out which words hurt people, still like to use them. They think it's smarmy and "PC" to have to say things kindly, or that it's too much pressure not to be able to punish freaks with words like *freak*.

Anyway, my parents would never even let me audition for *American Idol*, even though I can really sing, because they know Simon Cowell laughs at all the deformed people. It's complicated, since my mom and dad would never admit that my "situation" qualifies, but they still have to protect me. Because of this quandary, they finally broke down and agreed to send me to a performing arts high school last fall for my junior year, which is what caused this whole hideous nightmare in the first place.

Maybe my parents should have admitted that dwarfs are better off cloistered or hanging in some forest of Oz, and saved me the humiliation of having tried to pretend I'm fit to attend a flashy school. My parents are five feet six and six feet one, but they're on every board of every dwarf association in the world, and they use the words *little people* like there was never any other way to put it. They take me to "little people" conferences and manage to blend right in. So maybe from their dreamy bubble, it seemed possible that my "stellar academic performance" and charming personality would earn me popularity and favor among the rest of the kids, that I'd be a beloved Lilliputian among the Brobdingnagians.

That's not how it turned out. I should say right here, though, that what happened is not my parents' fault, and that I don't blame them.

They're probably frantic right now, or dead from ulcers or heart attacks. I know they're searching for me, and the thought of it makes me physically sick. I guess because I love them. But I can't come out of here yet, don't know when I'll ever be able to rejoin the world.

Because most of society, including Darcy Arts Academy, is nothing like my parents. You can get a sense of the difference if you take a look online. I'll give you an example. Google "little people" and you get 8 million hits, most of which are for stumpy Fisher-Price figures with no legs. If you look up "small people," you get under a million (but at least one of the first two is the charming lyric "short people got no reason to live," preceding a story about tiny ancient people who hunted rats and lizards near the Java Sea). Call it predictable, but if you search "midget," you get 21 million hits, about 20 million of which are YouTube videos of "midget fights," "midget bowling," or "midget Michael Jacksons." There's also the really nice website TinyEntertainer.com, with its "Rent a Midget" logo scrolling across the screen like breaking news ticker tape. And if you type in "midget girl," you get nakedmidgetsex@hoes.com. Maybe up in the big world it's difficult to understand why midgets might hate the word *midget,* but here, I'll help. The Little People's Association explains it like this:

the term has fallen into disfavor and is considered offensive by most people of short stature. The term dates back to 1865, the height of the "freak show" era, and was generally applied only to short-statured persons who were displayed for public amusement, which is why it is considered so unacceptable today. Such terms as dwarf, little person, LP, and person of short stature are all acceptable, but most people would rather be referred to by their name than by a label.

"Fallen into disfavor." I love that. So everyone can call me Judy, even after I get a job as a hot porno midget escort, because there's nowhere else for me to go from here. It's funny how I've reached the bottom of something, but up is still not an option.

My parents named me Judy accidentally, by the way, without realizing that Judy Garland was a dwarf mocker. Judy has always been my mom's favorite name, and who doesn't love that Klimt picture of Judith holding Holofernes' head? Maybe someday there'll be a picture of me holding Kyle Malanack's head, although it'll be a smudged newspaper photo, ripped digitally from the security camera of a parking garage or something. I doubt people will produce millions

13

of prints for dorm rooms. Although maybe they will. Some kids love a villain.

I *was* brilliant in school, by the way. You have to be smart as well as talented in some other, "artistic" way to get into Darcy. Maybe that will be the next story, when it breaks, when they find me here. The sequel. Lots of Darcy kids being like, "She seemed so, well, normal!" Except they'll have to stop themselves: "I mean, not normal, but you know, sweet"—except they'll have to stop themselves there, too, because I wasn't sweet, exactly, was kind of sarcastic, for a doll of a girl. "Well," they'll have to concede, "after what happened to her, I mean, who wouldn't lose it?" They all know what happened. It's too horrible to contemplate, and I wish I didn't know. What they should say is that I was too smart for my own good, that it would have been better to be an animal, not to know what I was missing, not to have been able to see my life. A little bit of ignorance would have saved me. What good is there in seeing your situation clearly if there's no escape from it? I'd love to hear the story of my academic genius, if there were any way of interpreting it other than that I've had to overcompensate every second of my life.

Here, news media, here's a sound bite for when you find me: if you're born saddled with a word like *Achondroplasia*, you learn to spell. If

14

the first boy you dare love pulls the worst Stephen King *Carrie* prank in the history of dating, then you run and hide. Because who can love you after that? Maybe your parents. But how can you face them, when you've all spent so much time convincing each other that you're normal?

All I'm saying is, if you're me, and you can't reach a gas pump, pay phone, or ATM, and your arms and legs are disproportionately short, and your mouth is too impossible to kiss without it becoming a public carnival, then you don't get to be included in anything but the now obsolete, original meaning of the stupid word *normal*. Which, believe it or not, according to the *OED*, is *rare*.

So I'm the rare dwarf at the Motel Manor on the outskirts of Ypsi, close enough to my parents that they should have found me by now, and maybe in more danger than I can guess at. And you know what? I don't care. I hope the story ends here. It's fine if it does. I mean, that way I'll be the dream come true of all those hopeful *Oz* watchers, waiting for a dwarf to hang.

*Thumbelina, Thumbelina, tiny little thing. Thumbelina dance, Thumbelina sing. Thumbelina, it makes no difference if you're very small, for when your heart is full of love you're nine feet tall.*

2 The hot pink eighties were already over when my parents moved from St. Louis to Michigan with my older brother, Chad, and opened a restaurant called Judy's Grill. It would be more touching if they'd named the restaurant after me instead of naming me after the restaurant, but whatever. I could pretend I was born before it opened, and was such an adorable baby that they couldn't think of a better name for the place where they'd throw globs of meat on a grill, but in fact, Judy's came first. My mother got pregnant the same spring they arrived, and stood behind the counter, with Chad in one of those mechanized swings that rocks a baby back and forth until he falls asleep watching animals rotate above his head. She poured coffee, served sizzling foods to customers just starting to become regulars, and loosened her apron ties more and more until she was too pregnant to work. Then she went to the hospital and had me. My dad found her sexy, even bloated with the fifty pounds she gained pregnant; there are pictures of him leering at her giant ankles, even one of him grabbing her Hottentot ass.

As for the birth, my mom was kind of a peasant about the whole thing. I mean, she spent only a week at home after I was born before she brought me to work, where she nursed me in the kitchen between shifts. Even though I had some medical problems, my mother stopped working only when I was actually being cut open like tropical fruit to have a trach put in because my tubes were too small to let me breathe right. I don't remember that, by the way; it happened when I was a baby. But my mom remembers it like it happened ten minutes ago, because every time I cough, I can feel her start running from wherever she is in the house. When I was healthy, she always had me at Judy's Grill with them. She was like the Chinese woman in that book *The Good Earth* that we read in eighth-grade English. The wife, I mean, who keeps getting knocked up over and over and going into the back room and giving birth by herself, gnawing off the umbilical cord and rushing back to work in the fields the next day like a slave, with the baby strapped to her back. My mom's that type. Uncomplaining, I mean. I think it's a point of pride with her. I'm a complainer, myself. But I guess my mom was also desperate to get back to work with my dad. She likes work. And she likes my dad. She never stops moving, racing, doing—except at night, when everything she's had to do all day is done—and then she reads *New York Times* bestsellers. But not brand new ones. Older ones that she checks out of the Ann Arbor District Library. When she's finished with them, she leaves them on my nightstand with the due-date cards sticking out like reminders that I have a deadline. Sometimes I read them. Not usually.

My dad thinks it's cute that my mom keeps so busy. He's busy too, but in a kind of understated way. He smokes a pipe and listens to Ella Fitzgerald and Louis Armstrong, and on his most hip days, Cassandra Wilson, who he found out about by watching a PBS documentary about jazz. My dad is the kind of guy who will do whatever the rest of us want to do, which means when he's not working or fixing things, he's mostly watching Michigan football with Chad, wearing the "M Go Blue" sweatshirt my mom bought him at parents' weekend. They're very proud of Chad for going to U of M and being a swimmer and so handsome and well-adjusted and smart. And even if they weren't, they'd still be the types to go to parents' weekend as if they had traveled from two thousand miles away, even though we live ten minutes from campus.

Maybe the busy hum of Judy's Grill was a relief for my mom, compared to life with me. She loves the grill with a pathological devotion; I wouldn't be surprised if she squirted her own breast milk directly into people's coffee mugs when she went back to work that first week after I was born. Maybe it was a happy, distracting refuge from the horrors of my babyhood. The grill is full of clutter, the smell of shimmering fries fresh out of the metal oil basket, the crunch of pepper grinders, chatter and smack of people eating. There's nothing to eat in hospitals; even when there's food there, it tastes like Lysol. And anyway, who has an appetite in a place where the walls look so much like the floor that you're swimming even as you walk? The U of M hospital smells, looks, and tastes like an antiseptic nothing. Judy's Grill is a hot red place.

No mom loves watching her tiny dwarf baby get strapped to a gurney, but my mom is pretty tough. My dad still talks about how she cleaned my trach tube every ten seconds for the whole year and a half I had the thing in. He apparently could barely handle it, not because it was gross, he swears, but because he was so freaked out that he'd do it wrong. My mom has always claimed that she had never loved anything the way she immediately loved me. Chad is expected to live with that part of the family lore—I mean, he got a fabulous life so why can't I at least get to be our mom's favorite? Plus, I'm a girl, and the way my mom tells it, she really wanted a girl "for herself," the idea being that Chad was for my dad. And it's true that Chad and my dad are perfect for each other. Chad's as noisy and fun as my dad is quiet. He drags my dad out to play football in the backyard, scandalizes him with obscene jokes, and does a brilliant imitation of

19

our mom: "Chad! Judy! Sam! I hear a riot! Someone's about to get hurt! And it's going to be Sam!" Her cute Midwestern accent, all nasal and young-sounding.

My mom grew up on a working farm, and she still lives on an animal clock, awake at the first flicker of light in the sky. She prefers chores when the air is still icy and silent, and makes us breakfast at dawn every morning before she and my dad take off for the Grill to feed dozens of other people all day. She also builds and fixes things—TVs, the roof on our house, the tiles in the bathroom. The only thing she leaves for my father to fix is the car, and she encourages him to do that as often as possible, even, I think, when it's not broken. For their anniversary once, she bought him a board with wheels on it so he can jack the car up a bit and roll underneath it. I think she finds mechanics sexy, and my dad is game. I mean, he fixes the car sometimes, or at least pretends to. Fills it with oil or something. My mom keeps a framed picture of him on her nightstand, even though if she wanted to, she could just look over at him, sleeping next to her. In the picture, he's rolling out from under the car, grease on his hands and a monkey wrench held up victoriously above him like it's a weapon.

But even though my mom likes my dad, what she loves most is the three of us. And she went all the way with the claim that she loved me unconditionally—by having another baby after me. I take my little brother, Sam, as proof that my parents weren't scared off the project. And my mom was rewarded for her bravado, because Sam is the best person anyone has ever met. We all love him most. It's hard to explain except to say that he's a delicately wired twelve-year-old with buckteeth and braces, that he weighs less than sixty pounds, has no irony, and takes hip-hop classes on the weekends at the rec center. He wears his Levi's so low they show his Hanes, and just generally tries so hard it's heartbreaking.

I can almost imagine Ann Arbor back before me and Sam, when Chad was a little baby and my parents were all hopeful and young. The place would have had more boutiques and fewer strip malls, the same stadium and roads, but I always picture it as an old-fashioned college town, music pouring out the windows of Hill Auditorium, dancers in the shadows at Power Center, the Brown Jug lit up on campus, open all night. That's where Michigan students sat drinking thin, pre-Starbucks coffee out of cream-colored diner mugs. Judy's Grill is right across from the Brown Jug, on South University. My mom and dad chose a red color pattern, pizza parlor lanterns, booths, and gingham tablecloths. Eventually they even got a jukebox, and some-times students hang out there when there are no tables at the Brown Jug, listening to the crappy oldies my parents picked—like Journey and REO Speedwagon.

Not to romanticize too much, though, because it's usually old people in there, gumming meat loaf and sipping stew through straws. Retirees never put money in the jukebox, so my mom plays them "Happy Together" and the Beatles for free. They love it. And they love me; I'm like the everlasting infant mascot of Judy's Grill.

Sometimes I think the Grill must have been an absolute Norman Rockwell print before I arrived. And then wham! All of a sudden there was a spontaneous genetic mutation, maybe in her egg, maybe in one of my dad's sperm. It's too gross to contemplate that part, since we all know where it goes, but did a dwarf sperm swim up to an average-size egg and hit on it like, "I have other things to offer?" Or was the egg a little bit small? Anyway, there it was. Some famous doctor my parents once had examine me in a hotel room at a conference told them it's usually the sperm's fault when your baby's a dwarf. I wonder if that made my dad feel guilty.

My mom knew she was pregnant right away because of the constant barfing, but they didn't know about "that" until later, at twenty weeks, to be precise, when the docs noticed "fore-shortened limbs" and something about my pelvis on the ultrasound screen. Maybe the technician at the U of M hospital was like, "Oh, let me get the doctor," because apparently you can tell from an ultrasound if your baby is "of short stature," which is pretty hilarious, because what unborn baby isn't of short stature? I mean, foreshortened limbs? Anyway, then my parents were probably like, "Is everything okay, technician?" and she was like, "I'll let the doctor explain," and the rest of their lives were mapped out from that moment: my dad's old-school-ness about the whole abortion thing, the baby they already had, how now his life would be affected by this shit, the deformed one taking up all the attention, the kinds of conversations they must have had, the final decision. Let's keep her anyway! Or maybe it's the way they present it now, like they didn't even consider putting me back. That my mom heard about my dwarfism and loved me even more. More than anything, even Chad, her lanky, healthy toddler. But it wasn't the Dark Ages. They had ultrasound technology, and when I first found out about that, in seventh-grade health class at Tappan Middle School, I started asking my parents all the time if they had considered a do-over, but that's not the sort of question where you'll ever get the straight answer you want. Anyway, now I've ruined their lives by ruining mine. So even if they didn't regret having me then, maybe they do now. Health class is the same one where our teacher once said, "Do you girls want to know the only thing you need to stay out of trouble?" and we were all like, "What, Mr. Katz?" and he said, "A dime," so we all looked at each other like, "What the hell is he talking about?" and he said, "Take the dime and put it between your knees and hold it there, and that way you'll stay out of trouble."

Speaking of trouble, I once read that parents of kids with childhood leukemia suffer more post-traumatic stress disorders and recurring nightmares than the kids themselves do. I can see why. Watching your kid suffer has to suck at least as much as suffering yourself. If my mom could give me her legs, I bet she would. And I'd take them, too, because I'm that kind of person. I'd rip them right off, and use them to tower above and hop over everyone like I was on pogo sticks. It's a fact, even though it's hypothetical, do you know what I mean? If she could, my mom would give her legs to me, and I would take them. And that's why I can never go home again, because having to watch me die of misery over this Darcy scandal might be even more hideous for them than it is for me, if that's possible. The funny thing is, I'm not a totally bad person, and I know it because if I could choose to make my little brother, Sam, live my life and me live his, I wouldn't. I'd rather this be me than have to watch it be him, even though he's a boy. Because if I had to watch him go through this, that would kill me. I don't know why I feel that way about Sam and not my parents. Maybe because he's little and they're grown-ups.

The horror show didn't start right away at Darcy, by the way. I was the happiest I'd ever been before I became the unhappiest. I think people are all that way; if you have the capacity to experience huge, engulfing joy, then you can also feel its equal and opposite level of pain. My diary entries are like the lines on a graph, shooting up and up toward Thanksgiving and then rocketing off the page by Christmas. Of course it's not a very useful graph for drawing conclusions, since I didn't record them plummeting; they just disappear entirely.

My parents were nervous the summer before I started at D'Arts, talking in whispers and then changing the subject when I'd come in after swimming at Fuller Pool with Meghan, my best dwarf friend, who I met at an LPA convention in Florida four years ago. Those are where little people from all over the place get together and become friends. Our parents met there, too, and liked each other—they're all average-size, although Meghan has a little-person older brother, too, and an average-size older sister. She comes every other summer for a week, and then I go to her place in Northern California. Whenever Meghan and I are together, we talk

25

about how much we wish we lived in the same place. She's an achon too, so we look alike and everyone thinks we're sisters and that's okay, even though we hate it when people assume we're sisters with, like, every other random dwarf in the universe. At that first LPA conference where I met Meghan, there were tons of teenagers, but she and I were the only two twelve-year-old girls. The next year, there were a bunch of younger guys, but no guys our age, and when we were fourteen, there were, like, no teenagers at all. It's random. Last year, I met a guy named Joel who was kind of okay, and we danced a few times and even went swimming late at night, but I was embarrassed that all the grown-ups there seemed to think that dwarf teenagers should get married right away in case no one else ever agrees to marry us. I mean, I danced with the guy like three times and tons of people were pulling my parents aside like, "I think they're a great couple, don't you?"

My parents, good on most things, said, "We're glad Judy seems to be making friends and having fun," and left it at that. They're not the types to try to match-make.

And even though they spent the whole summer worrying, my mom and dad gamely dropped me off on the first morning at Darcy, trying their best to comment cheerily on the "fabulous" student murals decorating the walls, and the "creative" vibe of the place. They kept up their tradition of staring the welcoming stare at anyone who ogled me, although I was finally like, "People are staring at me because my parents are at school with me. Please leave immediately." I told them I already looked like a six-year-old, could they please not make matters more unbearable by staying. But they didn't listen, and sat through the whole morning of meetings and orientations, including a private twenty-minute chat with the principal, Mr. Grames, and a school counselor named Mrs. O'Henry: "We have access to world-class medical facilities and are committed to our students' physical and psychological well-being, Judy. I hope you'll contact me right away with any concerns or if you need anything at all."

At lunchtime, they swept me away from the possible horrors of the cafeteria: my legs dangling from a bench, no one to sit with, some movie-worthy bully slapping my sloppy joe tray into the air and stealing my milk money. They took me off "campus" to Zingerman's, where we all ate turkey Reubens. I chewed four pieces of spearmint Eclipse on the walk back and spat them out in the trash can at the back entrance to the school. My parents insisted on walking to the door to drop me off, and tried to kiss and smother me as if I were leaving for a hundred years instead of three more hours of high school. But I fought them off and they left. I was desperately relieved to see them go.

Walking back in, I felt less sure of myself, though. The halls were bulging with kids hugging each other, throwing books into their lockers, slinging on fashionable backpacks, singing, leaping. It was like that old movie *Fame*, the one that has no plot at all and is just a montage of beautiful people in tights, alternately weeping and fucking and frolicking. I chewed more gum. One girl was crying, and an absolute soap star of a high school boy was hugging her. I thought *Spring Awakening*, just knew they serenaded each other and danced through fields together on the weekends. Their life was definitely a rock musical, and they were probably engaged, or at least "going steady." I felt sick, tried to focus on the student murals my parents had pretended to admire: swirling, spotted, punked-out zebras in rainbow colors, kids dancing, and a Greek goddess with her hair trailing all the way from one end of an orange hallway to the other. The lockers are all painted by students, too; one of the big bonuses of the place is that you're allowed to decorate the outside of your locker, not just the inside like at most regular schools. It's a big competition, of course, and there are stories of the most famous lockers ever, like Sophie Armaria's. She graduated ten years ago but people still reminisce about how she painted herself naked on her locker, in thick, glistening oil, so that the combination dial was one of her nipples. The school didn't know what to do. Did they "censor" her or celebrate her artistic freedom? Grown-ups are so idiotic. I mean, who cares? Finally they asked her (I'm not joking) to paint a bikini on the thing. She refused, and Darcy put some tape over the locker's privates. Unbelievable. Sophie, apparently even more deeply in love with herself than ever before, wrote "CENSORED!" in black lettering on the tape. When I first started, people were obsessed with a senior named Amanda Fulton's locker; she created a mosaic on it out of beads and glass tiles and photographs of her friends. She spent, like, her whole four years at D'Arts working on the thing. The photos look all 3-D, because she framed them and then broke the glass, so each face had at least a few shards of glass over it. It was incredibly cool, actually. I wish I were Amanda Fulton. Or at least one of her friends, framed for eternity (well, four years of high school) on that locker. Some kids who can't think of anything better pretend to be above the whole thing and paint their lockers black. Others "tag" them with fake street graffiti. The truth is, the whole scene is a little fake, but I spent the whole postlunch orientation meeting contemplating how I could amaze everyone with my locker decorations. Maybe I'd do something with tissue paper—make an enormous garden, blooming out into the hallway. Or a mint farm with boxes of Eclipse gum. Of course then everyone would steal it and chew it up. Maybe I would use marbles somehow. Was there a way to fasten marbles to a vertical metal surface? It was good I had this to think about, since otherwise the orientation was nothing but an excruciating, dwarf-peek-sneaking affair about "sensitivity to race and gender issues."

In other words, "We do not discriminate on the basis of gender, race, color, handicapped status, sexual orientation, religion, or national or ethnic origin, so you shouldn't shout racial epithets at the two black people allowed in or refuse to pick the dwarf for your kickball team." Everyone kept looking over at me, especially these girls I later figured out were Amanda Fulton and Carrie Shultz. They were dressed alike in superexpensive jeans, with all the seams sewn on the outside, and button-up blouses buttoned down enough that their black lacy bras were just visible. I tugged at the jeans my mom and I had bought in the children's department at Nordstrom's for my first day—they were the most expensive ones I'd ever had, $118. My mom had splurged, the whole time marveling with me over the fact that people would spend more than a hundred dollars on jeans for a six- or seven-year-old, who would presumably grow out of them in a month or two. Then we were both quiet, maybe thinking I'd never grow out of them, and what the hell, we might as well spend thousands of dollars on designer jeans for me. I had on boots with heels, too, orthopedic but full of the effort to look stylish, a black T-shirt, and a dark pink cardigan. The truth is, in the mirror that morning, I'd felt pretty cute. I have good hair, is the thing—light brown with blond streaks in it, and a pretty good face, too. I don't have the mushed nose, broad forehead look, and my eyes aren't too wide apart. I have long eyelashes, which are darker than my hair even when I don't put mascara on. And my mouth is round and cute, with straight white teeth. Lots of people in Ann Arbor are used to me, by the way. It's not like I have no friends, it's just that I stupidly decided to leave my high school and go to Darcy so I could become famous and make everyone be like, "Remember Judy? We never thought she'd be the next—whatever, Peter Dinklage."

But that first day at Darcy, I kept thinking of my friends, starting the year at Huron, only several miles away. Why had I left devils I knew for ones I didn't? I wanted to go to Darcy desperately, that's the funny thing. Darcy Arts is Ann Arbor's private school answer to LaGuardia High. It's for talented performing arts kids, so everyone wants to go. If you live in Ann Arbor,

31

getting into D'Arts is almost like winning *American Idol*. Not to mention getting in for free. D'Arts has this friendly pretense that its scholarships aren't need-based, so if you get one, everyone's supposed to be like, "Wow, she's even more talented than the rest of us stars." But I needed the money, so everyone else who has a scholarship probably did too. My parents aren't poor or anything, but D'Arts costs almost as much as college (everyone there is always mentioning that). And I guess poor kids do have to be even more talented, because there must be more of us applying than kids who can pay. By the way, you're allowed to call it "D'Arts" only if you go—who wouldn't want that? And I know I keep mentioning *American Idol*. It's not my dream or anything, it's just an example of giving teenagers a shot at what they want most in the universe. The stakes are very high, is my point.

My parents were shocked that I wanted to go to Darcy. But I thought it was time for me to break out. I mean, they've always been overprotective and suffocating. So I explained that it would be a "perspective broadening" experience for me, and the truth is, I kind of thought it would be exactly that. I mean, I was tired of the same hundred kids I'd known since Angell Elementary, even though there was something safe in staying on with them, even the meanest, like Scott Declan, who has pointed and laughed literally every time he's seen me. Which is roughly two billion, six hundred and ninety-three million times, since we've gone to school together since first grade. You'd think someone like that could eventually get a grip, but apparently not. At least I stopped caring what Scott did or said when I turned eleven. If only I'd realized how delicious that safety was. I thought an escape to a more sophisticated school might benefit me, and that maybe I could become an intellectual powerhouse or Shakespearean actor like Peter Dinklage. Because I love Peter Dinklage. I even have a picture of him from *The Station Agent* that I keep in my wallet. And like I said earlier, I can really sing. And I can sort of write, at least school essays. I knew they'd let me in anyway, because how cool would it be to have a talented dwarf on their brochure for the rest of time? And even if I was wrong about everything else I ever thought in my whole life, I was right about that.

Mrs. O'Henry, the school counselor, kept smiling at me from the stage during the orientation, and every time she said "Any questions?" she looked right at me all hopefully, like she was just so thrilled to have a real live special-needs victim there for her sensitivity demonstration. I was like the moment she'd been waiting for, except I didn't ask anything, because, for one thing, I was chewing gum, and you're not allowed to have gum so I was keeping my mouth closed. For another, I had already signed up for an arts education. I would have to sing and act and probably dance a dwarf jig in front of everyone in town—that would be enough attention for me.

As soon as the meeting ended, I scuttled up to the library on the fourth floor of the building and sat alone, the hunchback in a dollhouse bell tower, clanging away. I arranged my books in a stack on the desk, opened a notebook, took out my favorite pink pen, and wrote "Judy" and "D'Arts." Then I doodled patterns—tiny schools of fish, stars, and striped hearts—under my name. The silence echoed around me and I wished terribly to be in the car on the way home with my parents, or already at home, or even on the AATA bus up Washtenaw to our house. I clicked my orthopedic heels together, imagining the intersection where Washtenaw meets Stadium, the little dip in the road, the bike path, the left turn, down the hill, past the speaking-in-tongues church, to where our house is. I was climbing out of the car in my mind when I heard the voice. I turned, away from the dream of my brothers playing basketball in the driveway, and as soon as I saw who was talking I thought I'd been catapulted out of reality into that movie *Mean Girls*, because the girl standing there was so pretty and bitchy-looking that my bones froze and my blood fizzed through my veins like grape pop. She had streaky blond hair that looked all intentionally messed up, and was wearing black yoga pants, flip-flops, and a gray Darcy Arts hoodie sweatshirt, an outfit that looked on her like it had cost thousands of dollars. She was probably five feet ten barefoot. She smiled.

"Um, hi," she said.

"Hi."

"I'm Ginger Mews," she said, sticking her hand down at me. I looked at it for a minute before shaking it with my stumpy paw. Her fingers were long and thin, but the nails were bitten down below the line, all ragged and scabby. Some of them even looked freshly bloodied. Maybe we could be friends.

"I'm Judy," I said, and she nodded.

"I know. I'm on the social staff, I mean, you know, the orientation staff. I just came by to welcome you to D'Arts and see if you needed anything, and, oh, to make sure you knew that there's a party this weekend at Chessie Andrewjeski's, so, you know, we hope you'll come."

"The social staff?"

"Mmm. We just, you know, welcome new students and stuff."

We stood there for a minute, while I contemplated what to say. Only the dwarfs? Thank

35

you? Had Mrs. O'Henry sent her after the meeting with my parents, and if so, what had she said to Ginger, "This girl needs your gorgeous, socially well-adjusted help"? I didn't know where to look, didn't want to stare up at her like a weird pet or a flower growing wildly toward the sun, but I also didn't want to just look away, lest she think I was rude. Mainly, I didn't want her to leave yet.

"You want some pretzels?"

"Sure," she said, glancing around. Food was forbidden in the library. I took a bag of Rold Gold out of my backpack and passed it to her, so she could reach in and take a polite, obligatory pretzel and stick the dry thing into her mouth. It was a gesture of solidarity, and, after she did it, she pulled a chair over to my carrel and sat. Maybe we would be best friends. Now that she was sitting, eye contact was easier to manage. I relaxed about one octave, imagined asking her to fetch books for me from high-up shelves, watching her lunge into the chairs in my room at home. Maybe we'd have a love montage, sip from a shared shake at Judy's, my parents swooning in the background.

"So do you have any questions about Darcy?" she asked.

"Do you ever have dwarf-tossing contests?"

It worked. She laughed hard enough that I could see some pretzel packed into her back teeth, and I had another surge of the dream that we would actually be best friends. My hope was so great that sarcasm left me for a moment. Even if it meant I had to sell out my own dignity for all of time by making dwarf jokes, I was happy to do that if it meant Ginger would come over and laugh her huge blond laugh. Plus, at least I would beat everyone else to making whatever jokes were going to be made about me.

"Excuse me!" the librarian suddenly shouted. She was as skinny as a fireplace poker, with puddle-colored hair that looked like it had been poured over her head and then dripped down onto her shoulders. She wore frameless eyeglasses and a plaid cardigan, buttoned all the way up. I wondered if she had gotten the job because she looked so much like a school librarian, or if she looked that way because she had gotten the job. Maybe we all eventually become calcified chunks of our own essence.

"There is absolutely no food allowed in the library, girls," she told us. "Put that away immediately, or I'll have to confiscate it!"

Ginger looked at me and rolled her eyes and made a chomping motion with her mouth, tipping the pretzel bag back toward her throat. This time we both laughed. The librarian had gone back to typing away on a huge, ancient computer. It seemed to me that a school with as much money as D'Arts could afford a desktop made this century, but maybe they reserved their funds for Broadway-style props and sets.

"You have AP history now, right?" Ginger asked.

I stuffed the pretzel bag into my book bag. "Yeah."

"I'll walk you." She stood up and shrugged, her long, messy hair falling over her shoulders. I caught a whiff of mint and lavender shampoo. Her life seemed perfect. I guessed she was the happiest person alive. She walked me to AP history and said good-bye at the door.

"You're not in this class?" I asked, both surprised that she'd come with me just out of niceness and alarmed that I was about to be left alone again.

"I'm in retard history," she said, and then realized something—I don't know what exactly —that I might consider myself an actual "retard"? That dwarfs and retards feel empathy for one another so she shouldn't use language like that around me? Some birds-of-an-offended-feather-type thing? Anyway, she was like, "Oh my god! I didn't mean—I just, I'm—" and flushed a horrible, violent pink. She looked beautiful.

I put on my most casual expression ever, even though I don't like that word. "Don't worry about it. Please—hey—do you want to, maybe we can—"

I don't even know what I was going to say—have coffee? Schedule a playdate? Fall in love? Sit at lunch together? See each other again? Be best friends? But it didn't matter, because Mr. Troudeau banged his gavel of a hand on the table and I scurried into a desk like a squirrel, with Ginger already gone down the long hallway. I missed the first half of the lecture, some shit about how making the choice to remember and how we remember and write history makes us who we are—because I was busy making up my mind to go to Chessie Andrewjeski's party. I would wear my black corduroy miniskirt, pile my hair on top of my head, and make hilarious and sarcastic quips all night, until everyone at D'Arts recognized how much sophisticated fun I was. It would be the new, wildly popular me.

3 This goth girl at D'Arts named Sarah wanted to be my friend as much as I wanted to be Ginger's. Goth Sarah. She was one of those girls who feels like a freak on the inside and wishes to be one on the outside, so she can express or at least represent her inner self better. It's like the way some kids cut themselves, so they can feel a physical version of whatever psychological pain they either have or think they have. Sarah wasn't really super punk or dark; she was kind of watered-down angsty-looking. She was actually conventionally very cute, but had tried to mask it by dying her hair an oily seal black, puncturing every possible surface with hoops and studs, and ripping her fishnets. She looked riddled by bullets, but wore pink lipstick and striped polo jerseys.

I later understood that preppy-goth is a Darcy type, but Sarah was pretty original and seemed full of potentially interesting contradictions. When she smiled in precalc one day, I smiled back and then looked down quickly, in case I had misread her and was grinning ludicrously for no reason. But I wasn't—she really wanted to be my friend.

Goth Sarah told me once, right before Christmas break, that before she "really got to know me" she'd been amazed I was willing to go to parties. I liked her more after she admitted she thought that. I like those compliments, because they're true. I never like the kind that are like, "Oh, I didn't even notice you're three feet tall, because I'm disability- and color-blind and you're such a great person." I prefer ones like Sarah gave, of the "You're so brave to leave the bell tower; I'd never have the balls" variety.

I told her the truth in return, that once I got to Darcy, I started to like parties. Maybe I was just older, or the parties at Huron, the high school where I went for ninth and tenth grade, just sucked. Or maybe Darcy parties were all the same, and therefore safe and predictable. Because once I leapt out of the frying pan into the whole new-school fire, I longed for non-agonizing social situations.

Although that first party, the one at Chessie Andrewjeski's, was terrifying. That was before I knew anyone except Ginger, and she hardly helped. I remember that night better than almost anything else that's ever happened in my life, too, because it was the first time I ever saw Kyle Malanack. Sometimes I wonder—if I hadn't gone, would everything still be this mammoth disaster? I'm sure I would've met him eventually anyway; I mean, D'Arts wasn't that big and he was a huge star there. But maybe if I'd met him some other way, it could have happened differently. If we'd been in the hallway, or the lunchroom, or gym class, if he'd been falling off the climbing ropes, losing a race, too exhausted to swim his final lap. But I met him at Chessie's. There was nothing special about the scene; it was any party full of teenagers anywhere, except the D'Arts kids were cooler-looking than the ones at my non-performing-arts high. Chessie's place was out on Scio Church Road and hard to find, so my older brother, Chad, who was a freshman at Michigan, drove me and said he'd have his cell phone on all night. I could call whenever I needed him to pick me up and he'd rush back. If I didn't have Chad around, I'd be even less well-adjusted, because we don't have the pedals in our car raised, so I can't drive yet even though I passed my driver's test right away the first time. I mean, my parents would have had to drive me. It's unimaginable. My friends from Huron who can drive said they didn't want to go to a Darcy party. They were mad at me for changing schools, which is another story, and not that interesting. So I had no friends, no car, and obviously wasn't going to ask my parents to take me. They don't allow "parties where the parents aren't home"—as if there's such a thing as parties where the parents are home. But even if they had agreed to the party, they probably would have insisted on staying all night, like it was a sequel to my D'Arts orientation or something. I guess Chad's becoming more like them, because he's usually mellow and fun, but he was so nervous when he left me at Scio Church Road that he said, "Look, J., I'm just going to pull around the corner for twenty minutes, so if you need me to come back right away, I can. Why don't you go in and see if it's okay and then I'll—"

I cut him off. "I'll be fine. I have to go to high school on my own, even parties."

"I'm not saying I'll come in or anything. I'll just be down the road where no one can see me, until you call and say it's okay." For a moment, I contemplated telling him to come in and pretend to be my gorgeous boyfriend, but it was too Freudian and pathetic. So I got out of the car and went inside.

Chessie Andrewjeski, the girl having the party, was crying. Her parents were out of town, of course, and she had invited only a handful of people but the entire school had shown up, as well as dozens of kids from Huron and Pioneer and Community, the public schools. I felt annoyed that my stupid Huron friends had refused to come, even though there were plenty of people they would have known there, even a few I knew. Chessie was crying half out of genuine unhappiness about trashing her parents' house and half because of the glee of being a surprise sensation, popular enough to fill an entire suburban farmhouse. There were teenagers scattered everywhere, across the lawn, having sex in the upstairs bedrooms, someone passed out on the back patio, all the doors open, two kegs in the kitchen, and a bucket of punch so alcoholic it smelled like it might blind you. People were dancing wildly in the living room, and all the furniture was pushed up against the walls, everyone crawling over it like animals. The rug was black with grime from people's shoes and spilled drinks. But if you looked under the "girls gone wild" surface, which was easy for me to do since I was sober and actually below everyone who formed that surface, you could see that it was just a bunch of insecure teenagers guzzling alcohol and Kool-Aid from Dixie cups and freaking out about how "stressed out" they were about SATs and APs and rehearsals and auditions and résumé-padding efforts.

I'm lucky this way; being a dwarf may have ruined my life, but it used to mean I had a good shot at getting into a great college because my Little Sarah Hottentot essay was so potentially prizewinning. I had already used part of it to get my full ride to Darcy, and when I showed it to my AP English teacher, Ms. Doman, even though it wasn't for her class and wasn't related in any way—I just wanted to show off—she said it was the best high school writing she'd ever seen and if it wasn't so original, she'd accuse me of plagiarizing some Nobel Prize–winning author. So that was a good thing that happened at Darcy. Ms. Doman was a good thing.

Kids are always so "stressed out," even when nothing stressful is happening. My brothers, Chad and Sam, are careful about this; they know that complaining about their glistening lives in front of a dwarf is unseemly, so they almost never fuss. They're also not bratty and entitled, the way most kids are, especially at Darcy, maybe because the culture of a school that's anything other than a regular "feeder" encourages colic. You're so privileged to be there, you feel like you have to complain about something just so you don't have to think constantly about how lucky you are. It's a kind of overcompensation, I think, when I'm feeling generous about it. Or, when I'm not, I think maybe it's just the basic requirement of being a teenager, feeling like you get to have everything be perfect all the time, and when you have an algebra test or a hang-nail, the rest of the war-torn, poverty-stricken, deformed world ought to turn its attention to you.

When I first walked in at Chessie's, I felt less of the simultaneous buzz and chill than I had imagined I would inspire. Most people were already drunk, and maybe everyone had heard of me already. The ones who were in-the-dwarf-know looked down nonchalantly. One or two who hadn't been forewarned let a bit of shock flash across their faces. But in most cases, I was impressed with how fast even the most uncouth regained their composure.

These included three guys in the corner, one with puffy muscles that made him look like an inflatable parade float. The others were a sleek swimmer and a curly-haired fatty, all standing together in a corner laughing horribly loud, although whether at me, I couldn't have said. It did feel like they were looking over at me when they started laughing, but I try not to be paranoid. Reality is bad enough—why exaggerate it? Now I know those three were seniors, Chris Arpent, Alan Sarft, and Tim Malone. Elizabeth Wood, an anorexic junior with dark curly hair who had been cast as Juliet her sophomore year, came over to their group carrying three beers for them, two of them clutched in one hand. She handed the single-clawed one to Chris Arpent, grinning up at him before splashing Alan's and Tim's beers onto them.

"Oops! Sorry!" she sang out in a totally ridiculous musical theater way, and then snuggled up to Chris, the muscled action figure in a white button-down shirt and jeans. He had short dark hair and light skin, and his eyes had a bruised, artistic look that some girls, apparently including Elizabeth Wood, really liked. She had huge boobs, and I wondered how that was possible when she probably weighed less than a hundred pounds. Had she had a boob job already? I once read that it's not a good idea to have cosmetic surgery when you're still growing, but I know for sure that some of the girls at D'Arts did it. I stared at Elizabeth Wood for a while. Her face was really pretty for someone so thin; she had a miniature mouth, like she was a kewpie doll, and her eyes were far apart from each other, almost on the sides of her head, which gave her an anime quality. In fact, she was incredible-looking. I had heard that she was the girl in the fall production of *Fool for Love*, the one that started rehearsing in summer. Everyone knew she was going to be famous. I wondered if her parents were worried, and what it felt like to be her, scary or hungry or maybe driven and fabulous. I couldn't tell. She wore red shiny patent leather heels with jeans, and they were supposed to make her look like a supermodel, but they only kind of did—they also made her look like a six-year-old playing dress-up, or Dorothy, wearing the ruby slippers after she crushes the witch with her house.

On the other side of the room, a crowd of people was gathered around a table, flipping quarters into glasses, drinking and shrieking. I saw Ginger among them, and she saw me. She waved, stood up, and made her way over.

"Judy! I'm glad you came! You want a beer?"

she shouted, and then, not waiting for an answer, took off for the keg, leaving me alone again.

I looked around the room, trying to find a corner I could tuck into, and then settled on the bathroom, where I planned to lock myself in and breathe deeply. By the time I had squeezed through the throngs of legs, I reached up, grabbed the knob, and shoved the door open without knocking. And that's how I met Kyle Malanack. Peeing.

He turned.

"Oh my god," I said, "I'm sorry—I didn't—" He readjusted his eyes from where he'd expected me to be to where I was, and smiled. He made no move to yank at his zipper, and didn't seem alarmed that I'd barged in, seen him peeing, or turned out to be the size of a Cabbage Patch Kid.

"Come on in," he said, grinning and zipping calmly, slowly. "Here. I'll even wash my hands before we shake."

He turned on the sink while I continued to stand in the open crack of the door, mysteriously unable to move. It was like being electrocuted to the floor. I know that's melodramatic, but it's true, too.

He dried his hands off on a towel and held one down to me in a totally casual way. "I'm Kyle," he said.

I stretched a hand up, shook his. "I'm Judy."

Kyle's a person who misses no beats. "So," he

said, "if this were kindergarten, we'd be seated next to each other."

Then he picked up an expensive-looking video camera from the sink and started out the door. I wanted to stop him, keep him in the bathroom with me. It was the first time I'd ever had that specific feeling about a guy. It reminded me of being a cavewoman. Maybe if Kyle and I had been prehistoric, hairy people together, I would have wanted to trap him in a cave with me forever. Of course, if I'd been a dwarf and not had my wit and conversation skills to win him over, maybe he would have shoved the boulder out of the way of the cave entrance and escaped. Here's the thing. Call me stupid, but I loved him. I loved him right away.

"Actually," I said, "I think they alphabetize by last name, even when you're five."

He turned his camera on, smiled at me from behind it. "What's your last name?" he asked. He was filming now, but I decided I'd pretend not to notice.

"Lohden," I told him. "My name is Judy Lohden."

"It's nice to meet you," he said.

"You too," I said. "But I wonder what made you think of kindergarten?"

He passed this test, unveiling rows of gleaming teeth in a friendly smile and saying, "Just our names being lined up like that. Why do you ask?"

49

I smiled back, trying to hide the fact that I had nothing clever left to say.

He bailed me out. "By the way, my last name's Malanack," he said. "So we'd still be next to each other." I had heard this last name. He was the guy doing *Fool for Love* with Elizabeth Wood. Of course. Typical of me to fall in love at first idiotic sight with the prom king.

He was gone, headed back to the keg. No "Do you go to Darcy?" No "What a party; do you want to be my girlfriend?" I quickly slammed the door shut and bolted it, thinking, if you're a guy like Kyle Malanack, you don't care about the lock because you're so gorgeous and confident that anyone who gets to see you naked and peeing is just lucky. So you figure you'll keep the possibility and door open for all the people at the party, keep their hopes alive. But I was also thinking—did he not notice? Had someone already warned him? How was it that no surprise at all had registered on his face, that there'd been no dropping of his heartthrob jawbone? I climbed up onto the counter and took a look at myself in the mirror. Not bad. Green eyes, the eyelashes, light hair, and plenty of lip gloss. Maybe he'd actually thought I was cute.

Back outside the bathroom, Ginger had given the beer she said she'd get me to someone else. I went and got one for myself, and sat drinking it on a couch where I could tuck my legs underneath me and watch and listen for the rest of the night. But Goth Sarah came and sat with me, talked about a book she was reading, apparently about why girls starve themselves. Something about self-loathing. She asked me if I was a feminist.

"I'm not sure," I said, and then, just to be polite, added, "Are you?"

"Absolutely," she said. "I mean, bad guys hijacked that word, and now it's so horrible! Everyone thinks feminists are, like, shaving our heads and strangling men, but actually, all it means to be a feminist is that you think gender inequality still exists."

"Oh."

"And it so obviously does."

Kyle was leaning against the far wall now, in a semicircle with Ginger, Kim Barksper, and Alan. Chris Arpent was telling a story, standing on one leg and holding an enormous arm out, and everyone was laughing uproariously, except Kyle, who was smiling in a vaguely above-the-fray way. Then Chris snapped his arm in and threw his head back into a long, self-indulgent laugh at whatever the punch line of his own joke had been. I made a promise to myself to laugh more at my own jokes. I mean, if he could be so unapologetic about finding himself funny, then why couldn't I? Of course, he was great-looking and popular. Alan slapped him on the back and

I noticed Ginger put her hand on Kyle's arm, right where the sleeve of his T-shirt was pushed up.

"Don't you agree?" Goth Sarah was asking.

I nodded. "Sure," I said, but since I had no idea what the last thirty things out of her mouth had been, I couldn't take it much further than that.

Fortunately, she didn't force me to fake specificity. She said, "Only two every year are women—out of five hundred! America is just set up for men. I mean, once you have kids, you kind of have to drop your work."

"My mom works," I said, mildly. "With my dad."

"Yeah, mine works too," she said, "but she wanted to be an artist and then she had us, and well, what are you going to do?"

I shrugged. "I don't know, you?"

"I want to start a dance company that tours the world and helps girls and women."

Something shy came over Goth Sarah when she told me this, as if the mere mention of a plan she cared about made her vulnerable. I was impressed that she had such a detailed life goal. Usually when that's true, the person wants to be a movie star or something. I tuned in for real for a minute.

"That's cool," I said, "You've thought it through."

"Thanks."

We were quiet, and then for some reason she was like, "We did a reading of *The Vagina Monologues* last year after I brought it to Ms. Minogue, and it was like a total scandal."

I nodded, even though I have to admit that when Sarah said the V-word, I felt a shudder of embarrassment. I was glad they had done the play the year before so I would never have to utter the word in front of anyone myself. I mean, what were the chances of D'Arts doing it again?

Kyle was now standing alone with Alan, engaged in what looked like a deep conversation. Alan had straight, chlorinated hair, and was dressed so conservatively he could have been in a J.Crew ad. He was a swimmer, tan, covered with a sheer pelt of blond hair on his arms and legs. His shoulders were so wide and his waist so narrow that he reminded me of a grade school project my kindergarten teacher, Wilma Feinstein, had once made us do. We had to glue shapes together to make a person, and I had used a triangle for the body on mine, accidentally making Alan.

Goth Sarah was talking about the starving book again. I mouthed the words "I'll get a copy. It sounds great," while looking around feverishly, hoping for an escape. Since I had no friends at all, I had a lot of nerve. I don't mean to make everything about me all the time, but I felt like maybe Goth Sarah was obsessed with issues of body image or something, and assumed I'd be like-minded because my body is different from most people's. But I don't starve or even hate myself, so I thought maybe she'd be disappointed. Or maybe she was one of those girls like K. C. Hart at my old school, who wants everyone to know how unfazed she is, and shows it by befriending a weirdo. Actually, I know now that I was just wrong and insecure and an idiot—Sarah cared about the world, was interested in topics of actual depth. She also gave me more credit for being smart and deep than I deserved.

Maybe it was just the delirium of watching Kyle Malanack that made me uninterested in anything else, but I wanted Goth Sarah to leave me alone so I could devote all my energy to plotting how I'd convince him to fall in love with me. I'd have settled in that moment for simply figuring out his class schedule so I could change all my classes and be in his. But I kept nodding at Sarah and saying *uh-hunh* like I was listening while I actually watched Kyle. I thought she wouldn't notice, which is a lot like thinking no one can tell when you're falling asleep in class. You know, your eyes start vibrating and your head crashes down and you snap it back up again and say some totally incoherent thing to prove that you weren't asleep because you actually were and then you think—even though you know better—that no one else noticed. You almost congratulate yourself on whatever stupid thing you managed to say, like, "Wow, that was pretty quick of me, now no one will know I'm actually completely asleep and in a coma." And everyone in the universe knows that you were sleeping just like when it happens to someone else, you're like, "Why can't she stay awake or at least do a better job pretending?" Well that's how this was; everyone knew I was in love with Kyle. Sarah must have known right away. I couldn't look away—he was like the best book I'd ever read, keeping me up all night, tearing through pages. He flopped around the party, his bright hair a little too long and falling into his eyes and over his ears while he chatted with everyone. He wasn't the type to spend too much time with any one person. He drank two beers, hugged Elizabeth Wood and Kim Barksper, roughhoused with Chris Arpent and Tim Malone, sat for a few minutes with Triangular Alan in what seemed to be a meaningful talk, and then, all of a sudden, there was a big commotion out on the lawn. I followed the crowd out, and there were Chris and some other guy I didn't know, rolling around on each other, kicking and punching and fighting. Kelly Barksper was screaming for them to stop like it was some life-or-death thing or she was auditioning for *A Streetcar Named Desire*, and Elizabeth Wood was jumping up and down on the porch, saying,

"Someone help! Someone help!" Big, beautiful cartoon tears oozed out of her eyes.

Kyle walked down the porch steps fast, but super calm, too, and everyone parted like the sea for him. He didn't get excited or shout or do any of the monkey things teenage guys usually do. He just walked right to the middle of Chris and this guy, and kind of lifted Chris off the other guy and moved him out of the circle. He said something no one else could hear, and as soon as Chris heard it, he straightened up, brushed his pants off, and let Kyle lead him away. The other guy, someone from Huron or Pioneer, I don't know, was still swearing and waving his arms. He looked so stupid that people on the porch started laughing. Then one of his friends, way less cool than Kyle and too late, came over and took him around the house the other way. And that was it. It was pretty amazing, I have to admit, the way Kyle broke that fight up. He was only a junior, and kind of scrappy and skinny, especially compared to Chris, who was huge and a senior. It's only because Kyle was so cool that all his guy friends were seniors, and he was, like, in charge even though he was the youngest. Kyle and Chris walked toward a parked car and stood for a minute, talking. I watched Kyle's strong jaw, outlined in the streetlight, as he opened his mouth to call, "Hey, Alan!"

Alan appeared on the porch, hopped down the

stairs, and unlocked the car, and they all got in and drove off. I could feel my body straining, trying to leave my brain behind so it could chase Kyle down the street like a dog. I didn't want to go back inside and listen or watch anymore, so I called Chad from the lawn and while I waited for him I looked up at the blanket of stars hanging over Ann Arbor. A fall chill was already in the air and it smelled dark like winter: crisp leaves burning and the snow that's about to come. I like that combination of smells, fire and an impending icy Midwestern season. I don't think I could ever live anywhere that has constantly nice weather. The stars don't look as good when it's not cold. And places that have no transitions make you feel like change isn't possible. I believe in change, even now, even after everything that's happened. Maybe because I grew up in a place that can be scalding and freezing both.

Chad came to get me in so little time that he must have been sitting around the corner in his car all night. I didn't ask. He pretended he was about to "return" to a Michigan party, and then waited until I was safely inside our house before backing away. My parents were at the table, pretending they always have tea at midnight. Everyone in my family does a lot of pretending on my account. And I pretend not to notice.

"Oh, hi, honey!" my mom said, all casual.

"Hi, Judy. Did you have an okay time?" my dad asked.

I looked at him closely, my sleepy-eyed dad, sitting there with my mom, who had definitely made him stay up waiting for me, because then they could look "natural" at the table, rather than worried. And I loved him very much at that moment.

"It was good, Dad, thanks."

"Great, honey," he said. "Well, I guess we'll be turning in."

He stood to clear their teacups, but my mom kept her hand wrapped around hers.

"Who was there?" she asked.

"I don't know, Mom, everyone, I guess."

"Have you met lots of new people?"

I shrugged, opened the cabinet, and took out a package of Oreo cookies. Then I poured some milk and sat down. I took the tops off of three Oreos and stacked them up. I ate the open-faced ones, scraping the filling with my teeth. When I had finished those, I dipped the stacked tops in my milk one at a time.

"I met a cool girl named Ginger," I told my mom, "and one named Sarah."

This was something for her to hold on to—names. She relaxed and I excused myself and went to my bathroom, brushed my teeth, and looked in the mirror. In my room I put on black cotton pajamas with moons and stars on them and climbed into my bed next to the ratty monkey doll my grandma Mary got me when I was a baby. I named it Bunkey, which my mom says is because I was a genius who could rhyme, but is actually because I thought monkeys were called bunkeys until I was like eleven. I slapped Bunkey's arm against my face while sucking my thumb so much that the arm fell off and had to be sewn back on two hundred times.

I tried to sleep and couldn't. So I got up and put my ear against the radiator in my floor. This is one of the ways I know my parents pretend all the time. Because I can hear bits of the truth through the vents in our house. My mom was talking endlessly about me, as usual, and my dad was either listening or sleeping. I felt for him.

"—or whether it was what she actually did. Will they be—" My mom must have gone into the bathroom or something, because this was all I heard for the moment, but I kept my ear to the floor. She came back in the middle of a new sentence. "—safe. I don't trust—"

"She's a good judge of character, Peggy," my dad said. So he was awake.

"I'm not sure," my mom said, to my annoyance. "I don't know where she was, or whether it was somewhere we wanted her to be."

"Then she's just like kids everywhere."

"I'm going to ask her to tell me tomorrow— and not just—"

"Don't, Peggy. She needs space."

"I know that!" my mom snapped. "Don't patronize me, or act like I'm not on her side. She's—you know, she's—in a different situation from everyone else. I don't want her to get hurt."

"I think the possibilities for where she was and what she was doing are fairly limited and safe," my dad said. I was annoyed in a whole new way.

"Maybe we should ask Chad to talk to her."

Then there was a long pause, during which I got up and climbed back into bed, wondering whether Chad was on my parents' side. I didn't care that much at that moment, honestly, because I had so much thinking to do about Kyle. I could picture him with absolute precision: his face, somehow soft even with the jaw; his hair, not curly exactly, but not straight, especially where it was a bit too long; his dark green cargo pants and faded T-shirt; his white teeth and his eyes. What color were his eyes? I hadn't been able to tell, felt urgent about finding out.

People joke all the time about teenage love and how stupid and "not the real thing" it is. My parents even have a reel-to-reel of that horrible song "A Teenager in Love." But if I ever feel again in my life the way I felt about Kyle, I'll eat every word I've ever written or spoken. There's no way I'll ever feel this way again. And I'm glad. I think maybe the very not-realness of teenage love makes it *the only real thing.* Say what you will if you're a grown-up, that it's puppy love when you're young, that we aren't going to marry our teenage loves anyway, so they're just crushes, or that you have to spend years together, peeing with the door open, before love counts as love. But none of that matters. Because what's *true* about love isn't a quantity thing—it's a quality one. And the reason I know that is because I still feel like I'm actually going to die.

The Monday after Chessie's party, I spent the morning zoning out on a series of announcements at "meeting" from 8:00 to 9:00 and then precalculus from 9:10 to 10:46. Why do high schools always schedule classes in such a weird way? Is it just a way of punctuating further the obvious fact that this is not the real world? A refusal to run on the normal human time schedule, say from 9:00 to 11:00? Or even 9:00 to 10:45? In precalc, I sat, as I always do in every class, in the back row. From there, I could observe my gleeful actor and dancer classmates—the smart ones, I mean—talk about how, oh my god, this year AP bio was going to be so gross and we were going to have to dissect cats, and placements for voice classes were already under way and had you gone yet, and oh my god, mine went, like, so badly, and did you hear they're not letting any nonseniors into senior voice this year, and blah blah blah. Oh, and have you memorized your monologue for Ms. Minogue because she's such a bitch, last year she made Sonya Ross sob and run from the room. I stayed quiet, but I could see their logic about AP bio. I mean, last time I'd cut something up, in eighth-grade bio at Tappan Middle School, it hadn't been anything fluffy, just rubbery pigs. And since human beings have a habit of cutting pigs into bacon-shaped pieces and eating them, there's less love lost there than there is with domestic pet corpses.

At the mere mention of fetal animal dissection, I remembered Tappan suddenly, with the first nostalgia I'd ever felt for it, that sprawling concrete slab of a building with its unforgivable choice of school mascots: the Trojan. I could feel the energy of its colorless classrooms, rows of gray lockers, pervasive chlorine smell.

Once, in seventh grade, a guy named Joseph peed into a radiator vent in the basement and they had to send everyone home because the entire school smelled so terrible. It was that kind of place, everything connected and infectious. When we dissected those formaldehyde-reeking fetal pigs, my lab partner dropped our pig's heart onto my lap accidentally and then squealed and screamed like it had been her lap. Or her heart. I'm not squeamish. I picked the thing up and put it back on our table, like it was a piece of gummy candy.

Speaking of Tappan, my little brother, Sam, is there this minute, probably sitting through a math class too, learning fractions or decimals or metric measurements. I feel for him, trapped in middle school for another whole year. Or maybe he's in jazz band right now. I hope so. Tappan has an eighth-grade jazz band, and Sam went out at the beginning of the year for clarinet. They obviously let in everyone who wants to be in the band, but Sam was super nervous about the whole thing. I remember my mom baked a clarinet-shaped cake at Judy's Grill, with "Congratulations, Sam" written in frosting, next to the little dots she made for buttons. It even had an almond sliver for the reed. But when Sam saw it, he cried. My parents were as horrified as I've ever seen them. So was the manager, Brad. He inspected the cake, as if a rat or roach had just climbed out of it.

My mom, the only competent adult in the room, put her arms around Sam. "Why are you crying, honey?"

"I don't like it," he said.

"Like what?" my dad asked. "The cake?"

"No, the cake is nice."

"What don't you like, Sam?" my mom asked, really slow.

"The clarinet."

My parents stood there, stunned, groping around.

"Oh," my dad finally said. Good work, Dad!

"What do you like, Sam?" I asked, rescuing the adults for a change.

"Drums," he said. "I've always only liked drums."

"I know," I told him, "let's eat the cake anyway, and tomorrow you can tell them that you want to try out for drums instead."

I hope Sam is drumming right now, and not thinking about me, or dissecting animals or numbers. Although numbers can be kind of comforting. I mean, at least there's a predictability to the way they behave. But Sam hates math. That's why I always help him with it. I wonder if my mom's been helping him since I've been gone.

I remember that first day of math at D'Arts vividly, even though nothing happened that was worth remembering. Memory is funny that way; it isn't like a photo album, where high-budget moments get the most play. I mean, what I remember mostly about D'Arts are the textures, the way light looked coming in the windows in the precalc room, or whole days that were just days, when nothing went wrong or right—the day just happened. I remember our teacher, Mr. Luther, clearing his throat that first day and everyone staring gloomily at the board. Maybe part of the reason Mr. Luther's gestures are memorable is that he was created by a cruel cartoonist. It's bad enough to have to teach arts students math, but he had a greasy comb-over, and a cloth Izod belt he had refed through four overworked loops in his gray chinos, somehow managing to keep the alligator logo visible. He was as pointy and yellow as a number-two pencil, and I loved him right away, the way one underdog loves another. His affection for calculus was so sad and misplaced in this world that I couldn't help but want to share it. I tried to give him encouraging looks from the back row without ever actually raising my hand. I couldn't risk starting the year out like Tracy Flick, even though I knew most of the answers he was looking for.

I only want to be a performer because then I can stand in front of everyone else and be someone else when I do it. In fact, by acting, I can feel what it's like to be all the people I don't ever actually get to be. I don't have to admit anything. Even when I sing, this is true. As long as the words belong to someone else, as long as I've made them absolutely polished, they don't reveal secret things about me. People think they do, but they don't. And that's why being on stage makes me feel safe.

I know why math makes Mr. Luther feel safe —because unlike social interactions, or life, or anything big and overwhelming, numbers are manageable. They're tidy and sensible, not sprawling and panic-inducing. At least at the high school level, math can also be accomplished in private, small steps. It offers both one correct answer and a best method for arriving at it. The funny thing is, there's a correct answer in words, too. Sentences are like proofs in geometry—if you pick the right words, they lead to the precise point you want to make, whereas if you choose sloppily, you end up making the wrong point, or at least not showing or saying what you meant to. Mr. Luther was unlucky, because he was missing the half of his brain that can translate math into words. He could barely take attendance without flushing and gasping. But as soon as he had his back to us and was writing numbers on the board, he was as graceful as Fred Astaire, swiping at the board and turning occasionally to see if we shared his delight at how well things could turn out once they were in the safe language of chalk-mark clicks and digits.

After class, a pretty black girl next to me, who looked like she'd been dressed by her mom or some daft aunt, introduced herself. I stared at her yellow shirt and red sweater, thought of a traffic light. Her hair was in small braids that looked like they must have taken two years to put in. She had lip gloss on.

"I'm Molly," she said, "I've seen you around school—you're new too, right?"

"Yeah. I'm Judy."

"What do you have after this?" She tied the red cardigan around her waist.

"AP English," I said.

"Me, too. You want to walk over together?"

She started walking and her sweater was sideways and covered only one hip so I noticed that she was wearing blue paisley-print underpants under white pants. I guessed (incorrectly) that this was not a choice she had made on purpose. Now I know she dressed like that as a kind of in-joke with herself. Because Molly's a huge nerd, and when you first meet her, you can't imagine that she's, like, actually very inappropriate, but then it turns out that she is. It's especially surprising when she says crazy things, because she's such a goody-goody. I guess she's one of those people who has a lot of contradictions, so whenever you say something about her, you could kind of say the opposite, too, and have both be true. Of course, most of us are like that. I mean, we contain various versions of ourselves. Anyway, one of the versions of Molly liked to wear preppy white pants and another one liked to make up bizarre rhymes and wear panties that showed through. The preppy one was talking about how she was originally from Atlanta, and how her dad was a lawyer and a professor. I didn't know why she was telling me this.

"What about you?" I asked.

"What do you mean?"

"What do you do?"

"I'm mostly a writer, actually. I write poems, I guess. Have you done your auditions yet?" She took a Diet Coke out of her bag and unscrewed it and it bubbled all over the place. She leapt backwards to avoid splashing it onto her white pants.

"Was that a demonstration of your dancing?" I asked, and she laughed a loud, unembarrassed laugh.

"Yeah," she said. "Did I get into senior dance?"

"Absolutely." I stuck my leg out in front of me, pointed my toes.

"You're in!" she said, taking a sip of the pop.

"Seriously, though," I said, "have you gone yet?"

She nodded gravely. "I had both this morning."

"How'd they go?"

"Pretty good. I didn't totally mess anything up. I'll find out this afternoon. So . . ." She looked around awkwardly and I realized, to my dismay, that she had to turn left down the hall, and I was turning right. "I have to stop at my locker," she said, and gestured to the side of her, and, for some reason, up. Her arm seemed to float toward the ceiling as if pulled by a marionette string. I put the conversation out of its misery by darting down the hall, calling "See you in AP English!"

over my shoulder as I went. Having seen her arm move the way it did, I wondered if she'd done well in her auditions and was modest, or whether they'd actually been comically bad.

Every afternoon, they posted the results of all the morning placement auditions outside the auditorium, so everyone could see where they (and everyone else) had placed, and either be celebrated or humiliated. Or neither. Honestly, it was mostly neither. I mean, for the most part, we all got the sections we expected to, but even within those, some were better than others. Everyone wanted to be in Ms. Vanderly's junior voice, because she sometimes moved people into senior halfway through the year if she liked you enough or you were really good, because she was also in charge of senior voice.

I felt shy when I got to AP English, and found myself wishing Molly hadn't had to go to her locker. I took a seat, as always, in the last row. Then, out of the corner of my vision, I saw Kyle. He was making his luxurious way through the doorway of the classroom. My heart slammed into my rib cage, rattled the bars. He had his video camera again, trained on Elizabeth Wood, who was talking into it in a totally exaggerated and annoying way, and wearing a skirt so short and plaid that she looked like a porn star doing a parody of a schoolgirl. Kyle was all drowsy and tousled, like he had rolled out of bed five minutes ago. In fact he was rehearsing *Fool for Love* with Elizabeth, so I knew that he'd been at rehearsal from 6:00 to 8:19, when he had his first class. Maybe he had that carefree sleepy look because he was actually really tired. I guess that's one cost of stardom—if you're so hot and talented that you get to play the lead in *Fool for Love*, then you have to wake up at 5:30 to get to school in time to kiss Elizabeth Wood for two hours before your first class. That can probably be exhausting, even for the most vigorous of boys, like Kyle. It's also possible that he went to bed every night at 7:30, and wasn't tired at all, but cultivated the lidded look because it was so vulnerable and gorgeous.

Molly came back in, holding a notebook and a new, unopened Diet Coke. She sat in the empty seat to my left. Then Goth Sarah arrived, sat in front of Molly, and turned to us to say hi. I nodded, but was so distracted that by the time I tuned back in, Goth Sarah was talking about how teenagers are always made to be so cute and clever in movies and how she hates that even though she thinks of herself as cute and clever. Molly was nodding attentively. I was furiously busy watching Kyle. I didn't want to turn my attention away from him to utter a single sentence, even if it would have solidified forever my only potential friendships at D'Arts.

He wasn't leaving! He wasn't dropping

Elizabeth Wood off, to my monumental relief. He was in the room, and appeared to be staying. I couldn't believe it. He was in my section, and I imagined in the pro-noid psychosis he inspired in me that he had figured out my schedule and signed up because he wanted so much to follow up on his joke about being seated next to me alphabetically.

He turned from the front of the room, where he'd stopped filming Elizabeth and started bantering with Kim Barksper, the sweeter of the Barksper twins and the only one of the two of them who can resist bringing up four hundred times a day the tedious fact that they were once in a Doublemint gum commercial when they were babies. Kyle saw me. When we had eye contact, I thought my heart might shoot out of my chest like a cannonball.

And then he came and sat next to me. Even Sarah and Molly shifted around on the other side of me. Were they impressed? Surprised? Disturbed? Jealous? I have no idea—the surf was pounding in my ears. I glanced around. Stockard Blumenthal, famous for that absurd name and for apparently blowing Greg Bailey during the movie *King Kong* at Top of the Park the summer before freshman year when they were both, like, not even fourteen, seemed to notice too. Although maybe I'm imagining it, since why would she have cared where Kyle sat? To me, everyone was tuned in to his every move. But maybe she was actually thinking about how unfair it was that people started calling her Jock-hard Blew-them-all instead of Stockard Blumenthal. I mean, what if he was the only guy she'd ever blown? Why Blew-them-all? Especially since she's still dating Greg Bailey. Maybe they're trying to make a point. Last year they both got tattoos that said "OATS," and at first everyone was apparently like, "OATS? What the hell?" And then someone figured out that what it meant was "one and the same," like they had become two parts of one person. And people said how stupid that was and joked how they were going to break up and have to have laser surgery to have the things removed, but I think it's kind of romantic. And I bet everyone else probably does too, they're all just big haters.

Stockard was doing a showy mime routine in the aisle between the desks, and I could see her OATS tattoo on her ankle, but I didn't care, because Kyle set his camera on the desk and stretched his enormous legs into the space between us. I was suddenly aware of mine, dangling from my chair.

"Judy L.," he said, "how're things?"

"Good. You?" His eyes were gray, dark gray, like where the sandbar ends and the water changes to the color of drowning.

"You know. I can't complain." He smiled.

My mind raced around like a foaming dog, desperate to come up with something, a joke about our being seated next to each other, something about complaining, anything, anything. There was nothing. A fire started in my brain and burned it blank. Maybe we would get tattoos of each other's name on our ankles. Or better yet, the backs of our necks. I caught my breath just as the teacher walked in. She was shockingly young and beautiful, wearing dark lipstick and with her straight red hair pulled back into a neat ponytail and held by a silver barrette. She clicked to the front of the classroom, set some books and papers on the podium, and wrote her name on the board: Ms. Doman. Even Stockard sat down and appeared to be paying attention.

"Hi, guys," Ms. Doman said. "Why don't you come up and take a syllabus and a course pack?" And with this, she pointed to two stacks of papers in front of her. Syllabus and course pack! I was thrilled, just like everyone else.

Kyle looked over at me, blinked his nighttime eyes. "I'll get you one," he said, and galumped up to the front of the room before I could respond. Was this a typical offer? Or had he had the thought that I might not want to stand up in front of everyone and get myself a syllabus? Was he flirting? Was he a real person, or a figment of my low-budget-independent-movie imagination? He tossed the papers on my desk and wedged himself back into his chair. His hair flopped into his eyes and he breathed upward, trying to blow it out of the way.

"I need a haircut," he told me, and then, before I was required to say something · interesting or flirty in response, Ms. Doman cleared her throat. Her white throat. She had on a silver chain with gold and silver circles of various sizes dangling. One of her earrings was a gold circle, and the other was silver. She wore a big diamond on her ring finger. I wondered who her husband was. He must have been thrilled when she said yes. She had light freckles on her cheeks and probably her shoulders and back, too.

"This is AP English and I'm Ms. Doman," she said. Her voice was warm and bubbly, lower than I'd expected, something like a deep bath. She looked out at us, first surveying and then appearing to have decided something important.

"Before we even touch the administrative aspects of the syllabus and assignments, I want to talk about narrative," she said, making us all feel adult. "Why are stories important? Why have English classes at Darcy at all?"

Elizabeth Wood raised a fake-baked tan hand and Goth Sarah rolled her eyes. She was jealous, I thought. So was I. You have to be a certain kind of girl to raise your hand first in a class like that, on the first day.

"Because books allow us to have experiences we can't necessarily have in our own lives?" Elizabeth said.

*For when your heart is full of love, you're nine feet tall,* I thought.

"Indeed. Great. What else? Other reasons?" Ms. Doman asked.

Ms. Doman was one of those teachers who actually cares what students say, who collects answers from lots of people and then responds to them. She's not looking for the answer she's already thought of. Goth Sarah spoke without raising her hand. "Because those who fail to learn from history are doomed to repeat it," she said.

"Good." Ms. Doman smiled, but she seemed less impressed than she had been with Elizabeth's response. Maybe because the whole "doomed to repeat it" thing is a cliché. Or maybe because Sarah hadn't raised her hand.

"Can you explain a little?" Ms. Doman added.

"I mean, we have to read books or we'll make mistakes. If we read stories of how other people lived, we can figure out better ways to live. I mean we can look at other people's lives and not make the same mistakes they made. Or we can, like, use their examples as models for ourselves." I knew she meant the V-word play, hoped she would stop short of saying it out loud.

"Brilliant," said Ms. Doman, and I could tell she was thinking: "Wow, this is going better than I even imagined it would." I was kind of thinking that too, like Sarah had turned out to be smarter than I thought she would. And so had Elizabeth Wood. I had this experience a lot at Darcy, because the truth is, the kids there were pretty smart for the most part. I mean, once we were trapped in classrooms.

"If those are two reasons for reading, then what about writing? Why write?" asked Ms. Doman.

"Immortality," said some ass-kisser.

"Yes! What else?"

"So you won't forget something you want to remember," Molly added.

"Those are related, right?" said Katherine Hassel. "I mean, not forgetting and not being forgotten?"

I noticed none of the guys had spoken.

"They certainly are," Ms. Doman said. "So, what does it mean to call this class 'American Lit'?" This was the first I'd heard of that. I thought it was just AP English.

But Ms. Doman was such a good teacher that she taught hers as an American lit class. She thought it was too "institutional" to teach straight AP English. She promised that her class would also prepare us for the AP test; she just wasn't going to plan the whole syllabus around a stupid standardized test. She taught us contempt for tests, especially standardized ones, and never gave us quizzes. We just wrote papers for her. Ms. Doman wanted to be a college teacher, I think, so she pretended that we were college students and that this was a university class. Everyone adored her; I wasn't the only one.

"That you teach American writers?" Molly said.

"Okay, but it's more than that, too. What makes a body of literature American?"

"I think the relationship between culture and literature is two-way," I said, breaking my Tracy Flick rule, but feeling inspired and like everyone else in the class was a huge nerd, too, so why couldn't I live it up a little? Plus, right away I had a teacher crush on Ms. Doman and I couldn't resist showing her as soon as possible that I was smarter than anyone else in the class.

It worked. She looked at me glowingly and then looked down at her grade book, trying to remember my name. "Say what you mean, Judy," she said, and then, "Do you go by Judy or Judith?"

"Judy is fine," I said. Everyone in the class was staring at me except Kyle, who was looking at his notebook, and it occurred to me that they were grateful that I had raised my hand to speak, because now they got to stare with impunity, at least for a few minutes. I resisted the urge to smooth my hair down, felt the weight of my legs, tried to hold them still so they wouldn't swing. I cleared my throat a little, not in a gross way, but just enough to speak without coughing.

"I mean, we define American literature as American because it comes from America. But the idea of what America is comes from our literature. So it's two-way."

She smiled openly at me, the way you do at someone you know you'll fall in love with—a person you agree with more than you agree with anyone else. Maybe like the way I smiled at Kyle when we met at Chessie's party. I think Ms. Doman knew I'd be her best student, and she wanted me to know she knew. Maybe she wanted me to feel like that was enough, like my life would be okay if I could come up with smart things to say and write in American lit. Or maybe it went further than that; maybe she knew that it wouldn't be okay, that I'd be eaten alive at Darcy, and that she would love me by then and be heartbroken when it happened.

After class, I had my first D'Arts lunch with Goth Sarah, which was a relief, because even though she spent the whole hour chewing with her mouth open and telling the story of her on-again-off-again thing with a tall, black-haired guy named Eliot Jacobs, it meant I wasn't alone. I couldn't tell from the story whether they had done it or not, and thought maybe she wanted me to ask, but I didn't want to ask and

I didn't want her to ask me if I was still one, so I said as little as possible. I didn't see Molly; maybe she went off campus to Zingerman's or something, at D'Arts you were allowed.

When Ginger came into the lunchroom with Amanda Fulton and Chessie Andrewjeski, she didn't sit with me, but she did wave from across the room and smile. Kyle was on the other side of the cafeteria, taping some stupid thing Alan and Chris were doing, something that involved grabbing each other in headlocks and rubbing each other's hair. I was happy just to have a clear view of him, and I felt pretty sure that I could feel him turning the camera across the cafeteria every now and then, maybe even including me in a pan of the room.

"He's coming back right before Thanksgiving," Goth Sarah was telling me, about Eliot. "His dad was on sabbatical, but now he's finished and—well, wow—I can't believe he's coming back. He's great. He's, like, super evolved."

"So less of an armpit-scratching caveman than other guys?"

She laughed. "Exactly. I hope you guys will like each other. He's a really open-minded person."

I arched an eyebrow, wondering about the connection between that and our liking each other.

"Meaning?"

"He's okay with my, you know, whatever you

79

want to call it—bitchiness," she said, and looked down, embarrassed.

I was interested. "What do you mean, your bitchiness?"

"Well, you know," she said, looking flushed. "A lot of people find me, I don't know, too abrasive or radical or something." She shrugged, but I could tell she was hurt by whatever it was she perceived that people thought of her. And that it was a question.

"I don't," I said. "I find you weakwilled and not enough of a loudmouth."

She laughed and then, to my astonishment, climbed onto the bench so that she was towering over the room. Everyone looked up. She wadded the Saran wrap from her sandwich into a ball and threw it overhand, hard, across the room. It missed the trashcan by six feet and landed in the middle of the floor, but she yelled, "Three points, woo-hoo!" without any holding back, and threw her arms up in a mock cheer.

Then she climbed back down onto the bench next to me and opened a bag of barbeque soy crisps. Everyone, including me, was still staring.

"Wow. Well, I take back the part about the loud mouth," I said.

"I knew you'd rethink it," Goth Sarah said, grinning, and held the salty orange bag open to me. "Want one?" she asked.

I did. I love those things.

4 I've made a friend at the Motel Manor, a middle-aged guy named Bill, who has apparently been living here for more than a year. This is the kind of place that rents rooms by the week or month. Sometimes, late at night when there's no wall of sunshine between me and my terror, I think I'll be like Bill, just settle down and stay here for the rest of my life. It's only $106 a week; I could last a long time with the money I took.

I wonder who's paying for Bill's room. Maybe he has some money saved up from when he used to go to Alaska every winter to catch fish. That's what he told me when we first met in the hallway. He seemed harmless in some hard-to-define but certain way, so I stopped to talk to him when he said hi, and he told me he used to go every winter and work on an Alaskan fishing boat and then he would come home and "just live" the rest of the year on the money he'd made, once it wasn't fishing season anymore. I guess you can make a lot of money if you're willing to go to Alaska and work on a fishing boat. Although I don't really understand what it means to "just live," especially if you do it at the Motel Manor.

Bill is a good friend for me here because he's too daft to realize that I'm a teenager and shouldn't be here on my own, or that my story about being between jobs and "down on my luck" can't possibly be true, that there's probably a manhunt across the Midwest for a missing dwarf, or that I'm three feet tall. That's why I like him; in his worldview, I'm as normal as the next person. The truth is, there are so many freaks on this wretched strip of highway that I barely stand out. I like that aspect. And I bought enough cans of SpaghettiOs to live for at least another week before I have to emerge and walk down the street to Kroger.

The funny thing is, even though I started out by lying to Bill about the whole "between jobs" thing, I decided almost right after that to tell him my whole story, the way the reporters, and maybe even my parents and brothers and friends, would have liked to hear it. Bill doesn't know how lucky he is to be the recipient of the epic dwarf download. Which is why he's perfect. At first, I wasn't sure how to tell him, even. I thought maybe I'd start with the hardest part, but then I rethought it, and decided I'd do it chronologically. I mean, I hinted that things turned out badly for me, and of course he knows in whatever way it's possible for a guy like him to know anything—that I ended up here and that that's not good news. But I started with the beginning of my life at D'Arts.

I've already told him up to the part about

Chessie's party. Bill's a good audience for drama, probably not comedy. I don't think he'd get jokes. But he's kind, and he listens. And he nods a lot. Maybe he's on drugs and can't manage much information. That's basically why I decided I'd tell him—it's like practice in case I ever have to talk about it with my family, a rehearsal. During the whole nightmare, I managed to say impressively close to nothing for someone with such a big mouth. But I might have to explain it at some point, my perspective, I mean. Maybe to Sam. The thought of Sam makes me feel like my heart might bite its way out of my chest, fangs all over the place. He must be so grossed out and hurt and—I wonder if everyone at Tappan is making fun of him. I wonder if he's seen—I can't think about it.

If I survive this, and leave the Motel Manor, even if I can't ever bring myself to talk about it with Sam or Chad, I might need to tell my kids. I mean, if I ever have kids and they're daughters or teenagers or something. I could make it like one of the "morality tales" Ms. Doman liked to talk about.

Ms. Doman had this whole thing about how we have to tell stories about whatever happens to us, and then we can use those stories to decide whether our lives are happy or not, whether events have redeeming aspects or are totally hopeless, that it's really all about how we choose to shape and name things. If we can just make a bearable story out of what happens to us, then whatever happened becomes bearable. Ms. Doman once said that that's how people rebound after losing their entire families in car crashes and stuff.

But I can't do it, and my whole family isn't even dead; I'm just disgraced, so what's my problem? I mean, some nights I lie awake thinking about all the worse things that have happened to people in the world, and how can I feel this sorry for myself, etc. But none of it, no matter how gruesome, changes the fact that my life is ruined. So maybe suffering isn't relative. And I can't take Ms. Doman's advice, because every time I start to try to make a story out of it, let alone make one I "can live with" or that makes me seem like a person who might be happy again in the end, I start chattering like a wind-up toy, clacking around the room. Literally. The first time I talked to Bill about what happened, I got so scared while telling him that I had to excuse myself and throw up.

Sometimes, at night, when my mind wanders back to the video and what it looked like and how many people are probably watching it right now—this minute—my teeth actually start banging against each other like shutters in a storm. Every night, even if I sleep for a few sweaty hours, it's like I'm rewinding myself to start the anxiety again every time I wake up. So my new coping strategy is to watch *Friends* reruns all night, every night. It's not working. I'm not coping.

My mom says I have a bad habit of tying all my anxieties together, which makes them seem "systemic," rather than sorting them out and dealing with each at a time. My mom went to nursing school before she and my dad opened the Grill. She thought she wanted to be a nurse, but then decided she hated it before she had graduated. But she likes to use words like *systemic,* maybe to make herself feel like the whole enterprise wasn't a waste. And it wasn't. I mean, when we got hurt as kids, she always knew exactly what to do, even the time Chad cut his leg open on some terrifying submerged rock when we were swimming on vacation and my mother made a tourniquet out of her shirt and stopped the bleeding while we waited for an ambulance to come. Chad still has a scar so giant it looks like he used to have another mouth on his leg and they sewed that one shut, but at least he didn't bleed to death. The paramedics said that my mom had saved his life. It took them forever to get there, but I can't remember why. My dad almost fainted, apparently, did nothing to help. Poor guy. I guess he watched Sam and me, which is something, considering that we could have drowned while my mom was putting pressure on Chad's leg. I was only five at the time. Sam was a toddler.

In this case, who cares if my panics are systemic? There's only one giant one, and I don't see how its only being one thing makes it any better.

To make matters more horrifying, someone knocked on my Motel Manor door this morning. I didn't answer it, and they didn't come in, so I know it wasn't housekeeping. It wasn't Bill, either, because he's the only person I know here and he never comes to my door. It's like an unspoken agreement we have that if I want to talk I stop by his room, 214, and knock twice quietly and once loud and he comes out. Or we peek into the hallway if we want to see each other. He's almost always outside 214, smoking. I was scared it might be people looking for me —I don't even know who, reporters, I guess. There's no one I can stand to face, so I hid. In the closet. Maybe I'm losing my mind. I mean, when I think that out loud, even say it, *I hid in the closet,* it reminds me of *The Shining*, of how if you stay in a hotel too long, you go crazy. Of course I've been here only a few days. What if I stayed a month? A year? Forever? I wonder if the police are looking for me, but it wasn't them, because I know from movies that when the police come to your door at the Motel Manor, they shout "Police" really loud and bash the door open, and that didn't happen. Plus, I don't think this whole thing, my life that is, is a big enough deal for the police. Although maybe it is. Hard to say. But maybe it was just some jackass looking for someone else. Part of me thinks it might have been my mom, but wouldn't she have called my name? Or Sarah. It was gentle knocking, so I don't think it was, like, the media, coming to ferret me out. I don't know. The only certainty was it wasn't anyone I could tolerate seeing.

My second week at Darcy, I moved through the days on a cloud. It was "placement week," meaning we auditioned for voice and dance. Acting class was organized by grade: freshmen took freshman acting, sophomores took sophomore acting, and so on. Since I was a junior, I was automatically registered for junior acting. But for voice and dance, we had to try out. And even though in the school brochure, Darcy claimed that its "artistic productions are collaborative and inclusive rather than competitive," someone gets to play Juliet, if you know what I mean. So they auditioned us that second week of school for our classes and then a few weeks later for whatever the winter production would be in February. We all knew it would be some huge thing that cast everyone, what with the fall production starring only Kyle and Elizabeth and two other senior guys, who played the "old man" by putting baby powder in their hair or the other guy part by wearing a fat suit. The official reason for doing such an unfair star vehicle of a show in the fall was that it went up four weeks into school, so they had to begin rehearsing before the year even started. There was no need for a party line about why Kyle and Elizabeth got the leads; they were both perfect in every way, a simple fact accepted by the rest of us, like gravity or the sun rising. But D'Arts would make it up to us with a huge winter show. We'd all get fabulous parts, they promised, and have to rehearse for a million hours, probably including over Christmas break. But we had signed up to make such sacrifices. The "professional world" was so demanding, and everyone acted like even though we were in high school, if our families took a vacation that meant we weren't dedicated "artists." We used the word *artist* all the time there.

My fall placement auditions happened the second Tuesday of school, the second day of my second week. I had told the dance teachers I'd just take the absolute beginning-level class and therefore there was no need to audition me, but they made me go in anyway. Before it even started, I was already blushing to the roots of my hair, wearing kid-sized yoga pants and a tank top instead of the leotard they required, and I made my way through the moves in the most half-assed way anyone has ever seen. The sad secret truth is that I love to dance, but only at home in my bedroom, on the bed with a fake microphone, or in front of the full-length mirror in my parents' bedroom with Sam break dancing. I do not like to dance in tights in front of Ms. McCourt, whose anorexic daughter Katie goes to the school, or in front of Ms. Smith, the seven-foot Amazon dance teacher who used to be a professional dancer and still wears her hair in a bun so tight her eyes bulge like they're going to explode out of her head. Her entire being is singed with disappointment that she ended up teaching. I barely made it through the audition, and when it was over Ms. Smith just said, "We'll post the list later today," so I knew I'd be in the beginning dance curriculum, which meant I had to learn basic ballet, tap, and jazz. I wondered if they regretted letting me into D'Arts at all. Maybe I'd be an embarrassment to the school.

I promised myself that I would do better in the singing audition, but as soon as I had the thought, I felt sick because before I blew the dance audition I hadn't even had to think about the voice one because I'd been sure I would do great. Now my one song had so much riding on it. Why hadn't I just practiced the dance moves more? What if some weird thing happened and I did a bad job at the voice audition, too, and everyone thought they had let me in as a total pity move? Worse, what if they had?

I tried to breathe deeply as I went into the auditorium, and visualized the sheet music, since that always helps focus me. I thought how unfair it was that they made us do our placements back to back. I mean, I was still nervous from the dance one. The director of the music department, a wiggly noodle of a guy named Mr. Gosford, was sitting with Ms. Vanderly and Mr. Stenson, the two voice teachers. I was thinking, "Please, just let me get into Ms. Vanderly's section, so when I come out, I'll have good news." I didn't even know what difference her section made, but I wanted to come out proud. And no one liked Mr. Stenson. He was new at the school, and had a bald head with some scabs on it. Mostly, he had no power to put you in senior voice half-way through the year, which was apparently the best thing that could happen to a person. Unless of course you got in right away, which was practically unheard of.

The teachers were all in the front row of seats, right in the middle. It reminded me of that crappy movie *Flashdance* when the girl from *The L Word* has to audition for everyone even though she's a small-town girl who's never had professional training. They're all really skeptical until she runs up and down the walls, dancing all over them. Then they love her, of course. That's after the money scene, the one where she goes on a dinner date and sucks lobster out of the shell like an animal while fondling her boyfriend's crotch under the table with her foot. When I watched that movie with Chad and his high school girlfriend, Kate, I thought that scene was like the sexiest thing I'd ever seen. And so did Kate, apparently, because after that whenever she stayed for dinner, she ate with her hands and played footsie with Chad under the table like they were in *Flashdance*. My parents found this cute, grinned at each other, probably remembering when they used to play footsie in high school. Gross. Sam was the only one who never noticed, of course. He just gobbled his spaghetti and talked about his day at school while Kate picked red peppers from the salad and licked her oily fingers between each bite.

At my audition, I had one of those anxiety visions where you do something totally crazy in your mind, just to torture yourself with the possibility, just to wonder what would happen if you *actually* did it. I used to feel that same unbearable urge at Chad's swim meets. I'd imagine running down from the risers, tearing my clothes off, and leaping into the pool during a race. I couldn't stop thinking about it, the terrifying question of *what would they do* so huge I was almost elated to consider it. I think the thrill of contemplating that kind of thing is related to an idea my dad once told me when I was crying on the ski lift at Mount Brighton—that vertigo isn't the fear of falling off a cliff, but the fear of jumping. His point was to comfort me, to be like, "You know you're not going to jump, so why be scared?" But it only made me more scared because how do you know you're not going to jump? I mean, how can you know who you'll be twenty seconds from now? What evidence is there to prove that you'll know the upcoming you? What if the Judy I become in two minutes does a striptease for the voice coaches, shocking everyone in the room with her dwarf sexuality? *What would they do?*

I wonder if they would have noticed my body. This is conceited, but I think I have a get-out-of-jail-free card, so I'll just say it straight out. It's not only my face that's cute—I also have a cute-looking shape—I mean, I may be too small and my arms and legs are a bit short, but I have a little waist and kind of big boobs for someone my size and a nice round butt. Sometimes, I can tell that boys look at me and think "Wow," before they think, "Oh my god, did I think 'Wow' just now about that tiny person? And if she's such a kindergartner, then how come she has a great butt?" I can see the transition on their faces, because I've seen it so many times. Achons like me tend to have hourglass bodies; it's like a concession prize or something. That guy Joel at the Little People conference told his friend Ian who told Meghan who told me that I was the closest thing he'd ever seen to a living doll, with my long eyelashes and hot body.

So what would have happened if I had torn my clothes off and danced a wild flashdance at my Darcy Arts voice audition? I'll never know, because what I did was walk out on stage, stand as straight as I could, and open my mouth up to the lights like I might drink them. I had the feeling I always do when I'm singing, that the notes come from someplace other than my body—an underground current rising through my feet and up my legs, taking shape inside my lungs and diaphragm and then trumpeting out of my throat. Like, not to be too cheesy or anything, but my voice makes me nine feet tall. Because it's huge, and no one, including me, can believe this body contains it. My parents knew my singing was crazy from the time I was a toddler, so I was always in every chorus, had private lessons, and like I said, they splurged on the piano even though they couldn't afford it, so I could have more music in my life. Anyway, like this wasn't obvious anyway, I owe it all to them, because unless you study and practice there's no point in having talent, right? Someday I'll try to remember to thank them. Because I wasn't even that nervous during the voice audition, even though the dance one had gone badly; I mean, I knew they weren't going to be able to believe it when they heard me sing. Partly it's just an expectation thing—it's like when you see a book with a really stupid cover and then you're surprised it's deep or good or smart or whatever. When you see me, you're like, okay, there might be things she's good at, but having a huge, bellowing voice probably isn't one of them. But it is. It's just one of those things.

So I sang the old jazz standard "Four," with its terrible, rhyme-lunging lyrics and achingly beautiful melody, and hit it right out of the place. I could feel how well it was going; my voice soared through the auditorium. There was a stunned silence when I finished, like no one even knew what to say.

Then Mr. Gosford, the director of the music department, said, "Judith Lohden, that was incredible," and Ms. Vanderly and Mr. Stenson said nothing, but just beamed at me like we shared some great secret. Then they nodded at each other, congratulated me, and told me right away without even talking it over privately that they were putting me in the senior voice class, even though "such a decision requires a great commitment on my part." Maybe it sounds trivial, but at Darcy, it was a huge deal. And everyone knew about it right away. By the time I walked out of the auditorium, people in the hallway waiting to go next were like, "Holy shit—did you get into senior voice? Congratulations."

All I could think of was the certain fact that Kyle would hear about it. I mean, his best friends, Alan and Chris, were seniors, so they'd definitely know. They'd be in the class with me. Maybe Kyle would even get in! I wondered how good a singer he was.

I woke up Wednesday morning giddy with it, wondering if he would say something in American lit, or better yet, while passing in the hallway or at lunch. And he did. He walked by with Ginger, actually, and they both stopped and were like, "That is so cool about you getting into senior voice; it's been like five years since that happened." I even told my mom about it on the ride home, that's how excited I was.

Speaking of my mom driving me home, my parents promised me a used car of some sort once I've had my license for a while, but if I'd held my breath about it, I'd be dead. I mean, even to run away, I had to take the AATA bus. The truth is, I feel guilty about the expense of them doctoring the car so I can drive it—raising the pedals or buying extenders. I bet they were planning on doing it for my birthday. My parents work really hard and they have to pay for U of M for Chad, which is still expensive even though it's in-state and everything, and they made a huge thing about not making him live at home, even though it would have saved them money. He got into Cornell, too, but he didn't go. And I think maybe it was because he didn't want my mom and dad to have to pay that much more. He never said that, he just acted like it was too far away and all his friends were going to Michigan anyway, but I think he would have liked it in Ithaca. After he did a college visit there, he told me there were tons of cliffs. And that sometimes kids there paint bull's-eyes on the rocks below, because apparently lots of Cornell students kill themselves. But I think the suicide thing was a generous kind of sour grapes by proxy, Chad's way of saying to my parents that he didn't want to go there anyway, so it was okay if they couldn't really pay that much money and he ended up here instead.

Anyway, it's possible that my parents are still working on the car thing in secret, actually, that they plan to have it ready by my seventeenth birthday, which is in two and a half weeks, incidentally. It seems very sad now, if they are. If you'd told me I was going to spend my seventeenth birthday at the Motel Manor, with no chance of finishing high school or showing my face in Ann Arbor again, I wouldn't have believed you.

Sometimes on Tuesdays and Thursdays, I swam at school in the mornings. Mrs. O'Henry and Mr. Grames had okayed this unusual arrangement, and I loved those mornings of getting to school before anyone else (except

Kyle and Elizabeth, who were already there rehearsing). I would eat breakfast in the car, a Power Bar and a Naked cherry-pomegranate juice, and then my mom would leave me at the back door, which the custodians knew to leave open for Kyle and Elizabeth and me. I would go upstairs to the second floor to drop my books in my locker, which I had begun to decorate with ribbon and lanyard. I wove six-foot strands into friendship bracelet patterns at home, beaded the ends, and then borrowed a ladder from the custodian, Mr. Nicks, so I could climb up and Krazy Glue the beaded parts to the top of my locker. So far I had finished only one strand, because it was long enough to reach from the top of my locker to the bottom, and it took forever. I can imagine exactly the sound of the metal door locking shut, beads clicking against it.

Then I'd head down to the pool, on the level below the practice rooms, with my swimsuit and towel and goggles in a bag. When I walked around the school those swimming mornings, all the hallway drama was still potential, the school itself somewhere between asleep and awake. It felt conquerable to me when I was alone there during the quiet, felt like I belonged and like maybe even D'Arts belonged to me.

Sometimes, if I was early enough, I would walk by the auditorium and peek into the doorway where no one could see me from the stage. I could watch a few seconds of the beginning of Kyle and Elizabeth's *Fool for Love* rehearsals that way, before slipping down to the pool. I must have seen them in it at least a dozen mornings before the show went up, so when it did, for its skinny week of performances, I felt like his girlfriend even though everyone was talking about whether he and Elizabeth Wood were having sex for real. They almost had to have sex to do the play, so it wouldn't have been a big leap. I couldn't even entertain the thought, just stuck to the fantasy where I was her, in the play with him, leaning on his arm, kissing him, screaming at him, even. And offstage they flirted, sure, but I never saw him kiss her or hold her hand in the halls in a boyfriend-girlfriend way. He was nice to everyone. Especially me.

This might sound boring, but I loved those days, loved that I knew exactly where I'd be each morning, that my time was neatly stacked like unit blocks. That the hours couldn't surprise me, except with emotional drama. I dislike logistical surprises, because it's already complicated for me to do normal things, like find the right place to sit, or make my way through a crowd, or reach the Naked juices without taking my grabber out of my backpack. It's fine when I have to use it, I just like to know when I'm going to have to do those kinds of things.

The first time I walked into senior voice, I had to count my breaths to make sure I was still breathing. Chris, Kyle's big, handsome senior friend, was standing right in the doorway doing some kind of comedy routine for Carrie Shultz. Then Alan walked up, looking slippery, like he'd just gotten out of the pool. It's funny how we become the things we do, even start to resemble the places we do them. I mean, it's not like Alan swam all day, every day, and even I had been swimming that day, but he just looked like a pool. He had big blue eyes and the summer hair on his arms and legs and a green, chlorinated tint about him. He stalked over, his equilateral torso balanced on skinny legs, and Amanda Fulton came up from behind and put her arms around his pointy waist. I took a long time walking up to the door, because I was hoping the four of them would disperse, but even though I moved as slowly as I could, they were all still standing there when I arrived, so they had to kind of move over to let me by. I had the unsavory thought that I could probably have just squeezed right through their legs. Alan and Chris were enormously tall, even if you weren't me. Alan was wearing a short-sleeved white T-shirt with a picture of a pigeon that said, "Ceci n'est pas un pigeon," and gesturing with his arms, so that muscles rippled up and down them. It's funny. I never wondered what it would be like to be Alan's girlfriend, but I sometimes found myself wondering what it would feel like to be Alan himself, or in a body like Alan's. To be a boy, I guess, a lanky, wiry boy. Did his body just snap along as he walked? Or glide through the world? Did it feel good to be as athletic as Alan? Or as handsome as Chris? There was an effortlessness about Kyle, though, that neither of the two of them seemed to have. They were always thinking about being themselves. I know, because I'm that type too.

I wedged in between them, closing my eyes until I was safely inside the auditorium, where I climbed onto the stage and took a seat in the back row of risers. I felt faint. When the bell rang, Ms. Vanderly shushed us all and then made an impassioned speech about what a big deal senior voice is and how the fall concert is one of the greatest prides of the school, as important as the shows, and how that's why we get to have class in the auditorium even though freshman and sophomore and junior voice use a regular classroom. When she said "junior," she looked over at me. "I think most of you are aware that we have a junior in senior voice this year. Judy Lohden will join us because, as some of you may already know and all of you will find out, she is a huge talent." I think she flushed slightly when she realized she'd said "huge," but I was busy trying to tell whether Chris and Alan were paying close-enough attention to my glory that they could remember it and tell Kyle later. But when I looked over, Chris was throwing something—a wadded-up piece of paper?—at Amanda Fulton, and she and Carrie Shultz were giggling. I tried to smile graciously at Ms. Vanderly without looking like an ass-kisser. But she wasn't watching me anymore. She had sat down at the piano and begun playing scales. She turned to us and we sang up a scale with her notes, and then back down. I started to relax, worked on not looking at anyone else, and finally heard us singing. It sounded glorious to me, even though we were only doing warm-ups.

Getting to SV and leaving always sucked, and whenever Ms. Vanderly made me sing alone, I had near-death, pulse-racing moments. But when we were all singing together, I forgot about everyone—even Chris and Alan and Amanda and Carrie—and just listened to us, sounding like one big person.

My love of routine is part of why the Motel Manor life is not suitable for me. There are too many variables and too few systems. This morning, just like every morning now, someone knocked gently on my door again, and again I didn't answer. But later, when I woke up from a tortured nap with the TV on, there was an unmarked envelope under my door. I could barely bring myself to touch it. I looked at it for a long time, as if it were something alive and dangerous, a mail bomb or monster. Eventually I went over and picked it up carefully, using my index finger and thumb as if they were sterile tweezers. I felt unequivocal, didn't even smell it or look at it up close. I knew, whatever it was, I couldn't handle it yet, so I put it, unopened, into my diary, which I was keeping on the nightstand for when I felt like writing an entry. When that day comes, maybe I'll also feel like I can open the envelope. Right now, I can't imagine ever doing either.

Tonight I have no plans, except to eat SpaghettiOs, watch TV, and cry. Maybe I'll order pizza and ask Bill to hang out in the hallway and listen to me whine. The sound of my own whining makes me miss my mom. And Ms. Doman. Come to think of it, I really miss Goth Sarah, too. Maybe even Kyle. It's funny how when someone betrays you, it ruins your idea of the person, but doesn't make you stop loving him right away. Or ever, maybe.

5 I picked a Rickie Lee Jones song for my solo in the fall voice concert, and practiced it every day for an hour after school. I did this not because I was especially disciplined, but because I loved the D'Arts practice rooms. They were tiny cinder-block caves in the basement, one level up from the pool, which was in an absolute dungeon next to the gym. The practice rooms reminded me of monk dorms I once saw at a church in New York, during the same trip when my mom took me to see *Saturday Night Live*. The monk quarters were cool, marble, and simple. Likewise, each D'Arts practice room had its own piano, two stools, two chairs, and two music stands. And that was it. But it was everything you could need, even if you were doing a quartet, in which case two people sat on stools and two on chairs. Mostly, one person used the room at a time; there were sign-up sheets, but there wasn't much competition since most kids were rich and had way nicer pianos at home. But I loved them, and frankly, going from those quiet vaults straight to the Grill every night to meet my parents felt perfect. The private to the public, artistic hunger to greasy spoon. I looked forward every day to both, and to the moments between them, my mom or dad pulling up in the car,

ready to hear about my day and take me to the Grill, where a plate of whatever special they'd made would be hot, waiting. My mom always played Bruce Springsteen, my dad Ella Fitzgerald. I liked those ten-minute car rides alone with one parent, detailing for my mom or dad my tidy high school days. There were rumors that people used the practice rooms to have sex, but I had a hard time imagining that, considering that they had windows in the doors. I guess you could have hung a shirt or towel, but any teacher walking by would have knocked the door right down if you covered that window.

Ms. Vanderly knew I practiced down there more than anyone else. But she couldn't have known why. She was almost as popular with us as Ms. Doman. Ms. Vanderly was black with long, braided hair, broad shoulders, and a walloping alto voice. She had wanted to be an opera singer, but maybe that industry's as racist as every other, or her voice wasn't good enough, or she had had kids. Or maybe she just wasn't pretty in the right way. It's surprising to some people, but video killed the opera star, too. It used to be enough to be morbidly obese and have a fantastic voice, but now you have to be ravishing, too, or you can't get cast in an opera. So Ms. Vanderly, who's a huge person in every way, became a huge teacher. Unlike the skinny Ms. Smith, who considers herself too good for us, Ms. Vanderly used to be a fanatic about her own career and now she's one about ours. And she isn't bitter about the whole thing. She loves us and takes us seriously. In fact, now that I think of it, the teachers at Darcy were really good. Ms. Doman was like that too. Unpatronizing, I mean. I wish they'd gotten to have what they really wanted—Ms. Vanderly to be a professional singer and Ms. Doman to teach at the University of Michigan. I think they'd both have been good at those things. It's a horror that I also disappointed them.

I worked really hard those first few weeks of voice, singing my butt off and getting the best solo spot in the fall show. Ms. Vanderly announced that Carrie and I would walk out first, start the jazz medley, and then the rest of the group would join us, snapping and singing backup. Then, after that number, six of us got to do "real solos," and I was first. I swear, when Ms. Vanderly said my name, Amanda looked over at Carrie and sighed like, "More of this affirmative action bullshit?"

But then Carrie talked to me after class, so maybe I was just being paranoid. She walked out with Chris Arpent. He was carrying a cardboard box, and she said, "Thanks for hauling that around for me all day, Arp," and I couldn't help but wonder what it would feel like to call him "Arp" and have him carry my things around like a 1950s boyfriend. He said, "No problem," and then she saw me, and said, "Hey, Judy!" And I looked up like, no way is she actually going to talk to me, and what if it's to say something mean? And in front of her handsome senior Arp? I sucked a lot of breath in and got ready, and then what she said was: "That's really cool that you got the first solo—are you nervous?"

So maybe all that time she'd just been waiting for a chance to be nice. I have a good sarcasm radar and I couldn't detect even the smallest hum of it, so maybe she was just friendly or shy and I'd been wrong. Chris shifted his weight around with the box, and said, "Hey, Carrie, I'm going to go put this in my car—I'll take you after school," and she nodded, but stayed there with me, like she was going to finish the conversation. Alan and Amanda were already long gone. I didn't want to respond to her question if she was going to rush after her friends, but she made it totally obvious that she wasn't in a hurry.

"Thanks, Carrie," I said. "What are you going to sing?"

" 'Summertime.' I love that song."

"Yeah, wow, that's hard."

She smiled. "I'm going to do it all Janis-style," she said, and then she put her hands on her hips, thrust them forward, and shouted out, "Your daddy's rich, and your mama's good-looking!" Her voice sounded like a ton of gravel. It was pretty amazing. I mean, I knew she could sing a nice, clear soprano line, but I'd kind of thought she was a lightweight. This made me think she had real pipes. I laughed.

"Eat your heart out, Janis!" I said. "I'd love to hear you do 'Bobby McGee.' "

"I love that song!" she said.

We stood there for a moment, feeling cool together.

"So, what are you doing?" she asked.

"I don't know yet," I lied.

"Oh, really? There's a bunch of sheet music in the library, if you want to look through things. I could help you."

"Really?"

"Sure."

"Thanks for offering. I—"

A cell phone rang in her purse and she pulled the phone out and looked at the number. Then she rolled her eyes as if to say, "Ugh, but I have to," and picked up. "Oh my god, no way!" she said, "I'll be right there!" She waved to me and took off.

I hurried into the stairwell and down to the first practice room in the row. I closed the door and sat at the piano, feeling so safe in the quiet it was like sinking into a bathtub. I took out my sheet music and pink pen, and plunked out a few notes. My voice was still warmed up from class, and the truth is, I had picked my song—Rickie

Lee Jones's "We Belong Together"—and been practicing it in my bedroom the entire year before I even got into Darcy. I used to imagine auditioning for *American Idol* with it, knew every note so well I could have done the entire thing a capella and not been even slightly pitchy.

I also had two other songs absolutely polished, in case Ms. Vanderly turned down "We Belong Together." They were "Blue Velvet" and "Blue Valentines." Something about the texture of those songs was so longing that they made me feel old, wise, deep. Every time I listened to Tom Waits sing "Blue Valentines," I cried. I never played it in front of anyone, because that way it was like my own private blues. Plus, I had found it in my parents' moldy record collection, so I hardly wanted to arrive at D'Arts all like, "I love my parents' old favorite, Tom Waits; don't you dig his records too?" "Blue Velvet" was from that horrifying movie about the guy who huffs gas and molests Isabella Rossellini, who looks more gorgeous and heartbroken than ever. I saw that when I was like ten because Chad was watching it once when my parents were out.

I lied to Carrie about my songs so she could feel like she was helping me. I knew I would even take her up on the offer of the library, would look through sheet music with her, lead her to the Rickie Lee or Tom Waits, and make her feel she had picked them for me. Then she'd have something invested in my doing well. I turned my iPod on and the first chords came into my ears: the light, hollow drums, then the twinkling piano notes, more chords. I started with the second verse, because it had my favorite part, about the girl who wrote her name forever:

And now Johnny the king walks these
     streets without her in the rain
Lookin' for a leather jacket
And a girl who wrote her name forever
A promise that—
We belong together
We belong together.

I knew the piano parts, had studied classical piano with my bizarre teacher Mr. Mivicks, who came to my house twice a week from first grade until sixth grade to teach me scales and études and Suzuki studies. Then in sixth grade I graduated to a new teacher, named Mrs. Rosenstock, whose house always smelled warm and tasty like meatloaf. She taught me "Ragtime" and "The Entertainer" and Chopin nocturnes until last year, when my mom managed to convince Rashid Karim, a musical prodigy at the University of Michigan, to be my private teacher. He came to our house, since my parents had bought a used grand piano with money they scraped together for years.

I like Rashid, because he told me to call him Rashid right away, and because whenever he plays, he hunches his shoulders and his hair flops all over the place. He's always dressed immaculately, but his shoes are never properly tied. He loves music so much that even now that I'm almost seventeen and know better, I still have that little-kid suspicion that he never leaves the bench. Like in kindergarten when you're shocked to run into your teacher at the grocery store, because doesn't she live at school and sleep behind the chalkboard? Rashid always appears to have climbed straight out of our piano, and to live on concertos or nothing at all. My mom is constantly trying to feed him during our lessons, but he's not interested in food. He's thin as a pipe cleaner and has superhero ears. Since Rashid started teaching me last year, my mom has had to have the tuner come four times, even though he used to tune the thing once every four years.

On Friday, I showed Rashid my sheet music for the Rickie Lee Jones song, because I wanted to be able to accompany myself. It was pretty easy anyway, but I thought I'd play it for him and see if he had any pointers. He was not impressed.

"You should be focusing on the nocturnes we're doing," he said.

"But I have to do this for senior voice, for our upcoming concert."

"Why not sing opera? At least something

classical? Verdi?" he asked me. I shrugged, put the song away, and vowed never to tell him anything about school again.

On Saturday I woke up early, brushed my teeth before putting three pieces of spearmint Eclipse in my mouth. I did some stretching exercises while I chewed, and then finished *The Great Gatsby*, all before nine. I had nothing to do. My parents were at the Grill, so I put a parka on, and an old Michigan hat of Chad's, got my bike out of the garage, and rode down Londonderry to Devonshire, turned right, and took Devonshire all the way to Geddes. It was cold and bright out, Ann Arbor crisp. I crossed Geddes and rode into Gallup Park, still orange and red from autumn. I sat for a few minutes on the chilly bank and watched ducks attack toddlers holding bags of bread. By eleven I was freezing and hungry, so I walked over to the concession stand and bought popcorn and a hot chocolate. As I was pouring loose change back into my purse, I saw Amanda Fulton and Gary Sorenson walk by. I ducked behind the door and watched them—they were laughing and holding hands, headed for the pedal boat docks. She had a white parka on, with a fur collar, and a striped hat. What a cute date, paddling around the cold pond at Gallup Park. They would have to snuggle in the boat to keep warm. I imagined myself in a boat with Kyle, trying to reach the pedals, failing, and having to sit on the floor, pedaling with my hands. Perhaps not for me. I felt suddenly embarrassed to be in the park alone, even though I often rode to Gallup by myself. I had never before thought it was a sign that my life was a terrible black hole but now that seemed obvious. I didn't want Amanda or Gary—or anyone else—to see me. I sneaked back to my bike, finished the cocoa in one gulp, poured the popcorn out for the overfed ducks, and rode home.

No one called me that night, so I called my friend Stacy from Huron. She didn't pick up. I began to think I had made a giant mistake going to Darcy, that I would never make a friend, and that I might die in isolation my junior year of high school. Of course I never even factored in the possibility that it would happen at a creepy dump in Ypsi where they once found a dead baby. (Did I forget to mention that there was once a dead baby thrown behind the Motel Manor?) In those, my more innocent days, even dying of loneliness took place in a cozy purple bedroom with books and a beanbag chair.

My mom came home from the Grill and asked what I was doing, so I lied and said I didn't feel well. I went to my room, where I read *The Bluest Eye*, even though that unit was still three weeks away, looked up *theme, figurative language, symbolism, imagery, characterization, flashback, tone,* and *style.* I identified passages that exemplified the terms. It would save me time then, I thought, in case I was hugely popular by the time we read Morrison. I mean, what if by then Kyle and I were in love and I was the star of the huge winter show and had no time for homework? At 8:30, I finished rewriting 1 over x to the seventh and 6 over x to the fifth and –4 over 2x to the third as expressions that didn't look like fractions. I looked around my room: lavender walls left over from when I was seven and asked for a purple bedroom and my parents compromised; curtains my mother had sewn, with tiny buds on the fabric blooming into a line of actual flowers across the top. She had added lace to the bottom edges, and my bedspread matched. There were teddy bears flopping off the top shelf, books on the first tier, and on the middle one, a Hello Kitty alarm clock, my cell phone charger, and a framed picture of Chad and Sam and me at Mount Tam in California five years ago. Chad and Sam have me on a little chariot they made by crossing their wrists and hands into a seat. I look pretty, in a pale pink T-shirt and white shorts, my hair pulled back by a pair of cat-shaped sunglasses. I also have a garland of wildflowers around my head, tangled into the glasses. I am laughing, and so are my brothers. I can still feel that day; we bought dried kiwis and strawberries from a fruit stand on the way up the mountain, but I can't remember what we were laughing about. I looked up at the

*Little Shop of Horrors* poster from my eighth grade at Tappan; I had played a shabop girl and our drama teacher, Ms. Bickle, had the brilliant idea that in the opening scene, I should be carried in by the two other girls, on a kind of sedan chair they made out of their arms, like the one Sam and Chad made on Mount Tam. But the two other shabop girls, Christie Krutchen and Liz Schaberg, had no confidence that they could hold me, so they were terrible at it, plus they were supposed to be singing and dancing while they were carrying me. It was obvious from the first rehearsal that the whole thing was just a disaster. We were all panicked that I would fall off, but Ms. Bickle couldn't let go of her directorial vision, so we did it, and missed half the notes in the opening sequence because our throats were tight with fear.

I went to sleep at 10:30, listening to James Taylor. I would never tell anyone at Darcy that I like James Taylor, by the way. It would be incredibly embarrassing.

The next morning, my room was so bright at 6:00 that I sat straight up in bed wondering whether the house was on fire. As soon as I realized the only emergency was that I was awake that early on a Sunday with nothing to do except practice nocturnes for Rashid, I went downstairs and poured myself a bowl of cranberry nut crunch.

"Hi, honey," my mom said. She was in her nightgown, drinking coffee.

"Why aren't you at the Grill?" I asked.

"Dad's there. I have stuff to do here today. What are your plans?"

"Um, some homework. Whatever. Not much."

She picked up a copy of the *Ann Arbor Observer* from the counter in a gesture that struck me as overly casual.

"Things okay at school?"

"They're fine, Mom."

"We're so proud of you."

"Thank you," I said. I took my cereal upstairs to my room and ate it sitting at my computer, looking up Kyle's Facebook page. He was friends with everyone at Darcy, especially all the girls. Not to mention the millions of girls from his old school in Boston who are still posting messages on his wall like every two seconds. And who all have their perfect-looking pictures linked to his page. Kyle's picture of himself was even better than what you would expect: get this—him, age nine or ten, in soccer shorts and cleats, an absolute afro of silky hair, laughing into the sun and kicking a ball. It was everything a Facebook photo should be, sweet, cute, modest—it suggested the Greek god of a high school boy he was now, but he wasn't self-loving enough to put even a current photo up, let alone a good one. Whereas most kids post such a great picture of themselves that when you meet them, you're like, "Wait, I thought you were a supermodel." And I'm one of those kids. In my picture, I might as well be six feet tall, for all you can tell—smiling in a way that shows no teeth, kind of like a model smirk, all seductive and smart and flirty. I have Meghan's mom's "wicked" lipstick on. And the music I list is way cooler than what I actually listen to on a daily basis.

But Kyle's too genuinely awesome to have to overcompensate on his Facebook page. You could tell from it that he liked kids, was the kind of guy who wanted to have five, and as soon as you saw it, you wanted to have five kids with him. His favorite books were like that too, he put comic books first, showing that he was light-hearted and in touch with his younger self. He liked *Dune*, which I hate—that's a brown, boring book for boys—just the thought of it makes me thirsty. But he also put, right at the end, as if they were afterthoughts: *Catch-22* and *The Catcher in the Rye*. I made a mental note to bring those up subtly one day and test him. Of course, Ginger Mews and Amanda Fulton and Carrie Shultz and Elizabeth Wood and Stockard Blumenthal were all his friends, along with everyone else who had ever gone to Darcy, which was impressive considering he'd only been there since last year.

I looked at Chris Arpent's, which was pretty likable too, I have to admit. He liked Chris Ware, that hip cartoonist, and half of his profile pictures were a fat, kind of schlubby cartoon character that Chris Ware draws. In the only one that was actually Chris, he was staring into the sun, with his shadowy eyes looking especially dark and tortured. There were some pictures of him with his mom, who was very pretty, but I didn't see a dad in any of them. Other people had also tagged a bunch of pictures of him with a baby—his niece or cousin or something. She had cheeks so huge they appeared to be full of food for the winter, and he was laughing and kissing her in one picture. There was something about it that made me catch my breath—maybe the contradiction between the way he looked, all, I don't know, GI Joe, and the fat baby in her wool hat. It was very appealing. His page said he was "in a relationship," but didn't say with who. Maybe Carrie. Her page had a million things that she had written on Chris's wall, all like, "How are the Colts doing? How's your mom? Say hi to Alan," and other stupid shit that was definitely about him and his friends and whatever he was out doing and his interest in sports or whatever. There were barely any responses back from him. I felt bad for her.

Elizabeth Wood's page, by the way, was the perfect example of what I mean about Kyle's being so great. Elizabeth lacked his knack for making herself casual—she had a whole gallery of herself "modeling" and even put "modeling" as her "profession." I mean, come on. At least hers said "single," so maybe she and Kyle were just friends. Then my cell phone rang and I snapped my laptop shut, like someone could see me looking at Kyle or Elizabeth or something. (734) 201-5580. I didn't know the number. I paused before picking it up. I know it sounds stupid, but I felt like maybe it was Elizabeth Wood herself. Like, maybe she had heard me stalking her on Facebook, or thinking sarcastic things about her stupid bikini and smooth, long legs. I picked up.

"Um, hi," said a voice. "Judy?"

"Yeah?"

"It's Sarah, Sarah Taylor." Goth Sarah.

"Oh, hi."

"I got your number from the directory."

"Oh. Okay. So, hey."

"So, um. I'm not doing anything today, and I was just calling to see if you maybe wanted to come over and hang out." She didn't even wait long enough for me to respond before she was like, "If you're too busy that's cool—we can do it another time."

"No, no, I'm free. I'd like to. What time?"

Her voice had lifted. "Whenever? I mean, I'm just hanging out, reading *Gatsby*."

"Me, too," I lied.

I hung up and went to ask my mom to drive

me over to Sarah's. I was overjoyed. Even though Sarah was no Ginger, I was almost as grateful as my mom that I didn't end up spending the entire weekend alone in a pathetic homework bubble or playing Guitar Hero with Sam. My mom drove me over to a two-story on Rock Creek Drive, right off of Geddes, and on the way, I saw a dead dog with its eyes popping out of its head like a cartoon. I don't even know how I saw the thing so clearly, but I guess my mom had slowed way down for the stop sign at the bottom of Londonderry and Devonshire, and the dog was right there on the corner, which makes sense because it probably was running across the intersection when it got hit. It was a white dog, with so much blood on its fur it had a kind of neon look to it. It must have been dead only a few minutes when we saw it, otherwise all that red would have been black already, the way it looked in the pool on the pavement. My mom, who hadn't seen it, accelerated out of the stop, turning right onto Devonshire, and I asked, "Why would getting hit by a car make you bleed that much? I mean, doesn't getting run over just crush your bones or break your neck or something?"

"What are you talking about?" my mom asked.

"Did you not see that gory thing?"

"What gory thing, Judy?" She looked at me, worried.

"Watch the road, Mom!"

"What gory thing are you talking about?"

"Road-kill, Mom. A dog. With a collar and everything. Someone's dog! I can't believe you didn't see it."

"I'm busy watching the road," she said. She seemed relieved that it hadn't been anything actually scary. She signaled to turn right from Hill Street onto Geddes.

"I'm surprised how much blood there was. I mean, don't small dogs like that only weigh like a few pounds? There were, like, gallons and gallons of blood. An ocean!"

"Maybe it had a head injury. Heads are very vascular."

When we pulled up at Goth Sarah's house, her mother was out on the lawn, raking leaves. She looked like a catalogue model, with a red parka on and medium-length sandy blond hair yanked back into a messy ponytail. I wondered if Sarah didn't dye her hair, whether she'd be blond too. Her mother walked over to the car, her duck boots crunching gravel. She had no makeup on, and a pretty face. Her teeth were all white and straight, lined up in her mouth in an obedient way. I thought of what Sarah had said about her wanting to be an artist. I wondered what kind of art she had wanted to make. I climbed out of the car, feeling inexplicably shy. The rocks in the driveway shifted under my feet, making me think they might become quicksand and swallow me up. I checked my orthopedic shoes; still there. My mom left the car idling, rolled her window down.

"You must be Judy," Sarah's mom said, reaching down toward me, her hand in a gardening glove. I thought she was going to shake my hand, and felt a tremor of social awkwardness, but she put her hand on my shoulder instead. She managed to do it impressively naturally. I liked her right away.

"I'm Ann. Sarah's in the living room—go ahead on in. We're glad you could come over." She made her way over to my mom's window.

"Hi, I'm Ann," she said again, this time to my mom, peeling off a glove and sticking her bare hand into the window to shake my mom's. Sarah's last name was Taylor, so I immediately thought how ridiculous it was that her mom's name was Ann Taylor. Of course now I know that her mom's a big feminist and kept her own name, so her last name is Carlton. It's funny that even though my parents lived in New Mexico once and had their whole hippie era, my mom totally changed her name the day she married my dad. Of course her last name was Haverfinder, so who wouldn't want to change that? I'm going to keep my name, even if I ever get married. It's weird to change your own name after having it for a million years. I mean, my parents didn't even get married until they were like almost thirty. That means my mom was just suddenly someone else, after a whole really long life as Peggy Haverfinder. I think that's weird.

"I'm Peggy," my mom said, "Thanks for inviting Judy today."

"She's welcome to stay for dinner," Ann said.

I wandered up a stone path to the front of the house. The living room faced out into the yard, and was walled in glass, so I could see Sarah in there, lying on the couch reading a book. Next to the living room was a screened-in porch, and the rest of the house fanned out in a mess of wood paneling and two-story predictability. I rang the doorbell, watched Sarah swing her long legs off the couch, wondered, as I often do, what it must feel like to live in an ostrich body like that. To stand up and tower over couches and chairs. To be someone else.

She waved through the window before arriving at the door and opening it.

"Come on in," she said, turning not toward the living room but straight back from the door into the kitchen. "You hungry at all?"

"I'm okay," I said.

"I'm hungry," she said, and I liked her very much for this. I didn't know if she was or not, but it's always better to pretend you're hungry at your own house so that if your guest is hungry she doesn't have to admit it. She can just eat some of whatever snack you put out "for yourself." Sarah put some chips in a basket and poured salsa out of a Whole Foods container into an orange pottery bowl. The chips were the healthy kind, Garden of Eatin', so I figured her parents were like mine and shopped at the co-op and bought that nasty peanut butter with the oil floating on top. But the reason I liked her mom was also that she had brought up dinner right away. It's funny how if you're comfortable in someone else's house, you're a million times more likely to like the person. Whereas even if you love someone desperately, if you starve or freeze or suffocate when you're over at their house, you never want to go back. We're all basically animals, is the thing.

"Come on," Sarah said, handing me the chips and carrying the salsa. "I'll show you my room."

We went down a flight of stairs off the kitchen, into a basement that was quite bright as underground spaces go. There was a couch against the back wall, and a TV facing it, two bookshelves crowded with toys, a sock monkey puppet, and some baby dolls. There was a laundry room to the right, with a door that led out to the backyard, and two bedrooms straight to the back of the basement. The playroom or whatever it was at the bottom of the stairs had a yellow linoleum floor and smelled faintly of mildew but also like lemons and bleach, like something old and damp but that's just been washed, the way most Midwestern basements do, especially ones with no carpet. Sarah gestured with her shoulder to the one on the left. "That's my brother Josh's room," she said. She turned right and headed into the other bedroom, which was, to my surprise, painted pale yellow. There was a row of narrow horizontal windows along the ceiling of the room, letting a little line of light in. The floor was baby blue and plush. I considered the walls and rug. Maybe she was a big Michigan fan, but I doubted it. Then I saw that there were stenciled animals along the ceiling that broke only for that row of windows: alligator, bear, camel, dolphin, elephant, flamingo, giraffe.

I realized with glee that it was the alphabet. This was just her baby room, like mine, all those suddenly embarrassing little flowers crawling up my curtains and bedspread like squeamish reminders that I'd been an infant mere moments ago. The revolting purple carpet. The white, lacy Chinese lantern. I realized, looking at her baby animal parade and yellow walls, that I had expected Goth Sarah's room to be pierced and wearing fishnet wallpaper. But being a teenager isn't gradual, that's the funny thing. It happens all of a sudden, and your bedroom can't quite catch up with you immediately.

Underneath the stencils were two punk rock

posters and a framed collage of pictures of Sarah and a bunch of other goth girls I'd never seen. Next to it was a poster of Martha Graham dancing, and next to her, Isadora Duncan. Sarah had an open violin case with a shiny violin inside, and two huge bookshelves stuffed with books, many of them horizontal. There were books stacked on her nightstand, and some books open on the desk and others lying on the floor. Except for the scatter of books, her room was mostly neat. There was a bright red Stratocaster next to the bed.

"Wow," I said. "Can I pick it up?"

"Sure," she said. "That was my sixteenth-birthday present from my parents."

"It's unbelievable."

"You want to plug it in?"

"That's okay," I said, meaning no, not really.

I held on to it, played a few chords. She sat on the bed. I pointed the guitar at Martha and Isadora, thinking it was funny and totally predictable that she'd have them up, rather than posters of someone currently cool.

"You a fan of modern dance?" I asked Sarah.

"I'm a dance major so everyone buys me dance posters when they can't think what else to get me. I like the Isadora Duncan story," she said. "Do you know it?"

Everyone liked to talk about our "majors" at Darcy, as if. But Sarah said it sarcastically enough that I thought she had perspective on all that bullshit too.

"What story?"

"She died, you know, when her scarf got caught in the wheel of a convertible she was driving in."

"No kidding." I played another chord.

"She was in the car with a hot Italian mechanic. In Italy. The last thing she said was 'I'm off to love.'"

"Who'd she say that to?"

"Her friend on the street."

"I'm off to love, huh?" I could see why Goth Sarah liked this.

"Right. And then she was gagged to death by her outfit."

I wondered for a moment what I wanted my last words to be. "I'm off to love" was a pretty good choice.

"What did the mechanic do?"

"I don't know," Goth Sarah said. "He probably screamed. Or called an ambulance. Tried to unwrap her? He must have freaked out, right?"

We spent the rest of the afternoon in Sarah's room, gossiping about D'Arts. She hated Chessie and Carrie and Amanda, said they were all total bitches who belonged in a B movie. I said Carrie had been nice to me and Sarah shrugged. "Whatever, watch your back."

Then I ate the first of what would turn into

countless dinners at Sarah's house with her family. Her parents were mellower than mine, not low involvement exactly, but laid back. When they asked questions, they weren't the kind my parents asked, probing, social, embarrassing. They were like, what we thought of health care reform. Literally.

They called us when the pasta was almost ready, asked us to make a salad, but didn't boss us about how. I spun lettuce in a plastic white spinner while Sarah sliced red peppers into slivers. She made sure to cut all the white stuff out of the insides, and washed off every seed, then cored a tomato and chopped it into pieces as tiny and even as jewels. Sarah's a meticulous person, that's the funny thing about her. You wouldn't have thought so to look at her, because of her whole ripped fishnets thing, but even those were artfully constructed. She tore them up herself, deciding first exactly where the holes would go and then cultivating them. Whenever the tears were the wrong size, or in the wrong places, or just too numerous, she threw the tights out.

Goth Sarah's dad was a pale blond giant, lumbering around the kitchen in a friendly way, joking and small-talking while he handed stemless mushrooms to Ann. He threw the stems out, washed the cutting board, wiped the counter, and opened a bottle of red wine, saying he would "let it breathe" on the counter. He surprised me by putting five wineglasses on the table. Apparently, Sarah and her pimply, totally silent, chess-playing brother were adult enough to have wine. As soon as I met Josh, I thought he would benefit by meeting Sam, even though Sam was younger by at least a year. Sam wasn't cool either, but he was so much cooler than Josh that it was sad.

We all sat sipping wine and eating pasta and salad while her parents talked about politics and a trip they were planning to South Africa for Christmas. They both taught at U of M, her dad history and her mom environmental science. It turned out her little brother was an actual chess nerd genius of some sort, so they spent part of the evening planning out a tournament they were taking him to in October, while he scarfed his food like a wolf and then bolted from the table without saying a word. Sarah asked if we could be excused, and we went back to her room and watched old Michael Jackson videos on YouTube until it was time for me to go, when she drove me home in her mom's car. I was interested that they let her, considering we'd sipped some wine, but it had only been thimblefuls. I didn't say anything, of course. Sarah said on the way to my house that she thought her parents were about to surprise her at Christmas by giving her the car for her own, but she wasn't sure yet. She had to prove she could drive it around for a few more weeks without crashing or anything. I told her I thought my parents were going to get the pedals in our car raised soon, so I could drive too.

At home, I went straight to my bedroom, happy, the promise of my new friend and a week of D'Arts and Kyle Malanack floating above me like a pink candy cloud. It was nice to have had a distraction from thoughts of Kyle, but now that I was alone in my room, I was thrilled to be able to go back to thinking about him again, safely and quietly. I hummed Rickie Lee Jones's "Lucky Guy" while I packed homework and books in my leather backpack. Then I set out a yoga mat so I could stretch in the morning, and hung my Monday outfit up—jean skirt, red tights, and a soft, striped sweater.

The week flew. I was at least an assignment ahead in every class except AP bio, and I had so much to think about that I spent the days in a happy fantasy. Goth Sarah and I sat together every day at lunch, and on Thursday, Molly joined after volunteer-tutoring someone in precalc. D'Arts was big into "students as teachers," which meant smart people helping stupid people during lunch. When Molly arrived at lunch, she was like, "Why can't people just work harder?"

Molly thought everyone had equal talent, and whether you were good at stuff was a question of whether you were a lazy sack of shit or not. I sometimes wondered what she thought of me. Mostly, I was glad for her company, because it was good not to spend lunches or weekends in solitary confinement or even just with Sarah anymore. I mean, even though it makes me a bad person, I was a little bummed about the whole being BFF with Sarah so fast, if I'm being totally honest about it. I still wanted to be friends with Ginger, and my friendship with Goth Sarah disqualified me for ones with girls like Ginger. Everyone the least bit glittery had lost interest in me entirely. As usual, I should have appreciated what I had when I had it. And even though it's counterintuitive, Molly made that problem better, since when she was around, there were three of us, so it was more like we were a group, and less like the two friendless freaks had found each other and latched on. Whenever Molly wasn't tutoring during lunch she sat with us and sang weird songs about food and people in our class, and talked about who had said what in American lit and her mysterious crushes on Chris Arpent and Tim Malone, the class fat guy.

The second time we ever hung out at lunch, she was eating tidy rows of sushi from a plastic box her mom had clearly packed and she was suddenly like, "Do you guys want to hear a poem I wrote?" So we were like, "Okay, sure," and she took a folded piece of paper out of her pocket and cleared her throat and read this crazy thing about giant spiders that live underground and come out at night to hunt and eat chickens. The poem was called "Housekeeping," because the spiders keep this pet frog who eats ants and mites and other bugs they don't like. I think her point was that even though the frog is trapped, the spiders love him, and maybe he loves them, because she ended it like, "Beloved frog, you are the definition of a pet. Eat your grief quick, keep kept."

Sarah was like, "Wow. What's that about?"

"Brazilian spiders and their pet frog," Molly said, smiling, and I couldn't tell if she was being secretive or if that was just the whole thing of it.

It was a pretty good poem. Molly was like, good at being good at everything, but also bizarre and unpopular enough not to be annoying. She had gone to a private school in Atlanta called Atlanta Girls School, and apparently her dad didn't think D'Arts was "academic enough," so he was teaching Molly history on the weekends, kind of like homeschooling. It sounded horrible to me, but Molly said her dad was a genius, that he had written four books on American history and was a practicing lawyer and taught "the law," too. Whenever Molly talked about what her dad did, she always said, "the law." She was very proud of him.

When Molly invited me and Sarah over for a sleepover, we consulted and then said yes.

Molly's house was kind of like mine, except bigger and fancier. There were papers and pieces of mail on all the surfaces in the study and kitchen, but they were stacked neatly. And the living room was completely, fanatically clean, with a white couch and some expensive-looking lamps and glass sculptures on the shelves and tables. But the den was full of stuffed bookshelves and soft chairs. Molly's mom was in the kitchen, cooking complicated Thai food and wearing high heels. When we were upstairs, Molly said her mom was a "housewife," and Goth Sarah, unable to refrain, was like, "Um, I think, it's 'homemaker' or 'stay-at-home mom,'" and Molly shrugged. "My mom says 'housewife,'" she said, and Sarah managed to keep quiet, although later, when Molly went to the bathroom and we were alone, she told me she thought Molly's frog poem was actually about her mom. I wasn't sure.

Molly's dad came home while we were all eating shrimp curry and cucumber salad. He was very tall and formal, wearing a suit and a scarf. He had a man bag, too, that might have been a purse on someone else, but I couldn't imagine anyone making fun of Molly's dad.

"Hi, Robert," Molly said to him. Sarah and I looked at each other with wide eyes. Meanwhile, Molly's seven-year-old sister, Susanna, leapt up and knocked her chair over backwards to get to him, shouting, "Daddy!" He kissed her hello, then took his coat off, loosened his tie, and came over and kissed Molly and her mom on the tops of their heads. At dinner, he asked Goth Sarah and me about D'Arts and our life goals. Molly's mom, whom Molly called Barbara, asked a bunch of questions too, mostly about what we were reading. She had read everything. I felt nervous, like I was at a job interview or something, because her parents were so dressed up and intense. I longed for my house, where my mom danced around the kitchen in her socks and Sam put his feet on the table and made airplanes and "food people" out of potatoes and chicken legs. Maybe Molly was worried that we might be uncomfortable, because we all ate fast, excused ourselves, and went upstairs. Molly's room was cream and maroon, with a painting that looked like two giant boxes of color stacked on top of each other. She didn't have the embarrassing baby-room problem Sarah and I did. Maybe because she had moved here recently. Or maybe she was born a grown-up and her first words were *Barbara* and *Robert* instead of *Mama* and *Dada*. Or my first word, which, to my mom's great delight and pride, was *ood,* or Judy. My mom says this was because I always knew exactly who I was.

Molly's sister, Susanna, wanted to hang out with us all night. She was clearly weirded out by me, and made a lot of references to how high she could reach, maybe wanting to say that she was taller than me but realizing that it would be rude. Their mom made her put on Disney princess pajamas at 8:00, but said she could stay up until 9:00, and Molly painted her nails sparkly pink and let her play until their mom came to get her, so it was their mom's fault and not Molly's. Molly never said anything impatient or made her leave, even though we kind of would've been happier talking about D'Arts and whatnot. I liked Molly for being nicer to her sister than she was to us—that was right of her, you know? Even when Susanna finally stopped hinting about how she could get a book from the highest shelf and asked Molly straight out, "Why is Judy so short?" Molly didn't scold her. She just said, "You should ask Judy." So Susanna looked over and I said, "That's how I was born," and she accepted it the way kids do. Kids like facts.

I looked over at Goth Sarah and Molly to see if they were like, looking at each other with pity for me, but they weren't. They didn't even seem to think it was a big deal or that I might not like having it come up like that. They had a lot of faith in me.

Sunday morning we woke up at eleven and walked downtown. I'm probably not the first human being to have noticed that being in a herd is better than being alone and having to gnaw your leg off to escape your own loneliness. But I felt strange that morning, anxious to go home and be alone for real. Maybe because sometimes loneliness happens precisely when you're with people who should make you unlonely.

It was freezing out, so we went to a café, and while we were waiting to order, this old lady came up and asked Molly for help. At first I didn't get why she did it, but Molly knew immediately, the way I know when someone's about to be like, "Oh, aren't you cute," to me. She assumed Molly worked there, and Molly was polite about it; she just pointed to where the counter was, so the old lady could see the person you're supposed to order from—a blond girl in an apron. And the old lady kind of knew to be embarrassed, because she said, "Oh! I'm sorry, I thought you were helping these two," and pointed at Sarah and me. We weren't sure whether to be, like, horrified or apologize on behalf of the old lady, or what, but as soon as she was out of earshot, Molly was like, "Can I get you two anything? Ma'am? Ma'am? How can I help you?" to me and Sarah and we laughed, part politely, part for real since Molly was very funny about it.

After we sat and drank cocoa for a little while, I was finally like, "Well, I gotta get home," or something equally unconvincing and lame, so we all got up. Then, on our way out, we saw Mr. Luther, our long-suffering precalc teacher, run by. He was wearing yellow terry-cloth shorts with running tights underneath and a sweatshirt that said, "Team-Building Math Camp 1996." Before we could pretend not to see him, he waved. We all waved back. And no one said anything mean, even after he jogged away with his shorts riding up so high he looked like he was naked. Maybe simply because it would have been too easy. And all I can say about that morning is—how did we three know instinctively where the lines are between being funny and being brutal? I mean, why is it that everywhere I look, other people seem to be crossing those boundaries constantly? Jumping, falling, leaping over the line from banter into cruelty. Sometimes it's on purpose and other times it's by accident, but in any case, people savage each other. Maybe because they can't help it.

6 Sarah's parents were going to be out of town for her gangly brother's chess tournament, so she decided to have a Halloween party at her house. Every day after senior voice, she came to discuss the details, who we would invite (it would be open, we finally decided, that was cooler), whether we'd decorate (a little, not so much that we were like in sixth grade), who would get drinks (we'd have to rely on Chad, who had a fake ID and older friends in the fraternity he was rushing at Michigan). Molly joined in on these conversations, partly because she wanted to help with the party, and partly because she liked showing up at SV so she could see Chris Arpent. She was pretty brave about it, often came right over and was like, "Hey, Chris," even when he was standing with Carrie and Amanda and Alan. I would never have done that; I could barely bring myself to wave to Carrie, even after she was nice to me that one time.

The other funny thing about Molly was that she always came by right before her karate class downtown, and she preferred to change in the D'Arts locker room, so she was usually already in her white pants and jacket with her yellow belt tied all tight around her waist. To say that I would never, ever, in several hundred thousand light-years have put on a karate costume and bounced up to Chris Arpent in the hallway, and been like, "Hi, Chris! Look at me in my tight white suit. I'm on my way to practice an East Asian art you probably think is a cartoon, and now that I'm leaving, you'll likely do that stupid thing guys do where they lip-sync bad dubbing while faking kung fu" is the biggest understatement of all time. But that's not how Molly thought of it. I once asked, gently, if she thought those guys made fun of her karate costume.

"It's not a costume," she told me.

"Well, your whatever, suit."

"Why would I care?"

She said this in a totally matter-of-fact way, not even defensively. She actually genuinely didn't care if they made fun of her or not. I considered calling my mom and dad Peggy and Max, and asking them to homeschool me on the weekends, so I could be above the fray too. Needless to say, I never brought up Molly's karate outfit again, except to congratulate her when she graduated to a green belt. And then, amazingly, one day Molly ran by SV, wearing the green belt, and Chris was like, "Moving up in the world, huh, Moll? Don't kick my ass, you green belt, you." And she gave me a big I-told-you-so grin.

Every day after Molly left, Goth Sarah walked me down to the practice rooms. Then she did homework in the library while I practiced, and drove me to the Grill. She had nothing else to do after school and needed the extra driving practice since she was still showing her parents she could drive their car without crashing. I kind of missed having my mom and dad pick me up at school, but they liked it when I showed up with Sarah, because it made me seem like a popular teenager or something, so it was okay for all of us. And I was cool enough not to insist that my parents keep picking me up once I had a friend who could drive and offered to take me every day.

The night of our big party was one of those terrible subzero Halloweens that always happen in Ann Arbor. I felt sorry for all the little kids trying to trick-or-treat with their parkas ruining their costumes. When Chad and I were kids we used to try to come up with costumes that involved parkas—Michelin man, cloud, fat person, cotton candy. Weak, I know, but otherwise we'd end up working really hard on a costume and then put a huge coat right over it.

Goth Sarah and I had already decided to dress up as sexy witches, and had gone to Value World in Ypsi, where they have used dresses for like two dollars. It's hard to find slutty black dresses since I have to shop in children's departments, so I bought a long dress and cut it off. Sarah frayed the hem for me. Molly, doing her own weird thing as usual, was going as Mulan. She pulled her curls back into a tight ponytail and wore her karate suit, which was a little uninspired considering she'd been parading around school in it. But it was kind of tight and flattering, and she had a little plastic dragon necklace that was very cute. She looked like she could scale walls and sail over bamboo forests.

We spent the afternoon carving pumpkins, burning the seeds horrifically, while Molly made up a song about carving pumpkins with her friends who were bumpkins, and Sarah was like, "You're the one from the South," and Molly was like, "Atlanta is not the South, and there are way more bumpkins in Michigan," and Sarah said, "Not Ann Arbor, though," and then we strung up a few orange streamers and balloons, but they looked shriveled and depressing, so we tore them down and threw them out with the incinerated pumpkin seeds. We lit candles in our pumpkins' faces, put a giant bowl of candy out for trick-or-treaters, and hung a skeleton and two bats in the window. Chad had agreed to get as much liquor as he could with the $180 Sarah and Molly and I had pooled from allowances and clothing money and babysitting and various other embarrassing revenue streams. Chad had said, only half joking, that he would get us drinks only if he was invited, and I knew he meant he wanted to stay and watch out for me.

"Yes! Come and stay!" I said. "And maybe bring some of your friends?"

If Chad and his guy friends hung out there even just for a while, it would add a coolness quotient that is impossible to exaggerate. And maybe I would get some credit, since the U of M guys would be my contribution. Chad said he'd see what he could do.

I had told my parents I was sleeping at Sarah's, which was so commonplace that they didn't even think to ask whether her parents were there. This was lucky for me, because in spite of all the disastrous things I've now done, I always tried hard not to lie directly. For example, if my mom had asked straight out, "Are her parents out of town?" I would have had to say yes. And if they had asked, "Is she having a party?" I would have had to say yes to that, too, and they wouldn't have let me go. I don't know why I'm such a Goody Two-shoes in this way, but there it is. My parents have embedded in me a sense that straight-out lying is a terrible crime. Omission's just not as bad.

At seven o clock, after we'd eaten some left-over pizza and opened a bottle of Sarah's parents' wine, one we hoped wasn't too fancy, we started painting our fingernails and getting into our costumes. We were feeling very sexy, standing in our stockings with our nails drying and wine staining the sides of thin-stemmed glasses.

Sarah's dress was a filmy, hot pink thing, and she was wearing fishnets with seams up the backs. She put on platform shoes so enormous she looked like some kind of bizarre animal with hooves, and then, perhaps thinking I might be offended if she was literally ten feet taller than I was, she took them off. "Too hard to walk in," she said.

"Right."

"Let me see your dress," she said, and I turned to face her. I had gotten dressed in the corner of the room, and she and Molly had politely looked away while I did. Now they looked me over. The dress was quite tight around the chest, with spaghetti straps and a diving, scooped-out neckline that made me look like a mini Dolly Parton. It was short, so short that it made my legs look long, or at least longer anyway, and I had cute sheer stockings with the faint hint of white bones etched on them, a little Halloween touch that made the dress less of an obvious excuse to look hot. I planned to wear my best dress shoes, because they had the highest heels I was allowed in. I hadn't put them on yet, but I thrust my chest out.

"Don't gloat about it," Sarah said. "You look great. He'll definitely notice."

"Who?" I said, innocently.

Sarah and Molly looked at each other and rolled their eyes.

"Do you think we're both blind?" Goth Sarah said.

"Hunh?"

"I'm Kyle Malanack," Molly said, and then she half closed her eyes and batted her lashes before doing a little sleepy-looking dance, which ended with a flourish. "I am hot, hot, hot, I am tired but I'm hot. I'm your heart attack, Kyle Malanack, and I'm hot, hot, hot," she sang, thrusting her hips from side to side with each beat.

I could feel the blood rise up the roots of my hair. "That is so not him," I said.

At this, they both laughed so hard that I had to laugh too. Then Sarah looked at me seriously. "I mean, we're your friends. You can admit it."

"This is a safe space," Molly joked, grabbing her wine violently and then taking a delicate sip. Molly had an odd combination of grace and raucousness in her gestures. She could do a staggeringly accurate imitation of someone's way of moving, or dance across the room so lightly it looked like she was levitating or flying —but when she reached for things, there was a high risk of her dropping or shattering them.

"Whatever, Kyle's okay, I guess," I said, shrugging.

Molly stood up on the bed, and did her Kyle Malanack dance again, but this time she said, "I'm okay, okay, okay," instead of "hot."

When she was finished, Sarah clapped. The truth is, it was a very cute dance. Then Sarah turned to me. "You have a cardiac arrest every day when he walks into American lit."

"Or the lunchroom," Molly said.

"Or the hallway," Sarah said.

"Or the bathroom."

"Enough! He's cute, okay?" I said. Then I waited what I thought was an adequate amount of time before asking, "So, do you guys think he's coming tonight?"

Sarah began doing the Kyle Malanack dance with Molly, who was now singing, "Hey, look over here; you can't smile! You must give it up, because I'm KYLE!"

She paused to throw me a black witch hat, which I caught and put on. I looked into Sarah's mirror and twirled, so that the frayed edge of my witchy skirt blew out like Marilyn Monroe's. I felt electric, about to have a party Kyle might come to. Sarah came and joined me at the mirror, and we slathered our eyelashes with mascara and painted our lips dark red. When Molly said, "Congratulations, you look like professional hookers," we made her take a dozen pictures of us on Sarah's phone. Meanwhile, Molly demurely slipped on silver flats and wrapped her green belt around her waist.

"Why not wear a black belt?" I asked.

"Because I'm only a green belt."

"It's Halloween. The point is you get to be what you're not in real life. Do you think I'm an actual sexy witch?"

"I don't feel good about wearing a black belt until I've earned one," she said.

This time Sarah and I laughed and rolled our eyes. I mean, who wants to go as a green belt for Halloween? How can anyone be *that* ethical?

"What will Chris think?" I asked.

"He'll think I'm about to kick his ass with my hot karate," Molly said.

"And he'll be right," Sarah said.

"Do you guys know about his dad?" Molly asked us.

"What about him?" I asked.

"That he, like, totally walked out on them when Chris was a baby?"

"Really? How do you know that?" Sarah asked her.

"I overheard Carrie and some other girls talking about it, I guess. Carrie was all like, 'He's, like, abandoned, with no male role model! It's so sad!' "

"Wow," I said, "that's horrible."

"Maybe it's why he looks so tortured." Molly closed her eyes halfway and gave a little-lidded, Chris Arpent look that was pretty convincing.

I was busy putting my heels on, and when Sarah noticed this she immediately put hers back on and then we stood in the mirror for a moment, posing and flexing our calf muscles, Chris's tragic childhood already a distant memory. By the time Chad pulled up, I was light-headed from half a glass of wine. He was with Phil, whom Chad introduced as "the Philster," and Santana, two friends from his frat. They were wearing Michigan sweatshirts and baseball hats backwards, and I thought about how stupid and obvious that was and then remembered that we were "sexy witches," and wondered if they thought that was stupid and obvious. Of course, we didn't have names like Philster and Santana. Guys always have stupid nicknames.

Sarah cat-walked down the stone path in her front yard to meet them, the cold air whipping her hot pink dress up and freezing her nipples so they greeted my brother and his friends before she did. Molly and I hung back at the porch, feeling shy.

"Hi, guys!" Sarah called out, and her voice sounded amazing, and I realized how modest she was. Sarah barely talked about herself, or the fact that she was musical and talented. Until she met Chad and his friends, I'd never seen her be so forward, and it was funny, but now that she was dressed in a Halloween costume she looked more normal than she normally did in her weird goth getups. I also thought suddenly that it was a waste that she was punk at all, how if I'd been Sarah, I'd never have dressed in anything but

146

tight jeans and T-shirts that showed off how great-looking I was. Maybe I'm shallower than she is. I mean, maybe she's making some deeper point with the way she looks than just "I'm pretty."

By eleven, the house was mobbed with people, half of whom we'd never even met. Shit was getting broken and barfed on left and right, so Sarah and Molly and I were like, super worried but also proud that our party was such a success. We had never imagined that everyone from Darcy would show, including all the senior girls, Chessie, Amanda, Carrie, and everyone. I had just seen Ginger and was making my way over to her when Kyle appeared, looking flushed, maybe from cold, or maybe he'd already had a beer.

"I'm so glad you could come!" I told Ginger. My words slurred together in a way I found attractive. I had drunk two glasses of wine, the most I'd ever had. My cheeks were hot.

"Thanks, Judy," she said. "Great party."

"What are you supposed to be?" I asked.

She was dressed in jeans and a pale blue button-down blouse open almost to her chest. She had a baseball cap on, her long blondish hair hanging out the sides of it. At the opening of her shirt, her bra, also pale blue, was visible. It looked girlish—was probably one of those Calvin Klein wisps with no wire. She was impossibly tan for November.

"Um, myself," she said. She shrugged.

"If you turn the hat around, you could go as a frat guy," I told her.

She turned her hat around and smiled. I noticed she had no drink. I went to get her a wine cooler, and when I came back she was talking to Santana, gazing up into his college eyes. He had taken his cap off, but she was still wearing hers, backwards.

"Here," I said.

She reached her hand out for the drink. "Thanks, Judy. This is Santana."

"I know," I said. "He's my brother's friend. Where's Chad?"

"Dunno," Santana said, barely looking at me. "Wanna dance?" he asked Ginger. She nodded and handed me back the wine cooler. Santana led her into the pack of sweaty, grinding people and began to hump her leg. I was watching them with dismay when I realized I was standing next to Kyle. He was also looking in the direction of the dancers.

"That guy's in college," I told him.

"Pathetic," he said.

I laughed.

"Do you want to go sit somewhere?" he asked.

I looked up at him to see if he actually meant it, nodded.

I grabbed my jacket from Sarah's hall closet

and we went outside, where throngs of kids were gathered on Sarah's parents' back deck even though it was literally freezing. Everyone was smoking. Kyle found two chairs in the corner, pulled them up to a dusty table no one was using.

"So what are you?" he asked, gesturing to my dress. I had left my jacket open, in case he hadn't noticed yet how cute I looked.

"A dwarf," I said.

He laughed. "You're pulling it off," he said.

Then we sat there until I thought I'd die of either awkwardness or hypothermia.

"So, uh, what are you doing for Thanksgiving?" I asked.

He shrugged, like he didn't know. "You?"

"I guess I'll spend as much time as I can with my little brother, Sam. I guess I've kinda been ignoring him because I'm too busy with voice rehearsals and schoolwork and piano lessons and stuff." I said this not only because I couldn't shut up, but also because I wanted to remind Kyle that I was in senior voice, and that I was brilliant in school. That way how could he resist me? Kyle looked at me for a weirdly long time.

"How old is he?" he finally asked.

Other people began to invade our cold and dusty table.

"Hey, man! I've been looking everywhere for you!" Chris shouted at Kyle. When Kyle didn't really respond, Chris and Alan started doing shots of Jägermeister from a bottle they'd carried out. Alan was bragging about how he was going to L.A. over Christmas break with his dad, and maybe he'd "take some meetings" while he was there. His plan, which I knew because everyone talked about it constantly, was to go to Stanford, major in film, and grow up to be an oily Hollywood producer. I had heard a rumor that Alan's dad, who I guess was a big-shot rich guy of some sort, had lined up summer internships for both Alan and Chris at production companies in L.A. This would be a big promotion for Alan, who I knew, from seeing him and his blond leg hair all summer, had been a lowly lifeguard at Fuller Pool. I went there every day with my friend Meghan from California. Alan was always either reading or pretending to read what he called the "trades," *Variety* and *The Hollywood Reporter*, and he and Chris, who was apparently going to go to UCLA and then be a famous stand-up comedian, were both also writing screenplays in their spare time. I had heard Chris talking before SV about how he couldn't talk about his, the idea being that it was so great and high-concept that someone might steal it and get the movie made before he could graduate from high school and take over Hollywood while at his unpaid internship. I had overheard enough self-loving snippets to know that Alan's screenplay was about a Stanford swimmer who is so irresistible and fabulous that some hot girl stalks him and tries to kill him. I guess no one told him that there's already a very stupid movie about exactly that. I don't know what Chris's screenplay was about, because it was such a state secret— probably a gorgeous guy with huge muscles, short dark hair, and bruised-looking eyes who gets stalked by a desperate supermodel. I mean, come on.

"He's almost twelve," I said to Kyle about Sam, even though it was too late.

But he was still waiting to hear, his face calm and still like a lake at night. I thought how smooth Kyle was, and I don't mean smooth in the terrible way. I mean like you could have skipped a stone across the surface of him.

"Twelve, huh?" he said, the corners of his mouth rising in a smile. "What's he like?"

Kyle Malanack seemed so not like a fake person. I mean, he's the kind of guy who asks what your little brother is like. And when he asks, you're certain it's because he's curious. And he deserves real props for both things—I mean, for being curious and for asking. Most people aren't curious about each other, unless there's something sickening or hideous to be curious about. And most people talk about themselves endlessly without asking questions. Or when they ask questions, it's like totally perfunctory and they don't really listen to the answer. Kyle Malanack is the type of boy, and I mean, he's a high school boy, who asks "What's he like" about your little brother, Sam, and when you say, "He wants to be either president or a rap artist," laughs with his head thrown back and you can see all his teeth and you can tell he sees how much you love your brother and that if Sam were his brother, he would love him too. And that's why you believe, even after it turns out to be false, that Kyle Malanack loves you.

Then he asked, "Is he a little person like you?"

I felt my breathing get faster, my heart pop a little in its cage. I really didn't like the question. But why? I mean, wasn't he just saying what we'd both been thinking anyway, that if we got married and had kids, they might be dwarfs like me?

And how did he know to use the words *little person like you?* Did he even know that LP was a phrase with capital letters? Or was it just how he thought of me, as a person who's kind of little, rather than a dwarf or midget?

"Nope," I said, "both my brothers are tall."

"Your parents, too?" he asked.

"Everyone in my family except me." I felt suddenly drunker than ever and realized my wineglass was empty. I wanted another glass.

"So it's not genetic?"

He asked this in a kind way, the way you

might ask someone about her job, or dog, or vacation. I shrugged unhappily. "It might be, I mean, you don't have to have a genetic condition to pass it on to your kids." I couldn't help but feel like now he might not want to have kids with me.

He took a swig of beer, noticed I had no drink, offered me a sip of his. I took the beer, so excited that he'd offered me a sip that it overrode my hatred of the taste.

"Do you have siblings?" I asked.

He looked confused by my question, but only for a moment, and then he looked totally freaked out. I had no idea how this could have been an offensive question, but I was instantly sorry I had asked.

"I'm an only child," he said. He took another gulp of beer, and something about the way he drank it made him seem like a little kid to me, like it was milk or something.

"So are you in town for Thanksgiving too?"

"Nah. I think I'm going with Alan to his grandparents' in Grosse Pointe." He said this as if he had just decided it, finished his beer, pulled another out from under the table.

I didn't say, "What about your family, aren't they in Ann Arbor?" I knew from Ginger and his Facebook page that Kyle had lived in Boston until this year, that he was new in the school. Past that, I knew nothing about him.

"Oh, cool," I said.

"Yeah. Maybe me and Alan'll catch a game or something."

"You like football?"

"I like to watch it," he said.

"Ann Arbor's a good place for you, then. We have season tickets to the Wolverines—"

I almost got to "if you want to come some-time," but before I made it there, from across the table where Chris and Alan had started a game of quarters, Chris threw a coin at Kyle, hard, but Kyle dodged it and then got up and put Chris in a headlock. Then they jumped off the deck and started rolling around in the yard. Alan shouted out to Tim Malone, "Dude, look at the lovebirds." Everyone looked, of course, so Kyle and Chris let go of each other right away and came back up to the tables and resumed their conversations or drinking or whatever they were doing.

Teenage boys are hybrids of people and monkeys. This kind of interaction was a daily occurrence at school: the homoerotic banter followed by physical contact, followed by someone calling the whole thing what it was (love, desire for contact, although put in fouler terms, usually), and then an embarrassed retreat back to the solo corners of teenage boy–dom, the lone seat at the lunch table, or the classroom desk, or wherever. I sometimes think, especially now after the whole sex thing, that life would be easier for all of us if boys just had sex with each other. I mean, I guess lots of them do do that, but I mean the ones who don't, the ones who think they're so straight, so into girls. Because maybe sometimes it's what they want. And if straight boys want to sleep with their friends once in a while, that would be fine, right? I mean, other than ruining their idea of themselves, it wouldn't cost anyone else anything. Then they wouldn't have to use girls, or sex with girls, as a way to bond with each other instead of bonding with the girls. Because I know I'm not the most experienced person in the world, but that's what I think guys are doing sometimes. I don't know why no one told me. No one ever talks about this stuff. And maybe it's surprising to everyone and not just me, because the brochures and website for Darcy are all full of pictures of people dancing across stages, singing in brightly colored musicals, or studying on the neon green lawn, but there are a lot of sketchy things happening there, and I don't just mean people fucking and then never talking to each other again—I mean, like, gang bangs.

And when I say "gang bang," I mean any sex that involves one girl and more than one guy. Because even though I'm only almost seventeen now I know what that kind of sex means. I didn't even know the term *gang bang* until I heard it in a song Chad was listening to, and when I asked him about it, he said, "Oh, that's group sex."

And I was like, "What is group sex?" because I was only thirteen when this happened.

And he was like, "More than two people having sex," and I couldn't even imagine what that meant, really, because my parents had read me that stupid body book for girls, and it had "sex" in it, but only the kind where you and your husband are in love and then you make a baby, by putting that in this, yadda-yadda. The body book for girls did not have gang bangs in it. And either Chad didn't really know what he was talking about or he wanted to protect me from the truth, because gang bangs aren't just a group of people having sex because everyone wants to. At Darcy, *gang bang* means boys and other boys having sex with a girl—and really, she's just a fake thing, a conduit between the people who want to have sex with each other but can't—Kyle and Chris, for example. Or Kyle and Alan. Or Alan and Chris. Maybe those are just the guys' way of experimenting, or "practicing," as we used to call it when I was twelve and thirteen, at Tappan, and we used to gather in Stacy Levinson-Monroe's basement and French kiss each other and slide our nightgowns off our thin chests and "practice." But we never used real guys in those experiments, just played a little bit with each other, seeing how it would feel, making sure we'd be "good at it" if the need ever arose. We never talked about those nights after they happened, not once. Or acted them out at parties. And we didn't take it to mean we were gay, even though the kissing felt good. And I'm not saying that Kyle or any of his guy friends is gay, because I think they're straight if what that means is that they'll marry girls and have kids and live in the kinds of places where no one's allowed to admit to being gay anyway, even if they are. I just mean I don't get why they have to use girls instead of just admitting they're sometimes in love with each other. Maybe it's because they're teenagers, or maybe guys are just chicken in general. But for whatever reason, the boys I know were too scared to use each other for their practice.

Ginger invited herself over the Monday after the party. I wondered if she had seen me on the porch with Kyle and that was why. Like maybe because he was interested in me, she suddenly found me interesting for real too. Because I had invited her over once before, but she'd said she had to be somewhere else and not said where and I'd assumed it was a lie and that she just didn't want to come to my house. But then during lunch, she came over to where I was sitting with Goth Sarah and Molly and stood in front of us.

"Hey, Judy, I could come over this afternoon,

if the invitation still stands," she said. I was pretty surprised, but I tried to shrug and said, "Sure," like it was nothing. I didn't have a voice rehearsal that afternoon, because the freshmen were apparently not at all ready for their fall concert and were having extra rehearsals in the auditorium. And I could give up my practice room time for Ginger.

Molly didn't care at all—but I could tell Goth Sarah didn't like Ginger coming over to talk to us and also probably noticed that I was happy not to go to the practice rooms for Ginger, even though I never skipped that hour for Goth Sarah. Sarah kind of had a thing about some of the other girls at D'Arts, even though she was big on women uniting and taking over the world together instead of fighting with each other. I guess someone had started a rumor about her at Scarlett Middle School, that she had gotten crabs at Interlochen summer camp. Which is completely stupid—I mean, she was twelve. Maybe it was lice or something, and they blew it out of proportion. Everyone gets lice at camp. I know the one time my parents let me go to overnight camp for one traumatic week, I came home with bugs absolutely leaping off my head. Or maybe she didn't even get lice that time; maybe it was nothing at all and those girls just made the whole thing up, I don't know. But I guess everyone believed it and thought Sarah was dirty and gross. And Sarah still held a massive grudge, which I could kind of understand, even though it was clearly time to let it go. Ginger could also just make you feel bad about yourself, even though she didn't mean to. Something about her reminded me of the Cheshire Cat, maybe her ability to materialize suddenly, looking somehow more than three-dimensional. Her ratty clothes felt like an insult to the rest of us, a statement about how easy it was for her to come to school in her pajamas and still look a thousand times more gorgeous than any of us (except Elizabeth Wood), no matter how much effort we put in.

I knew I should invite Goth Sarah and Molly to come over to my house that afternoon too, but I couldn't bring myself to. I didn't think Molly wanted to come or that Sarah would be able to be nice to Ginger, and I didn't want the whole afternoon to be an awkward nightmare. And isn't it okay to have more than one group of friends? So we said nothing about it for the rest of lunch, just rehashed the fun, mundane matters of our party: Tim Malone had flirted with Molly all night, and we were sure he was about to ask her out. Kelly Barksper had unbuttoned her shirt all the way down to her jeans and done a dance standing on the couch in front of a group of guys; Chad's friend Santana humped everyone in sight like Sarah's house was the dog park. Susie Schultz had made out with both Mike Conner and Ian Sarbell; Elizabeth Wood had passed out, but not before barfing all over Tyler Phillips and the jade plant in Sarah's parents' foyer. Another giant stain had appeared mysteriously on the living room rug, so Sarah and I had moved the couch over two feet to hide it. Maybe her parents would never notice, or we'd say Sarah got food poisoning from ordering pizza too many times while they were gone. It had taken nine hours to clean her house on Sunday, and Chad had come to pick up the kegs.

As we were leaving the lunchroom, Goth Sarah snuck her cell phone out of her purse, even though we weren't allowed to have phones at school unless they were locked in our lockers or they would get confiscated until the end of the week. Molly was like, "Sarah! I can't believe you have that thing with you again. Put it away—are you crazy?"

"Whatever," Sarah said. "If they take it, it's worth it—Eliot just texted me!"

Then Molly rushed off to her locker because she had to get notes for an open-book Latin test, and I guess Goth Sarah had been waiting until we were alone, because she was like, "Be careful of Ginger Mews. She's a bitch."

I wished Molly had stayed; she would have been reasonable. "Really?" I asked.

"She's just the type to, like, steal friends and boyfriends and start rumors."

"Everyone dates each other's boyfriends in high school—there's only like twenty boys in the whole class. And what do you mean, rumors?" I wondered if she'd mention the crabs thing.

"Nothing. There was just this thing last year where she told everyone that she had seen Jessica Lambkin making out with some old guy and it became this huge mess."

"Had she?"

"Had she what?"

"Seen Jessica with some old guy."

"That's not the point. I just mean, even if she had, why ruin Jessica's life with it?"

"Why would that ruin Jessica's life?"

"The guy was her dad."

"Let me get this straight: Ginger saw Jessica Lambkin *making out* with her dad."

"Jessica's dad."

"Her own dad. Jessica Lambkin was making out with the man who sired her."

"What?"

"The guy whose sperm made her."

"I know what *sire* means. Stop being so pretentious."

"Jessica was French-kissing her own father?"

"That's what Ginger Mews told everyone," Sarah said.

"Wow. That's really horrible."

"And it wasn't true. I mean, maybe they were kissing and hugging or something, but they couldn't have been, you know, making out. But it was one of those stupid things—and once Ginger said it, everyone talked about it so much that whenever you saw Jessica, you were just like, *ew*. Even if you didn't think it was true."

"That's really stupid. That whole story is just incredibly stupid. You do realize, don't you, that this is why everyone thinks teenagers are idiots." I stood and walked over to the trash can at the entrance to the cafeteria.

Goth Sarah followed me and stood there while I dumped my lunch out. "Actually, people think that because when you're a teenager, your brain isn't fully developed yet," she said. "I saw it on PBS. They used to think your brain was, like, finished growing once you weren't a little kid anymore, but then they realized that this part"— she tapped on her forehead—"right behind your forehead, where you control everything you do —that part isn't 'fully matured' or whatever in teenagers."

"What's your point?" I asked. "That we *are* stupid?" I spat my gum out.

She laughed. "No. I mean, their point on PBS was that the forehead part is like the boss of your brain, and the older it gets, the better you are at judging what you shouldn't do. Your brain is all exuberant when you're young, but then it gets you know, adulted out with rules or what-ever. Some kind of disgusting white film starts covering your brain as you get older, mummify-ing your thoughts."

"Really? Gross."

"Not until you're in your twenties," Sarah said, grinning joyfully. "So we still have a while with our underdeveloped brains." I loved Sarah's fact hoard. She watched a lot of PBS, and more than once I had seen her reading science books in the library and hallways—ones that weren't assigned.

But I couldn't resist saying, "If that's true, then isn't it wrong to hold a grudge forever just because someone once said some stupid shit about you when you both had infant brains?" I asked.

"Touché!" Sarah said, but now the bell was ringing and she dashed down the hall because as usual she had to go hide her cell phone in her locker, and was going to be late.

Maybe Sarah was right that Ginger had done something bitchy to Jessica Lambkin, but even without the whole brain argument, can you really define a whole person by one cruel thing she does? I ignored her warning, of course, and Ginger came over that afternoon. When we got to my house, it was totally quiet; Sam was with my parents at the Grill, and Chad was living full-time at his dorm now, coming home only to do laundry or have dinner whenever he had nothing better to do. I poured us some raspberry pop in the kitchen, and then Ginger and I took it and some potato chips up to my bedroom, where we sat listening to Bob Dylan.

I wished I had torn down the white curtains with lavender flowers, or changed the matching bedspread to something cooler, although I didn't know what that would have been. She poked around the room a bit when we first came in, looking at the pictures I had tacked to my bulletin board: me and Sam swimming at Silver Lake; my parents getting married in St. Louis, the arch visible behind them; Chad at his graduation from Huron High, still shaved bald from nationals; Meghan and me at the LPA conference the summer before, with Joel in between us, raising his eyebrows like, "I'm in a picture with two hot girls."

"Who's that guy?" Ginger asked, pointing at Joel.

I yawned. "Some guy I met at a conference last summer."

"Did you fuck him?"

In spite of myself, I felt the blood rush to my head, and hoped it wasn't visible. I tried to sound nonchalant.

"He wanted to," I lied. "But I didn't want to lose it to him."

Ginger nodded, as if this was not only an

appropriate response, but also the answer she knew she'd get. "Guys are pigs," she said. She came over and lay down across my bed. Because it was low to the floor, she had to fall a long way down, and she looked oddly disproportionate. I shifted my weight in the purple beanbag chair I was sitting on, felt its millions of tiny pellets shift, pour, and regroup. I thought maybe the thing about pigs was something she had heard her mother say. It sounded like that, like something that hadn't originated in Ginger's mind or mouth.

Dylan was singing, "I've walked and I've crawled on six crooked highways."

I debated whether to be like, "Yeah, I know, I know," which would have been completely false but maybe cool and unawkward, or ask the real, genuinely curious, "What do you mean, pigs?" I settled on the latter.

"You know, they just use you."

"For what?"

She laughed, as if I'd been joking. "Sex, of course," she said.

"But don't girls have sex because they want to, too?"

"Yeah. But we also want other things, and sex is *all* that guys want."

I thought of Chad and Sam. Sam wanted salamanders, and Chad? Time with our dad, and swimming pools and footballs and, from what I

165

could tell about him and his new U of M girlfriend, Alice, back-scratching. I couldn't bring myself to agree with Ginger, even if it meant we'd never be friends. I stayed quiet.

"You should be careful," she said.

"Careful of what?"

"Guys at Darcy."

"Okay," I said, turning away so she couldn't see my expression. I was embarrassed, didn't know what she was warning me of, exactly, but I didn't like it.

"Hey," she said. She swung her flamingo legs off my bed and found her purse on the floor where she'd tossed it. She opened the zipper. "You want?" She took something out of a ziplock bag and held it out to me. It was a tiny cigarette, all wrinkly and crazy-looking. It took me a minute.

"Is that marijuana?"

She laughed. "Yeah," she said.

I blushed again. "Sure."

She fished around for a lighter.

"Um, Ginger, maybe we should go out back—I mean, my mom might not like it if she could smell it when she gets back."

"Sure," she said. All of a sudden, I wished Sarah were over instead of her. I didn't have to pretend to be cool in front of Sarah. And I know it's stupid, but I had never smoked pot, and I was a little worried about whether it would freak me out or make me paranoid or something.

We went out to my backyard, which is mostly trees; they back all the way up to Washtenaw. Chad and Sam and I used to think it was enormous, like acres and acres of land, when we were small. We got CB radios once for Christmas, and played with them for two hundred days in a row, calling to each other from across the backyard. A couple of times we even overheard truckers talking. Once, Chad strung a wire from the tallest tree to the shortest, and put a pulley on it, and we climbed the tree and held on to the pulley and slid down over and over until the pulley snapped while Sam was on it and he fell and broke his arm. I remember he got a red cast. Sam always got hurt. Whenever we rough-housed or went wild after dessert, our mom would be yelling, "Someone's gonna get hurt! And it's gonna be Sam."

Walking out into the backyard with Ginger, I wished I were a little kid again, with Sam and Chad, our mom yelling from the deck, "Someone's gonna get hurt!" I wondered if Chad had ever smoked pot. I guessed so, wished I had asked for advice so I could have been prepared for this. I mean, I had smoked cigarettes once with Meghan, sneaking off behind the hotel at an LPA conference. She had menthol ones and I kind of liked them. I hoped, as Ginger and I climbed the rope ladder into Chad's old tree house, that the experience of smoking those would make it look like I wasn't a total infant.

She climbed into the hole in the middle of the tree house floor; I was behind her on the ladder. As soon as my head popped up into the house, I saw the cobwebs and bugs that had taken over the floor. Ginger shuddered and moved herself over to a corner.

"Whatever," I said, hoping to make her feel as stupid about being squeamish as I did about being inexperienced. I brushed some of the mess away down the hole, and she came out from the corner, where she had been squatting on her tiptoes. She took a lighter out of her pocket, sat down, lit the shriveled cigarette, and took a puff. She appeared to have filled her entire body up with smoke, because she got taller and taller as she inhaled, and held her breath for a long time before she blew out a thin stream of smoke and shrank back down to normal size. Then she handed me the thing. I had a vivid flash of how much better a time I'd be having if Molly and Goth Sarah had come over.

"Go ahead," Ginger said. I tried to hold it expertly between my fingers, without burning myself. She leaned her head back against the wall of the tree house and I watched her smooth throat, then put the joint in my mouth too far, so it was more like eating it than smoking it. I breathed all the way into my lungs, almost slurping the whole thing right into my windpipe. I could feel something black and feathery shoot into my body, like a hot pile of raked leaves, burning down my throat and into my body. I hated it, began coughing, gagging, trying to get the taste and smell and feeling out of my lungs.

"Oh my god," Ginger said, looking over at me. "Are you okay?"

"I'm fine," I hacked out. "Totally good." I stopped coughing finally, and waited to see what would happen. Maybe I would completely freak out and be unable to speak. I thought I might sit under the table in my parents' dining room, or eat everything in the kitchen, or my eyes would turn red and veiny and I'd be a complete junkie.

Instead, I felt nothing.

"You want another toke?" Ginger asked.

I shook my head. "No, I'm good," I said.

Ginger took a few more tokes and then we climbed down.

"Are you high?" she asked.

"Yes," I said.

"Good," she said.

We walked through the backyard, and she started giggling, so I started to fake giggle, hoping that's what you did, and she said, "So your brother's friend called me."

"Yeah? Santana?"

"Uh-huh."

"And?"

"We're supposed to hang out this Friday night."

"Wow. Really?"

She gave me a nonchalant look. "Yeah, I mean, he's okay and everything, but honestly, I wasn't sure I wanted to, so I waited two days before I said I'd hang out."

I couldn't resist. "Because he's forty and should get a girlfriend his own age?"

She shot me a sideways look. "I just don't know if I like him. What about you?"

I deflected. "Did you and Santana hook up at the party?"

"Nothing major," she said, and we hit another impasse. I had no idea whether Ginger and I agreed on what *major* meant—I mean, I had seen them making out in front of everyone. But I didn't want to explore the terms. Mainly, I was relieved to know they'd hooked up at all, since that probably meant she hadn't left with Kyle.

"Did you hook up with anyone?" she asked.

"Not at the party," I said, blushing. "I was too busy hosting, I guess."

We went upstairs to my room, and as I closed the door, I heard my mom's car pull into the driveway, and Sam, pulling the empty garbage cans up the driveway. I climbed onto my little stool to look out the window.

"My mom's home," I told Ginger.

She looked at her watch. "Wow," she said, "she

gets home early. My mom works till like nine or ten every night."

"My dad's doing dinner at the Grill tonight because Sam had something he had to go to. Do you want to stay for dinner?"

"If it's okay with your mom," she said. She giggled again. "I'm *hungry!*"

I guessed that this must be related to the smoking, so I said, "Yeah, me too!" and she gave me a knowing look, like we had a secret together, and I was glad we'd done it, even though it had sucked and had no effect on me at all. Maybe I was impervious to pot, I thought, maybe it doesn't work on little people. Then there were keys in the door, shoes in the hallway, voices pouring up the stairs.

"Judy? You home, sweetie?"

I tried to smell my hair and clothes, to see if they smelled like pot, without Ginger noticing. I took a pack of Eclipse out of my pocket and frantically chewed several pieces.

"Don't worry," Ginger said. "There's no way she'll notice. I mean, it was only one hit and we were outside for a long time after."

Sam came bounding up the stairs to my room, his coat still on.

"Judy! Do you want to see it?" he shouted to me, pushing the door open. "Oh!" he said when he saw Ginger. He shrank back like a tiny weed. "Sorry, I didn't know—"

"That's okay, Sam. Come in—this is Ginger."

He looked down at the floor, nodding so that his straight hair flopped over his eyes. I could tell he found Ginger pretty, and that this unnerved him. The truth is, Ginger might be the prettiest person I've ever met, and either she doesn't try or she tries so hard that it makes it look like she didn't even have to try. I mean, she wears almost no makeup, had the kind of skin so clear you can basically see through it to her veins, floppy blond hair, and all small features except for her lips, which are so puffy that they look like some kind of sea monster attacked her and sucked on them until they swelled up. Well, that's not an attractive way to put it, but the point is, her lips are huge and everyone wants to kiss them because they present themselves so assertively. The result is that Ginger looks like a commercial for whatever she happens to be doing or eating or holding. Now she was selling my bed, sprawled across it like a giant when Sam came in.

"You can show both of us," Ginger said. She propped herself up on her elbows.

"Show us what?" I asked.

"Whatever you were going to show Judy," she said to Sam.

I liked her for saying this to him, rather than answering me. It seemed respectful, made Sam feel dignified.

"Oh, that," he said. "It was just a move."

He looked up, and I was amazed and alarmed to see that he did, in fact, want to show Ginger and me his "move."

"Go for it, Sam—show us," I said.

He took his coat the rest of the way off, revealing a Kanye West T-shirt so absurd and big and aspirational on him that I wanted to wrap him up and protect him from whatever Ginger was about to think. But she was smiling.

Sam began jogging in place and then threw himself down on the rug in my room and tried to spin himself up into a headstand of some sort. It didn't work out very well, but, perhaps in an effort to save face, he vaulted himself from a triangle kind of yoga pose into a regular head-stand and then came crashing down, leapt up, and did some more jogging. I applauded.

He stood there, blushing.

"It doesn't really work on the carpet," he said, picking up his jacket.

"No, no," I said. "We could tell it would be great on a real floor. Very impressive." But he was looking at Ginger, who had a huge smile on her face.

"That was great," she said. "You'll be breaking on stages across America, no doubt. You should audition for *So You Think You Can Dance*. Or at least go out for D'Arts." She used a very serious voice to say this. Sam regarded her for a moment, trying to tell whether she might be mocking him and deciding, from her unblinking performance, that she was not.

At dinner, my mom watched Ginger carefully, with an interest I couldn't place. She asked lots of polite questions about Darcy, some less polite ones about Ginger's parents, who, it turned out, were divorced, both remarried, her mom redivorced and her dad living in Texas with a young wife Ginger said she hated. I was totally shocked, had assumed Ginger had an absolute picket fence around some perfect family in a white house. My mom, although not surprised, was also not impressed, and when Ginger left after dessert and a bit of lingering, my mom put on a flat voice that sounded like she was helping me run lines: "It was nice to meet her."

Then she waited for what she thought was long enough before she asked, "When is Sarah coming over again? Do you two have any plans?"

Adults are so obvious. It's weird that the teenage brain is considered underdeveloped. Maybe the more we develop the less capable we are of hiding our mostly pathetic motives. Or maybe we just give up, stop trying.

"No," I finally said. And went up to my room, listened at the vent to see if my mom would tell my dad what I knew she thought of Ginger, that she was a bad influence on me, or that I had "fallen in with a bad crowd." I was so sick of the idea of being careful. My plan was to feel thrilled about having smoked pot. But instead all I heard was my mom and dad bickering about Christmas and who was staying in what room when everyone visited and whether some people should stay in a hotel and whether Chad would want to come home or stay in his dorm over the holiday. My mom was furious that my dad wasn't helping figure everything out in advance without being nagged to; my dad was annoyed that she was nagging him. He never thought planning or setting anything up was a big deal. Of course he didn't have to do the planning or setting up, and maybe that was why. Or maybe if she had nagged him less, he would have taken more initiative.

Listening to them, all I could think was, "Can I please keep my exuberant brain forever?"

7 I was so nervous the night of the senior voice concert that I couldn't stop asking Chad if teenagers could have heart attacks. My pulse was like 210, pounding in my neck like an alien trying to escape. Chad said teenagers never die of heart attacks.

"You're going to be great," he kept saying. "The nervousness is the sign of a true genius." He said he was so nervous before his swim meets that he sometimes threw up, and the more nervous he was, the better he did.

"I'm not nervous when I dance," Sam said.

It was a cold, rainy night and the pavement in the parking lot shimmered as we walked up to the school from the car. I had on boots, black skirt, white blouse, and red tie, since those were the colors the seniors were wearing. I had dark lipstick on too, like Ms. Doman's. She had told us she was going to bring her husband. And since we all wanted to be married to her, this was interesting for us.

Everyone was there—and I mean the entire school, every teacher, student, sibling, parent, and custodian, all crowded in the hallway outside the auditorium. Mrs. O'Henry was all dressed up in a long maroon dress with buttons shaped like flowers, and she waved to my parents and me. Then I saw Ginger and some woman with enormous hair. When the woman turned, I stared. Her face looked like plastic that had been melted and molded, and now could never be moved. She was weirdly ageless, and resembled, in the way that all victims of plastic surgery do, Michael Jackson. Maybe it's the absurdly tiny noses that make people look like that, shadows of their original, real noses hovering above the new ones. Like the way you have limb anxiety when your leg gets cut off but you feel like you still have a leg. Maybe you break your face's heart when you chop off parts of it, and it longs for the other half of its original nose. The woman with Ginger had eyebrows so high up across her forehead that they looked suspended by puppet strings. I wondered how she closed her eyes to sleep, because she had practically no eyelids left.

"Hey, Judy, this is my mom," Ginger said, and the woman reached out and shook my hand and then my mom's hand, and after I recovered from the shock of Ginger having a mom who looked like that, I thought how her hands betrayed her, looked like they belonged to a fifty-year-old woman who had been married and divorced twice and was raising Ginger alone. Her boobs, on the other hand, looked like they were about to torpedo off her chest and puncture anything in her path. My mom took a tiny step back.

"Hi, I'm Mimi," said Ginger's mom.

"Hello," my mom said, in her flat voice, and I was furious at her for acting like a snob, even though I was stunned by Ginger's mother too. My mind was surging forward. For one thing, as soon as I met her mom, I thought maybe Ginger had a scholarship too. For another, maybe she wore sweatpants and stuff all the time because she didn't have that much money to buy fancy clothes. For a third, maybe she was insecure, embarrassed of her mom. Of course, it was sweet that her mother would show up at the senior voice concert when Ginger wasn't even in it. Maybe she just wanted to see the school. Or had Ginger been hiding her from us and now her mom had found an excuse to meet everyone? I would have to analyze with Molly, who was smart about other people's parents. Sarah was too mean about Ginger to be able to help.

"Thank you for having Ginger over," Ginger's mom was saying, and I couldn't stop thinking about how weird it was that Ginger's mom wore so much makeup and had such a crazy-single lady look with the big painted nails and everything when Ginger was so pretty in her sweatpants without trying. And then I thought how Goth Sarah was the opposite of her mom too, because her mom was all plain while Sarah was so Goth. This made me wonder if I was the same as my mom or different, and maybe it's just because it's hard to see yourself, but I couldn't decide. The truth is, even now, I don't know if either half of me is like my mom. Is the regular Judy half of me like my mom, even if the dwarf half isn't? Even if I weren't a dwarf, would I be like her? When I think about it, it gets hard to say what either of us is even like.

I did know one thing: my mom was being unfair by thinking just because of the way she looked that Ginger's mom couldn't be doing a good job. My mom never said she thought that, but I could tell. But she was wrong, because I know now that Ginger's mom is actually a good mother, and maybe my mom had an after-school-special idea about her just because she wants to be younger than she is. Of course, I kind of had the wrong idea about Ginger and her mother too, so maybe I am like my mom.

I saw Kyle walking into the auditorium by himself, and was thrilled that he had come, even though it was impossible to know who he'd come to hear; I mean, all of his friends were seniors, so it could have been anyone in SV.

Then Ms. Doman came in with an old man, and I wondered who he was—her dad? A new teacher? Then I saw that he had his hand on the back of her waist, and a jolt of terror shot through me like an arrow. That hundred-year-old man was her husband! My mom made her way over to them, dragging me by the hand like a five-year-old.

"You must be Ms. Doman," she said, and I was embarrassed that she would say such a boring thing to the most brilliant teacher in the school.

"Are you Judy's mom?" Ms. Doman asked, holding my mom's gaze like a movie star in love.

My mom nodded and put her arm behind my head, which is her way of putting an arm around me. This way, she doesn't have to crouch down, but also doesn't appear to be patting my hair like I'm a pet of some sort.

Ms. Doman leaned forward, glanced around politely, saw that no one but her ancient husband was in earshot. "Judy is the best student I've had in twelve years of teaching," she told my mother. I thought my mother might leap into her arms.

"Thank you so much for telling us that. We're very proud of her, of course."

Mr. Doman harrumphed and Ms. Doman opened up the side of herself that was next to him. "Judy, Ms. Lohden, this is my husband, Norman Crump."

"Norman Crump?" my mother asked. *"The* Norman Crump?"

"The one and only," Ms. Doman said, half sweetly and half bitterly, as if she knew he was famous but wasn't impressed anymore after years of having to pick his undershirts off the back of her desk chair or something.

"It's nice to meet you both," Norman Crump

said in a gentle way, and I felt bad for having had mean thoughts about him before he'd even opened his mouth. What was wrong with me? As if to make it worse, he turned to me. He had an afro of gray hair around his head, and wore round frameless glasses. I wondered if he had been cute when he was young, thought probably only in a so-ugly-it's-lovable way. He had a big, weird-shaped nose right in the middle of his face; it looked like someone had made it half an hour before out of modeling clay and put it on him as a disguise.

"Emma has shown me some of your writing," he said. "I hope you'll be a writer someday."

"Really? Thank you!" I was unable to mask my babyish delight, even at hearing him call Ms. Doman "Emma" in front of me. I tried to recover my dignity, but made everything worse by adding, "I mean, coming from you, that means a lot."

Norman Crump is a Michigan hero. He's a writer who sets all of his novels in Ann Arbor, and describes the town perfectly every time, making it seem like the center of the universe, instead of just a top-ten university town like Madison or wherever else college students gather in the Midwest to drink beer and get educated. He always has young people having sex in unmistakably Ann Arbor locations: the stadium, Gallup Park, on the steps at Hill Auditorium. Maybe he and Ms. Doman frolicked all over the town when he was young. Although when he was young, she wasn't born yet. So maybe he did it with someone else and then married Ms. Doman as soon as she turned eighteen. Old famous writers always marry their students. Maybe Ms. Doman had been the prettiest and most promising one in his class, so he had married her. I couldn't think of a polite way to ask how they'd met, although I was curious. What if I asked and he had been her nursery school teacher? No one wanted to have that conversation.

My parents went into the auditorium, where we saw Mr. Luther taking a seat by himself. He was so wrong for being a schoolteacher. It was like he was a sea sponge, removed from its natural habitat and unable to survive in the world he had picked. I hoped he was gay and had a boyfriend, but was just too shy to bring him. I hoped the boyfriend was sweet and sociable and helped Mr. Luther interact with whatever world they lived in when he didn't have to be at school. As long as he wasn't just alone all the time, living in the math room, slinking out from behind his desk to attend our events. I told my parents to go sit with him and headed backstage, where all the seniors were chattering giddily and putting on lipstick. Alan was rubbing Amanda Fulton's shoulders and bare neck. I stood in the wings, waiting for Ms.

Vanderly to gesture to me and Carrie to come out, and trying to breathe deeply even though every time I did, I inhaled so much dust from the thick dark red curtains on the stage that I thought my throat would close off entirely like a clogged bathtub drain. Ms. Vanderly was on stage introducing us, and then she turned a beaming smile toward the wings. Carrie and I looked at each other, nodded, and walked out snapping. We started the whole concert with the intro to "Take Five," and honestly, I was so nervous I felt like I might black out. But the audience was dark enough that I could pretend they weren't there, that the blazing above me was sunshine coming through my bedroom window, and I bolted that introduction out, all the boo boo shoo be doo bops, listening for Carrie's voice and trying to make sure we matched, that I wasn't drowning her out. I could hear her slight, high voice like a glittering string above mine, and I relaxed. We sang, "Still, I know our eyes often meet / I feel tingles down to my feet," and I could feel Ms. Vanderly's proud eyes on us from the wings.

Then everybody came out, and we did four numbers together before the six of us doing real solos exited and lined up backstage. I came out first again, the spotlight so bright in my eyes I couldn't see anything. I took a steadying breath and sang "We Belong Together," the whole song out into absolute blankness that could have been my room or the shower or outer space, except my parents and Chad and Sam and Kyle and Ginger and her mother and Molly and Goth Sarah and what I considered to be the rest of the world were all watching, listening.

I came back to consciousness during the last verse:

> Shall we weigh along these streets
> Young lions on the lam?
> Are the signs you hid deep in your heart
> All left on neon for them?

Then it was a blur. The audience was standing and screaming, and we were done, had sung our solos and the finale and felt like rock stars even though the fans were our parents and brothers and teachers and their hundred-year-old husbands. Backstage was like being inside a hot air popper. Everyone had rushed back there and was hugging and screaming and congratulating each other. I spotted Kyle right away; he was standing near the doorway to the auditorium with Chris and a woman I guessed must be Chris's mom. She was fine-boned, wearing a simple black dress with a cream cardigan over it, and black boots with a lot of stitching on them. Her hair was pulled up into a gold clip, and she had on soft pink lipstick.

Both of her arms were wrapped around Chris, and she looked like she might die of love and pride. To my surprise, he didn't seem to mind, was returning the snuggle, unembarrassed. I wondered how his dad could have left them, if she had lots of boyfriends, if Chris was jealous. Alan was there too, but before I could figure out who his parents were, mine arrived to smother me with compliments.

I could see past them that Kyle was making his way over, although maybe he was just headed to the door to leave. But in any case, as he walked by, he was like, "Judy Lohden, congrats, man, that was great!"

My parents were standing there like cardboard cutouts of themselves. I said, "Thanks, Kyle!" really fast, and my voice was all high-pitched and squeaky so I tried to cover it up by saying, "So were you," which was horrible because he hadn't been in the concert because he wasn't in senior voice. But instead of being like, "I mean, I know you would have been good," or whatever I could have said to unembarrass myself and continue making it worse, I managed to stay quiet. This was good, because it meant I could keep hearing my name in his voice. It echoed in the dark, empty chamber of my mind. Ginger was standing there too, and she was like, yeah, good job, Judy, and even though I was grateful that she said it, because now the stupid thing I'd said to Kyle wasn't the last thing anyone had said, I pushed her voice away so it wouldn't ruin Kyle's. Because my name sounded different when he said it from how it was when anyone else, including me, said it. In his voice, it was crunchy, like car wheels on a gravel driveway.

My parents took Molly, Goth Sarah, Chad, and Sam and me to the Grill that night, where Brad, the manager with floppy blond hair and a unibrow, already had banana splits ready for Chad and Sam and a mint chocolate sundae for me. He asked what Molly and Goth Sarah wanted, and Goth Sarah was like, "Coffee, please, black," and Molly ordered lemon sorbet. I saw my parents look at each other. I'm not allowed to have coffee, maybe because it stunts your growth. I felt like a little kid, eating my stupid frothy sundae while Molly and Sarah spooned sorbet and sipped coffee. We sat in the front, listening to the rain pound down on the roof and gossiping about the concert.

"He's a thousand-year-old fossil," I said.

"Yeah, but he's amazing. I mean, did you read *Under Babylon*?" Goth Sarah asked. My mom was so impressed she could barely contain herself.

"I didn't," I said, "but my mom did."

"It's a wonderful novel," my mom said, "I've been encouraging Judy to read it for years!"

"My dad has that book at home," Molly said. "I'm going to check it out."

"Norman made a point of coming up to us to say what a fabulous job you did tonight, honey," my mom said to me. This made me think of Kyle's voice saying, "Judy Lohden, congrats, man," and my stomach flipped like a pancake.

"You were dope!" Sam said. "I mean, no one else was as good, and they were seniors! Everyone in the audience thought so."

"Thanks, Sam."

"So, is Ginger coming over again?"

I was surprised he would ask this in front of Sarah and Molly. I saw Sarah shoot Molly a look like, "Of course," but Molly grinned.

"Who's Ginger?" Chad asked, and I started to say, "You know Ginger—" but Sarah was staring at me like, "Shut up," and then thankfully my mom said, "Ginger is a new friend of Judy's" before I could say, "The one your hideous friend Santana freaked at that party we didn't tell Mom and Dad about."

"A *hot* girl," said Sam. Molly and Chad and I laughed, and even Sarah had to admit that it was funny with a begrudging snort, but my mom shook her head. She looked at Sam meaningfully. "That's an offensive way to talk about Judy's friends."

After she said this, she looked at Sarah and Molly, and I was wondering what she could be thinking, maybe something along the lines of: "Well, at least neither of you is hot enough to get objectified by my twelve-year-old son."

Then Chad was like, "I have to take off. I told Alice I'd pick her up after her study group. Congratulations, J., you were great. Molly, Sarah, nice to meet you two." I liked this; he was pretending he hadn't met them before, at the party our parents didn't know had happened. He even winked at us. I bet Molly and Sarah loved that.

"So, Judy," my dad said, as Chad walked away. "Where'd you find that song?"

I felt in this question something about what it must be like to be a parent, to realize that your kids' lives actually take place without you, in dark practice rooms, in their bedrooms, in their private, inaccessible imaginations and minds.

"I've been listening to nothing else for three years, Dad," I said, punishing him for no reason. I never cut my parents any slack at all. And I'm sorry for that now.

"Oh," he said. "I'm surprised I've never heard it before, then."

"I had never heard it either," Goth Sarah said, and I wondered if this was true, or if she was just kind and wanted to make my dad feel better.

"Me, neither," Molly said.

We drove home in the kind of warm car glow that exists only when your life hasn't been totally ruined. I remember it now, because it's raining outside the Motel Manor, and the window in my room is leaking just enough so that the gray paint on the windowsill is bubbling and the carpet next to the window is sopping and black.

If I close my eyes as tight as I can and rub them until dots of light form, I can still see Sam next to me in the backseat the night of the SV concert, and the backs of my parents, my mom with her arm stretched between the seats. It was warm in the car with Sam and my parents all safe. And I had just had the thrill of being in the senior voice concert. My mom was playing with the little bit of hair curling down into my dad's collar. She was thrilled, because of the concert and my polite friends, and because she had seen all three of her kids that night and we all seemed happy.

"You want a haircut, Max?" she asked, playing with my dad's hair.

"Do I need one?"

My mom always cuts my dad's hair. I don't think he's ever had his hair cut by anyone else. My parents met the summer after high school and got married when they were twenty. Those were their "hippie years," when they moved to New Mexico and made belts and definitely smoked a lot of pot while their one pig and six chickens ran around the yard. They didn't stay, because I guess it wasn't a great life for Chad. I wonder if all the pot-smoking I'm guessing they did was related to my foreshortened limbs.

Later that night, I heard my parents in the bathroom, setting up the haircutting salon, and Sam thumping plastic strums to "The Boys Are Back."

I didn't listen to the vent, just lay down on my stomach on my bed and wrote a long entry in pink in my leather diary—a gift my dad had gotten me at the Ann Arbor Art Fair. I wrote all about the concert, Norman Crump, my voice, the way it sounds coming from my body and how it must sound different to people who aren't inside my body. And Kyle. What he hears when he listens to me. How I think he's a good listener, so unlike most boys. I wrote about AP bio, how I'd gotten Rachael Collins as my lab partner, and how I liked her because she was tidy and reserved, with short dark hair and a big vocabulary. She worked on the school paper, wrote a current events column, and saved most of her words for that; she didn't talk much. I suggested naming our dead cat "Cletus the Fetus," not so much because I wanted Rachael to think I was funny (although I would have liked it if she had), but because joking about the rubbery plucked cat made me feel less miserable about carving up someone's beloved pet, or worse, a helpless stray. Our teacher, Mr. Abraham, who was constantly touching us with his moist, fat hands, posted cat-part pictures on the class website and made jokes about "partbook" being like, our "facebook." Grown-ups who use Facebook are embarrassing, and even if Mr. Abraham had known better than to be on Facebook himself, we still wouldn't have found him cool for knowing what it was. It's better not to pander to teenagers, since we have super sharp pander radars. But Mr. Abraham probably wouldn't have been embarrassed to learn that we thought he was a loser anyway, because there are two kinds of people in the world: people who get embarrassed and people who embarrass others. And Mr. Abraham was definitely the latter. He'd probably be thrilled to know that he and Cletus the Fetus are characters in my diary.

I wrote a lot about that cat, even drew diagrams of him. I don't know why; maybe I wanted to honor him in some way, after violating him with all that cutting and labeling. We started with his mid-ventral muscles: transverse abdomens, rectus abdominus, internal oblique, external oblique. The more we hacked away, the more he looked like a chicken. It reminded me of that horrible thing people say when they eat creatures no human should eat, like frogs and rabbits, how they "taste like chicken," and I decided never to eat meat again. Rachael almost threw up when we cut up the jejunum. I don't know why she found it grosser than the urinary bladder, maybe the unfamiliar word grossed her out. People hate things they've never heard of.

Right before I fell asleep the night of the concert, I flipped to the back of my diary and wrote out the lyrics to my Rickie Lee Jones solo, even though I'd had them memorized for years. I have a habit of flipping ahead, writing notes to my future self: "How are things now? Did you pass the math test? Did the boy you liked end up falling in love with you, too?"

> Are the signs you hid deep in your heart
> All left on neon for them?

I don't know what made me write those down that night. Maybe I sensed that soon all the secret signs in my heart would be utterly neon —for the world to gape at and label.

8 My second American lit paper for Ms. Doman was on Pecola Breedlove, and how race, fate, and longing ruin her before the plot even starts. If you're ever feeling bad, reread *The Bluest Eye*, because Pecola Breedlove has such a tragic life that it makes even what happened to me seem like a sneeze. The funny thing about literature is that if you have a name like Breedlove, you're fucked. There's no way an author calls you that without making you breed your father's baby after he rapes you on the kitchen floor. But the part of that book that kills me is how she loves the blond doll. How she wants to be what she can never be. That's life-ruining enough, I think. So my paper was kind of on that, and Ms. Doman read it out loud to the class, even though it was six pages long.

Then she followed me down to the auditorium, because we had auditions for the spring show, *Runaways*, an utter piece of shit with the single advantage of a cast of dozens of teenagers. It was because of *Runaways* that I started seeing Kyle every day after school, not to mention Chris and Alan, who were always picking him up, working on the senior show, swimming, or doing whatever it was they did in the building after hours. It's funny how being at school after school gives you a lawless feeling. Even if you're there for rehearsal or something utterly, nerdily school-related, the energy is a jittery, giddy sort, unlike the trapped vibe of daytime. *Runaways* also made us feel reckless, as if we were actually kids living on the streets, rather than our lucky private school selves dusted with a little makeup to look dirty.

I vividly remember the day we auditioned, because I got cast as a deaf black guy named Hubbel, after doing some comically bad fake sign language. And because Ms. Doman and I had a conversation that made me nervous.

"Judy," she said, in an oddly serious tone, "can we walk down together?"

"Sure! Are you casting *Runaways*?"

"No, of course not—they don't give the book-worms any say!" she said, smiling. "I just wanted to watch you guys do your thing. Are you nervous?"

I nodded.

"I'm sure you'll be divine. You were stunning at the voice concert, Judy. Really stunning. But you know what?"

"What?"

"I hope you'll think about being a writer."

"Thank you."

"Don't thank me. I don't mean it as a compliment. I mean it as an assignment."

"Okay," I said.

She waited for a minute, kind of watching me. We had arrived at the auditorium and were standing still outside the door. I felt uncomfortable.

"How're things going?" she asked, and something about the fake casualness of it reminded me of my mom.

"Really good!" I said, and it came out too high and too fake, as if they weren't good, but they actually were, so I was weirded out by myself. Why did I sound like I was lying to Ms. Doman?

"If you ever want to talk to me about anything, just come by, okay? Doesn't have to be just the books we talk about in class." She pushed the auditorium door open and we walked in.

I wanted to say, why would I? But I didn't want to insult Ms. Doman, and I had a little chill of fear—that she knew more about me than I knew about myself, the way your parents think they do but don't, and the way some grown-ups actually do.

"Can I ask you something?" I asked as we sat down. I put some spearmint Eclipse in my mouth.

She looked at me warmly. "Of course, Judy. Anything."

"I hope it's not a rude question. Um. When did you marry your husband?"

She smiled, a bit bewildered, but maybe touched, too. I held the package out to her, in case she needed gum or encouragement, but she waved it away politely.

"I married Orb when I was thirty-two, five years ago."

"Orb?"

"Everyone calls Norman 'Orb'—it's a nickname."

"Oh."

"Why do you ask, Judy?"

"Just curious."

"You thinking of getting married?"

"Not until I'm thirty-two."

"I'm glad," she said. "Not that it's any of my business, but you can fall in love many times before you get married. True love isn't a once-in-a-lifetime event."

As she said it, she watched me for a reaction, and I tried hard not to show one, because the truth is, I thought it was a very depressing thing to say. I want true love to be a once-in-a-lifetime thing. Maybe just because she married an old famous dude, she has to think she might find love again, or that she had found it before so it's okay that this isn't it. But that's not how I feel about it. Or maybe she has true love with Norman Crump, and I'm just young and stupid. The horrible thing about being young and stupid (among others) is that you can't know what you don't know. But you can have a sense that you don't know shit. This is a curse I notice most of my classmates don't have. They seem to think they know a lot about a lot of things. I don't know why I have to be like a magical elf of a teenager, but I somehow know it's impossible to know much until you're way older than we all are. I hate that. Both the fact of it and the loneliness of being the only one who seems to know it.

In fact, the whole experience of *Runaways* gave me a dizzying epiphany about being young and stupid. For one thing, it made me think of a Young People's Theater show I had done in third grade, a musical adaptation of *Animal Farm* in which my friends Julie and Caitlin and I played sheep who sang about the rule of law. We were all eight years old and thought we were fantastic. I didn't even care that I was like one foot tall, singing, "No animal should sleep upon a bed, or wear a coat or hat upon its head. / No animal should drink of alcohol or hurt or kill another animal. / All animals are equal cha cha cha. / All animals are equal yah yah yah." Now that I'm almost seventeen, I realize what a butt-numbing disaster that play was—and my parents must have died, sitting through it nine times. But at the time, I thought it was like the best thing ever and that there was nothing they would rather do than watch me with my wooly earmuffs on, all night, every night. So what am I going to think of *Runaways* eight years from now? Or even eight months? Eight days? Impossible to say. What will I think of myself?

As Hubbel, the deaf black runaway, my first lines were "I had to run away! I had to! You do it because you get scared! Scared of yourself!" They were incredibly melodramatic (and now, I realize, ironic), and since Goth Sarah got the part of my interpreter, she spoke them while I "signed" silently. I didn't know what deaf people sound like when they talk, and didn't want to do anything people would think was a joke, or make fun of anyone. So I tried during the audition, and the one time I did the actual play before I actually disappeared, to keep the fake sign language subtle and kind of sad.

Maybe that was Tony-worthy genius, but I have to admit I felt like Ms. Minogue cast me as Hubbel because she thought he and I were both disabled and I could Method-act his alienation or something. Or it was payback for getting the big senior voice solo. I couldn't feel sorry for myself, though, because Molly got chorus, which I thought was totally unfair, and if I'm being totally honest here, kind of racist. I mean, she was the only black girl in our class and she was really good and they should have given her a real part. I wondered what she and her parents thought, if they were all used to life being unfair and talked openly about it, or whether they all just pretended it was okay that she was "chorus member three" like we pretended in my family that everything was okay.

Kyle played a bad-boy druggie, which was easy since he always looked half asleep, except now, because he was suddenly paying close attention to me during the numbers when we danced near each other. I knew it the way you can, like in a *Planet Earth*, *Life*, *National Geographic* way—like, I don't know, I was a scrumptious baby alpaca and could feel some groggy but hungry wolf eyes on my back. Maybe that's overstating it. But he was watching me.

And then, after rehearsal one day that first week, Goth Sarah and Molly and I were sitting in our usual spot at the end of the hallway next to the theater and almost to the fire escape, and Molly was improvising a song about Sarah, to the tune of "Yankee Doodle," that went: "Sarah Taylor went to town, riding on a hedgehog; she got hungry by a swamp and ate a hairy bullfrog," Sarah was laughing hysterically, and I was eating a cookie because I was totally starving. And then Kyle came over and stood in front of me, not saying anything, just smiling, like we both knew something was coming. Molly stopped singing. I offered him some of my cookie because I didn't know what else to do and he was like, "Sure," and I broke the cookie in half and the halves were totally uneven so I gave him the bigger half because I didn't want to seem like a pig, and he was like, "Thanks, Judy Lohden!"

Chris Arpent heard this and walked over, and when he saw Kyle eating the cookie, was like, "What am I, chopped liver?" Which kind of reminded me of my grandma Mary. I gave him the other half, and he took it and didn't say thanks but said to Kyle as they started walking away, "C is for cookie, good enough for me." Goth Sarah rolled her eyes, but Molly was like, "You're going to hate on Cookie Monster's song? That's cute! He's in touch with his inner child!" And then they looked at each other and laughed and Molly nudged me with her elbow and sang, "K is for Kyle—kinky good for me!" They waited for me to respond, but I didn't, and finally Molly asked, "You okay?" and I tore a page out my notebook and wrote in pink, "I'm deaf, can't hear you bitches," and held it up. Molly laughed her shout-laugh, grabbed the paper from me.

Chris didn't thank me after gobbling up my cookie, but he started saying hi in SV and whenever he showed up at *Runaways* rehearsals to hang out with Kyle. Meanwhile, I never ate another cookie, because I didn't want to have one and not give them any, but I also didn't want to do it again, because it would have seemed like I was eating the cookie just so I could get them to talk to me. Of course, not eating the cookie for them is just as stupid as eating a cookie for them, but at least they didn't know about it that way.

And then on the Tuesday before Thanksgiving, Kyle stood right down the hall from me while Goth Sarah was talking about Eliot Jacobs and how he was like, super into Japan and read books about tea ceremonies and how to organize flowers so they would look especially something—well organized, I guess. He had apparently planted a garden at his mother's house in Ann Arbor, and Sarah said it was the most relaxing place she had ever been, and that he practiced some Japanese religion called Shinto, which was much cooler than being a Buddhist, because that was already such a cliché in America, but most Americans had never even heard of Shinto.

Kyle was standing with Greg and Stockard, listening to Greg say he was going to get some good shit over Thanksgiving and get "hiiiiiiiigh," and laughing politely, but then he wandered away from them and over to us. He had had me on his radar the whole time, the way I'd had him on mine. I reached up and touched my earrings, silver moons my mom got from a place called Anonymous Angels that hires disabled people in third-world countries to make jewelry. Kyle was eating Fritos and held the bag out, but I shook my head. I didn't want to smell like corn chips in front of him, even if he smelled like them in front of me. He had his camera on his shoulder, but it was in the case, turned off for once. Most days, he appeared to be making a documentary about the making of *Runaways*. I was tempted to make fun of him, but something in me said not to, that it wasn't a joke for him. I never wanted to hurt his feelings.

"So Judy Lohden, guess what I got?" he said.

I shrugged, tried to arch my eyebrows in the way I constantly saw Elizabeth Wood doing.

"A car."

"No kidding. Do you have your license?"

"Yup. Got that, too."

"How will you make the most of it?" I asked.

He smiled right at me, like he was smiling into my mouth. It's hard to describe.

"You want a ride home?"

"Only if it's a convertible," I joked, trying to drown out the pounding of my heart, in case he could hear it. I still love myself for coming up with that.

"If you consider my parents' used Toyota Camry a convertible, then it is."

"I consider that a Mustang," I said.

"So I can drive you home, then?"

"Sure," I said, "thanks."

Then he went to grab his computer bag and I swooned against the wall.

"Wow," Goth Sarah said. "Maybe he wants to ask you out for real."

"Yeah, maybe," I said, thinking *for real?* I mean, maybe she and Eliot drank tea naked and whispered to each other in Japanese in his mother's garden, but a ride home from Kyle was a serious date, as far as I was concerned. I was soaring around in my mind. I excused myself to call Rashid and cancel the piano lesson I had after rehearsal. It was the first time I'd ever done that. I wondered if he would tell my parents, and whether they'd be mad. Maybe this was a transition into the life of the new me, the one who skipped her responsibilities to get rides with Kyle Malanack.

He and I walked out together, and I imagined everyone must be talking about it. Kim Barksper was standing talking to Ms. Vanderly. Kim saw us and waved in what seemed like a genuinely friendly way. Maybe they weren't in love. Or maybe she thought there was no way he could be into me like that, so she didn't care if Kyle drove me home. If I'd seen them leaving together and getting into his car, I would have cried.

We said nothing walking out to the parking lot together, and I had the fleeting worry that I would be so boring he wouldn't be able to stand it and this would be my final and least successful audition ever.

He didn't open the door for me and I was glad. I hoisted myself up into the car, grateful that it wasn't an SUV, since that might have meant him lifting me in himself, a totally unbearable thought. When he closed his door, the world outside the car disappeared. His hands on the steering wheel looked strong and clean. I had the weird thought that we were both young.

Kyle pulled his seat belt across his chest, snapped it on, and started the engine. Tom Petty jumped out of the CD player. I was surprised by this nerdy choice. What else did he have in there, Eric Clapton? I wondered whether he watched *American Idol*, hoped so, wanted to watch it with him. Maybe now that he had driven me home, we'd be boyfriend and girlfriend, would spent weeknights doing homework at each other's house, weekends driving from party to party together. My heart flooded its cavities.

"What did you think of Ms. Minogue screaming at Kim?" I asked Kyle.

"She always does that kind of thing. At least Kim didn't cry until later."

"Oh, so she did cry. Everyone was talking about how she managed not to."

Ms. Minogue had screamed at Kim Barksper that her performance was getting worse instead of better, that she was lazy, and that being pretty wasn't going to be enough to get her by in "the real world," so why did she think it was okay to rely on it at Darcy?

Maybe I was the only one, but during this episode I had had a moment of tremendous, drowning jealousy. I mean, how great would it have been to have Ms. Minogue announce in front of everyone that I was pretty, as if it were such an established fact that it could be used against me? Of course this would never have happened, because I was pretty, but not the kind of pretty that would make anyone bring it up as a criticism or a compliment. Not to mention that I had memorized the script the night Mr. Gosford announced that we were doing *Runaways*, and was off-book by the time we auditioned (I held my script anyway, though, way too ass-kissing to show that I had memorized anything). I was Ms. Vanderly's favorite. In fact, I was the pet of every teacher at the school, except Ms. Minogue, who I tried to avoid, and Mr. Abraham, who barely knew who we were. It was a good situation for me in a way, because even though all the teachers loved me, the other students never hated me for it, since I was too much of a mascot to be a real threat. And maybe they all thought it was only fair that I should be good at school and singing, since what else would ever go my way.

"How do you know Kim cried?"

"I saw her in the hallway."

"Oh." I felt jealous again, imagining Kyle comforting her. "I'm sure you made her feel better." I tried to say this nicely, as just a compliment, but he must have heard the angst behind

it, because he looked at me sideways, in a confused way.

"What does that mean?"

"Just that you're nice."

"Oh. Thanks."

"No problem. It's just the truth."

Here, we both waited for what felt like a long
time.

I lost the stare-down or won the friendly, who-
will-save-our-conversation contest, depending on
how you see it. "In fact, come to think of it, why
are you so nice to me?"

He was pulling up to a huge house that
looked like it had been built five minutes ago,
entirely out of blond wood.

"Why wouldn't I be nice to you?" he asked.

"Good point."

"Hey, by the way, do you want to come over
for a snack or something before I take you
home?"

I smiled, but felt a flutter of something like
fear. He hadn't even asked me where I lived,
hadn't invited me until we were already at his
door. Had he been so confident I'd say yes? I
thought for a minute that I should say no, take
me home now instead, but I didn't want to.

"I guess you thought I'd say yes."

He laughed in an odd, flat way, turned the
engine off, and got out. I couldn't decide what he
meant by the laugh. I think he thought I'd been

making a joke, so in that sense, it was a polite gesture. But I hadn't really been joking, exactly, so the more genuine the laugh, the ruder it was. He didn't offer to help me out, and even though I could have used a hand, I was kind of glad. Kyle never once patronized me. I opened my door and jumped out and then body-slammed the door shut. I followed him up three wooden steps to a front door flanked on either side by enormous windows. I could see the foyer on the left and on the right, the living room, a soaring, modern room with a balcony over it. We walked in, and Kyle threw his book bag on a bench and his shoes on the floor, even though the house was so spotless I felt like I might have to tiptoe through it, straight to the shower, and scrub myself before I was allowed to sit down. I took my shoes off too, lined them up neatly at the window. A giant flat-screen TV was embedded in the living room wall, across from a black leather sofa with silver feet. I would have put lots of money on no butt ever having been perched anywhere near that couch. I looked at my socks, made sure they had no lint or dust on them. They were striped. Looked pretty clean.

"You want something to eat?" Kyle asked. I did not. We went into the kitchen, lit by a giant window in the ceiling, and he opened the fridge and poured a glass of milk. "You want milk?" he asked. I remembered how when he'd had the beer at Chessie's party, I'd imagined him drinking milk. I don't like milk, shook my head no. "You want something else? We have everything," he said. I peered into the fridge as he put the milk back, saw that they did, in fact, have everything. Their house looked like an advertisement for a house, rather than a place where anyone lived. The contents of the fridge were lined up so neatly it was almost as if they'd been alphabetized and organized by a robot.

"I'll have lemonade, if that's okay," I said. I thought in the impossible event that Kyle kissed me, I'd like to taste lemony, rather than like punch or diet soda. Milk seemed worst to me, but obviously he wasn't thinking ahead, or didn't care if I thought his teeth were coated with white film when we kissed. And he was right. I would have kissed him if he'd had Rachael Collins's and my fetal cat in his mouth.

He poured me lemonade, and went to the cupboard for some Smartfood popcorn.

"This okay?" he asked, shaking the bag.

"Perfect," I said, thinking there was no way I was going to eat anything, since my stomach was on fire.

"Let's go upstairs."

I followed him up a flight of carpeted stairs, also lit by a skylight. He took the stairs two at a time, thundering up to his room.

"Show off," I said.

He looked back down at me and laughed in a friendly way. Then he came back slowly and reached his hand out to me.

"Sorry!" he said. "Here."

I let him take my hand, and the moment our hands touched, electricity shot through my hand, up my arm, and straight down my body, pouring heat into my stomach. I frankly thought I might faint down the staircase. But I managed to climb the stairs, taking them as slowly as possible in case he never touched me again. I wanted to make the hand-holding last as long as it could. At the top of the stairs was an enormous canvas, painted with a design so modern it gave me the hillbilly I-could-have-painted-that feeling, before I squashed it. And when I looked closer, I realized it looked kind of like the shape of a light blue baby, floating against a darker blue background. But I couldn't be sure. It gave me a bad feeling.

"Cool painting," I said. Kyle let go of my hand.

"Yeah," he said. "My parents are into art. My dad used to collect it."

"But now he doesn't?" I asked.

"No, I guess he still does," Kyle said.

Something about his voice made me change the subject.

"Where do you practice lines?" I asked him, kicking myself as I said it. It was too boring, too obvious, too like—I want to fantasize forever about you in this house, about my having seen it, about—

But he seemed to appreciate that I had steered the topic away from his dad's art collection.

"In my room." He pushed a door open, and there it was, glory: the only disorderly part of the house. I felt relief at the sight of a mess, as if there was potential that anything could be alive in this drafty museum. I wondered what his parents thought of Kyle, his sport socks thrown on the floor. Maybe they never came into his room. Or maybe they found it cute that he was sloppy, that it was part of his being "artistic." He wanted to be a filmmaker, everyone knew that he was going to be a big director, and even though he didn't talk about it, everyone said he was going to D'Arts so he could learn "every aspect" of the business, that is, how to act—and apparently also how to dissect cats, because he was taking AP bio. Other than his desk, the rest of the room was a storm of stuff, sweatpants thrown over his chair and bed and books and papers all over the floor. His room reminded me of Chad and Sam and their rooms, Chad's ratty Snoopy doll and Sam's car-shaped bed and salamander terrarium.

Kyle slumped down onto a sofa next to the window, rested his arm along the back of it. He looked relaxed and sleepy, like himself, for the first time since we had come into his house. A

TV faced him. He patted the cushion next to him. Was it so obvious that this was why I had come over? Was he going to kiss me? Disbelief shot through me over and over, in little jolts. I sat and glanced around at the walls.

A *Sopranos* poster. And another of Robert De Niro from *Raging Bull*. Across the room from where we were sitting was a desk with a white Apple laptop and about twenty DVDs stacked there. They were labeled with dates, but that was it, and they were the only thing he kept neat at all. But I could tell that he would have to do a lot of work to escape being a complete sociopath about neatness, because the rest of his house was so still and immaculate that you felt like if you coughed or something, floor-to-ceiling windows and priceless pieces of modern art would shatter.

Kyle picked up a remote, turned the TV on. A blue HBO screen came up.

"Do you have on-demand?" he asked me. I did not, but I nodded.

"You ever watch *The Wire*?"

I hadn't. "Yeah, once or twice."

"You want to watch an episode with me?"

I didn't. "Sure, I'd love to."

He put it on, and then put his arm around me. I reminded myself what Chad had said about how teenagers can't have heart attacks. I hoped he was right. And that if he wasn't, and my heart exploded, I would at least have kissed Kyle before it happened.

Sometimes, climbing onto the bed at the Motel Manor, I wonder, would I take back that day? I don't think so, even now. Call me crazy. I wondered on the couch why he wasn't at all nervous about what I thought of him. Maybe it was totally obvious that I was so in love with him I was about to combust spontaneously. Or maybe he figured I had so much to be embarrassed about that I wasn't the type to judge other people. Sometimes people like to be my friend for this reason. They don't realize you can be both really short and fucked up yourself and also quite judgmental and bitchy. Too bad for them.

"Where are your parents?" I asked. It came out all scrunched up, like now that my heart was in my mouth there was no room for words in there.

"At work," he said, and again his tone made me feel like I couldn't ask anything else about them, so I didn't.

To the left of his room, I had noticed another bedroom. Because the door was open, I could see a big four-poster bed with a cream-colored bedspread on it and a beige carpet. It looked like a hotel room. The curtains were open in there, too, and I could see the branches of an oak tree, touching the side of the house and the window.

I thought if there was a bad Michigan storm, the tree might come right in the window and impale Kyle's parents while they slept. Or just smash open the whole side of the house and expose them. Maybe they'd fall out of the house. I'm not usually a morbid person, but there was very weird and scary energy in Kyle's house.

"Maybe it's stupid to watch this from the middle," he said suddenly, and turned *The Wire* off. "If you've only watched it once or twice. You should really watch the whole thing in order."

For the first time I thought he might be nervous. He got up and went to his desk.

"Whatever," I said. "I'm happy to do whatever you want."

This came out kind of sexier than I'd meant it to, and I could feel my skin turn to lava. I looked out the window.

Kyle was sitting at the desk and scrolling through songs on his laptop. Maybe he had put his arm around me as a gesture of friendliness, the way I might put mine around Sam. He settled on Ella Fitzgerald and Louis Armstrong, plugged some speakers in, and music flared into the room. Darcy Arts kids were always like this—showing off that they have classic taste. Kyle would never have been the type to put on anything trendy.

Tomato, tomato, potato, potato. We were quiet for a minute.

"Do you want to sit down here?" Kyle asked. Now he patted the bed next to him. I looked at it, judging quickly that it was low enough that I could get onto it, but high enough that I would have to climb like a Munchkin. I smoothed down the shirt I was wearing, a fabulous red Lucky Western button-down with pink roses on the cuffs. I wanted to make sure it didn't rise up over my jeans as I hoisted myself onto the bed. Kyle waited. I put both hands on the mattress and pressed down, raising myself up, and then climbed as gracefully as I could until I was perched next to him. I was grateful that he had offered me no help. The staircase was bad enough; if he had had to lift me onto the bed, then he might as well have tucked me in and read me a story, too.

I sat on the bed like a tiny bird on a high wire, and looked around. There was a picture facing down on the nightstand next to his bed, and I was like, "What, is that a picture of your girl-friend or something?" maybe just because I was so nervous. I leaned over and picked it up and saw a girl with pigtails held by rubber bands with red marbles on them, squinting and laugh-ing into the sun next to a pool. She had a cherry-print tank top and jeans shorts on, and was sprawled out on a big white reclining chair. I could tell right away that the girl—with her skinny legs and a smile full of pointy baby teeth—

was probably six or seven or something. I said, "Oh, sorry," because I was embarrassed, and he was like, "Yeah, whatever," and his eyes looked like the marbles on her ponytail holders, and I didn't ask anything else about her, not even her name.

Then Kyle leaned down and started to kiss me. Heat spread through my mouth and into my body—so much of it I thought I might boil over my own edges and burn his house down. I didn't know where to put my hands, was glad for a million things: that he hadn't said anything embarrassing like "I want to kiss you" or "Can I kiss you?" like Joel had said to me at the LPA conference. Kyle didn't pretend it was anything other than what it was, an obvious make-out session. I felt feverish, tried to absorb the moment, to enjoy it as much as I possibly could, to remember everything about the way it felt so if it never happened again, I could live off the memory of kissing Kyle Malanack for the rest of my life. But I couldn't enjoy it. Where was I supposed to put my hands? I wrapped them around the back of his neck, which was hot and smooth. I felt the hair at the nape of his neck, more babyish than I had expected. His hands were moving on the buttons of my Lucky shirt, undoing them.

"Is this okay?" he asked.

I nodded, went to help him with the buttons.

As soon as I did, he let go and reached to take his own T-shirt off, stretching it over his head. When neither of us had a shirt on, he moved up to the pillows and motioned for me to join him. I lay down, face to face with him, and it was almost as if we weren't horribly mismatched. His legs went on forever, but I couldn't see them, and now that we were lying down, it mattered less. He put his arms around my back and pressed my chest to his, all skin and pulse. His fingers were on the strap of my bra, a pink cotton, simple one I definitely wouldn't have worn if I'd known Kyle would be fumbling, plucking, guitar-strumming it. Should I help him? It was taking way too long, but I didn't want to be aggressive. Finally, I reached back with one hand and unclasped it for him, and he said, "Thanks," and then we both laughed. I was really glad we laughed. I wanted very much to do a good job, to fool him into thinking I had had my shirt off before, that I wasn't dying of embarrassment. I didn't even wonder whether he'd had other girls with their clothes off in his room, just assumed he had been Don Juan since he turned seven. That's how sexy he was. Although as soon as my bra was off, I was horribly uncomfortable that it was sunny outside, that I had a freckle on the side of my stomach, and freckles on my chest, and probably farmer tan lines from last summer. And I wondered what he thought of the way I looked —too big, too small? I was so tense, I was lying there like I'd been freeze-dried, so I focused on being flexible, and while I was doing that, I noticed a frantic quality to the way he was moving and undressing. He unbuttoned his fly and kind of shoved my hand in there. I had no idea what to do, so I moved my hand up and down, but it was basically stuck in his jeans and boxers anyway, so I could barely move it, and I was glad, since I didn't know how to move it without hurting him. My mind raced. I had once heard someone—Was it Meghan? Stacy from Huron? Someone likely to be right about such things? I couldn't remember—say you could never touch a guy without first putting lotion on your hands, or they got "dick burn," which was something like rug burn. I didn't want to give that to Kyle. But I wasn't going to ask him for lotion, either. While I was thinking about this, he undid my jeans and put his hand inside my underwear, moving his fingers for like two seconds before he was like, "Should I get a condom?"

Maybe this is amazing, or maybe not, but I didn't hesitate. It was like smoking with Ginger. I mean, I wasn't going to be good at it, but I didn't really want to be like, "No, I can't, I'm too pure," or "I never did it before." Plus, what's so great about being a virgin when you're about to be seventeen, especially if you're me? I did think the condom question came up suddenly, but I was mainly just glad that I had already decided, in the driveway, that I would go the whole way if it came up. I could even hear myself calling Meghan in California the next day and being like, "I lost it to the hottest guy in the school, yeah yeah, average size, yeah yeah, Kyle, the one I told you about." I even thought I'd tell Sarah and maybe Molly, and that if the school found out, well, so be it. Meghan and I had already thought we'd probably lose it the summer we were seventeen—that seemed about right, or at least senior year—so if I got a jump on it by a few months, what was wrong with that? Especially since it was *Kyle*. Kyle. I mean, I loved him. And I thought he either already loved me, or would soon.

Maybe this makes me a slut or whatever, but I wanted the whole experience, and didn't think I would ever have a chance to lose it to anyone lovelier than Kyle. So while I entered an even deeper level of panic over how I'd manage the next step, I watched him put the condom on. He did this kneeling over me, naked, and I had the same thought I'd had the first time I met Kyle Malanack, that he was the most un-self-conscious person in the universe. Here he was, on his knees above me, wrapping that hideous flesh-colored balloon around himself as if it were the least embarrassing thing that had ever happened. I mean, I was so mortified I thought I might faint and fall off the bed, and I wasn't the one spread-eagled and basically standing up. I also wasn't, you know, turned on. So that made me think about acting, about what I would do if I *were* turned on. Maybe move around a lot? Wiggle? Make noise? There was no way I was going to make noise. And in fact, moving around a lot sounded horrible too. Then I figured, whatever, it was already slutty enough that I was sleeping with him on the first date—and it wasn't even a real date—I didn't want him to think I was like a nympho or anything. So I just kind of lay there, waiting, but then I started worrying that lying there like that was unsexy. But he was on top of me, fumbling around for what seemed to me like an awkwardly long time. I tried to help by arching my back but I was kind of scared and super weirded out and the light had changed and the room seemed suddenly brighter and I wondered what he could possibly be thinking and even what I was thinking. Then I started really freaking out, like *what am I doing here and did I say yes to this and who am I and will I regret this later,* but by the time I was having those thoughts, he had put it in and it was so painful somewhere up near my lungs that I took a sharp breath that made noise. That gave me something to think about, because I was wondering was that noise unsexy, but Kyle was coughing or moaning or something and then he stopped moving. It was all very uncomfortable. And since I'm being totally honest here, kind of gross. I wanted him to get off me, even though it was Kyle. Because by then I felt like I didn't know who he was and even if I had known at some point, we were both different people from who we'd been then anyway. I tried to remember sex scenes from movies, even Internet porn I had once accidentally walked in on Chad watching. I wished I had paid closer attention, watched more, read my parents' *Joy of Sex* more carefully. I mean, I had read it, but all it had was pictures of a skinny, hairy guy climbing all over a hairy girl like they were missing links trying to create the next human in the chain. And what did that have to do with me? What did girls do when guys were slumped like that? I hadn't seen any pictures of a beautiful guy like Kyle coughing and slumping in the *Joy of Sex*. I considered scratching his back like Alice always did to Chad, but I didn't know how that would go over, and all I wanted was to get up and put my jeans back on and run home and lock myself in my room so I could think this over and decide what it all meant. That's the thing about me. I prefer things once they're already over and I'm working on understanding them. I wish I were faster at that—like, I could understand things while they're happening—but I always have to read the whole book and write the entire paper before I even know what the hell I'm thinking.

So I just stayed still in Kyle's bed, waiting for it to be over so I could know what to think. I just lay there like a dead person. Thankfully, after ten seconds, Kyle rolled off me and stood up, pulled his boxers and jeans on. I sat up then, super relieved that he had finally given me the chance, and scrambled for my underpants and jeans.

"Sorry," he said.

I was confused by this. Had he been able to tell I hadn't liked it?

"No, no, that was—" I said, even though I wasn't sure what we were referring to. I didn't want to admit that it had been bad, was worried that he'd said sorry, because I thought that meant he'd known it was bad too. I had already pulled my jeans back on and was rehooking my bra. A wave of nausea washed over me.

"Um," he said, "was that okay? Are you okay?"

I looked him over and nodded. I suddenly really liked him again. Liked the way he said "okay" in his friendly, sleepy voice. That he was worried about whether I was okay. We barely knew each other, I realized. Then he took it to a whole other level.

"You don't have to answer this," he said, "but have you ever done it before?"

I wished I knew which answer he would like better—I would have supplied it. I tried to buy time.

"Are you serious?"

He looked serious. "Yes, why not?"

What would I have said here? Who else would ever have wanted to? No one's ever liked me except Joel at the LPA conference and we were fourteen?

I didn't want to be that pathetic, and it wasn't totally true, I mean, an average-height boy named Ian had kissed me and put his tongue all over my mouth and face once during a game of spin the bottle in seventh grade, and that had to count for something—I mean, I thought I might drown, there was so much spit. It was like getting water up your nose. Later he asked me to go to the video game arcade with him, but I'd said no, because I couldn't reach the joysticks or the change machines, and I didn't want to have to watch while he realized it once we got there. He never talked to me again. But that didn't seem like a good story to tell Kyle, either.

So I said nothing. He looked into my eyes, in the same serious way he always did.

"Anyway, you don't have to tell me," he said, and that made me be like, "No, I've never done it before."

"Oh," he said, as if he felt really bad about having been my first. "I'm sorry it was so—you know," he said, and I realized, in one of those epiphanies that's so obvious it makes you stupid to have had to have it at all, that he was thinking about himself, not me. That there had been something bad or wrong or not cool about how he had done it. And maybe that's why the whole thing grossed me out suddenly. Maybe it was the way he collapsed. Or maybe he finished too fast or something, and I should have said, "This happens to guys all the time," but that would have meant I had done it with guys all the time, and I didn't want to say anything like that. Plus, I had never been totally sure what that meant anyway. Maybe he had totally sucked in some way I didn't know about. I was glad. Not to be mean, but at least he wasn't as worried about whether I'd been sexy as he was about whether he'd been. It hadn't even occurred to me that Kyle Malanack would care at all what I thought, even of him naked, even of him having sex. As soon as I'd had this thought, I had the next one, which was that I had slept with, had sex with, lost my virginity to Kyle. I could not believe that it was true, that it had actually happened this way. His room was so bright. I looked around it again, at the details, trying to memorize them so that when I started to sort this out in my mind for the rest of time, I could supply myself with the pieces that would prove it fact. Then I let myself wander into dream territory: Maybe it would happen again. Maybe he would offer to drive me home the next day and the next.

"Have you?" I asked suddenly.

"Have I what?"

"Ever, you know, before."

He nodded. Was it someone from D'Arts? Elizabeth Wood? Or Kim Barksper? I hated the thought of either one of them in his room, his bed. Maybe it was someone in Boston, from his old school. But I couldn't ask.

So I retreated into the bubble bath of my fantasy. We would arrive at school on Monday in love, write notes to each other, eat lunch together, and hold hands walking down the hallway. Of course, when I came to this part I had to block out the part about my short arm reaching up into his long one, looking from behind like a little girl and her father. We would comment constantly in American lit, making it seem like we meant the books, but actually meaning our love. We would raise our hands so many times that Ms. Doman would have to shush us, and then we'd be forced to have meaningful eye contact that everyone else could see. My stomach was somersaulting—with thrill, nerves, horror, everything. I'd never felt that way before, the way I felt after that first time with Kyle, and I don't expect—or even hope, really—to feel that way ever again. I mean, a lot of that feeling was fear.

If you had told me at any point in my life up until that day that I would lose my virginity to Kyle Malanack, not only would I not have believed it, I also would have thought that whatever happened as a result would be worth it. That's the funny thing about earlier me's—they're so naïve, those domino girls falling over into a dead row behind the me who exists now. I used to like to throw my mind backwards. I'd think, "Okay, if you showed some earlier me a video of my life now, would she be happy?" The reason I liked to play this game was that the answer was always yes. The younger me's would have been impressed: that I had turned out pretty cute, that I got one of the coveted shabop girl parts in *Little Shop of Horrors* at Tappan, that I was valedictorian there, that I won a Lilah Terrace Fellowship to D'Arts, even that I had turned out brave enough to change schools like I did. When Ms. Doman read my paper out loud to the class, I thought, "Look at me now, all you younger Judys! Look at the soaring dwarf—if you could only have told me when I was younger that this would be happening, I would have cheered. I would have danced on the roof of a car like they do in *Fame*." Because I would have been that excited for myself. But now I hate that game. I never want to play it again, because if you'd shown me the me I am right now, how would I have been able to look myself in the eye?

9 I've been watching TV nonstop because I can't stand to think. So I happened to see an episode of *Celebrity Apprentice* from the bed in the Motel Manor, and let me just say that if this were the movie of my tragic life, that's exactly the clip the director would have had me watching. Because in case you think the *Wizard of Oz* problem was just the result of it being like the 1900s when that movie was made, you're wrong. *Celebrity Apprentice* was having a contest for who could design the best ad about laundry detergent. (How can TV producers stand themselves?) For some baffling reason, they decided to call it "Jesse James and the Midgets," and right when I turned it on, this complete asshole Hershel Walker was like, "What if we let Little People wash themselves in all detergent in a bathtub and you hang them out to dry?" And then Clint Black was laughing, "I'm trying to envision how we'd hang them out to dry," and Joan Rivers, whose face is hanging off her bones to dry, said, "Well, I have a terrace. We can hang them out on my terrace." And then she tried to move her paralyzed mouth into a laugh, and failed. My takeaway from this is that anyone who thought that people in America aren't still dying for a dwarf to hang needs to

think again. It's like a national fantasy or something.

I ran straight to Bill's room and knocked twice quiet, once loud, and he opened the door and came out into the hallway and we sat down together and he lit a cigarette.

"Do you mind if I have one?" I asked.

"It's not good, not good," he said, meaning smoking.

"I know. But I'll just have one."

So he lit a cigarette for me, and I puffed and choked until it was halfway gone and then stubbed it out. Whatever Bill thought of this performance, if he thought anything at all, he politely kept to himself.

"Do you want to talk?" Bill asked.

"I guess so," I said. "Would that be okay?"

"Of course," he said. "I like your story. I like it, even though it's sad. Parts of it are happy, too. Parts of it."

I liked this idea, even had the thought that I would like to make a kind of percentages chart of the ratio of happy to sad parts of my story. I mean, if you don't think of it as a plot, then maybe half is happy and half is sad. The fact that the happy stuff is ancient history and the terrible parts are recent makes me feel like the entire thing is a sour mess, but I like Bill's attitude better. It reminds me of Ms. Doman. So I decided to focus on a happy part: Sam.

After I lost it to Kyle, I was more grateful for Sam than ever before. That night after Kyle's house, I went to the Grill and helped Sam with his homework while my parents did the dinner-time rush. Being with Sam was like returning from an alternate universe to a safe one. Plus, he was the type who could tell I was jittery with delight, but didn't know the kinds of prying questions other people might have asked. Mainly I asked him things. That's how it's supposed to be with people who are younger than you, by the way. Adults who talk about themselves endlessly in front of young people are unacceptable narcissistic freaks. They should do the asking.

I remember Sam was hunched over the desk in the back office at the Grill, poking the keys on the laptop. "What are you working on?" I asked, reaching up and putting my arms around him.

He kept tapping with his finger, typing one letter at a time. "Lists for my project."

"Lists of what?"

"Stuff I need from Mom and Dad."

"What's the project?"

"Science. Do you want to know my hypothesis?"

"Of course."

"That if Earth were a different shape, then the effect of climate change would be different."

"How'd you come up with that?"

"I was just thinking, you know, how we could fix the whole problem. I don't just mean, like, recycling or whatever. I mean a bigger solution." He looked up at me with round brown eyes, blinked. "And then I realized, what if we could do something magical, like change the shape of the planet? I mean, that would be so much better."

"Why, though? Why would that help?"

"I don't know yet. I have to figure out what shape would make it better."

"So what stuff do you need?" I asked. I peered over his shoulder at the list on the screen: milk cartons, baking soda, balloons, newspaper, paste, paper, cardboard, glue, weather map, ruler, globe, rewritable DVD, laptop. I thought of Kyle's neck and my stomach flipped.

"What are the milk cartons and balloons for?"

"I'm going to build different-shaped Earths out of those. For the square Earth, I'll use the bottoms of milk cartons. The round one I have to do out of papier-mâché."

"Why do you need a globe?"

"So I can draw the right places on the Earths."

"Why do you need baking soda?" I hoped there were going to be volcanoes.

"To put with water and soak the milk containers. And then when I've built the Earths, I'm going to shine light on them to see how the sun would shine on Earths that aren't round. The cubical Earth will be cold, right? Because it'll only have light on one side? And the round Earth will be warm, which is better for plants, but worse, too."

"Can I help?"

"You want to?" He looked at me happily.

"Of course."

"You can help me draw the maps and then write up the results."

"Who taught you to say 'write up' like that?"

"Mr. Frank," he said, proudly.

"You're a true scientist," I said. "I'll go get you the milk cartons and baking soda from the kitchen. And you should add poster board to that list, so we can do a big write-up of the results, with digital pictures of the Earths."

"But we'll have the actual Earths there too, and a digital slide show."

"We should hang the Earths from poster board anyway, so they're there in three-D. We'll build a diorama with the Earths and then put the poster board behind them, explaining how the project worked, with pictures of where the light shone on each of the Earths. You can put it next to the projector."

He beamed.

I went to the kitchen to fetch his things, and my mom kissed me on the head.

"Do you want pasta, honey?" my dad asked. He was cooking.

"Sure," I said, even though I was too giddy to be hungry.

An old woman sitting at the counter drinking Lipton tea saw me come out of the kitchen carrying crayons and pasteboard.

"Are you working on a project for school, cutie?" she asked me. My dad and I grinned at each other.

"Yup," I said.

"Well, I'm sure you'll do a great job. I bet your teacher loves you!" she said as I disappeared back into the office to find Sam.

The next day was the Wednesday before Thanksgiving, so we had no school. Kyle didn't call, but I knew he was going to Grosse Pointe with Alan, so I pretended that it was okay. I had no appetite the entire weekend and was wasting into a primordial version of myself, even though I usually love Thanksgiving and hang out endlessly at the Grill, gobbling my parents' food. At Thanksgiving dinner, the bird glistened on the table like it had been shellacked for a week. It reminded me so much of Cletus the Fetus that I didn't even pretend I was going to eat a single bite. And I kept getting up to check compulsively whether Kyle had changed his status on Facebook from "single" to "in a relationship" (which of course he hadn't, and neither had I). I also called Meghan a few times, thinking I would tell her what had happened and that she would be even more thrilled than I was. I knew what she'd say, things like, "I knew he'd fall in love with you—you're so gorgeous and brilliant and I knew everything would work out and you're like the homecoming queen at your acting school" and blah blah.

But each time I heard her voice on the phone, I changed my mind about telling her. I mean, she knew I had a crush on Kyle, but I didn't want to tell her I'd lost it. Not on the phone, I told myself. She was begging her parents for a ticket to come see me in February when *Runaways* went up, so I'd wait and tell her then, when I saw her. Maybe we'd be in love by then.

Of course my mom sensed that something was up with me, so the whole time she was scooping oranges out of their peels and refilling them with mashed sweet potatoes and cranberries that would burst in the oven to form red polka dots, she kept asking, "Do you have news for us, sweetie? About the play, or school, or senior voice? What's happening with you?" And I just said things were good and that was it. The truth is, I ignored my family that weekend, wasn't grateful for any of the best things in my life, and couldn't wait for D'Arts, American lit, rehearsal, the first sight of Kyle's sleepy face.

But he missed class the first Monday back. When I got to rehearsal I was trying not to hyperventilate while Goth Sarah told me about

Thanksgiving with her grandparents in Minnesota. And then there he was, leaning against a wall, super casual as always, talking to Kim and Kelly Barksper and Ms. Minogue. He looked up when I came in, saw me. He nodded in my direction, even gave a tiny smile, and then went back to talking. Eventually Rachael Collins came over to me with some small talk about AP bio and I couldn't watch him in peace anymore. But I was also relieved to have something to occupy me. Maybe that smile was an invitation. Maybe he agreed that now we had both shown restraint, it was time to talk. To hang out again. That's what I took it to mean.

After we were done blocking, Ms. Minogue gave us notes. She didn't have any for me, but she told Goth Sarah that she was upstaging me as my interpreter, and that she should try to be more "understated." Sarah grinned in my direction. As soon as notes ended, I hung around in the hallway, looking at a plaque on the wall commemorating two seniors who had died in a freak car accident four years before. I had seen the plaque and the photo next to it before, but had never spent that much time looking at it. I felt kind of guilty doing it now, just so I could wait for Kyle to come out and see if he wanted to leave with me, but I couldn't help it. The thing was gold, and it said in carved letters, "In Loving Memory of Mindy O'Grady and Samantha Robinson."

I had been twelve when they died, but knew about it then because Chad was in high school at the same time they were, and anyway it was on the news. Mindy was driving, and it was hailing and they skidded around an icy curve and crashed into the half-frozen river. Chad told me he heard that by the time the divers and paramedics got there, the car had sunk and they had to get under the ice, and they couldn't find the car, and the girls drowned. I remember he was crying when he told me, and he kept saying maybe if it hadn't been so cold, or if the car had spun out of control somewhere else, or if they'd been found sooner, or if it had been a four-wheel-drive car, or if any small detail had been different—then maybe they'd still be alive. Chad cried again later, too, while we were all watching the 11:00 news. He hadn't known them personally, but every kid in the city cried, because it could have been any of us, and because on some level we knew that their parents' lives were over, and because our parents were so upset that no one even knew how to pretend it was going to be okay. There's nothing okay about two teenagers being dead forever. In the photo next to the plaque on the wall at D'Arts, Mindy and Sam are on the lawn, smiling into the camera like they're immortal. Of course. Because they're young. I don't know who made up that saying about "youth is wasted on the young," but I don't agree. It isn't wasted on me, for example, because I'm enjoying it, and because I can feel it going by.

And this is really shallow, but I was still looking at their picture when Kyle walked by with Kim Barksper and they left, and I could hear myself wishing I were dead and then I reminded myself that some people actually were dead and I promised never to have another thought like that again. And every time those thoughts bubble up, even now, I think of Chad crying when those girls died, and how my mom sat there silently, with her arm around him, letting him cry and not even saying anything to make it better, and I know that what happened to me is different, because maybe it won't be eternal.

Kyle left rehearsal early the next day with Chris and Alan, and on Wednesday, we didn't talk at all. So it was never going to happen again, had been a fluke, or so terrible that he not only didn't want to be in love with me, he never even wanted to say hello to me again for the rest of our lives.

The days were a miserable, thick slog, until Thursday, when, after rehearsal, he nonchalantly was like, "You want a ride?" I wished I were the kind of person who could have been like, "I'd love one, but I have other plans," but I'm not and I couldn't; I said yes, called the Grill, and left a message saying I'd be a little late, because I was hanging out with a friend.

Then I went back to Kyle's cold, silent palace. This time we didn't even get popcorn or fake that we were going to watch HBO, just climbed onto the bed. I noticed that the framed picture of the girl was gone. His camera was sitting on the nightstand instead. When he got up to go pee, I crawled across the bed to look at his tidy desk. There was something weird about an oasis of clean in his room. The dated mini-DVDs were still stacked immaculately. To the right, on a shelf above the desk, was one by itself, labeled "Claire." It was the only one with anything other than dates on it. I heard Kyle coming back down the hall toward his room and I leapt to the other side of the bed and pretended to have been staring out the window.

He came and sat on the bed next to me, put an arm over my shoulder, and leaned in to kiss me. This time the kissing was quite soft, his mouth sleepy like the rest of him, but he also pushed me down onto the bed, and I thought how odd the contrast was between his kissing and his, I don't know, pushing. It kind of made me think maybe there was a fight happening between his personality and his body, because even though his mouth was kind of soft, the rest of him was pressing against me so hard it hurt. I peeked to see what he was doing or thinking, but his eyes were closed, so I closed mine, too. Then he jerked up suddenly and took his T-shirt off. One of his knees was between my legs, and he used it to push them apart and then he lay down on top of me and put his hand first under my shirt and then under the striped skirt I was wearing, and then he took both off and suddenly I was naked for the second time in Kyle Malanack's bed, and I kept thinking, "It's the second time, which makes it even more real. Enjoy this, absorb this—this is actually happening," but I couldn't enjoy it, because even then I knew it was too good to be true and there must be something weird and wrong. It was more uncomfortable even than the first time. And here's the funny thing: when he put it in and it hurt and I put my hand over my mouth so I wouldn't say "ow" or something unsexy, he took my hand off my mouth, and even as he was going faster and then doing his creepy slumping thing, he was like, "Is that okay? Are you okay?" and I was glad the lights were on. I said I was fine.

And that's when he rolled off me and flicked the light switch next to his bed. The room was dark, and we were lying there silently for a minute, and then I was like, "Kyle?" and there was no answer, and I realized he was asleep. So maybe he was actually just really sleepy all the time. Because I don't think I've ever fallen asleep that instantaneously, especially at a moment like that. So I lay there, bionically awake, watching his clock click its red digits, wondering whether it was weird that right when I thought how glad I was for the light, he had decided to turn the lamp off. And then I forced myself not to be a superstitious idiot, and shifted my mind back to the fact that I actually, formally wasn't a virgin anymore. I mean, the first time was so quick and surprising that I wasn't sure it had counted, but now we'd done it twice and even though the second time had been quick too, there was no doubt that the boy I had lost it to was Kyle Malanack. And even though it was as dark as a cave in his room and he was sleeping and I felt a little scared, I still knew if I'd been able to choose anyone in the entire universe, it would have been him. And I had faith that it would feel good later, once I wasn't such a virgin anymore. I mean, I had hated kissing the first time I'd kissed a guy, and now I liked that. I hoped that sex would get fun, the same way kissing had, although I wasn't sure how many practice sessions that would take, and I was kind of worried either way. I mean, I didn't really want to have sex with Kyle all the time if it was going to be like this, but I also didn't want not to, if that would mean we weren't in love. Maybe we'd be more comfortable with each other soon, and we'd be able to talk about things, although I hadn't even asked him why he hadn't called me. I mean, it had only been a week, and it wasn't like we'd said we were boy- and girlfriend. I didn't want to push it. But when I woke him up forty-five minutes later (after I'd gotten dressed and climbed up onto his sink to wash my face and put on new lipstick and use his toothbrush to brush my teeth) and asked him if he'd drive me home, he was all cute and groggy. He said sure, of course, and stretched out and then sat up. He apologized for "falling asleep like that" and asked me if I would be willing to do him a favor.

I'm tempted to lie about what I said, because it's so sickening and stupid and revealing, but today I confessed it to Bill at the Manor Motel, word for word. And he just nodded like, okay, that's what some people say, even when they don't know what the favor is going to be. So I'll admit it here, too. What I said was, "Anything. I'll do anything for you."

# 10

I smoked pot again at a party the Friday after Thanksgiving, this time with a bunch of people on the deck at Kim and Kelly Barksper's house. Which is funny, because if I were someone other than me, and didn't know the story from the inside out, I can see how I'd be like, wow, she started smoking pot and having sex, no wonder her life fell apart! But it wasn't like that—I mean, I smoked twice, and it never had any effect, and the sex was supposed to be because I was in love, so it was just a coincidence. This is one of the reasons that adults are stupid. Because they create these nonsense propaganda narratives out of what's actually just our lives when we're teenagers.

Mainly, I was obsessed with whether people could tell I wasn't a virgin anymore. Molly and Goth Sarah definitely suspected something was up, and the truth is, I wanted to tell them, was even planning to, but how could I? I mean, every time they saw Kyle and me near each other, he was ignoring me—like at rehearsal on the days when he didn't drive me home, or left with Kim, or at the twins' party, when he was sitting with Kim, which killed me, wearing gray cargo pants and a crisp blue T-shirt that showed under his unbuttoned coat. His hair was longer than usual and he had pulled a gray winter cap over it, so there were curls sticking out the bottom of the cap. I thought of the curls at the nape of his neck, and felt incredulous that as far as Goth Sarah and Molly knew, he had driven me home twice and that was it. If I had told them we'd done it, they would have died of shock, although they also would have forced me to face the truth, which was that his not calling or paying attention to me in public wasn't actually okay.

Elizabeth Wood was with him and Kim at the Barkspers' party; she was talking about "her career"—I could tell by how her perfect, kewpie doll face moved. I turned to Goth Sarah to be like, "Look, Elizabeth is demonstrating her passion for acting," and Sarah laughed as if it were funnier than it was, which made me feel mean and slightly better for about two seconds, before I just felt mean and therefore even worse. Kim and Kyle were listening to Elizabeth's monologue. I was hoping for a way to go over and join in, but I couldn't bring myself to. I kept thinking of Kyle in his room, all sleepy, with just me there. But no one seemed to notice anything different about me— or him, obviously—and this made me feel like it hadn't even happened.

Even though I had hated Ginger's smoking seminar in my backyard, I was grateful for it at Kim and Kelly's, because now I had actually smoked once before and didn't look like a total loser. This time I held the smoke in my mouth again, and it had no effect again. I think Molly was kind of surprised to see me try it. She turned the pipe down, unapologetically, casually, the way she wore her karate suit, or took classes with her dad on the weekends, and as usual, no one judged her. Goth Sarah puffed like a pro, although she took only one hit, maybe because she was driving. I wondered if she had smoked before, or if she was good at faking it. Kyle didn't smoke; whenever the pipe came to him, he passed it to Kim. But I must have seen him refill a milk glass with whiskey at least five times.

In fact, it was at Kim and Kelly's that it occurred to me how much he drank. He drank a lot. But he wasn't a loud drunk; he just got quieter and quieter. Chris Arpent did the loud drunk thing for him, maybe, for all of us. Chris stood on the deck that night, shouting about how it makes no sense to call it "going commando" when guys wear no underpants. I have to admit, he was kind of hilarious, standing with his body in a commando pose, one arm stretched out in front of him, miming that he was holding a gun, and then turning to the guy behind him, like, "Dude, where's your underwear? What? I'm a commando too, and I'm not free-balling all over the battlefield."

I was laughing until Goth Sarah leaned over to me. "He didn't think of that himself, you know. It's from—"

"Well, it's pretty funny anyway."

"Do you want to go soon?" she asked, and even though I didn't, because I didn't want to create the possibility of Kyle's leaving with someone else, I said, "Sure." I'm not the kind of friend who makes you stay at a party if you're having a horrible time. My friend Stacy, at Huron, was like that. Whenever we went anywhere, I knew if I was leaving with her then I might be trapped for like ten years in a place I hated if she was having too much fun to want to leave with me, or liked some guy and wanted to wait and see if he would leave with her instead. In which case I would have to call Chad or my parents to come get me. And she was totally the type to get super drunk at a party and leave with some guy, and leave her car there, even if she was my ride.

Molly had to babysit for her little sister, Susanna, in the morning, so she couldn't sleep at Sarah's. I said good-bye to her, and she used it as an excuse to get up and walk over to where Chris was sitting. Inspired, I went over to Kim, pretending I wanted to thank her, but actually to warn Kyle I was leaving—in case he wanted to stop me.

"So, Kim, thanks for having us," I said. And I

said it right during a huge lull that no one was expecting in the conversation on the deck, so everyone heard it and it was really stupid, but then Chris started laughing and laughing. And then everyone started laughing, so I pretended I'd meant it as whatever joke they thought it was, and Sarah and I left. Kyle didn't say anything, and I couldn't tell if he'd been laughing or not. "Yeah, Kim," Chris said, "thanks for having me." I didn't get it, but they were all high, so maybe every stupid thing seemed funny. Kyle smiled at me, gave a little wave as I left.

At Sarah's, we let ourselves in and ate some grilled shrimp we found in the fridge. When we were finished with our snack, we went downstairs, and I got Sarah's desk chair and pulled it into the bathroom to wash my face and brush my teeth. When I got back to her room, she had already folded out her metal trundle bed and raised it up so the two beds were side by side. And once I had climbed up onto my side and we were lying there on her matching twin pale yellow sheets, she was all of a sudden like, "It's totally not worth it, worrying about him so much all the time."

"I don't worry about him all the time," I said. "I mean, I'm not even sure if I like him that much," I said.

"You can tell me. I mean, did anything happen that day he drove you home?"

I couldn't bring myself to say no, but couldn't manage the truth, either.

"You know, we hung out for a while, that was all."

"Hung out? What am I, your grandmother? Did you guys hook up?"

"Maybe a little."

She screamed with glee. "You did?! You hooked up with Kyle Malanack!? You are kidding me! Are you excited? Horrified? Glad? Angry? Have you guys talked about it?"

This was like dipping my toes in the swimming pool and knowing immediately that they would have to be amputated. The water was much too cold. I can't overstate how much I regretted having admitted anything at all, and I frantically backtracked.

"I mean, I don't know if it counts. We just kind of held hands or whatever."

"Held hands? What, in the car?"

"I don't know if it was even holding hands, really. I mean, he kind of brushed my hand as I got out."

"Oh," Sarah said. She must have been so weirded out. I feel bad, even now.

"Hey, Sarah?"

"Yeah?"

"When have you smoked pot before?"

"With Eliot, twice, why? When have you?"

"Just that one time when Ginger came over to my house after school."

There was an unpleasant moment of silence, while we both remembered how rude I'd been not to include Sarah. I was sorry I'd brought it up, but also relieved that the conversation had moved away from Kyle.

"How was that, by the way?"

"Smoking? It sucked."

"I meant Ginger coming over."

I turned over in the bed and pulled the covers up to my shoulders, stuck one foot out—the right one. I like to sleep this way; it keeps my body temperature exactly right and makes me feel like there's a possibility of escaping the sheets.

"It was just okay. She's kind of weird, I think."

"Yeah, no shit."

We were quiet again.

"Judy?"

"Yeah?"

"Are you mad at me?"

"Why would you think that?"

"I don't know—it's just, I feel like you don't really—"

"I'm just incredibly tired." I faked a huge yawn that became real halfway through. Needless to say, I wish I had confided more in her when I had the chance.

Sunday took ten years. I went home to our silent house and read and spent an hour picking two pictures to upload to Facebook, imagining that Kyle might see them. One was a picture I'd taken myself, of me holding the camera out and kind of smirking; the other was from the Halloween party—Molly had taken it of me and Sarah sitting on her bed in our sexy witch costumes. I couldn't wait for Monday, to see our fetal cat or sit in American lit, to catch a live glimpse of Kyle anywhere. I had made up my mind to talk to him, and this felt like a plan. Maybe it would go okay. Maybe we would be weekday boyfriend-girlfriend. I even thought I could live with that. Sunday night, I reread *Charlotte's Web*, one of my favorite books, but even though I love that story, it seemed unbearably childish and optimistic now. I had the feeling, while I was reading it, that I had floated up above myself and was watching Judy read the book, but I wasn't me anymore. Maybe that's what they mean by growing up; it was like there were two of me, one the same me I'd always been, and the other one suddenly too old for her.

Monday came but Kyle never approached me. I was wearing my black corduroy miniskirt and boots, and I tried to say brilliant things about *The Crucible* in American lit, but my words betrayed me and came out garbled. Kyle was across the room, in track pants and a white T-shirt, looking at the blackboard. I noticed he was wearing new sneakers, wondered if he'd gone to buy them with his mom, or by himself.

When I spoke, he barely turned around, but then neither did anyone else. I mean, we had all stopped being that curious about each other, unless there was real gossip. I want to say that I felt like my heart was breaking that day, but since I now know what that actually feels like, I'll just say that I felt very bad. After a run-through of the moronic bilingual song "Where Do People Go When They Run Away," I found myself standing onstage next to him. *¿Dime, donde van? Tell me, where do they go? And what do they say to each other? Do they sit in the theater all day like sad old men?*

"Um," I said, hating myself for being pathetic, and wishing, wishing I were tall, that he didn't have to bend down to make eye contact with me. But I didn't even need to wish that, it turned out, because he looked straight out, over me, even after I asked, "So what's happening?"

"Nothing, why?" he said, still not looking at me. I walked off backstage.

Two more weeks passed. It was as if we had never met. I began to wonder whether I had imagined our encounter. I went through the school days in a numb haze, stopped raising my hand, even in American lit. I ate lunches off campus, alone. In the evenings, I labeled papier-mâché globes with Sam, couldn't bear to leave the house except for school and rehearsal. I didn't call Sarah or Molly, didn't want to tell them anything, didn't want anyone to know. I slept one entire weekend, told my parents I was sick, which was true. The next one I spent at the Grill, "studying" for finals, avoiding Sarah, even though she called a million times and I missed her. I practiced in the mirror how I would tell Sarah when she got back from South Africa over Christmas break. I would act like I had thought it through over the vacation and could now explain—or that I had gotten over it. Maybe, I thought, I would actually have gotten over it, and I would be able to laugh about it with Molly and Sarah. It seemed doubtful.

Christmas break came. Time kept moving the relentless way it does. That used to scare me, I have to say, and it still does. I used to think, all the time, that even if I sat under my parents' dining room table and did nothing and spoke to no one, time would still move, and I would still grow up. It's hard to explain, especially the part about the dining room table, but that's always how I thought about being unable to control the slipping away of my own hours. Before school even got out, Kyle's family went to St. Bart's; I knew from his Facebook page and chatter at school. Molly went to Atlanta, and Sarah went to South Africa. We all had to be back the second week because, like I said, you weren't even really allowed to travel if you went to Darcy, because rehearsals started up the second week of break.

I spent the entire agonizingly long week and a half at the Grill with my parents, who didn't take any time off, including Christmas Day, because they liked to make hams and turkeys for their regulars, who I guess were so old they didn't have friends left, or couldn't travel to see their families, or whatever. Or students who couldn't afford to go home. I usually loved Christmas dinner at the Grill. Everyone had the same food, so it felt like a huge family holiday, even though some of the people were strangers and we were all eating in a diner. My parents loved it too; they were always in great moods, even though it was a spine-cracking amount of work, cooking fancy food for that many people.

It snowed seven of the nine days, until the Huron River's edges froze into jagged patterns of ice and a wall of white rose outside our windows, taller than I was.

When we got back to rehearsal in January, it was still six days until school started. Everyone was giddy because we hadn't seen each other in a week. Most of the juniors had crazy tans, some fake and others real. Everyone was talking about where they'd been, what they'd done over the break. Kyle was wearing a white polo shirt and had one of the real tans. It made him look preppier than usual, more like a game show host than his usual bedraggled director self, but it also looked on him like he hadn't had to work to get it, had just been playing or doing his thing, and the sun had attached itself to him like we all wanted to. He was in an especially joyful mood, bounding around like a puppy, with his teeth electric white next to his tan. Everyone was in the best moods ever, and I felt left out, totally alone. My happy days at Darcy were over.

It's not like Kyle was rude; I mean, he was very friendly to me those first days back, said hi, said, "Great job, Judy," one day after a full run-through. But he didn't call me and I didn't call him. I wanted to, even just to make the point that I didn't think girls should have to wait for boys to call us. But I couldn't bring myself to make that point with Kyle. So it had been over a month since I'd been to his house, and when I saw his name flash across my cell phone screen, I almost had a heart attack.

"Hello?"

"Hey, what's up?"

"Not much." My heart was a jungle drum. I wondered if he could hear it pounding in the background, like traffic, if the sound would drown out my voice.

"Um," he said, "I was wondering if you want to come over for a little bit."

"When?"

"I don't know," he said, "whenever. How 'bout now?"

"Oh. Okay," I said. I already had my jacket on and was out the door.

I took the bus to his house, where he met me at the front door. The place, as always, was totally silent and this time pretty dark. He looked different from the way he was at school; his tan seemed yellow and faded, and his affect was moodier, weirder. I saw as we walked by the kitchen that there was a plate of dinner on the table, wrapped. Seeing it made me feel sad for Kyle, so I asked, "How're things," meaning *I really missed you and please make up some excuse for why we haven't seen each other since before break,* but he looked at me and said, "Good," which I took to mean that he hadn't missed me. But I pretended at the time to think he had anyway, that he hadn't been able to admit it for some deep reason I couldn't guess at. I had to believe this so I could justify what happened next, which is that we went to his room. But this time he took a long time getting to the sex part.

We listened to music for a while, and watched some TV. I asked about his trip and he said it was fine.

"Just fine?"

"What do you mean?"

"It wasn't great?"

He shrugged. "I don't really like hanging out with my parents, you know?"

I thought about this, about how much I did like hanging out with my parents. So much that I kind of took it for granted, thought everyone liked their parents and people who said they didn't were just pretending, since it's not that cool to adore your mom and dad. But the way he said it was very matter-of-fact, and I knew it was true. I mean, he hated it every time they even came up. He never told me that, but I could tell.

This was no exception, because that's the moment when he was like, "Do you want to . . . ?" and then he kind of gestured toward the bed, and I was surprised, because he hadn't asked that the first two times, and it seems like the kind of thing you ask the first two times and maybe not the third time. But maybe he needed a way to change the subject, and it would have seemed weird to start kissing me while we were still talking about his vacation or his parents or whatever.

So I shrugged and nodded, and I kind of leaned into him, because we were both on the couch already. And we started kissing, and it was the best time yet—maybe because he had asked. Or because it had been so long and I had thought we would definitely never even talk again, let alone kiss on his couch. Or maybe just because we had already kissed twice before and I knew more what to expect. Then he unbuttoned my

253

shirt and pulled his T-shirt over his head. We slid our pants off, and I grabbed a blanket from the back of the couch and draped it over us, which made me feel safer, somehow. We did it on the couch, with him on top of me just like the other two times, but this time it felt pretty good, and I moved a little bit under him, even arched my back up, and as soon as I did that he collapsed on top of me. He didn't say sorry that time, though, and I was suddenly like, "Why did you call me?" even though I should have asked that before I went to his room. Or to his house. Or never asked it at all. Or asked the opposite, why he hadn't called me all those days he hadn't.

"Why not?" he asked. He had his sleepy voice back on.

"Was it just because you wanted to—"

"To what?"

I couldn't get the words out. Even now, I can't decide what they would have been—*have sex?* Ew. *Fuck?* Of course not. *Do it? Hook up? Make love?* I mean, oh my god. Why has nobody in the history of humankind been able to work this problem out? Isn't there some way of saying it that isn't completely gum-cracking and immature, disgustingly vulgar or like what my parents probably whispered to each other in the hairy seventies?

"To—to—you know . . ."

He sat up and shrugged, pulled his sweatpants on without putting any boxers on underneath or anything. In spite of the awkwardness and my attention being mostly elsewhere, I had the thought that this was both gross and something girls wouldn't do. I turned away from him on the couch and, keeping the covers over me, pulled my own clothes back on, underpants first.

"Can I ask you something else?" I asked.

He shrugged again, and I felt kind of angry.

"Does that mean I can't ask you anything? Or that I can?"

"Sure," he said.

"What was the favor you said you wanted me to do?"

"It's kind of a long story."

"I've got nothing but time."

"I want you to make a tape of me."

A little flutter of something went through me, but I didn't know if it was excitement or fear. "A tape?"

"Yeah."

"What kind of tape?"

"I just want to say something to my parents, and I need someone else to tape it."

"Why not Alan or Chris?"

At this, he tensed up and shrugged. "I don't want them to do it," he said.

"Are you going to kill yourself?"

He laughed. "Do I strike you as suicidal?"

"Sometimes the warning signs are tough to read."

"You're a good reader," he said.

My heart vaulted into my throat. "Is that why you like me?"

"It's why Ms. Doman likes you."

"And you?"

"I think you're nice."

"I'm not that nice, really."

"I think you are."

"But why me? I mean, lots of people are nice."

"Just because."

"That's all the favor is?"

"What did you think it was?"

"I had no idea."

"Yeah. I have something I need to say to my mom and dad, that's all."

So maybe he loved me, trusted me, knew we were both smarter than anyone else in the school, knew I wasn't shallow, something. Something deep. I still think that's sort of what he meant.

"Can I ask you one more thing?" I asked.

"Yeah."

"Did you just want to have sex, or did you want to do it with me?"

I meant this to be just a question, but it came out like a bullet, and he was mad. Maybe I would have been mad too, if someone had asked me that while I was all commando in my sweat-pants right after having sex with that person.

"What do you think?" Kyle asked.

"I don't know," I said.

"If I'd just wanted sex—" He stopped.

"What?"

"Nothing."

Was he going to say, "Why would it have been with you?" I mean, it would have been true, and a good point. He could have slept with anyone he wanted to, why on earth, if he just wanted sex, would he keep calling me?

He stood up, went and got his camera. He clicked a new mini-DVD in before handing it to me. He turned it on, opened the lens cap.

"I'm gonna sit here," he said, and patted his desk chair before sitting in it. "Maybe you could stand and film me?"

"Okay," I said. He came back over and bent down over me to show me how to push RECORD. I could smell his hair and his skin when he leaned down—a mixture of soap and sweat and lovely, tousled boy smell. I inhaled for as long as I could before he returned to the desk chair. He looked serious, the way he looked in *Fool for Love* right before he grabbed Elizabeth Wood and started kissing her.

"Is it recording?" he asked me.

I nodded, didn't say anything in case he didn't want my voice on the video.

He cleared his throat, looked down, and then looked up again, right into the camera. I tried to hold it steady, keep his sweet face right in the middle of the screen.

"Mom and Dad."

Kyle swiveled the chair around until he was facing his desk, and then he picked the letter off his desk in a very deliberate and dramatic way. He turned back to the camera, and he opened the letter. Why had he sealed his own letter to his parents?

He looked up from the page. "I'm sorry," he said. "I'm really sorry."

His eyes started to close a little bit, and I blinked too, thinking, "Oh my god, he's going to cry." But instead, or maybe to keep from crying, he looked up at me and said, "Okay, turn it off," so I pushed the red button and the camera stopped recording.

"Are we done?" I asked.

"Yes," he said. "Thanks."

Then we sat for a moment.

"Are you going to tell me what that was about?" I asked.

"Not right now. You wanna go get something to eat?"

"Can you tell me why you tape everything all the time, at least?"

He shrugged, went to get his sneakers, and started to put them on. I thought he wasn't going to answer me at all, but then, as he was tying his second shoe, he looked up. "That way

I can keep things, you know? I mean, have them even when they're whatever—over, or gone."

I didn't respond, because I knew he had gone on an icy, fragile limb to say that to me, and I didn't think I could honor it properly, or get the answer right. I wanted him to keep telling me everything, especially now that I thought he might be sad. We put our parkas on and drove downtown in silence, the windshield wipers squeaking snow off the glass. Then we sat at the Brown Jug, where the windows were foggy with cold from outside and he ate cheese fries and drank Coke. I had hot chocolate. We were very quiet. I don't know why he was, but I couldn't think of what to say. I wanted to go back to the conversation in his room.

I was finally like, "So, *Runaways* is opening crazy soon," and he nodded. "Too bad rehearsals have been going so badly," I said.

"Well, you know what they say," he said, meaning that bad rehearsals mean good performances or whatever.

I couldn't stand it, felt like we were in a bad TV movie, and since we were clearly never going to see each other again, I decided to cut to some central questions.

"Would you take me to the cast party?"

Kyle looked genuinely baffled. "What?"

"Would you take me to the cast party?"

"What cast party?"

"The one for *Runaways*."

"What do you mean?"

"I mean, would you go with me to the cast party?"

"I didn't even know there was a cast party. The show hasn't happened yet."

"I mean, you know, hypothetically. If there were a cast party, would you take me?"

"Sure."

I couldn't control myself. "Sure because it's hypothetical? Or sure like, when it happens, we can go."

"No one really takes anyone to a cast party. We all just go."

"But I mean, would you go with me even if it meant people seeing us together?"

He shrugged. "Sure. We're out now, aren't we?"

We sat in silence again, shame lapping up against me, threatening to drag me under and drown me.

"Let's pay," I said. "I want to show you something."

So we got the check and he was like, "Let me get this," and I was like, "No, no, we should split it," but he didn't listen and paid for it, and I thought this made it more like a real date. And then we walked across the street to Judy's Grill, where my parents were behind the counter, laughing with some customer. As soon as the door opened, they looked over at me, surprise registering on their faces before they tamed it, but I saw how on my mom's face it stayed hope, or delight or something, and then turned to fear. My dad went right back to the business of pouring coffee for someone after saying, "Hi, Judy," but my mom can't hide anything from me. She tries really hard, but her voice was high-pitched and squeaky when she said, "Hey, sweetie! Come in, we'll feed you." My mom never says "hey"—she just said it because I came in with the most beautiful boy anyone had ever seen, and even though she wanted it to be true as much as I did, she already knew it wasn't, couldn't be.

" 'S okay, Mom, we just ate. I just wanted to introduce you guys to Kyle." I didn't say *friend,* because I wanted to leave open the possibility that he was my boyfriend. I didn't say boyfriend, obviously, because he wasn't my boyfriend.

But Kyle stuck a hand over the counter and smiled his big, trustworthy smile, all those straight teeth consoling my parents. "Hi," he said. "It's great to meet you, Mrs. Lohden, Mr. Lohden."

"Call us Peggy and Max," my mom said. "Can we fix you something?"

"No, thank you," he said. "I actually have to be getting home, just wanted to drop Judy off. See you at school," he said to me, and bolted.

But I thought he'd kind of passed that test, too. I mean, he'd met my parents at least, had seen what it looked like to love me, and now they knew who he was. I felt like it made him accountable.

I went into the kitchen and helped Sam label cardboard Earths. My mom came in and asked, "Are you and Kyle dating?"

"Dating?" I wondered what that even meant.

"You know, are you having a romance."

"Ugh, Mom."

"Are you?"

I looked her right in the eye. "Yes," I said.

I was as proud as I've ever been about anything, even felt defiant for some reason. But then my mom was so quiet I finally had to be like, "What, Mom?"

She shrugged. "Nothing," she said, "as long as he's kind to you."

"Why wouldn't he be?" I asked. I thought of the video he'd asked me to make, of how much he trusted me, how he'd already started telling me whatever his worst secret was. But my mom and I just stared at each other for a few minutes, fighting, neither of us willing to say the words.

My dad brought me a Greek salad and chicken noodle soup and fries, and I sat at the especially high red stool all the way at the end of the counter, waiting for Sam to come and sit with me. A friendly-looking fat guy came in in the meantime and sat down next to me on the stool I'd been saving for Sam. He smiled a big, overcompensating smile and said, "Good things come in small packages," like I needed to be comforted by him. Like I'd never heard that one before. Like, I don't know, he knew me, was allowed to talk to me. Why is it that everyone in the world feels like they're allowed to talk about my body —*to me?* I thought of saying, "Oh? Not huge packages? In that case, maybe you should hold off on the fries," but I could see my dad throwing me our knowing grin from behind the counter.

So I just said, "Yeah, thanks," and turned back to the food my dad had made for me.

Kyle waited another two weeks before he called me again. I hated this pattern, but at least once I saw it as a pattern, I found it endurable. And once again, as soon as his name flashed across my cell phone I was out the door. I didn't realize on the bus over there that it would be the last time I would go to his house. It was Friday, February 5, the day before Meghan was coming, three days before *Runaways* was going up.

When I got there, Kyle opened the door and led me straight into the kitchen. His hair had gotten longer and was curling down over his ears. He blew some curls out of the way of his eyes.

"How are you?" I asked, because he didn't say anything.

"I'm okay," he said, all mushed together, like one word. He opened the freezer.

And I said, "Kyle? Who's Claire?"

Cubes of ice fell out of the tray into the freezer and onto the floor.

"Shit," Kyle said, but he made no move to pick them up, just clutched the few he'd managed to rescue to his chest and put them into the glasses.

"Can you not tell me?"

He took a bottle of whiskey out of the cabinet, and poured both glasses full.

"Wow," I said. "I guess my parents are coming to get me."

"Why don't you just stay?"

"Really? You want me to sleep here?"

"Why not? My parents aren't back until Monday."

I stood completely still for a minute, trying to think. "Oh, um, where are they?"

He looked at me strangely. "Boston. Why?"

"Oh, okay, so . . ." I felt oddly dizzy.

He waited, didn't rescue me.

"So, okay," I said again. "I guess I'll call my parents and say I'm staying at Sarah's?" I went to get my cell phone and called the house, knowing they'd be at the Grill, and left the lie on their voice mail. Then I texted Sarah, saying

I'd told my parents I was sleeping at her place and could she cover for me. I knew I'd have to explain, but I didn't care. When my phone buzzed twenty seconds later and "Goth Sarah" flashed across the screen, I didn't pick it up.

Kyle was standing at the counter, looking at me.

"You want to hear about Claire?" he asked. Then he turned and walked into the living room with his drink clinking and sloshing, and turned the giant flat TV on. *The Talented Mr. Ripley* was on, and someone was beating someone else to death with a bat in a boat. I could hear Kyle slurping down his drink. I sat next to him on the couch, stared at the TV, held on to my glass.

All of a sudden, Kyle put his glass down.

"You know, you're not the only one with problems," he said.

I want to say that he shouted this, because that's what it felt like when he said it, because I was so shocked by it, but he didn't shout. He's not really a shouter. He more like steamed it, and I thought of his constantly calm demeanor. Maybe he had a geyser inside him, waiting to erupt and kill him and anyone else within a mile. He usually seemed so sleepy and mellow. But that night at his house, he was anxious, from the moment I arrived. Maybe he knew what he was about to do, and was defensive, trying to justify it. Or maybe it happened because he was anxious and angry, and not by design.

"What does that mean?" I tried to keep my voice even, but my heart was flapping and beating, trapped in my body. The TV noise seemed suddenly nagging and loud.

"I just mean that being small isn't the worst thing that could happen to someone."

Now I was angry. "No shit," I said. "Did you come up with that yourself?" I'm glad I was mad enough to say this to him.

"I just think you act like a victim sometimes."

"Yeah? Like a victim? Compared to what?"

"I'm just saying, everyone has problems."

"Everyone has problems. Really, Kyle? Thank you. Do you think I'm, like, comparing my short self to the Holocaust? Is that what you mean by I'm not the only one with problems?"

This was very mean, of course, because I knew whatever he meant was about his own stupid problems, ones he must have wanted to tell me about, but I was so mad that I wanted to belittle his thing preemptively with the Holocaust. And it worked, because whatever shallow shit he was referring to had to be smaller in scale than the Holocaust, so he was embarrassed that I had made the very point he was pretending to have to make for me.

"I meant something else," he said, "which is that other people, even regular people like me, have problems too. You're not the only one."

"Right. You said that already. And I never asked you to help me with my problems," I said. "I'm not even the one who brought them up. Maybe you're the only one of the two of us who thinks my life as a short person is a problem. I mean, I'm just short. At least I don't treat other people like shit."

"Fuck it," he said.

"What do you mean, 'fuck it'?"

"I was—forget it."

"Forget what? Do you want to tell me what happened? Or what that video was about?"

"Nah, skip it."

"You should tell me."

"Why?"

"Because."

"I'm not sure I can."

Now he sounded pitiful. "Why me, Kyle? I mean, I know you said it's not about me, but you could have made that video yourself with a tripod, obviously, right?"

"Right."

"So wasn't asking me to tape it for you just a way to practice telling someone?"

"I guess."

"Have you ever told anyone else whatever it is?"

"No."

"Why not?"

He shrugged. "I dunno. It's private, I guess."

"What about Alan and Chris?"

"Would you tell those guys your secrets?"

I was amazed that he said this about his friends. "Of course not," I said, "but those guys aren't *my* friends."

"Do you tell *your* friends everything?"

"No," I admitted. I thought of how little I'd told anyone since I had met Kyle. And again, I had the thought that he and I were alike, that he liked me, felt connected.

"You can tell me your secret if you want," I said. "I won't ever tell anyone. I absolutely give you my word. But if you don't want to tell me, that's fine too."

I meant this, and he could tell. And it made him want to tell me. It's like Bill not caring about my dwarf story and therefore me wanting to tell him the whole thing even though there are lots of people who want to hear it and I don't want to tell them. People are stupid in this way, but it's just a fact. The less people ask you, the more you reveal.

"You've already guessed, right?" Kyle asked.

"No. How would I guess?"

"I don't know. I've always thought you kind of knew anyway."

"Because I'm an elf?"

"I meant that as a compliment. And you heard me apologize about Claire."

I asked, "Who's Claire? Your girlfriend?"

He sighed.

"Did something bad happen?"

I could see his Adam's apple move, and felt suddenly like it was hard to breathe in the room, like I was falling into a dark hole.

"I promised my parents I wouldn't tell anyone."

"Oh."

"Claire was my sister. And we moved here because she died."

"Oh my god," I said. Why would his parents have made him promise not to tell anyone that? What kind of psychopaths were they? He waited.

"Kyle. That's horrible. I'm really sorry."

"It was my fault," he said.

"People always think shit's their fault even when—"

"No, but I mean it was actually my fault."

I felt like he'd touched me with an electric prod. It was almost gentle, the feeling of that shock—like the point of someone's finger had just come lightly into contact with my skin, and yet my spine straightened and my hair stood up in a prickle that kept going. I felt weirdly tall, sitting there. My voice came from somewhere far away.

"What does that even—"

"I hit her. I— She was in the driveway, running out to greet me."

He stopped, and I had a sudden crystal-ball flash of his house in Boston. There was snow falling, or hail, ice on the driveway where she was running out to greet him and slipped under the wheels of the car. Or maybe the house was dark on a summer night, not even the porch lights on, her pink Schwinn parked up against the garage door. She was in a nightgown, running out to the car, hearing the sickening thunk of her own body against the hood. Had he pinned her to the garage door? The Schwinn crushed and mangled? The house switched to autumn, his sister hiding under a pile of leaves Kyle drove through.

"You don't have to tell me this if you don't want," I said. "Let's talk about something else. Let's go downtown and—"

"I still can't believe she came outside so late."

"Of course," I said. "And if it was dark—"

"She heard the car. I was late and my mom was freaking out. That's what kept her up."

"It wasn't your fault," I said. "You couldn't have—"

"I was really drunk," he said.

"Oh," I said. I thought for a moment.

"My parents covered it up." We both sat there, very still. Kyle finished his drink. I looked at mine, untouched, and took a burning gulp. It tasted like flowers and wood smoke. I coughed a little.

"What if your parents come home?" I asked.

"They're in Boston until Monday," he said again.

"Really?"

"They're never here."

"Why don't you ever have parties?"

He looked at me. "You want to invite a few people over? Let's do that."

So it was my idea, I guess. He was like, why don't you call up Sarah and Ginger or Molly or whatever, but I didn't. I just drank more throatfuls of whiskey while he called his friends. This is going to sound like I'm lying, but I barely remember anything else about that night. I kept drinking the smoky whiskey, that much I know. And apparently Alan and Chris showed up, and we watched some of one of the *Saw* movies, and drank more whiskey, and then we were playing cards or something—I don't know what, but something happened at a table. And then the rest is not only history—it's *the* history of my whole life. I'm like that girl who gave the president a blow job once. I mean, she had an entire life, but then it was defined forever by that one thing. Just like mine will be by this—the one night of my entire life I can't remember. Even if that wasn't true, it would still seem unfair that the first time I ever got really, really, like black-out, forget-what's-happening drunk, I was in such bad hands. I mean, other kids do that all the time and they get to wake up the next day and go on. Am I cursed?

I asked my mom, before I ran away to the Motel Manor forever, if she thought I might be under some horrible jinx, and she said absolutely not, that she thought I was lucky and would have a wonderful life and remember this as a painful but character-building moment. And when she said it, I couldn't be sure whether she actually believed what she was saying herself, but I had this terrible sensation that the floor was disappearing from under me, that I was spinning, falling slowly into space, where gravity didn't work the way it's supposed to. I knew what this feeling meant: that your parents can be wrong about things. I knew my mom was wrong about this, in an engulfing, bad-dream kind of way. I'd had that sense before, over something way stupider and less deep—when my dwarf friend Meghan and I were talking about shaving our legs. Meghan has dark, curly hair and is always talking about how hairy her body is and how she has to get waxed constantly, and I told her what my mom had said, that men "like a little hair," which I'll admit is really disgusting if you think about it. And Meghan was like, "No, they don't." And I was like, "My mom said they do." Meghan rolled her eyes, and I knew right away that she had a point, that maybe my mom was wrong, or at least that she had a very strange idea about the way men think of hair. Or something. Because this wasn't something my mom said to make me feel better; it was something she actually thought—that men "like a little hair." Which of course means my dad—ew. Anyway, I told Meghan the rest of everything my mom said because I couldn't shut up, even once I realized I was on the wrong track: that you should shave your legs only halfway up, because it's better to have hairy thighs than to have prickly thighs. And Meghan was like, "Someone needs to send your mom a memo telling her the seventies are over."

And I knew, the way you can about truth, that Meghan was definitely right and my mom was wrong. And even though it was about the dumbest thing ever, the floor was gone and I floated away without that great feeling you have when you're a little kid—that your parents know everything and can protect you. I'm glad I lost that safe feeling, of my mom always being right, over a ridiculous revelation about how far up my thigh to take a razor. Unlike my virginity, which I lost to Kyle in a horror movie, and then, in an even more dreadful sequel, my actual innocence. Which is not the same as virginity, by the way. But which I also lost to him.

# 11

I was running out of SpaghettiOs, so I knocked on Bill's door before dawn this morning, pretending I just wanted to ask if he wanted me to get him anything at the twenty-four-hour supermarket, but hoping he would offer to come, because the truth is, even though I had my grabber and could have managed to carry my stuff back, I really wanted some company. Maybe Bill sensed this, because as soon as I said, "I'm going to get some groceries," he pretended I hadn't just woken him at five in the morning, and he turned to get his shoes.

"I'll come. I'll come," he said. "I can carry your things. I'll come and carry your things."

Bill's weird habit of repeating things isn't annoying, by the way. It's very sweet, actually, as if he thinks over and over of kind things he can do for people, and sometimes the things vary and other times they don't. But he says them right away, to make sure he's offered. And then, again, maybe to make sure you've heard. I mean, it's a little *Rain Man*, sure, but who am I to cast stones? Who is anyone, for that matter?

It was barely daylight when we walked down East Michigan almost a mile to Kroger's, a dwarf and her crazy, thoughtful friend. Cars whipped by at highway speeds, almost running us over until one car slowed and I thought for a panicked moment it might be someone who knew me, or reporters, or I don't know what. But then some rude person shouted something out the window at us. Thankfully I wasn't able to make out what it was, and if Bill heard, he didn't show any sign of having thought it was about us. Or caring, anyway. I loved this about him. But then as soon as we arrived at Kroger and were pushing at the broken automatic doors, a kid pointed at me and jumped up and down trying to get his mother's attention. "Don't point," his mother said.

Bill saw this happen and turned to me. "He likes you."

"Right," I said. "Kids and dogs always *like* me." I tried not to say this in too mean or sarcastic a voice, not that Bill would have gotten it anyway. He's too good-spirited to understand me or to imagine that dogs literally think I'm another dog, or a treat or something. They come up and sniff me like—"What is this fabulous dog-size human I've found?" They can kiss me on the lips without having to jump up or even stand on their hind legs. More effortless slobbering and hump for your buck. Kids think I'm a kid at first, and then when they realize I'm not, the possibilities for what I might be instead are endless: hobbit, garden gnome, or adult small enough to be bossed around by them. In any case, it's loads of fun, and who wouldn't point? Some kids just want to gloat because even though I'm obviously older, they're bigger. I'm over it. But if I ever get married and have average-size kids myself, I'm going to show them who's in charge.

Bill got a cart and started pushing it, and I climbed up onto the bottom shelf of the dairy fridge and pulled out a small carton of milk. He reached down and took it from me gently so he could put it in the cart. I felt exhausted suddenly, like my bone marrow was giving up on me. Living alone was terrible. I mean, this was only the second time I'd ever been grocery shopping without one of my parents. And I hated it. I wanted desperately to go home, to hide in my house, even though maybe there were throngs of cameramen camped out on my lawn, wanting to make my life into more ugly videos. Just the thought of that made me want to sleep. But at the thought of sleep, an image of the bed at the Motel Manor popped into my mind, and fear climbed my spine like the rungs of a cold ladder. Up, up, up. I took a breath, gathered myself, considered asking Bill to lift me into the cart and push me through the store, but it seemed too humiliating. Not in front of Bill, I mean, he wouldn't have cared, but just everyone else in the store, especially that kid who had pointed, who was right behind us now, screaming for candy.

I felt trapped, too scared to go back to the

motel, too scared to go home, too scared to do anything. I felt myself hopping up onto the railing of the cart and holding on while Bill pushed our milk and me to the canned goods aisle. I heard myself ask Bill to get two cans of tuna. He put them in the cart carefully, and while he was doing that, he asked me, "So did he ever call?"

"What?"

"The man in the story," he said. "The man. Did he call on the phone?"

"Kyle, you mean?"

"Oh. Yes. Maybe Kyle. Did he call?"

I didn't know what this question meant— whether Bill wanted to know if Kyle had called me back in the day, like after we did it? Or wanted to know if he had called me lately, at the motel or something. His utter inability to understand time as a linear thing was comforting to me. It didn't matter when Kyle had called, at least not in Bill's and my universe. That he had called at all, ever, still counted for something here.

So I said, "Yeah. Sometimes he did call."

"Oh, good. That's good. That's good news," Bill said. "It's nice, to get calls. It's nice."

"You're right. It is nice. Thanks."

"Then what happened?"

"To me, you mean?"

"To the man?"

"Well, he did something kind of cruel."

"Oh."

"He and his friends took advantage of me. Or maybe his friends took advantage of him and me. I'm not sure. I don't know if he meant to; I mean, I think it might have been their fault and not his, but I—"

It was the first time Bill had ever cut me off. "Are you all right?" he asked, as if that was more important than whether Kyle had done it on purpose, or by drunk accident, or force of peer pressure or something.

"Yes, I'm all right, thank you. Could you, um . . . ?" We had made our way back in a circle to the produce section, and I pointed at some apples.

Bill took a plastic bag from a spinning roll of them six feet above my head. He put some apples in the bag and then tossed the bag into the high cart so effortlessly he looked like an Olympic athlete.

"Apples," he said as the apples settled between some tuna cans and relish, and then, "Thank you."

We walked by the flower freezer, and I picked out a gardenia. I love gardenias, because they smell gorgeous, and even though it was nine dollars, I wanted something alive in my room. Maybe this was a good sign that I wanted to keep living too, at least as long as it takes to find out what will happen to me. Maybe because I don't want to miss the end of my own story. Or maybe because I don't want the idiotic pigs on *Celebrity Apprentice* to have the last laugh when I'm hanging off a terrace somewhere.

Bill put the groceries on the counter, and I dug into my bag for my wallet, which I found but then promptly dropped while I was fumbling for bills. My beloved picture of Peter Dinklage fell out. I looked at it there, on the floor, and knew suddenly, in a terrible and certain way, that I would have to leave it there, that I didn't deserve to carry him around anymore; what would he think of me now, ruining the reputation of the very word *dwarf*? I know it's silly, because of course no one can represent everyone else, and I'm not every dwarf in the world any more than I'm every teenager or every girl. Not to mention I could have gotten another picture of him from a magazine or online, which is how I got that one, but I felt so ashamed of my life at that moment in the lonely Kroger that I couldn't bring myself to put the picture back in my wallet. Of course I felt sick deserting my hero there too.

Bill didn't seem to notice any of my paralysis, just waited patiently while I came back to life, collected everything but the picture, reassembled the contents of my wallet, and handed him forty dollars. He paid, and then carried the groceries all the way back to the motel, where the desk clerk was back and there were several people milling around but no one spoke to us and I kept my eyes pinned to the floor and ran up to my room, vowing never to leave it again. Bill set the bags down outside the door.

"Thank you," he said. "Thank you, Judy."

"Are you kidding? Thank *you,*" I said. "I mean, for putting everything in the cart and for being so helpful all the time and carrying all my stuff," I said. "Why don't you come in? We can have some juice or something."

He came in and sat politely on the bed. I rinsed out the glass by my bed and the one I'd been using to hold my toothbrush so I'd have two, and poured Red Machine berry juice from one of the Naked bottles into both cups. I offered one to Bill, thinking how glad I was to have met him, even if he was a complete freak.

"Looks like blood!" he said, and took a big swig of the juice.

I was drinking when he said this, and suddenly had hiccups. So I bent over and tried drinking the juice backwards from the top of the cup. Usually that really works, but this time it didn't, so I kept hiccupping. Bill didn't say anything about it. Maybe he didn't notice. We sat there quietly for a while, drinking our blood juice. I thought about how AP biology was happening now without me. I wondered if Mr. Abraham had seen the video. Probably. My stomach went hurling through space at the thought, which led to the next one, one I'd had so many times it was like breathing: of Mr. Luther watching it, Ms. Doman, Ms. Vanderly. Of how sickening they must have found it, and yet how they went back to Darcy, kept teaching their classes. How everything went on anyway.

I was holding the gardenia I'd bought. "Remember how you asked what happened then?" I said to Bill, hopefully.

"What happened? What happened?" he asked. He sounded nervous.

"No," I said, "it's okay. I just meant the story I was telling you. About my high school and that guy, Kyle Malanack?"

"Oh yes. Oh yes. I remember. I know that story. That's a good one. That's a good story," Bill said.

"Thank you. So—what happened was that our play opened. The play we were doing was called *Runaways*. And my friend Meghan—you know, the one who's also a dwarf? From California? Well, she was in town for opening night, because even though it was a high school play, for us it was kind of a big deal."

Bill nodded. His juice was finished and I opened the second bottle I'd bought, poured the blue goo into his glass, thought of Dr. Seuss, the Goo-Goose chewing. Bill smiled, took a sip. I thought he might be hungry, too, so I stood up, left the gardenia on the bed, and got the cheap can opener I'd bought at Kroger, used it to pry the top off some tuna, which I stirred into a bowl. I added an individual package of mayonnaise he had retrieved from the skyscraper of a deli counter. I took out four pieces of bread and two slices of American cheese, twisted open a jar of pickle relish until I felt the pop under the palm of my hand. I was glad my mother wasn't seeing this; she's a believer in nutritious food. Of course, she's never had to live at the Motel Manor or walk down East Michigan to hunt for a meal. I slapped the cheese on the bread, scooped some tuna onto each sandwich, put a spoonful of relish on top of the tuna, and covered it with the second piece of bread. I don't like the relish stirred in; I like the surprise of a huge clump of it, like pickles on a hamburger. I put the sandwiches on paper plates I'd bought my first day there and had started reusing since I only had six.

I set one in front of Bill. "Your tuna platter, sir," I joked.

"Thank you. Thank you, tuna and juice," he said.

I sat back down on the edge of the bed and took a bite of my sandwich. It was pretty good. But then as soon as I started telling Bill the story again, something about eating the tuna sandwich seemed disrespectful. But when I thought about that, I realized it was only insulting to me, since I was the tragic character in the story. And maybe it was a sign that I'm callous and unfeeling about my own history, because I was hungry. So I disrespected myself by eating a tuna sandwich while I told Bill the worst part.

Meghan had talked her parents into buying her a plane ticket to come for the opening of *Runaways*, and to letting her skip three days of school to hang out and visit D'Arts. She was scheduled to arrive the day after Kyle told me about his sister and we got drunk at his house.

I woke up that Saturday morning naked, on Kyle's basement couch, which had been folded out into a bed. To say I had no idea where I was is an understatement. It took me three full minutes of the kind of panic I thought was reserved for near-death experiences, just to regain actual consciousness. Five minutes into being awake, I felt pretty certain that I was human, that it hadn't been an alien abduction, that I was in a body that belonged to me. After ten minutes, I looked down at myself, found I was still there, alive, familiar.

"Oh my god, I'm a dwarf," I said to myself, and almost laughed. I mean, you can't deny that that's pretty hilarious. I wish someone other than me had been there to hear it. But even before I could enjoy my ability to make myself laugh during what would turn out to be the worst memory of my life, I had to put my head in my hands. Because it was pounding, screaming. My eyes hurt, shards of amazing pain jabbed at them from inside my brain.

"Where are my clothes?" I wondered. I sat up, and the room spun so horribly that I had to lean over. That made me think I might throw up, so I rested my weight on my arm at the edge of the sofa bed for a moment, and that's when I saw Alan.

He was asleep on the floor next to the bed, wearing a pair of boxers with prints of dogs on them. He didn't even have a sleeping bag or anything, just one of the huge couch pillows under his head. It was at that moment that I knew for certain I was going to throw up. I heaved myself off the side of the bed into a standing position, and staggered into the bathroom, where I sat down on the floor again, rested my throbbing head against the side of the bathtub. There were tan bathmats on a tile floor, and matching tan towels hanging so high above me that they looked miles away. The room was wobbling like a canoe, so I sat for a while before crawling over to the toilet and barfing. I felt slightly better. I wished desperately that I had my own car, could not see calling my parents and admitting that I hadn't slept at Sarah's, or waking Kyle. I was too dizzy to walk, so I crawled back out into the room where

Alan's nightmare triangular body was still lying on the floor. I dug around like an animal under the sofa bed and finally found some of my clothes. I threw them on, backwards, inside out, not caring, focusing on the pain in my head, trying to ignore everything else I felt and saw. I barely looked at Alan, stood up, shaking a little bit, and climbed as fast as I could up a short flight that led me to Kyle's palatial foyer. I had to brace myself against the banister twice. My purse was on the bench right at the front door, so I opened it and looked at my cell phone. No missed calls. I put it in my pocket and headed for the front door. I had no plan, but wanted to get out of that house as fast as I could and never see it again. In the reflection of the enormous foyer windows, I could see the living room behind me, and a body asleep on the black leather sofa with silver feet, and felt my stomach turn over again. I tried not to, but couldn't help myself and turned and looked. It was Chris Arpent. I couldn't tell whether he had clothes on or not, since he was covered with a throw that had been resting on the back of the couch. One of his hairy legs was sticking out of the blanket, and he looked like a giant, muscley insect. I had some kind of physical memory when I saw that leg, knew that I had seen it before, or touched it even, but that thought too I pushed back into my bones.

I tried to think, but could not. My mind separated from my body in a kind of revolt I'd never experienced, and propelled me to the front door, which I reached up and opened. I scrambled out onto the porch, leaving the door open behind me, hoping an intruder would come in and steal everything in the house, maybe even kill Chris and Alan. I couldn't quite hope for Kyle's death. I stood there for a minute, trying to orient myself, the world coming at me the way I guess it does when you don't know what you did the night before or how long it's going to take you to recover from whatever it was. The morning light was soft over the trees in the front yard, sprinkling shadows of leaves over the wooden porch and the side of the house. But it felt offensively, impossibly bright. It was very cold. I hobbled down the stairs into the cul-de-sac, wondering where his preppy mom and dad were, whether on vacation or a work trip, why they were both out of town so much, what it felt like to be Kyle, popular and tragic and abandoned.

I walked out of the circle and onto the main road, looked at a street sign: Beckinsdale Court. With no other choice I could think of, I called Chad. But it was 5:26 a.m., and he didn't pick up. So I called Sarah. I knew she slept with the cell phone next to her bed, in case Eliot called, and sure enough, she answered. Her voice sounded horrible on the phone, all craggy and scratchy and asleep.

"Helllllllooo?"

"Sarah!" I whispered, "It's Judy. I need your help. Can you come get me, please?"

She was instantly awake, the way you are when someone calls you with an emergency. I could hear her sitting up, scrambling around.

"Judy? Where are you?"

"Kyle Malanack's."

"Oh my god," she said. "Okay. Um. Where is that?"

"Right off Huron Parkway—on Beckinsdale Court. Across from Huron High," I said. I blinked at the light again, looked at the street sign and then down the road to the nearest intersection. I couldn't see far enough to read that sign. "Turn left when you get to Bridgeway College."

I could hear her opening her front door. "I know where that is. Don't move. I'll be there in ten minutes," she said.

I sat down on the curb. "Stay on the phone with me, please," I said.

"Oh, okay. Jesus, Judy. Are you okay? What the hell happened? What are you doing at Kyle Malanack's house at five in the morning?"

"I'm not sure," I said. "I think I might still be drunk."

"Okay," Sarah said. "Okay. Um. Where's Kyle?"

"I don't know. Sleeping, I guess."

"Um, okay, Judy. I have to hang up now so I can drive. Just wait for me there." She hung up.

The light began to shift over the street, getting brighter. I started worrying that Alan or Chris or Kyle would wake up and come outside and find me, and whatever had happened would actually have happened. What if they drove out onto this main road, and saw me sitting here like an orphan? If I could just escape entirely before they got up, I thought, no one would ever know and then whatever it was might as well not have even taken place. I was grateful for the cold, even though it was hurting my eyes and nose. It froze the headache and nausea a little bit.

Years passed before Sarah pulled up. She did a dangerous, screeching U-turn and I opened the passenger door before the car had even stopped moving. I appreciated the turn because she was usually such a goody-goody about her safe driving. Her car radio said 5:48 a.m., and we tore down the street and took a right turn immediately. As soon as we weren't on his street anymore, I felt a little bit of relief. We drove by Gallup Park; the Huron River was still lit with the kind of light that had just woken up, and all the houses and buildings we passed were still asleep. The world was in place. My head was beating so intensely I thought someone might climb out of my forehead, and I leaned forward in the car, took my seat belt off so I could rest against the dashboard.

"You okay, Judy?" Sarah asked again.

"I think so," I said.

"What the hell happened?"

"I'm not sure, honestly."

"Do you mean you're not sure at all? Or you don't want to tell me. Because either thing is okay, just tell me the truth."

"I mean I literally don't remember."

"That's not good."

"No, it's not."

"Do you think you and Kyle, you know, hooked up for real, like—?"

"Yeah."

"Have you before? I mean, other than the hand holding or whatever?"

"Yeah."

"Oh."

She was quiet, hurt, but I had bigger things to worry about.

"There's something worse, though," I said, figuring I'd make up for some of my silence with increased disclosure.

"What?"

"Some of his friends were there this morning."

"Who?"

"Chris and Alan."

"Were Kyle's parents there?"

"Of course not."

"So, so what about Chris and Alan being there?"

"So I think maybe something . . ." I trailed off.

"Something what?"

"I don't know. I don't feel well." I leaned my head against the window, and when I looked through the cold glass, I saw my parents' house with my dad's car in the driveway, and realized it would make no sense if I arrived home at six in the morning.

"Wait, Sarah? Can we go to your house?" I asked. "I told my parents I was sleeping there."

"Oh," she said, "okay." She put the car in reverse and drove out of my driveway, and I felt relieved again for some reason. Maybe because I knew that Kyle's house and my house were two places I could never be again without having to admit that whatever had just happened—had actually happened.

"I have to be home by ten," I said, thinking out loud. "Meghan's coming today—remember? I have to go to the airport to get her with my mom."

"Oh, right, cool. When am I going to get to meet her?"

"Tonight, if you want. Hey, Sarah?"

"Yeah?"

"Thanks a lot for coming to get me. You really saved my ass."

"No problem. Um—"

"I'll tell you everything as soon as my head stops exploding."

"So you do remember what happened?"

"Not last night, but I'll tell you the stuff before. I wish—"

What I meant was, if I had just told you, then maybe you would have warned me and I would have listened. Maybe none of whatever happened last night, whatever horror it was, would have happened. But even as I said it, I was thinking, I still haven't told Sarah or Molly or Meghan anything, so maybe if I keep on that path, and continue to say nothing, we can all just pretend nothing happened. Hell, since I didn't even know what had happened, it would almost be true.

Sarah's parents were still asleep, so we went to her room and pulled out the trundle bed. I collapsed onto it and slept until 9:30. When I woke up, light was coming in sideways through the row of horizontal windows along Sarah's ceiling, blinding me and then lodging deep in my forehead.

"Sarah?" I heard her come down the stairs. She peeked her head around the corner into her room, looking oddly unlike herself. She had a headband pulling her hair back, and no makeup on. Maybe she had been washing her face or something. She looked very pretty and clean, like a young picture of her mom.

"You feeling any better?" she asked. I shielded my eyes from the light.

"I think I'm going to die," I said.

"Let me get you some Excedrin—those really work," she said, and she turned back into the hallway. I heard her in the bathroom next to Josh's room, opening drawers and turning on the sink, thought what a good friend she was. She came back in carrying two Excedrin in the palm of one hand, and an orange plastic cup in the other. I propped myself up on some pillows, feeling like I might throw up again, and swallowed the pills down with the water.

"Lie down for ten more minutes," she said, "and that will kick in. Then I'll take you home so you can meet your mom in time to get Meghan."

I wished I were Sarah, without wishing she were me. How nice would it have been not to have been me that morning, or any of the mornings that followed it? Someday I want to be the one taking care of my friend, rather than the basket case getting cared for. That said, I wouldn't wish what happened to me on the evilest villain in the universe, so maybe I'll never have a chance like Sarah had.

When she dropped me at my house, with the rest of her Excedrin bottle in my jacket pocket, I gave her an impulsive hug before staggering out into the driveway.

"We'll get through this," she said, and I knew right away that I would always remember that she said "we'll" instead of "you'll."

I managed to say thank you as I walked up toward the house. When I got inside, I was relieved to find it empty, and a note from my mom saying they were at the Grill and that she'd come get me at eleven so we could pick up Meghan.

I took four more Excedrin, not realizing you're not supposed to take more than eight in twenty-four hours, and put my head back down on the pillow. When the pills finally hid my headache under a numb bag of sand, I struggled up, took another shower, put on clean corduroy jeans and a sweater, and picked up my phone to call my mom. I had nine missed calls from Sarah and seven from Molly. So Sarah had told Molly. I couldn't blame her. But I couldn't bring myself to call them back, even after listening to their messages. Sarah's were like, "Let us take you out tonight and cheer you up," and Molly's were all, "Dying to see you guys this weekend—call me!" because she didn't want me to know for sure yet that Sarah had told her.

I went into my mom's bathroom and used all her makeup. By the time she got home at eleven, I looked like I was wearing stage makeup, and felt slightly better.

"Wow," she said, "you got dressed up for Meghan!"

I nodded. We drove out to the Detroit airport, small-talking. I used my best professional acting talent to hide everything until I left her in the car and went into the baggage claim to collect Meghan. But my mom was suspicious. She kept casting glances at me sideways and asking if everything was all right. And my phone vibrated so nonstop in my purse that it was as if the bag were a living animal throbbing on my lap. I glanced each time to make sure it wasn't Meghan, but it was just Molly and Sarah, over and over. I thought they were probably together, calling on a rotation.

"Why aren't you picking up your phone?"

"Because you and I are in the car together, talking." Even I could hear how unconvincing this was.

"Did something happen with you and Sarah?"

"No, Mom, everything's fine."

"What did you guys do last night?"

"We just hung out, okay?"

"Okay. Was Molly there?"

"No, she had to babysit her sister."

"Are you sure you're okay, Judy? You look— I don't know, tired, maybe."

"I was up late."

As soon as we pulled up outside the baggage claim, I bolted from the car. Inside the airport, I had a rush of the thought that I could leave. I could just board a plane and fly to some other land far away and never return. Or at least not return until a hundred years from now, when no one would care about whatever had happened last night. I'd be like Rip Van Winkle. Or Sleeping Beauty. Except the mere thought of Sleeping Beauty getting kissed reminded me of Kyle and the floor started melting under me. I was like this, in chaos, when Meghan shouted my name from across the room.

I looked up and she was clomping toward me in huge, illicit heels, waving. She threw her arms around my neck and kissed all over my face, definitely leaving lipstick marks everywhere. She looked fantastic, all tan and wearing a tight yellow sweater and jeans with her high-heeled boots. Under any circumstances other than the ones I was now under, I would have asked right away how she had talked her mother into them; they were definitely not orthopedic.

"Oh my god! Judy! I'm so happy to see you!"

"Me, too," I said.

She backed up and took a look at me. "Oh my god. What's wrong? Are you okay?"

"I'm really glad you're here," I said. "I'm fine, just super hungover."

"Wow, hungover, really? I guess your life has gotten exciting, huh? You'll have to tell me." She grabbed a black roller bag with a pink ribbon tied to its handle and heaved it off the conveyer belt. "That's it," she said. "Your folks outside?"

"My mom," I said.

She looked at me. "Are you sure you're okay?"

I gave up on my keeping-it-secret-forever plan instantly. I wished I had told her about Kyle from the very beginning, so she would have background, could help more.

"I think something bad might have happened last night," I said.

"What do you mean?"

"I don't actually know."

"Well," she said, sounding concerned but happy, "we have five whole days to talk about it. And your play! I can't believe I finally get to see you act." She started moving toward the door, yanking the bag along.

"I know. Thank you so much for coming."

Something in my voice made her turn and stop. "Was it something really bad last night?"

"I can't remember."

"Did you *do it?*"

"Yeah, but—"

"But what? You lost it *last night?*"

"No, before. A few weeks ago, with the guy whose house I was at, though."

"No way! You lost it!? Was it the guy you told me about? The peeing-at-the-party guy? I can't believe you didn't tell me—I thought we had a pact! You bitch!"

She slapped me on the arm, delightedly, but when I didn't respond she sobered up. "So if you'd already lost it to him, what was so bad about last night?"

"His friends were there, and they're not cool at all."

"Are you guys, like, dating? Hanging out with his friends and everything?"

"Not really, that's the thing."

She waited.

"I think something crazy might have happened."

"Like what?"

"I woke up naked, not with Kyle."

"Oh. With—?"

"Meghan?"

"Yeah?"

"What if I—?"

"What if you what?"

"You know—fooled around with this other guy?"

"Did you wake up with one of his friends?"

"Only sort of, I mean, I was alone, but he was kind of right there—he was—"

"Was he naked, too?"

"He had on boxers."

"Where was Kyle?"

"I don't know. I ran."

"You ran?"

"I mean, I didn't literally *run,* but I left quickly."

"How'd you get home?"

"I called that girl I was telling you about— Goth Sarah? And she came to get me. I didn't look for Kyle."

"Maybe that's all good, though, right? Maybe you were just too drunk, so Kyle put you to bed somewhere else because he didn't want to, you know, when you were too drunk to be into it. I mean, this other guy wasn't, like, with you when you woke up, right? Maybe—"

"I don't think it was all good," I said.

I stopped there, because I couldn't bring myself to say out loud to anyone, even Meghan, why: that I felt unlike myself, that I hadn't been able to find my underpants, that I remembered *something,* a kind of hazy picture of Alan near me. I didn't say Chris had been there too, and that I'd known exactly the way his body moved, in the instant I saw it upstairs on the living room couch, even though I couldn't remember why or how that was true. None of this was possible to say, even to Meghan. I knew I had seen a puzzle of Alan parts too, and I knew it because they were different from Chris's and Kyle's; Alan stomach, hips, legs. I didn't think I was imagining any of it—how could I have seen that stuff so clearly in my mind? And Kyle had been there. The worst part was that I thought I remembered laughing. Had Kyle been laughing? And if so, at what? Had I been laughing too? Maybe we had all just been joking around, having a good time. Or maybe I was just going crazy now, and none of it was real. I hoped so. Meghan and I walked outside the terminal, where my mom was circling. As soon as she came back around, she waved from the front seat of her car. Meghan waved back before lowering her voice and saying to me, "Why don't you call Kyle and ask what happened?" We walked toward my mom.

"I can't bring myself," I said.

"Ask him at school on Monday, then. We'll find a way." She opened the door to my mom's car. "Hi, Peggy!"

The whole way home, Meghan and my mom chatted cheerfully about her older brother's baseball playing and her older sister's college, and Meghan's art class or something, while I put my phone on airplane mode, and then leaned my head against the cool window and talked myself out of throwing up.

That night we had dinner at the Grill with Sam, and even though I felt terrible about it, I didn't call Sarah or Molly. Seeing Meghan, who had nothing to do with D'Arts, and didn't even know the people involved, was too big a relief to be sacrificed by getting back into the real conversation about it, whatever that was going to be. I couldn't imagine going back to school, and Sarah and Molly were evidence that that would have to happen. Plus, Molly was so—I don't know, good, I guess. I just felt like she might be judgmental. So I avoided them both, thinking they'd assume it was because Meghan was a better friend and now that she was in town, I wasn't interested in hanging out. I didn't sleep at all that first night. I felt bad about Sarah and Molly, and brink-of-death panicked about Kyle. Meghan slept in my bed and I paced the room for like ten hours, checking my computer and phone every five minutes, opening books only to close them again, watching the silent, still street glitter under the lamps out the window. Time is a heavy, thick thing at night, and it moves like glue. That was the first Kyle Malanack all-nighter I'd pull. I took six more Excedrin, exceeding the limit again, which is part of what kept me up, since those things are like 80 percent caffeine. I also chewed two entire packs of gum.

On Sunday, I turned my phone on, and had sixteen messages from Sarah and nine from Molly, who wasn't pretending anymore. "Call me right when you get this," she said. "Did something happen? Are you okay?" I didn't call back.

Meghan and I spent the day downtown, shopped at Urban Outfitters and Barnes &

Noble, had lunch and dinner at the Grill with dozens of old people and a couple of Michigan students who sat on the same side of their booth and alternately sipped from their drinks and made out. As soon as they started kissing, I felt my stomach twist, wondered whether whatever had happened at Kyle's would make me horrified by love for the rest of my life. When an old woman clucked disapprovingly at them, loudly enough for everyone to hear, Meghan threw me a knowing grin, not realizing she and I weren't on the same side anymore. I was like the old lady now, disturbed that I had to watch their disgusting session. Of course, her reason for thinking it was inappropriate probably wasn't that she had woken up less than forty-eight hours ago with a gaggle of naked teenage guys, unable to remember what she'd done. I wished I were the old lady, and then saw Meghan looking curiously at me. I wondered if I'd ever be able to explain how I felt—to anyone. The mere thought of trying made me feel exhausted and lonely.

I didn't see anyone from D'Arts, and I worked on convincing myself that even if something had happened, as long as I never mentioned it again, and no one else did either, I could just pretend it hadn't, and go on. I would just pretend. Pretend. Stay quiet.

The idea that that might work gave me a little comfort for a day.

**12** Because people are fundamentally animals, it makes sense that I knew before I knew for real—that something was very wrong, like I-can't-make-it-go-away, parasite-clinging-to-your-insides-gobbling-up-your-life wrong. I mean, more than what-had-happened wrong. I mean lasting, scary, something bigger than I had ever imagined.

There was the way the hallways seemed suddenly to expand and contract. They were long and daunting and dark, even before precalc, when morning light blasted in from the windows and lit the school like a stage. There was the way several seniors who had never talked to me moved their bodies a bit closer to each other when they saw me, the sharper voices they used, a weird, silent laughter underneath their "Hello, Judy." The fact that they said hello at all, which they had never done before. Maybe it was just Meghan, I hoped, maybe I had just multiplied the dwarf thing to the next power by bringing her to school. Or maybe it was because *Runaways* was going up that night, February 8. Yes, maybe that was why the building had that stomach-turning energy. Everyone was just nervous, that was all. All day I felt like my stomach was a bleeding ulcer, like I might fall, like the floor was uneven, moving. I kept telling myself it was *Runaways*, that I was just nervous, too, I mean, it was the first show I'd done at Darcy.

But then Goth Sarah cornered me in the doorway to American lit and was like, "What the hell is going on? Are you okay? Are you mad at me?"

"No, no," I said, "I just couldn't deal with it this weekend. I'm so sorry."

Right as Ms. Doman was about to start class, Molly came in and looked over at me, like "What the hell?"

I looked back at her, mouthed, "Sorry." I passed notes to both her and Sarah, saying, "I'm sorry, and I'll explain everything I can asap." Molly turned and nodded, but when I passed the one to Sarah, she read it and her expression didn't change at all and she just stuffed it into her notebook without looking up at me or writing back. Meghan was watching us like a puppy at a Ping-Pong match.

On the way to AP bio, I told Meghan that Sarah was mad at me and had every right to be, and that hopefully we would all hang out, at lunch and after school and before the play and as much as possible before Meghan went back to California, and I'd fix it.

"Why is she mad?" Meghan asked.

"It's a long story," I said, "but she's been a

really good friend and I never tell her anything. Kind of the same with Molly, I guess."

"Why?"

I shrugged. "I don't know. Maybe because I don't want any of it to be true."

Then she went to the library to do homework, since Mr. Abraham didn't allow visitors in his top-secret dead-cat lab. I went to AP bio alone and dissected Cletus the Fetus's vascular system with Rachael Collins, and it was the happiest hour of my life, because Rachael and I have that kind of relationship where even though we're high school lab partners and it seems like we see each other constantly, she's so polite and quiet that we still barely know each other and so we didn't have to talk about anything except anterior ventral veins. I made labels: cephalic, jugular, axillary, subclavian. But toward the end of it, I started thinking of my own neck, of what an autopsy of my body would look like. And as soon as I began to think of that, I thought of myself on the table, that black slate or whatever-it-was table, naked, cut open by my classmates, them laughing and labeling my jugular as they sliced it open but no blood came out, because I'd been deblooded like the cats. And as soon as I imagined that, and I mean really imagined it, the way you can sometimes understand death and forever in the dark of your bedroom as a little kid, the smell of the cat hit me. And it smelled like clammy, chemical death, and I gulped down a bunch of air, trying to push the rising nausea back down, but the more I swallowed and breathed the more dead cat and veins and stomach and muscles came into my body through my lungs and I could feel my skin prickling and rising in a chill, and even that made me think of cats, the way they arch their backs and the hair stands on end, and Rachael was like, "Are you okay, Judy?" And I realized all the blood had drained out of my body and I had to excuse myself and run to the girls' bathroom.

I locked myself in a stall, and right away considered staying there for the rest of the day, or even the rest of the year. I could write an "out of order" sign and stick it on the wall and hope it would keep people out forever. I sat on the toilet, pulled my legs up, wrapped my arms around my knees and buried my head in them. Even though it smelled like pee, being away from the pickled cats was such a relief that I felt the nausea subside a bit, and I sat there for a long time, maybe even fifteen or twenty minutes, focusing my mind on outside things: a coral reef I had swum in when Chad and Sam and I were kids; the image of my mom's purple terry-cloth bathrobe hanging from her and my dad's bath-room door; the leather cover of my most recent diary, with flower imprints and a thin strap. I thought of blank pages of paper, my pink pen, scripts, the smell of books. I kept my mind on good smells, maybe because the bathroom reeked more and more, maybe because of the cats.

Then the bell rang and the doors started opening and girls came in to chat and put on frosted lipstick and I heard a stream of pee and then Kelly Barksper's voice come out from a stall like, "Did you hear what it was of? Oh my god."

But no one responded and she was like, "Kim? Are you still in here?"

And then she left her stall, didn't even wash her hands, or at least I didn't hear the water running, and then the door of the bathroom opened and closed again and I didn't hear anything else. But the nausea was back, so bad and intense that I had to climb down from my perch and throw up into it. I was bent over the toilet, retching, praying no one would come in, when I remembered suddenly that Meghan was there, that she'd been in the library waiting for AP bio to end, that she'd be waiting at lunch for me. So I dizzily wiped my mouth with a piece of toilet paper, thinking how scraps of it would probably be glued to my face for the rest of the day. Then I inhaled and opened the stall door, just as Elizabeth Wood and Amanda Fulton walked in. When they saw me, I knew for sure that something horrible was going on, because of the way they stopped and stood absolutely still, staring at me. Amanda's mouth was open, like she was going to say "oh my god," but nothing came out.

Elizabeth pulled herself together before Amanda did, was like, "Oh, *hey, Judy,*" which was enough evidence because she'd never said hey to me before, and certainly not all fake-casual like that, so I was like, "Oh, hi," and bolted from the bathroom as fast as I could, worrying, even at a time like that, that they would notice I hadn't washed my hands. Without even checking the mirror to see if I had barf on my face or toilet paper stuck to my mouth. I went straight to my locker and checked in the mirror, and I looked fine, actually. A little pale around the eyes and flushed in the cheeks, but okay. I swished some mouthwash and swallowed it, put a piece of gum in my burning mouth.

I realized I hadn't seen Ginger all day—maybe she was absent. I was thinking about this when I saw Meghan, standing in the hallway, looking around, confused. People were staring at her as they walked by on their way to lunch, but she's used to it too, so I didn't have to say anything like "Sorry I brought you to my school and then left you in the hallway for the sharks to devour." Maybe they were just staring at her because they couldn't believe there were two dwarfs in the world and thought she was me, like, since when did Judy have tan skin and curly dark hair? When I walked up, Meghan's face lit up and I had the thought that she really loved me and it would be so nice if she could just live in Ann Arbor and we could go to school together and shut the rest of the world out. Or shut the world out and never go to school again, just hang out and read books.

"Judy—you okay?"

"Sorry. I got kind of sick—something about the cat freaked me out all of a sudden, so I went to the bathroom."

"You okay now?" she asked.

"I'm over the cat thing, if that's what you mean."

We made our way to the cafeteria, and when we got there and walked in, it was literally like we were in a movie, and I mean a really over-stated, crazy one about high school dynamics, where everything that happens is so obvious that you want to hit the writer over the head with your lunch tray. Except the person writing the story about my life was doing a little high-school-humor joke about irony, since I was the protagonist and didn't know what the hell was happening. Isn't that what irony is, when everyone else knows something horrible that's going on with you but you don't know it? Like Oedipus killing his dad and about to fuck his mom and the whole audience like, "Oh my god," and him like, "Life's too good to be true"?

Because when we came into the cafeteria the entire room froze. Conversation died like someone had blown a fuse, and the smell of whatever nasty food they had prepared hung like a toxic curtain over the room. My stomach clamped and I had the panicked thought that I might throw up right then, in front of everyone. The entire room was watching me. But I didn't throw up, and the freeze lasted only one single, mind- and soul-wrecking second, before people went back to talking and Meghan started to say, "Wow, I guess two dwarfs are—" but got cut off because Goth Sarah had seen us and come over from the table where she'd been sitting alone.

"Judy! What the fuck happened on Friday night? People are talking about it."

I started coughing when she said this, and couldn't stop. She whacked me on the back. When it finally looked like I wasn't going to choke to death, I said, "What are they saying?" and made my way to the line, looking at the glass counter, all steamed up from the "pasta" they were serving, which looked more like a red Jell-O mold with some bow-tie-shaped noodles floating in it.

I pointed to it and a plastic box of salad, and the hair-netted woman on the other side clacked some blocks of food onto my tray. I thanked her, slid down the line, paid.

"Um, Sarah, this is Meghan. Meghan, Sarah." They stopped for a moment and exchanged real smiles, before we all remembered we were in a horror movie.

"Judy, did you"—Sarah's voice dropped to a scratchy whisper—"hook up with Chris? Or Alan? Did you—um, did you guys—are you okay?"

At this, Meghan looked from side to side to see if anyone had heard, but no one seemed to have, so she went back to staring at the neon pasta she was carrying.

We made our way back to a table in the corner, where Sarah's bags were. As we walked, I felt a million insect eyes on my sides and face and back, prickling me like a heat rash. I felt jittery, like I might drop my tray. Which would have been fine, since I couldn't imagine eating a bite of food ever again.

We sat down and looked at our food. The red pasta reminded me of the cat and my stomach lurched. Sarah didn't say anything, just watched me.

"I hooked up with Kyle three times," I said. "Those times he drove me home, and then one other time, okay? And I went to his house Friday night, obviously," I said. I was angry, even though of course none of this was her fault, and it had nothing to do with her at all. She was the only person near enough to absorb some rage.

"Yes, I deduced that when I picked you up."

So maybe she was mad at me, too. I put one bow-tie noodle on my spork.

"Judy?" Sarah said.

"What?!"

"Why can't you just tell me what's going on? Is it because of Molly?" I was baffled by this for a moment before it hit me. If I had hooked up with Chris, then I had betrayed her. I couldn't help but feel, selfishly, that that was the least of my problems.

"No, it's not about Molly. Or you. I promise. Ask Meghan. I mean, I haven't been able to tell you what happened Friday night, right? Because I literally can't remember."

Meghan nodded at Sarah. "It's true," she said.

Sarah said, "Was it something kinky and freakish?"

"Why would you ask me that?"

"Because you were so secretive to begin with! I mean, I asked you if you and Kyle—you know, weeks ago before the Friday-night thing, and you told me he brushed your hand! I mean, brushed your hand? Did you lose it to him? I would have been thrilled for you—you could have told me."

"I know. I didn't mean—it was just, I don't know, kind of private. I mean, nothing's been happening, except we were kind of, I don't know—dating, I guess."

311

"You were 'dating'? Is that like 'brushing hands'? What does that even mean?"

"Okay, so we'd had sex."

Sarah took this in. It seems funny now, but she had to take a moment to do the math—and I watched her be like, "Oh my god, she lost it to Kyle Malanack," before she remembered that it wasn't time for celebrating that fact anymore. I wished more than ever that I had told her when it had still seemed like potentially good news.

"But what about Friday night? What about the taping thing?" Goth Sarah asked. She ate a bite of iceberg lettuce with pink Thousand Island dressing on it. My mind reeled backwards and then forwards. Meghan was watching me. I could feel myself blinking very fast.

"What do you mean, 'the taping thing'?" I asked.

"Oh, come on, Judy. If you don't want to tell me anything, that's fine, but don't lie about it directly. Aren't you the one with the whole 'no direct lying' policy?"

"Sarah." I looked straight into her eyes. "I don't know what you mean."

"Oh," she said, the weight of whatever it was coming at her. "I thought—I mean, I assumed you—"

The bell rang and Molly came running up, half dropping her precalc book and a chaotic stack of tutoring notes. "Oh my god, Judy!" she asked. "What is going on? What happened?"

I had never heard her so lathered up. "I don't know yet," I said. I turned back to Sarah. "Assumed I what?" I asked Sarah, trying to keep my voice even.

Now it was Sarah's turn to hedge. "I don't know exactly," she said, and I didn't know whether that was true. "But I heard that you and Kyle taped yourselves—I mean—"

"Taped ourselves what?"

"I don't know Judy, but I'll find out, okay? I can't skip right now—it's my presentation in—"

"Sarah! Who—"

I guess Sarah figured everyone already knew anyway, or if they didn't, they were all going to find out. She said, "Kyle or Chr—one of his friends, I guess." She glanced over at Molly, who was staring at us, one of her eyebrows raised in an angry arch.

"There's some kind of video of you guys, Judy," Sarah said. "A, you know, *video*. Do you want me to pick you up after block three? I'm so sorry—I have my presentation in AP history today so I have to—"

She started toward her locker, turned back, and said, super intensely, "Come find me in the parking lot after the bell. I'll get you out of here, okay?"

Molly looked over at Meghan suddenly. "I'm Molly," she said.

"Nice to finally meet you."

Then Molly turned back to me, and I thought she was going to freak out about Chris or criticize me. But she said, "We will sue their fucking asses off," she said. "If there's a video, or whatever— my dad—we will tell my dad, and he will—"

"Wait," I said, "let's just, we don't even—" I appreciated her loyalty and ability to look past the Chris debacle, whatever it was, but I didn't like the sound of anyone telling anyone's dad anything. I wanted to escape—just with Meghan. The bell was ringing.

"You should go to class, Moll," I said. "We'll talk about it tonight when—" I had a flash of *Runaways*, the opening, everyone gathered, holding hands for warm-up.

"They will not get away with this," Molly said.

My hands had started to shake, and Meghan, either noticing this or just coincidentally, took my hand and started pulling me toward the door.

"We'll see you tonight, okay?" I said to Molly, and then, feeling bad for so obviously wanting her to go, added, "We can talk about it then." I wanted to be alone, and frankly, for a reason I couldn't have articulated, being with Meghan was as comfortable as being alone. Molly walked away reluctantly, glancing back, and I thought how she should be glad to be able to walk away, how relieved I would have been to be her, to be able to leave this mess even for a few minutes.

Meghan dragged me outside into the parking lot, and we started walking through it, picking up speed, toward the field.

The most sickening feeling I've ever had came over me. I still remember it, like a hot, filthy envelope smothering me and then sealing itself, holding in all the nausea of my Saturday hangover, the horrible spinning bathroom at Kyle's house, the dead cat stretched out on the black table in AP bio, the smell of the girls' bathroom, and something else, something defiled, decaying. I started to writhe in my skin.

"What kind of video do you—" I asked Meghan slowly. I tried to remember where Kyle and I had been in his house. His room? The basement? The living room? I felt like maybe if I could remember the setting, I might know what we had done, but a black curtain dropped in my mind.

"I don't know," Meghan said, cutting me off. "We'll have to see it, okay? Whatever it is, we'll see it and we'll be okay. It can't be as bad as you're imagining."

"I wonder where Ginger is," I said absently. I had the feeling through that entire day that if I could just put everyone in his or her proper place, things would be okay. But there were all sorts of people missing. In fact, I hadn't seen Chris or Alan either, although I knew they were there because Sarah had seen them. There was no way I was going to senior voice. Kyle hadn't been in American lit. Where had he been?

Meghan and I got to the field behind the school and I cut class for the first time ever and sat there, stunned, trying to guess what was about to happen to me, based on guessing what had happened to me before. Neither was easy or pleasant to imagine. Time felt like a frappe, thick, icy, granular, grinding in a blender.

My mind was on a loop. What video? What kind of video? What had I done? A video of us talking? A video of me naked? How bad was it? I couldn't imagine what that video looked like. Where was it? It took me so long to sort out even what those words meant that it wasn't until Carrie Shultz walked by Meghan and me on the field, where we were waiting for Sarah to be done and drive us far away, and said, "How're things?" in a voice like six octaves deeper than her normal one, that I realized I had to get a copy as soon as possible. I had to see what it was, to know what everyone had either heard about or seen. Had everyone seen it? Why was Carrie's voice all weird like that? Because of Chris? What did she think, or worse, what did she know? I began to freak out.

"They're okay, Carrie. How are you?"

She said nothing, walked off.

"Was that as bizarre and awkward as I think it was?" I asked Meghan.

"I dunno," she said. "Is she like a super weirdo?"

"I don't remember," I said. I didn't think so. "Do you think she's seen the video? Do you think she knows about it? Do you think everyone has seen it except me? Oh my god—what if—" The hysteria was mounting in me like lava and I could imagine the horrible images breaking open the top of my head, erupting my brains and blood out. It would spill over the sides of me and harden into a black crust.

"We have to see it," Meghan said.

"I know."

"Call him."

I took my cell phone out of my purse and popped a piece of gum out of the package before I dialed Kyle's number. It rang and rang and his voice mail picked up. I hung up, chewed the gum. As soon as the bell rang, Meghan and I stood up and went straight out to the parking lot to wait for Sarah. She came right after the bell, unlocked the car, and we climbed in. She didn't start the engine right away, though, we all just sat there for a minute. I felt safe for the first time that day, locked into Sarah's car, with Sarah driving and Meghan in the backseat, all of us about to be far away from D'Arts.

I inhaled. "Oh my god," I said. "What's happening?" I slid down in the seat.

"I don't know, Judy," she said. "Let me take you home. We're called at seven."

"I'm not coming."

"What do you mean?"

"There's no way I'm coming tonight."

"You're going to drop out of *Runaways*? Drop out of D'Arts? Slow down. We haven't even seen the video yet, and we don't know who else has seen it, if anyone. Pretend nothing happened, go tonight, perform anyway—I mean, all our parents, teachers, everyone—"

"Um, Judy, I think you should do the show too," Meghan said from the backseat. "Don't let this ruin everything. If you don't go tonight, everyone will know that something's going on. It will just make things worse, and besides, maybe focusing on the play will make you feel better."

"How did you find out about the video?" I asked Goth Sarah.

"Tim Malone said something as you walked into American lit," she said.

"Tim Malone?" I asked.

She nodded.

"How the hell did Tim Malone know? What was he saying?" I heard myself ask.

"I don't know, Judy, I guess he's friends with those guys."

"Don't spare me. I want to hear what they were saying."

I could feel Sarah make eye contact with Meghan in the rearview mirror.

"That it was the latest celebrity sex tape," Sarah said quietly.

I tried to take this in. "Tim Malone said that? He called it a sex tape?"

"Yes."

"Oh." I listened to the sound of my own breathing for a minute.

"How did you know it was me?" I asked.

"I just do."

"How?"

"It was clear."

"They used my name."

"More or less."

"Don't take me home," I said.

"Where do you want me to take you?"

"Take me to the Grill."

She turned so abruptly that the tires squealed, drove to South U. and slammed the brakes on in front of the Grill.

"You going to be okay?" she asked.

"I want to see if my parents know."

"What if they do?"

"I'll kill myself."

"Don't be crazy. We'll work this out. You'll be fine. This kind of shit happens all the time. We have to get in touch with Kyle." I punched his number into my phone, got his voice mail. This time I asked his mailbox please to call me.

Then Sarah said, "What a complete asshole."

"I'm not sure," I said. It was as if my brain couldn't send a realistic message to my mouth fast enough. "I think he has another side." I heard how pathetic this sounded, but hoped, unbearably, that he'd be able, in some way, to explain.

"A side other than the one that made a video of you? And apparently invited Alan and Chris over to get in on the action?"

"That's not how it was. I mean, it was my idea to—I mean, I called you and Molly, or Ginger, but—" I couldn't remember if that was right. Had I called anyone? I remembered he had said I should call my friends. Had I? Why hadn't I?

"He's had a very hard life," I said, hating myself as the words escaped.

"*Kyle Malanack* has had a very hard life?" Goth Sarah said, incredulous.

"His sister died."

"His sister died? What are you talking about? His sister died? And this is the first anyone's ever heard of it? And what does that have to do with taping you having sex?"

"Maybe he just needs to preserve, I mean, to keep track of—we don't even know yet if he did anything, right? I mean, maybe it wasn't—" I stopped myself. Overwhelmed, I opened the car door, climbed out into the street, and walked toward Judy's Grill with Meghan. I didn't wave to Sarah. The bells on the door rang as we came in and my mom, behind the counter, looked up. She was surprised to see me.

"Hi, girls!" she called, genuinely happy. "You hungry?"

So she didn't know.

"No," I said, "I just stopped by to say hi before we get ready for tonight."

"Meghan, you hungry, honey? Do you want a burger?"

"I'd love one, thank you."

"You have butterflies, sweetie?" my mom asked. "Chad called to say he's bringing Alice."

"Great," I said. I went to the office computer, straight to Google, and typed in my name. Meghan stayed out front with my mom, either protecting me or waiting for her burger. Nothing came up except the usual hits, the pathetic writing awards, the Lilah Terrace Fellowship to Darcy, the happy-dwarf article from when I was a kid. I went to YouTube, typed in "dwarf sex tape," but YouTube doesn't allow that sort of shit. I wondered if it was online, how people were finding it. I went back out to the counter, dejectedly. Meghan was eating fries. She looked at me, raised her eyebrows like, "Did you find anything?" I shook my head.

"I made you a BLT," my mom said.

"I said I wasn't hungry."

"I know," she said, "but you should eat some-thing before the show."

I didn't say anything.

"I'll put it in the fridge. If you change your mind." She walked back out.

Meghan said, "What did you find?"

"Nothing."

"Good. So it's not online, at least."

"Well, not yet."

Sarah came back an hour later, with her wet hair in a ponytail and a gym bag over her shoulder. Molly was in the front seat, waiting. When I had told them Meghan was coming, they had been like, "That'll be fun—why don't we all get dressed together at your place before the play?"

But now it was somber, awkward in the car. Meghan and I climbed up into the backseat, and nobody really said much past "Hi," before Molly was like, "Are you okay?" I said, "I'm fine."

"Do you want to talk about it?" Molly asked, and I thought how she sounded like a shrink on TV.

"Not really," I said. "Can you put some music on?"

I saw her and Sarah make eye contact in the front seat, before Molly turned the radio on, loud. I wondered what their narrative about me was—that I was a horrible friend, certainly, but past that? I tried to turn my mind off. I can't remember what was playing; I was just grateful for the noise. When we got to my house,

Meghan hung out on my bed looking at photo albums and talking to Molly while I showered. Molly was half putting her stage makeup on. To my great surprise, I heard her ask Meghan, "What's it like being a little person there?"

"Same as anywhere, I guess," Meghan said. "I mean, people in Berkeley are nice and crunchy, so mostly they either don't care or pretend not to care."

Then Sarah turned on the hair dryer, and I couldn't hear anything else. Sometimes Molly's straightforwardness put me off. Why was it so easy for her to be so friendly and such a goody-goody, always asking and telling everything that was on her mind, without ever apologizing? Of course, as soon as I had this thought, I recognized that the problem was mine. Then I kept thinking, if only I hadn't fucked Kyle and maybe his two idiot friends and there weren't a video of me circulating, then this would be fun, being here on the opening night of my first play at Darcy with Goth Sarah and Perfect Molly and Comfort Food Meghan, curling our hair and gossiping. I began to feel grateful that I hadn't seen the tape yet. I guess I knew it was my last chance ever to have a normal life, even for a few hours. I could pretend I hadn't seen it, because it wouldn't be pretending. I could pretend, in front of my family, for at least tonight, that nothing was happening. If I was going to go through with *Runaways*, then maybe I didn't want to have watched it beforehand, even if everyone else had.

I called my mom, said we were going early, that Sarah and Molly were taking Meghan and me. She was thrilled, of course. Sarah drove extra slow and stopped at every yellow light on Washtenaw. Maybe she felt vulnerable, like now that this terrible thing had happened to me, everything bad could happen to all of us and we weren't immune even from car accidents. It was also a wet, cold February night, so maybe she was just worried that the car would hydroplane or something. Molly kept changing the radio station, and I fought a totally unfair urge to scream at her to leave it alone.

School was a circus. As soon as we pulled into the D'Arts student lot, and I had opened the door and jumped out of the passenger seat, I saw Kyle. I could taste my heart in my mouth. I considered running up to him and demanding an explanation. But he was standing with two grown-ups who, at least from the back, looked like parents. His dad was wearing a dark pink jacket with gray flecks in it, black suit pants, and shoes so gleaming and black they looked like giant, live beetles. His mom was in beige wool Banana Republic–type slacks, brown pointy boots, and a long cream coat. They were both very preppy from behind. Sarah and Meghan dragged me into the school, but I could barely rip my eyes away from the sight of Kyle and his mom and dad. A white, scalding panic came over me.

Inside the school there were more parents in the halls, and kids everywhere. We went backstage, where everyone was bustling crazily, painting makeup on, giggling, getting into costume in front of each other, warming up. I saw Kyle, without his parents now, but he was looking down, texting as he walked. This time I went straight up to him, and said, "We have to talk," and he barely looked at me, just kept his eyes on the phone.

He said, softly, "Yeah, I know" but then we both saw Ms. Vanderly and Ms. Minogue come in, so Kyle said, "How about after the show?" I wished he had said my name, that he had said, "Yeah, I know, Judy," or "How about after the show, Judy?" but he didn't. Maybe because still knowing or saying my name would have made him accountable. Or maybe he just didn't think of it.

Ms. Vanderly made us stand in a circle and then she was like, "Ginger Mews has flu, and sadly won't be able to be here tonight, so her understudy, Molly, will play the role of Izzy. I know this is a surprise and a challenging adjustment for opening night, but I have absolute confidence in Molly and know that you all will work as an ensemble to support her and make sure the performance is top-notch. And I have a get-well card here for Ginger, who will no doubt be very disappointed to miss tonight; we'll pass it around the dressing room so everyone can sign it."

I felt a surge of relief that Ginger was just sick and it had nothing to do with me. And that Molly would get a real part. In spite of my having been annoyed at Molly earlier, I hoped Ginger wouldn't get well too fast, because we only had six performances, and I wanted Molly to get to do at least three of them. It was only fair. Of course I never considered the possibility that I'd miss the rest of them too, and that my understudy, a mousy girl named Sonya, whose regular job it was to be chorus member seven, would play Hubbel.

After the buzz died down following Ms. Vanderly's announcement, we did our voice exercises and Kyle moved far away from me, maybe so he wouldn't have to hold my hand, and I thought I was going to cry. Everyone was watching us and it was totally obvious that this was about to be the worst story ever to hit the school.

Then, as I walked out of the backstage area right before my entrance, I heard him say my name. He was like "Judy," and I took a sharp breath in and whipped around to see him standing behind me.

"I just wanted—"

"Take your places!" Ms. Vanderly yelled. She was right in front of me, and she turned around and saw me, facing the wrong way, waiting for Kyle to speak.

"Judy, dear," Ms. Vanderly said, and put her hand on my shoulder to lead me into the wings. I was first out on stage, as usual. But I kept my face turned toward Kyle, and he said, "Judy, I didn't—"

Ms. Vanderly was pushing me gently. "Didn't what?" I asked. "Didn't what?" But Kyle had turned so he could cross backstage and get ready for his entrance from the left. I rotated "didn't" around in my mind. Didn't what? Do it? Mean it? Make a tape? Was he apologizing? And if so, for what? My fear crystallized into something solid.

The show was a surreal nightmare. I was a robot, didn't care, didn't get my sign language right, think, stay in character, hear my own voice singing, or feel my body moving. I didn't consider Ms. Doman, Norman Crump, Ms. Vanderly, Mr. Luther, or my family, even afterward, when everyone was congratulating everyone else. If anyone noticed how unprofessional and bad I'd been, they didn't say so. Which made me think for a moment that maybe I had never been good at anything and every compliment I'd ever gotten was a patronizing lie. But I had so much agony on other fronts that I tried not to follow the path of that thought too. I'd save the am-I-not-even-a-good-actress-or-singer torture for after I had figured out what the Kyle disaster was and what it meant.

My mom had brought me a bouquet, which I carried around for two minutes before feeling so numb and humiliated that I asked Chad's girlfriend, Alice, to hold it. She looked sporty and pretty in a light brown ponytail, wearing a Michigan sweatshirt and skinny jeans. When I handed her the flowers, she was nice about my making her do me a favor, said, "No problem, I totally understand," meaning my not wanting to carry them, but I thought about how little she could possibly understand about that night. How it was lasting forever. How I was desperate to hear the end of Kyle's sentence, to find a copy of the video or, better yet, hear him say there was no video, that it didn't exist, had all been a joke. But I couldn't find Kyle anywhere, so I turned my desperation toward leaving. All I wanted was to get out of the school and never come back. I practically dragged my confused family out the door, with Meghan's help.

Of course, leaving offered me no relief. I went home, hurt my parents' feelings by showing no interest in the usual debriefing about who had been especially great in the show. I didn't want to go to the Grill for ice cream. Meghan and I went straight to my room and stared at each other, each thinking there was nothing we could do and how were we going to make it through the night. Then Meghan, who I think felt terrible that there was nothing she could say to make this better, went to take a shower. As soon as she was in the bathroom, I thought of one thing I wanted to do. It was almost midnight, but I called Ms. Doman at home.

To my horror, Norman Orb Crump picked up.

"Who may I say is calling?" he asked.

"Um, Judy," I said. "I'm her student. I'm sorry it's so—" I kept thinking, Orb. Orb. Orb. Like some weird drumbeat in my mind. I kept holding the phone with my left hand and put my right hand up to my head to stop the noise.

"Okay, Judy. Let me locate her. Hang on."

I thought, *locate?* Then there was a pause and Ms. Doman's warm, deep voice. "Hi, Judy! You were wonderful tonight. I didn't have a chance to tell you afterward how fabulous—"

"I'm sorry it's so late," I said.

"Are you okay?" she asked suddenly, and her voice had gone from zero to sixty, like she was instantly super, super worried.

"I'm not sure," I said. "I have kind of a problem I was hoping I might be able to talk to you about. Could we meet tomorrow?"

"Of course—do you want to come to my room first thing in the morning?"

"Um, I'm not feeling well, so I don't think I'll be at school. Could we maybe do it in the afternoon?"

"Absolutely. Tell me how I can help."

"Can you meet me somewhere other than school, please?"

"Judy, is this an emergency? Do you need help right now?"

"No, no," I said, "after school tomorrow is fine."

"Where are you now?"

"I'm at home."

"Oh, okay. Good. Why don't you come over to my house at two thirty. I'm done early on Tuesdays. I live on Ferdon, near Burns Park— 136 Ferdon—do you need directions?"

I felt the black cloud shift a bit, so it wasn't directly over my head anymore.

"I can look it up. Thank you so much, Ms. Doman." I said. "I'll see you at two thirty."

It was only after I hung up that I wondered whether Norman Crump would be home when I went over. I hoped not.

Meghan came out of the bathroom wrapped in a towel.

"Who was that?" She sounded hopeful, like maybe it had been Kyle and he had made this all okay.

"My AP English teacher."

"Seriously?"

"Yeah. I really like her. And if everyone's about to find out anyway, I think I want to talk to her first."

"Are you going to go to school tomorrow?"

"Hell no. But I have to pretend to my parents I am."

"What do you want to do now?"

"I don't know," I said. "Watch TV?"

We stayed up all night, until Meghan betrayed me by falling asleep at four, still sitting up. I watched the sun come up out my window. At six, I woke her.

"Hey," she said, looking around. Then she took me in for real, and I saw her remember that my life was ruined, in one of those icy surges that gets you right when you're warm and vulnerable, in between asleep and awake. They keep happening to me every single morning of my life now. I sometimes wonder, from my dirty perch in the Motel Manor, whether they'll ever stop happening.

"Did you stay up all night?" Meghan asked me as soon as she was lucid.

I nodded.

"Poor baby. Do you want me to get up and shower and dress first?"

"No, 's okay," I said. "I'll go first and you can sleep a few minutes more."

She rolled back over and burrowed under the covers while I showered and dressed. When I

331

was ready to go downstairs, I shook Meghan's shoulder and she woke up and got into the shower.

I had breakfast with my mom and Sam, who were talking about the play, and how vast my range is. "I mean, a deaf black guy!" Sam kept saying, until I had a rare moment of real annoyance at him.

"Enough!" I said, and he was crushed.

My mom looked me over, surprised and irritated. "He was giving you a compliment, Judy," she said. " 'Thank you' will suffice."

"Fine," I sulked, "thank you."

He pushed his chair back and went to get his backpack. I told my mom that Meghan and I were going to ride bikes to school, so she kissed my forehead and took Sam to school and herself to the Grill. The house felt empty and cold after they left, and I added snapping at Sam to the list of things I was feeling bad about. I rinsed my cereal bowl as Meghan came down the stairs.

"Everyone gone already?"

I nodded.

We rode our bikes to Gallup Park, over the train tracks, over the little wooden bridge, and then around the park until we came to the little island in the middle of the Huron River. We tucked our bikes behind a bush and sat on the riverbank. I wanted to hold that moment, stay there forever, hidden with Meghan, my new bike and my old bike she had ridden waiting to take us if we ever wanted to leave. We sat like that until we were too cold to sit outside anymore, even though it was a warmish day for February. Then we huddled in the concession stand, eating popcorn and cookies and drinking Swiss Miss hot chocolate, the powdery, chalky kind you mix with water. I watched the hard marshmallows bob at the surface of the foam cup, little bits of chemical foam forming a film around them. I took a sip.

"Let's go back out," I said to Meghan, and she nodded. We walked back to the island, our hands wrapped around the cocoa cups.

"Do you think it's because you're little?" she asked. And I felt a surge of tremendous gratitude for her, since this was a question only she could ask me with real empathy and impunity.

"I don't know," I said honestly. "I don't know what it is, yet. But I think Kyle—I mean, I thought Kyle, I think Kyle liked me just because."

"I'm sure he does," she said. "And even if it's part of why he likes you, then that's the same as liking you for who you are, right?"

I shrugged. "I guess so."

We'd had this conversation before, when some older guy had asked Meghan on a date and we'd decided it was way too gross, and then when that guy Joel kissed me at the LPA conference, and when Meghan went to homecoming her sophomore year with an average-size freshman guy and they made out at the end of the night even though they'd been "just friends" when they decided to go. We had never come to any conclusions, and I doubted we would now, either. I mean, was it worse for someone to like you because you were different or in spite of your being different? And if the person actually, genuinely liked you, then what difference did it really make? We came in and out of quiet for several pointless go-arounds on this topic, without any information about what had happened with Kyle and without making any progress. Then it was time to bike to Ms. Doman's house, and I realized on the way that Meghan had brought up our ancient chat not only because it was more or less relevant than usual, but also just to distract me. I threw her a smile over my shoulder, noticed she was struggling on her bike. The truth is, the ride to Ms. Doman's was really far, but I must have been like, bionic with shock or something, because I barely felt the miles go by. Meghan was gasping for breath by the time we got there, and she's in good shape. Neither of us runs, really, it's bad for the knees and hips and joints, but we both swim and Meghan plays field hockey in California.

When we pulled into the driveway, Ms. Doman

was standing at the window, and I knew she already knew. Everyone at school knew, and she had found out. She came out on her porch to greet us, wearing jeans and a dark pink sweater and a long necklace of light pink and silver beads, all different shapes. Her hair was pulled off her neck in a messy ponytail; she looked stunning. But her eyes turned down when she saw me, as if she was sad, not to see me, but about something related to me. It was my first taste of knowing I had disappointed her.

"Come in, Judy. I'm so glad you called me, so glad you and your friend stopped by." We followed her into a bright yellow kitchen, with multicolored rugs on the tile floor and a white fan suspended from the ceiling. I could see the living room to the right of us, a comfortable room with a giant maroon couch and bookshelves against every wall. There were lamps on either side of the couch and two reading chairs and no TV that I could see. I wondered if she and Norman Crump sat on the couch together at night, reading by lamplight. If they did, that was nice. There were lots of pillows on the couch and a homemade-looking pink striped afghan thrown over the top of it.

I felt miniature suddenly, walking into her cheerful, cozy kitchen, as if I might be mistaken for a speck of dust on the floor and vacuumed up. Maybe she sensed this, because she pulled a couple of chairs out from behind a little round wooden table next to a door, and gestured for me and Meghan to sit on them. I sat down, looked out the door at a deck lined with potted trees. I rested my elbows on the flowered placemat in front of me, while Meghan looked around awkwardly and Ms. Doman put a red tea kettle on the stove. She brought a plate of chocolate chip cookies over to the table and set it in front of us while we all waited for the kettle to whistle. No one spoke. I was wondering whether this was okay or incredibly awkward, when the water boiled and screamed.

Ms. Doman turned a knob on the stove, and I unwillingly put a bite of chocolate chip cookie in my mouth. My throat felt so tight I couldn't imagine being able to swallow anything ever again. Ms. Doman was standing in front of me and Meghan, holding a giant box of tea bags, all lined up neatly inside.

"What kind of tea do you like?" she asked. Meghan pulled a dark purple bag of berry zinger from the box and I took peppermint. Ms. Doman had cinnamon. We were quiet while she put the bags in blue mugs, and then poured boiling water from the kettle. She set that on the table when she was done, on a penguin-shaped trivet. Then she had nothing left with which to busy herself, so she sat on a chair opposite mine and next to Meghan's, and handed me the honey bear as if it were the conch in *Lord of the Flies*, as if to say, "Speak."

"So, um, I hope you don't mind us coming by," I said.

"Of course not."

"I, um, I wanted to talk to you because—"

Here she decided to help me. "Because of what's happening at school."

"Right," I said. I felt relieved that she had finished the sentence for me, as if now I would have to say nothing else and she would tell me what the hell was happening at school and what to do about it.

She sighed. "Tell me what happened, Judy, so I can help."

I took a deep breath. "I think I did something stupid," I said. "I mean, something I wouldn't normally have done, except I was. Well, I had a few drinks with a friend, and I—well, I—"

"With Kyle Malanack, right?" she asked. She took a sip of her tea, and I thought, someday this will all be over. We'll be drinking and eating and we'll have recovered from this. I'll be okay. But as soon as she put her teacup down, my life zoomed back into focus and I lost the feeling that I'd ever get over this.

"With Kyle, right. He and I were kind of, you know—" I cleared my throat. Why had I decided to tell Ms. Doman? "We were seeing each other," I said. "And, um, I went to his house, and you know how he likes to make movies?"

"Yes," she said.

"Well, I think we were kind of, you know, fooling around or whatever, and his camera was on, and, I don't know. I think his friends came over and maybe we were all kind of drunk and now—"

"Judy," she said. "Nothing that happened, whatever it was, was your fault. You do understand that, don't you?"

I shrugged.

"Whatever happened at Kyle's house—if you did not explicitly say to Kyle, 'This is okay with me'—wasn't okay. And it wasn't your fault. Whether you drank or not, it wasn't your fault. If you did not give Kyle your absolute, conscious, and unequivocal consent to do whatever it was that you did, or to be taped doing whatever it was you were taped doing, then he and his friends are responsible for what happened. And I mean legally responsible." She paused for a moment before adding, "Judy, because some of the adults at school have already heard rumors about this, I think we need to tell your parents as soon as possible."

My mind was flooded with thoughts, none of them pleasant. I had a vivid memory of Kyle asking, at least several times, if I was okay. He was always asking whether I was okay. And I was always saying yes. I wished that we had not gone to Ms. Doman's house. It *was* my fault, and her thing about consent reminded me of it. I mean, I wasn't a victim, anyway, and I don't mean that in the stupid, TV-movie way. I didn't think I had been like, asking for it or whatever. But I also knew I'd said yes. Okay, so not to the video, maybe, but to Kyle and probably Alan and Chris, too. I hadn't invited Sarah or Ginger, because I wanted all of Kyle's attention, and now it was mine. I had wanted everyone, Chris and Alan included, to think I was cool and sexy. Didn't that desire make me complicit? And who even cared? Whether it was my fault or not, how was I supposed to get out of it now? Who did she mean, the adults at school? Had she already known? Worse, had she seen the video before I even had? I swallowed.

"Have you seen it?" I asked, my eyes lowered. I could see streaks of original tree in her wooden table. I thought about how the rings around a tree trunk tell you how old the tree is. I wondered what woodcutter had chopped the tree down to make this table, wished I were a tree, thousands of years old, that my whole small and stupid life-time were one ring, a blink, over, meaningless. Or that I were a woodcutter. I wished I were anyone but myself. The smell of tea began to make me sick.

"No," Ms. Doman said, looking at me. "I have not watched it." She meant to tell me that she had been given the opportunity to watch it. Otherwise she would have used the word *seen,* instead of *watched.*

I nodded. "Was there a copy at school?"

She looked at me, as if trying to figure out what I meant by this.

"Have *you* seen it, Judy?"

"Not yet," I said.

"I will not watch it, Judy, and I think most of the other adults who find out about this—will also make that choice." She did not need to say "including your parents," because we all knew what she meant. She thought for a moment before adding, "Maybe you should make that choice too."

"I think I have to see it," I said.

She nodded sadly. "I can understand that. Would you like me to tell your parents for you?" she asked. "Because they're going to find out, and I'd like it to come from you or me, rather than Mr. Grames." The principal. Had he heard? How? Who would have told him? Worse, had he seen the video? I wondered for the millionth time how bad it was, what exactly they had taped me doing. The possibilities, though blurry, seemed endless. I thought for a minute I might fall off the stool, I felt so dizzy. I couldn't speak.

"This is going to be okay," Ms. Doman said, and I didn't believe her, but was glad she'd said it nonetheless. "How about this?" she continued.

"How about I call your parents and just warn them that something is happening, and then you can tell them whatever level of detail you're comfortable with. Would that be okay? Would that help?"

Meghan was nodding before I could start. I nodded too, feeling horror and relief in equal measures. If Ms. Doman called my parents, they would know it was serious. They would also know that grown-ups at school still loved and forgave me, and maybe she would tell them the same thing she was telling me, that it was going to be okay. I began to climb down from my stool.

As if she had heard me thinking, Ms. Doman said, "This will be okay, Judy," again. "I promise. No matter how bad you feel right now, or how embarrassed, this will pass. You have a huge, brilliant life ahead of you—full of love and meaningful experiences—and this will not ruin it."

I did not find this comforting, although it didn't make me love her any less. *Embarrassed* seemed like such a flimsy, insufficient word. Embarrassed! I mean, destroyed, maybe. Honestly, her words seemed to me to be making the whole thing both too small and too big at the same time. For example, they made me think that she was worried I might kill myself, and that if she was worried about such a thing, it probably meant that suicide was worth considering.

She stood up from her chair and walked over to mine, bent down, and hugged me, sitting there, for what felt like a long time. Then she hugged Meghan, too. We both stood up, and Ms. Doman walked us to the door, waved from the porch as we backed our bikes away from her house and out onto Ferdon. I could see that her eyes were glittering, and I hoped she would hold in whatever crying was coming until we were out of sight. She did not. She was still waving as we rode down the street, but the tears had started pouring down her cheeks and I could see them as I pedaled away. I moved my legs faster and faster. The whole ride home, my mind raced. Trees went by on either side of me, cars, houses, windows. I thought how there were whole universes in each house, entire families with complicated lives and relationships and problems. Millions of people not me. This made me feel slightly better.

But as soon as we pulled onto Londonderry, we saw both my parents' cars in the driveway and my stomach dropped through the sidewalk and landed somewhere near the core of the earth. They shouldn't have been home for another hour at least. Meghan and I parked our bikes and climbed slowly off and I punched in the passcode to the garage. The door rumbled open and Meghan and I wheeled the bikes in. Everything felt like slow motion.

"Here we go," I said to Meghan.

"You'll be fine," she said. "It's much better they know. I think they might have to get you a lawyer or something. You need them to help."

My mom opened the door between the kitchen and the garage. Her face was drawn and white, bruised-looking.

"Where have you been?" she asked. "We were frantic."

"We were at the park," I said.

"Why didn't you tell me you weren't going to school? Mrs. O'Henry called this morning to ask why you were absent—your father and I have been driving around since eleven, Judy! Where were you?!"

"I'm sorry, Mom, I didn't realize—I—" Had they told her anything? Or just that I was missing school? Unsure of my footing, I decided to be angry.

"It's not like I'm the first person in the world to skip class once in my junior year, you know," I said. Then my dad appeared behind her in the door.

"Hi, honey. We need to talk," my dad said, and I knew it was worse than the skipping school thing, that Ms. Doman had just called and that this, my mistake, was going to be the worst thing that had ever happened to them. My dad's eyes were red around the edges; he had been crying. It is impossible to overstate my horror at this realization.

"We're not angry that you missed school," my mom said. "We just need to know if you're okay. Have a seat." My dad tried to look brave, and I have to hand it to him, he wasn't crying now, and he never once cried in front of me. It's not his fault that he couldn't hide from me the fact that he'd been crying before he saw me. He looked like he had pink eyeliner on. I kept thinking—both Ms. Doman and my father had cried over this. How was I ever going to recover, even from that small side effect?

I sat at the table. Meghan was like, "Excuse me," and then walked out of the kitchen, super quietly. I watched her go, thinking she looked smaller than usual and feeling terrible for involving her in this whole mess, and also bad for myself that she was leaving the next day and that then my despair would be complete. I closed my eyes, opened them again, realized this was real, that it was actually happening.

My mom said, "Judy, honey, do you want to tell us what happened?

"Didn't Ms. Doman just call? What did she say?" I had a shattering feeling in my heart. This is what they mean by heartbreak, I thought.

"She said you're in some trouble at school," my dad said.

"Yeah. I guess that's true."

"What happened, honey?"

"He made a video."

My mother closed her eyes, composed herself.

"Kyle, you mean?"

"Kyle."

"A video of the two of you."

"Did Ms. Doman not tell you anything?"

"She said she thought you would want to tell us the details of what happened."

"Right."

"Why did he make a video?" my dad asked, surprising me.

"We'll have to ask him."

My mom clarified. "You didn't know he was making it," she said.

"No. I didn't know."

"Is it a sexual video?"

"I think so. I haven't seen it."

"Were you, um, were you?"

"What, having sex with him?"

Meghan had reappeared at the mouth to the kitchen; maybe she had rethought it, decided I might want her there. Or maybe it was unbearable waiting in the other room for it to be over. I gestured to her to come in.

"I don't know, Judy. I don't know what I meant to ask."

Tears had started a string of water down my mom's cheeks. She made no move to wipe them, as if by ignoring them she could deny that she was crying. My mom hardly ever cries. I couldn't remember the last time I'd seen her cry, in fact.

I felt myself float up above the room, watched the conversation with a detached feeling. Her face contorted into a kind of personal battle; the top half crying and the bottom not admitting it, not letting it. She said hello to Meghan as if nothing was happening.

"Can I get you some hot chocolate, Meghan?"

"No, no, please—don't go to any trouble, I—"

"Isn't it pretty obvious that I was having sex with him if he made a sex tape?" I asked.

My dad scooched his chair back and stood up, went to the stove to watch the pot of boiling water.

"Is that what the video is?" my mom asked. Her eyes were pinned to me. I thought of how much she worried, how she talked to my dad late at night about how I was going to get hurt. How now she had been right.

"You haven't seen it?" I asked.

"Of course not," she said.

"Have you had a chance to see it and you just decided not to?"

"No," she said. "No one told us there was a video until now."

"But given the chance, you won't watch it."

"No," she said, without even pausing. "Your father and I won't watch it."

My dad cleared his throat and I thought maybe he was going to weigh in about whether to watch the video. But he asked, "Did you love this boy, Judy?"

I was surprised that my dad would have been able to find his way so quickly to the question at the center of things. But I didn't want to tell him that I loved Kyle, even though I thought it would make him feel better.

"Are you worried about my virginity?"

"No. Did you love him?" His voice was so sad that I gave in.

"Yes," I said.

My father nodded. "I'm glad," he said, and even in the first, grief-drenched moments of this whole thing, I appreciated him. For wanting to know most of all whether I'd been true to myself. And caring that I had. Caring more about that, in fact, than he ever cared through the entire ordeal about what anyone else said or thought.

And for not pointing out that I had been stupid to love Kyle in the first place. Or that my mom had been right that I was a basket case, unable to protect myself from the evil world. To my dad, it was better to know I wasn't a self-destructive slut. I hadn't done it because I knew he'd tape me, or because of peer pressure, or because I hated myself and wanted to lose my virginity to a sadist. I'd just been wrong, thought Kyle was lovable.

"Did you know, honey?" my mom asked. "Did you two decide together to make the video?"

I was grossed out by this question, since it suggested to me that there was a place in my mom's imagination for the possibility that people could "decide together" to make a sex tape. And I was furious again at having to repeat what I'd already told her.

"Of course not! I already said I didn't know. You already asked me that. Do you think I'd agree to making a video of myself having sex? Are you insane?"

"Of course I didn't think—I just hoped—" My mom cut herself off.

"Hoped what? That I was a porn star rather than a wretched victim?"

At this, Meghan flinched. I was too much, even for the people who loved me most.

My dad rejoined us at the table. I saw him inhale, preparing himself for whatever they were about to say.

"Honey, we're just trying to protect you," my mom said. "We're going to have to get rid of the video, and get a lawyer. We'll figure it out." She looked over at my dad, desperately.

"Figure what out?" I asked.

"How best to defend you from whatever's coming," my dad said.

"Whatever's coming? Isn't the horror show already here? I mean, I don't give a shit what happens from here on out—everyone on the planet has already seen that video—except me! It's probably already on MidgetHos.com! My life is completely ruined!"

This made my mom stand up and come over to my chair. She put her arm around me and moved the chair out from the table. "Let's go upstairs," she said.

I climbed down and let her lead me to my bedroom. Meghan followed us. My mom sat on the bed with me and rubbed my back for a few minutes, silently. She didn't ask me anything else, and eventually she leaned down, kissed me, and stood to leave.

"Honey, we'll help you fix this. This isn't unfixable. Your dad and I will call a lawyer, get rid of the video, and deal with whatever the potential criminal aspects might be. We'll—"

She was off and running, list-making, organizing us out of whatever had happened. But I was thinking, potential criminal aspects? I didn't say anything, couldn't tell her that it wasn't only Kyle, that there might be others, too. It was too sickening, too sordid, too much. I just nodded, thinking I would listen to my parents later, hear whatever they actually thought. Maybe I would have to decide whether to press charges against Kyle and Chris and Alan, like in the movies. I had an image of myself in court, naked, everyone talking about whether what happened was my fault. The doorbell rang, and my mother went to answer it. A moment later, Sarah appeared in the doorway. She looked like someone she loved had died.

"Holy shit, Sarah," I said. "What the—"

She came into the room and closed the door.

"I have a copy, Judy," she said. She took a DVD out of her purse and handed it to me. I looked at it. It was unmarked, which surprised me, although I don't know what I was expecting, Kyle's handwriting? "Me and Judy Fucking"? "The End of Judy's Life"?

"How did you get this?" I asked Sarah.

"From Alan."

"You called Alan?"

"I went to his house."

"You went to Alan's house?"

"Right."

"And how'd you get him to give it to you?"

"I threatened to tell his mother or call the cops."

I closed my eyes. "Have you watched it?"

"Part of it."

"Because it's too terrible to watch the whole thing?"

"I didn't think it was my business," she said. "Um, Judy?" she started.

I was holding the DVD, frozen, unable to put it into my computer.

"Yeah?"

"I'm not sure you should watch it, actually."

"I know," I said. "I appreciate all your help. But I have to. I can't be the only one who doesn't know what it is. I mean, I can't live with that, either." I leaned down, started to put the disc in, and then turned back up to the two of them, standing behind me, looking terrible.

"Do you guys mind if I watch alone?" I asked. "I mean, I'll—"

"Of course not. Tell me what we can do to help. Anything," Meghan said.

She reached up and took Sarah's arm and led her into my little bathroom. I could hear the water running.

As soon as they were gone, I had the distinct sense of standing on the edge of something, the knowledge before I even put the DVD into my computer that it was about to change my life forever, that even watching it would be an utterly disastrous event. There are certain things we're never meant to see, and this was one of them.

I put it in the drive, and my computer whirled and then the screen turned blue, offered me some choices, start movie, resume movie, exit. I thought how I'd like to exit, pushed START MOVIE, let the tiny forward arrow pulse with my choice to watch, and then came the bed, the room, the walls, the people. For a minute, I had a surge of hope, because our faces weren't clear, that we weren't recognizable. Maybe no one would know it was me. But then I realized that I was three feet nine, standing next to that foldout bed in the basement, the one I'd woken up on. I was wearing a T-shirt I didn't recognize, very long on me. I couldn't tell whether I still had my corduroy skirt on underneath. I was standing there, kind of swaying, laughing. Kyle was already on the bed, under a sheet, and I climbed up next to him and pulled the long T-shirt over my head, like a stripper. I did have the skirt on. Kyle was watching me, peeling the sheets back, and I lay down next to him on my side, and then, to my surprise, turned onto my back as if we had agreed on what was going to happen next. It was all strangely choreographed, looked like it had happened the way it happened because there was no other way it could have gone. Kyle climbed on top of me and pushed the skirt up and started moving his body up and down like an enormous puppet. Then another figure was standing next to the bed. Alan. I heard myself breathe in, but couldn't tell if it was the me watching or the me in the video. I squinted my eyes as if I might be able to block out what was about to happen, what had already happened, by not watching it. But I couldn't. So I saw Alan stand at the side of the bed and unzip his jeans. I saw him pull them down and his underpants off. He was naked, and I remembered it again—his legs, his body, familiar and yet utterly strange. Kyle climbed off the weird miniature woman in the video, and she turned over toward Alan, moved her mouth close to where he stood at the edge of the bed. Then the video cut, and I was there, close up, clear, smiling, saying, "Lohden. My name is Judy Lohden." I looked really pretty in that shot.

They had edited it. They had cut in the footage of me meeting Kyle at Chessie Andrewjeski's party. In the bathroom. The chair I was on and the floor dropped out from underneath me, the walls began to melt. Everything felt like slush. Midwestern-highway-style, polluted, melting, poisonous slush. They had edited the video so I would name myself, grin like an idiot at the end. They had, he had—taken the time to make sure everyone would know it was me. Why?

It cut back to the dark room, the bed. After Alan, Chris Arpent came into the frame, his muscles so big they were discernible even in the blurry, badly lit video. He was wearing nothing but boxers. He walked over to the bed, and—the bathroom door opened and I frantically shut down my computer, turned to see Meghan standing there with Sarah behind her, still in the doorway to the bathroom. I got off the chair, but as soon as I was standing, I felt boneless, flesh all the way through, Silly Putty, Gumby. I sat down on the floor. Meghan came toward me. I had no idea how much time had passed since I'd begun watching the video, since they had gone into the bathroom, since—maybe it had been five minutes, maybe five hours. The world started spinning faster and I thought I might faint.

Meghan said, "I'm so sorry, Judy. I just, you

know, heard you crying, so I wanted to ask if I could help, if I—"

I reached up and touched my face, hadn't realized it was wet.

"Is it horrible?" Meghan asked. She crouched down so we were both on the floor.

"It's unbelievable," I said. "They—someone edited it." Sarah had emerged into the room and now she sat on the floor too.

"Did you see that part, Sar? Did you see where I say I'm—"

She shook her head no, but I didn't know whether to believe her.

Meghan wrapped her arms around me and then Sarah moved in closer, and the three of us just sat there on the floor, not saying anything else.

But after several minutes—or again, maybe hours—like that, I stood up. "I have to watch the rest," I said.

"Do you want us to—?" Sarah gestured back at the bathroom.

"No," I said, "stay."

So we all stood in front of my desk. I didn't sit at the chair again, just leaned forward and clicked the PLAY button, and watched the remaining minute, during which Chris came into the shot and climbed onto the bed, me, moved like a monster. I turned the sound up—not loud enough to bring my parents knocking on my door, I hoped, but loud enough that I could hear laughing.

After six seconds of it, Meghan covered her face with her small, tan hands and cried.

# 13

If the media's love of me is any indication, maybe I was in fact meant to be a movie star. I am the tragic heroine of their stories, the victim. No one is spinning this with any kind of she-was-asking-for-it angle, because apparently I'm so deformed and undesirable I couldn't have asked even for abject humiliation. Everyone has run with it like I'd been lobotomized, unable to make a decision for myself.

When the news first broke, you could tell it was a hit reality-TV show in the making: "Authorities at Darcy Arts Academy in Ann Arbor, Michigan, say they are investigating charges that a sexually explicit videotape circulating among students shows three male students engaged in sexual relations with a sixteen-year-old disabled girl from the school. It is unclear whether the act was consensual or whether the boys will face prosecution."

Some of the stories are more salacious than others, but the reporters all pat themselves on the back for not naming Kyle, Alan, Chris, or me "because of our status as minors," and mine as a potential rape victim. The whole not-showing-the-face thing. None of the TV news can do anything, because they can't show any of us. They must be grinding their teeth, covering the coverage instead of the actual sex story they'd love to show. They've all clearly seen the video. The first time I saw a TV reporter mention it, I was sitting on the bed, and by the time I realized I had heard the words *video we received of a disabled girl from a local private performing arts school* I was already under the covers, shaking. I couldn't even come out to find the remote, so I couldn't turn it off and had to listen to them rhapsodize about their decision to show no footage and name no names.

Everyone uses words like *disabled,* whatever that word even means, and half say I'm a dwarf, because that's what makes the story so brilliant. I mean, everyone loves a teenage sex scandal— all that smooth skin and innocent crime—but what could be better than one that's also a circus freak show? Even I can see the appeal.

My fourth day here, I read a letter in the *Detroit Free Press* from Norman Crump, Ms. Doman's husband, asking why they were covering the story at all, and proposing that any coverage is invasive, unethical rubbernecking. I could tell from the writing that he considered it a heroic move to put his name on a letter like that, and I bet my parents were happy. Maybe they even celebrated the letter, read it out loud, felt grateful. But to me, he was just getting in on the action.

And why are all the reporters making me out to be such a victim? I mean, no one has given me any credit for being sane or independent enough to run away. I feel like they should write that I'm brave. Because less than twelve hours after I watched the video and Meghan and I listened to my mom sobbing like she was going to die and telling my father she wanted to leave the state forever and didn't give a shit about Judy's Grill and wanted to bring me up in the witness protection program and I don't know what and my dad was all quiet, listening, comforting her, finally telling her she had to calm down, had to be quiet, that she would wake us, as if we were sleeping. Listening to my dad tell her she had to take something and her going into the bathroom and the water running—what did she take? Sleeping pills? I mean, they hadn't even seen the video yet. And the next night I made the most decisive move of my life, even faster and with less hesitation than I had decided to smoke with Ginger or climb up into Kyle's bed. My mom and I had dropped Meghan off at the airport, a totally changed person after spending those horrific days with me. I, selfishly, was glad she had been there. Because I thought she, more than anyone else, knew who I was. Or at least who I had been. After Meghan left, promising to call every hour for the rest of my life to check on me, my mom confessed that she had to go to the Grill for twenty minutes to take my dad the key to the safe or something. She would be right back, she promised, he could handle the dinner rush alone, and would I be okay? For a few minutes? Anxious for any break at all from her withering, well-meaning scrutiny, I practically shoved her out the door. And as soon as I heard her car drive off, I threw away forever my already broken good-girl record by taking five hundred dollars from the cash box I knew she hid in her closet. I unzipped my giant backpack and packed seven clean outfits, including the $118 jeans from Nordstrom's, a CNN T-shirt Molly had given me for a nightshirt, my toothbrush, twelve Power Bars, a bottle of water, all my gum, and *The Bluest Eye*. By the time my mom came home from the Grill, I had stuffed the full backpack into my closet and climbed into bed, where I spent the entire after- noon and evening, fake-sleeping. My cell phone was under my pillow on vibrate, and it rang a million times, Ginger half of them, Sarah and Molly the other half. Meghan wasn't home yet, so her hundreds of calls didn't start until later that night. I didn't pick up for anyone, not a single time, although I did wonder why Ginger was calling. I waited all the way through dinner, still pretending to be asleep. My mom came and checked on me ninety-five times, but I never moved under the flowery duvet. I felt bad about

Sam, especially since I hadn't apologized for snapping at him at breakfast the day before, but I couldn't see a way to get through dinner without lying directly. Not saying good-bye made me feel guilty, but I couldn't say good-bye without them stopping me, so what could I do, really? As soon as I heard my mom and dad go to bed, I walked downstairs and right out the front door. It was so easy, I wondered why I had never run away before, and then I remembered that my life had never been hideous enough until now. Maybe I'd had no agency the night Kyle taped me, but now I was an outlaw of my own making. As soon as the outside air hit my skin, I felt better, freer, stronger.

The night was silent, the church asleep, the trees in our backyard dark and all *Wizard of Oz* in the night. I wished I had red glittering shoes, could click them together and be somewhere safe. I wished I had an emu, or a noose. I needed something, magic or not. I crossed Washtenaw and boarded the first AATA bus that came along. There was one guy on the bus, sleeping, and the bus driver, who looked so tired I thought she might fall asleep at the wheel, too. If she noticed me get on, or had any thoughts about my being a little person, she kept it to herself. The doors swung shut and I hopped up onto the first seat, the one reserved for disabled people. I rode down Washtenaw again, the nine millionth time in my life, past the once-gas-station-now-coffee-shop, past the rec center where my mom works out, past the Barnes & Noble, past Huron Parkway, where I would have turned off to go to Kyle Malanack's house, past Arborland, and onto 94E. I wondered if the police were at Kyle's house now, and what questions they would ask if they were. Although maybe if I wanted the police to ask him anything, I would have to be the one to call them. And what would I say on the phone? This guy I'm in love with made a video of me with some of his friends? If I said that, how would I prove I hadn't wanted to? And even if I could establish that, then would I be a powerless, pitiful victim? And a victim of what, exactly? The sex? The tape? What had they done by accident and what had they meant to do? I tried to put it out of my mind, to imagine everything would resolve itself without my involvement. When the bus sped up, a feeling of genuine exhilaration came over me. I was free! I could go anywhere, do anything.

But ten minutes later, I was scared and hungry. I thought of the cops again, of calling them, of a trial. Would there be a trial now? What if I found out Kyle had orchestrated the whole thing? What if there were other tapes? Had he taped me those first few times, too? I looked out the window: Ypsilanti, a place I had been twice— once to a music festival with my parents, during which I had jumped in one of those inflatable bouncy houses, and the other time to go Halloween shopping at Value World with Goth Sarah. We drove by the huge penis of a water tower. When I saw a McDonald's, I got off the bus. The parking lot was empty and littered with beer bottles. I went inside, and ordered a six-piece McNugget Happy Meal. It came with a plastic Barbie mermaid named Kayla. According to the package, "secret items from the ocean" were going to appear on her body if I dipped her in cold water. I sat there, totally silent, dunking rubbery, reconstituted chicken into rubbery, reconstituted BBQ sauce. I had the distinct sensation that this was another video, a movie of my life that I was watching, and in a minute I'd turn the TV off and be safe on the couch with my mom and dad and Chad and Sam.

Then I heard laughter, and realized that the kids working behind the counter had noticed me. I didn't care. No one could see or say anything about me that hadn't, at this point, already been seen or said. As long as they weren't violent or going to kill me, I didn't care. And frankly, even then I wasn't sure if I cared. The sound of their laughter reminded me of the video. I closed my eyes, thought how it had been one day since I'd seen the video, and how now my life would be a million more days long. I wasn't sure if I could get through them.

I got up and left quickly, not bothering to throw away my fries or Happy Meal box. I left Kayla the mermaid on the table and hurried out into the blank parking lot, feeling only cold. It was windy. I didn't want to stand there, waiting for a bus, so I started walking. I could sense suddenly how I might have looked from the outside, to my mom, for example, like a little kid, walking along the highway in Ypsilanti at one in the morning. As soon as I saw the Motel Manor, I went inside, decided to live there for the rest of my life, and why not? It was $106 a week. I could stay a month with the money I'd brought in cash, and I had my mom's credit card, too. I was hoping not to use it, because if I did, they could track me down right away, but in case they needed a deposit or something, proof I could pay, I was holding it, ready to show it to the clerk.

She took my $106 in cash without asking any questions, or even looking at me really, and reached over the counter to hand a heavy metal key down to me. The place was a dingy fun home, full of warped mirrors, peeling paint, and insects. There was a dilapidated couch across from two chairs in the "lobby," occupied by a sleeping man who was either homeless or a hotel employee. It was impossible to say which. No one seemed concerned that he was there. Of course there was no one to be concerned, really.

The desk clerk was so tired and haggard that she looked barely alive. I thought of Judy's Grill, the buzz and fuss of the place, my mom behind the counter, smelling like shampoo and talcum powder and french fries. I contemplated boarding the first bus back in the direction of my parents' house, but then I propelled myself forward to room 204, thinking I had to give it at least a night—*it* being the new, independent, defiant me. I couldn't be Judy Lohden anymore, smarty, chore-doing, upstanding daughter. Now I was a tough runaway, so I'd have to last at least twenty-four hours. And in spite of myself, I wanted Kyle to hear that I had disappeared, to worry. I wondered if he would worry.

The stairs to the second floor were concrete, with a slab of gray carpet thrown over them, not properly secured. It was peeling up, flapping where it met the banister on one side and the wall on the other. I had a special close view of this because the stairs were deep enough that I was like a tiny mountain creature on them. The top step was wet with something—blood? pee? coffee? rainwater?—so wet that it squished under my boots. I hoisted myself up to the landing and walked down a dim hallway to room 204, where I had to stand on my absolute tiptoes to reach the lock, mysteriously located above the door-knob. The door creaked open into a room of more darkness. I groped around in the dark for a light switch and found it, about three inches over my head. The light hummed and buzzed, barely lighting a dirty gray carpet. There was a double bed with a brown blanket on it, across from a very small television set on a table with two folding chairs. The bathroom was to my left. I dragged one of the chairs into the bathroom, where I used it to stand at the counter. I saw myself in the mirror, red-eyed, lost, unrecognizable. Then I plugged the filthy sink and filled it with water, took my cell phone out of my jeans pocket, with its million missed calls and names and voice mails all lit up like horrible reminders of a world I'd once belonged to—some of them were even from my former friends from Huron, so I knew the news was literally everywhere— and I dropped the phone in. Some bubbles rose up, as if it had been alive. I named the bubbles: Ginger, Sarah, Molly, Elizabeth Wood, Stockard Blumenthal, even Rachael Collins, as unfair as that was. I never wanted to think of anyone at D'Arts again, never wanted to see a single name or face from the school. Kyle and his friends I couldn't bear to think of at all. I felt relief, watching it underwater, drowned. I was uncontactable, hidden, safe. I walked back into the hideous bedroom and climbed up onto the bed, so exhausted I wasn't sure my arms could even handle the task. But they did. Then I had an image of myself climbing onto Kyle's bed. I collapsed onto the Motel Manor bed with all my clothes and shoes still on. I didn't even bother to peel the covers back. Not to mention washing my face or brushing my teeth. I felt all my routines short out, and my old self vanish. I mean, I am so deeply not the kind of person who sleeps in my clothes or skips face-washing or teeth-brushing. But there it was. And for the first time since that Friday night at Kyle's ice palace, I slept. It was a hot, sweaty, cold, wakeful sleep, during which I had the dream I've now been having over and over since I ran away. In it, I'm in a courtroom, watching Kyle and Chris and Alan admit what they did. There are thousands of people in the audience. The principal, Mr. Grames, is giving a presentation, holding a red pointer he shines first on the video and then on my body. He makes me stand up so everyone can see that I'm there. I'm wearing a sheet or something—something loose and thin that might fall off.

"Judy was naked!" Mr. Grames says, and the video plays, the red dot of his pointer following the lines of my body like a bright bug crawling on me. "We can see here what happened." And it's so real I now can't remember what the differences are between my nightmare video and the real one. They're both appalling, me arching my back, turning to face Alan, huge on the wall of some dream courtroom, everyone looking at each other with their mouths open, like they're

366

about to drink my humiliation, devour me. Then a judge who looks just like Mr. Luther but isn't him, says, "She was a virgin! It's not her fault! She was a virgin! It didn't count. It didn't count. It didn't count."

He says it just like that, three times, and then in the dream I put my head into my hands and Kyle gets up and he's laughing, and he says no, she wasn't, she's a slut and why is everyone so surprised that she got drunk and gangbanged me and my friends?

And then I stand up on top of a table, and the sheet feels like it might fall off, and I start to say no, no, I had sex with Kyle only three times and that was because I thought we were in love. But my throat closes, and my teeth are locked together so tight it feels like they might break. And I'm thinking, in the dream, my teeth are going to shatter and I can't talk. So I stand there totally silent in my sheet, with my locked jaw. And even in the dream, where logic is all fucked up, the truth is so humiliating that I know on some level it's better for everyone to think I was a willing participant. Because then I was just fun and crazy and doing my own thing, right? Rather than being violated? Then, when I finally risk opening my mouth, hoping to make this point, all my teeth start to fall out after all. And because I know the sheet will slip off if I move my arms, I keep them pinned at my sides and let my teeth spill down and bounce all over the desk like marbles. I don't even bend to pick them up.

I never fall asleep anymore without having some version of this dream. Sometimes, Mr. Troudeau, the AP history teacher, pounds a gavel until I put my hands over my ears. I look over at him, to say, *please, stop,* and it turns out he's pounding his hips into the desk like he's fucking the drawer. Then I look out at the audience and everyone is laughing. Ginger, Kyle, Alan, Chris, their moms, my mom, even Goth Sarah and Meghan—they're all laughing that laugh and sticking their tongues out.

Even though I keep having these dreams—or maybe because of them—I sleep so much at the Motel Manor that whenever I wake up, sometimes to the sound of someone knocking gently, I never know who or where I am. I can't tell what's a dream and what's real. And in those utterly disoriented moments, I feel half happy. But then I remember reality, and I sink under thousands of gallons of water. I pull the covers back over my head and try to fall asleep again, because even though the dreams are terrible, I live for that one moment a day, when, between being asleep and being awake, I don't remember. Even when I'm sure the knocking is real, I never answer the door.

Sometimes, I get up and go out into the hallway to find Bill. I read papers Bill brings me, and spend hours watching TV. The news has been the only way for me to follow my own story, and I think this might be the definition of having an out-of-body experience, reading your own life, as misreported by people who know nothing about you. My third day here I read that D'Arts was "cooperating with an investigation by the state attorney's office, interviewing parents and students close to the case."

By my fifth day, D'Arts was holding a "closed hearing." According to the *Detroit Free Press*, "A tribunal named by the school board heard evidence on whether three male students, all seniors, acted inappropriately or broke the law by videotaping a fellow student at a party." Someone named Caitlin Newbury, who is apparently the D'Arts lawyer, had the custodian "bar a reporter from attending the hearing." What does "bar" mean? Did Mr. Nicks, the eighty-year-old janitor, have to shove a journalist out of D'Arts? Was the hearing held at school? Or in a courtroom like in my dream? And either way, didn't they need me there? In the article, Mr. Grames was quoted saying that the school was cooperating closely with law enforcement officials, toward deciding whether and what criminal charges should be pursued.

All I could think was, what about me? What about letting me ask Kyle directly if he had done it on purpose, who had edited that horrific video and why? Wasn't that kind of all there was to it? I mean, this article ended by saying that school officials had "declined to identify" who would hear the case. Calls to my house were "unreturned," and my parents were not commenting. No one was, as the case was "ongoing." Just that word gave me the under-the-dining-room-table, seeing-if-time-stops feeling. I wondered for a moment whether my life had stopped being ongoing, and realized that even though I was living out the rest of it at the Motel Manor, alone, away from my family and story, it was still moving forward. So can someone please give me an example of something that isn't "ongoing"? Is there something in this life that's ever clearly, unequivocally finished? And is it just because I'm young that I have to ask that? I mean, here's a horrible possibility: even death can't exactly finish us. Even if I died, which would be one step closer to no life than this Motel Manor existence is, that video and this story would still live without me. My death would just be part of that ongoing tale. And maybe it's counterintuitive, but that makes me want to come out of hiding, show everyone that I'm alive and, if not in charge of, then at least a participant in my own ongoing life.

Today the *Detroit Free Press* said that Kyle and Chris and Alan have been expelled from D'Arts, but no "criminal charges are being pursued."

Being pursued! If that crappy writer had been in American lit, then Ms. Doman would have written in the margin, "Don't use passive voice unless there's a compelling reason." I mean, "being pursued"? By whom? I had assumed that such charges would have been pursued by me, and that they still could be. But the paper was acting like I'm not even real, just grammatically implied.

Maybe because I ran away and wasn't there to explain that I find the entire thing utterly sickening and was in a coma when it happened, the world has decided that we all agreed both to have sex and then to make the video. In which case I can see why there's nothing criminal about it. Maybe the world thinks I wanted this to happen. When I have thoughts like that, my veins freeze like the pipes in our house, right before the ice makes them explode and flood the basement. I can't believe my parents, who I assume were involved in this "hearing" in some way, would have let everyone leave believing that.

None of the articles I've seen has mentioned my disappearance. They're not allowed to name me, or show my face, so they don't even say I "wasn't available for comment" or anything, although they all say that about my parents. They all complain about "calls to the family" being "unreturned." Sometimes I wake up at night, sweating, thinking, what if my parents' lawn is covered with tents, reporters in and out of sleeping bags, shining flashlights, peering into the windows in search of me or my parents or brothers? What if every other room in this motel is full of camera crews or something. My two small, dirty windows overlook an airshaft and garbage dump, not even the parking lot, so I can't see if there are crowds in the front. I've left only twice, both times to go to Kroger, and once was my second night here, after dark, and the other time was that Saturday morning, predawn, with Bill. Maybe by now there are throngs. Or maybe I've just watched too many big-budget movies and real life is slower and flatter than all that. Maybe it's just what I've noticed, now that I'm the object of stories I know something about, which is that reporters actually report on one another's stories all the time, instead of coming to investigate the truth. They copy whatever everyone else wrote, and you see all the mistakes get repeated verbatim. Maybe I never noticed this when I was reading about stuff I also knew nothing about, but once you read about something you know something about, you can't believe how slack and inaccurate most articles are. In addition to making me want to come out and set the record straight, it makes me never want to read the paper again, since now that I know it's all fiction anyway, why bother? I'd rather read a good book. I mean, I don't know much about the culpability of the Catholic

Church, or oil spills, or banker crimes, but now that I've read the stories about me and my school, I can't imagine that reading the papers is the best way to learn much of anything about any of these other categories, either. I'm no expert, even on what happened to me, but I do know that I'm not "disabled," and that D'Arts is not "a breeding ground for scandals among the designer-drug-addled children of Ann Arbor's elite." The unnamed perpetrators are also not (a) "all seniors at the elite Arts Academy," as I've now read dozens of times, or (b) "childhood friends of the disabled victim," even if "sources close to the investigation" say so.

I've also realized that even though everything in the world is ongoing, or maybe precisely because that's true, nothing lasts. The story is migrating to the back pages these days; I guess if you can't print photos or name names, the sexy, empty headlines only grip people for so long. And there's no shortage in America of homo-phobic politicians molesting their young male staffers. A super prolific one has graciously taken the front-page spotlight off of me this week.

Mainly, what I want to know is something the media also can't seem to figure out, which is who the "hearers" of the hearing were, what they heard and decided, and whether any of it matters for me. The truth is, I can't know any of that without my parents. I need my parents, and I think I have to get out of here. Were they there? Was Mr. Luther? Mr. Troudeau? What about Kyle's parents? Kyle? Chris? Alan? Who picked and how? What could they possibly have said to one another? Did those guys get to tell their sides? Sometimes, if I let myself flutter near the fire, I imagine Kyle announcing to a room full of people, including my parents, "I was drunk." He says it in the same voice he used to tell me about his sister. But when he said that, his point was like, "it was my fault," and when he says this, it's the opposite, his point is, "I don't even remember what happened and how can it be my fault, I was drunk." The thing is, I was drunk too, and I still can't exactly remember what happened, so maybe he genuinely feels that way too. And what I want to know is not even about the sex, really—I can guess at what happened there, and whether I said I was okay or not doesn't seem to me to be the point. I mean, even if I said it was okay, it clearly wasn't. Whoever created the word *consent* has never been videotaped doing something she didn't mean to. What I want to know is whether Kyle is the one who edited the tape, if he was cruel enough to include that clip of my name. In my happy imaginary version of the hearing, it comes out clearly that the whole enterprise was Chris's or Alan's fault, and—surprise!—Kyle still doesn't know how it happened: "When I woke up, these guys had gone through all my tapes! I had no idea they made this thing." Or in the B version, he made the tape itself, but it was for him, a private way of keeping a record, keeping track, keeping me. And he never meant for it to get out.

I don't care about the expulsions, or at least I feel in my body like I don't. Dropping out of the world has made me numb, I guess. Or maybe getting expelled isn't a big deal. Is it? So they don't have to go back to school? Who cares? I kind of wonder what Kyle is doing with his empty days—watching the video on an endless loop, congratulating himself? Does he find the whole thing sexy? Or funny? Maybe not, maybe he feels bad about it, was trying to deny it or apologize for that night. Part of me, maybe the desperate, ridiculous part, still thinks he and I will have a conversation about this someday, that he'll be able to tell me something that makes it better. Not that that makes it okay necessarily, since how could it? But at least that makes it possible that this actually happened for some reason other than he's a monster and I'm cursed. Maybe he's in therapy now, becoming a better person, or figuring out why he did what he did. Maybe part of his process will be to come find me someday and say he's sorry. One of the things my mom told me that interminable day Meghan left was that the school had asked that I be "evaluated," by a shrink, I guess. My parents and

I were supposed to come in for a meeting with the school. I asked my mom if she and my dad were being "evaluated" too, and she shook her head, said, "No, I think just briefed."

Did Kyle's parents get briefed? Did he get evaluated? Maybe his family has moved again, to hide another nasty crime while he finishes high school elsewhere. I have no idea what Chris and Alan are doing, but they've both already gotten into colleges early, so it probably barely matters for them. Maybe they're writing new "real life story" screenplays in a coffee shop downtown, the expulsion a kind of artistic trophy or extended vacation. I've never met anyone who got expelled before, so I don't know what it means. Probably they'll all go somewhere where nobody knows what they did at D'Arts, just like Kyle already did after his sister died, if that hideous story he told me was even true. Maybe everyone knows that secret now that I told it to Sarah.

Sometimes I think about whether those guys are scared I'll press charges. But then I would have to talk—in public—about the whole thing. And not just that hideous night, or the video, but also the sex with Kyle—from before. I'd have to admit how it was on the first date, and then he would say it hadn't even been a real date, that he had just offered to drive me home and I had been pathetically in love with him before that, and it would be true. Chris would be there too. He would look handsome and troubled, with his shadowy eyes and beautiful mom. She'd put both her arms around him the way she did that night at the senior voice concert, and he would return the hug in his vintage I'm-a-macho-guy-but-I-love-my-mom way, and who would possibly believe he should be locked up? To say nothing of Alan, soft-spoken rich kid Alan, with his brown arms and hair so fine it would remind everyone of a kindergarten school picture. Everyone in the world would be there, gaping at us like we were starring in yet another sordid video about my life. And the audience would know that I'm not only a slut to my core, but also a rat. And whether I succeeded or not, everyone would know that I had tried to send Kyle and Chris and Alan *to jail*. Now at least I have the moral upper hand, I think. And if I stay quiet, maybe it will all go away faster. Which is what I want most. Sometimes, especially at night, when I think they might be celebrating each day that passes, I want to dial 911 and shout down the wires that I didn't agree to any of it, didn't want any of it, that my heart is on fire and I'm actually burning down with unhappiness and injustice. I thought Kyle loved me, and if he didn't, well, then even everything from before was an attack too.

But, maybe because I'm me, I can always fast-forward to whatever end the fantasies come to —all of us on trial, them regretting it, their lives being wrecked, even them going to prison forever—and none of it restores my dignity, erases that video, or improves my life. Maybe that's the conclusion my parents came to, too, and that's why nothing criminal is "being pursued." It's just a guess, but a pretty good one, I bet.

If it were true that misery enjoys company, then I guess I'd hope for those boys to be ruined, to go to jail instead of college. But somehow, maybe weirdly, it just seems like their lives being over isn't really a silver lining for me. So maybe I'm not the kind of person who would rip someone else's legs off to be tall after all.

At least I have Bill. And if I ever leave the Motel Manor, I'll have my parents back. And Sam. I miss them so much I've been waking up crying. I never knew that that could happen, that you could be crying before you're even awake. I always thought the mind had to tell the body to suffer, but even my whole body is heartbroken. I miss Meghan and Sarah and Molly, even Ginger. And I want to go home. I can't stop wondering how Kyle can live with himself after what he did. I mean, I can hardly stand to sleep at night or be awake during the days myself, but I keep thinking when I'm crying in the morning, "Get up anyway, Judy. You're going to be okay." Because at least what keeps me up and makes me cry isn't something disgusting I did to anyone other than myself.

# 14

It's been 9 days since I ran away, 216 hours; 12,960 minutes. This morning I woke up before it was even light outside, not crying for once, and put on my last clean clothes—and when I say clean, I mean filthy, because I've just been washing out the same outfits and wringing them out to dry them in rotation. I chewed some gum, sat on the bed, turned the TV on. News. People dying, markets collapsing, everyone losing their jobs. I waited for the gentle knocking, ready.

And when I heard it, I swung my legs over the side of the bed and jumped down, walked toward the door.

"Who is it?"

"It's me."

I opened the door and there was Goth Sarah, looking totally calm, unsurprised to see me. She was carrying a Whole Foods bag. I hadn't seen a human being I knew—other than Bill—in nine days. And since I'd ruined my phone, I hadn't even heard anyone's voice. More than once, I had wished for an old message from my mom or dad or Sarah, for one of their saved voices from before all this. Now, standing in the doorway of my room at the Motel Manor, Sarah was so familiar and so strange at the same time that it was like seeing someone arrive from being dead for a long time. I didn't say anything, because I couldn't. The tears started underneath my eyes, boiled over, and poured down my face. She watched me, deciding whether to pretend not to notice. She was wearing ripped gray fishnets and a sleeveless black lace dress with a white T-shirt underneath it. She looked skinnier than I remembered, smaller. She reached her pale arms out and hugged me.

"Hi, Judy," she said, into my hair. She was crying too.

"Hi."

She pulled back, looked at me. Her eyes were puffy, with circles under them. She didn't have any makeup on, rare for her. "So I brought you some things," she said, wiping her eyes with the back of her right hand.

"Thank you."

"Just some clean clothes, Fruit Roll-Ups, Power Bars, Naked juices, you know."

"Wow. Thank you." I swallowed, backing into the room, wondering if she would follow. Now what would we do? She kept looking at me, her eyes wide and tired.

"So," I said, "how did you find me?"

She shrugged.

"Do my parents know where I am?"

"Uh," she said.

"What are you doing here?"

"I came to make sure you were okay."

"Right. So they've known all along?"

She shrugged.

"How did they know?"

"I'm not really supposed to say that they know."

"Okay, so if they did know, how would they have found out?"

"Maybe some guy would have called them and told them you were here."

"And when would that have happened?"

She smiled a superwarm smile, shrugged again.

"A while ago," she said.

"A while like two hours? Or like nine days?"

"Can I come in?"

I nodded, backed fully into the room without taking my eyes off of her. Because I was terrified that if I looked away, even for a second, she would disappear, and I would be alone again. And I wouldn't know whether she'd even been there for real. Being alone can make you lose track of what's real and what's not. Maybe because most of what's "real" gets confirmed by how and whether we talk and write about it. Until the moment I saw Goth Sarah at the Motel Manor, Bill had been the only person who stood between me and absolute solitary confinement. Now that I had seen someone I knew, even though it meant my horrible story was true again, I couldn't believe I had made it through nine days alone. What if she left and I was never brave enough leave the motel again? I couldn't bear the thought of spending another second there.

Goth Sarah slowly sat down on the bed, and I climbed up next to her. She put an arm around me.

"So they've known the whole time where I was," I said.

"It still counts," she said.

"Right. So what—are they here? In the hotel?"

"No. They're at home. They just sent me."

"Every day."

She nodded. "Didn't you get my note?"

The envelope. I leaned over and took it out of my notebook, still unopened. Sarah watched. "I'm sorry," I said, "I didn't know who it was from, and I was too scared—"

"That's okay," she said, "you don't have to . . ."

I opened the envelope and unfolded the piece of paper inside, thought how well I knew Sarah's handwriting, how it reminded me of American lit. And lunch. The hallways. All the note said was, "I'll keep coming back. Don't want to intrude, so just let me know when you want to talk or if you need anything, okay? xoxo, Sarah." At the bottom was a little doodle of the two of us, standing side by side on a little path that reminded me of *Harold and the Purple Crayon*. There was a moon above us and a line at the end of the path that suggested the horizon.

"Thank you," I said. "I wish I'd opened it when

you put it there." This wasn't true, exactly, but it felt okay to say it anyway.

Sarah just nodded. I folded the note neatly and put it back in its envelope.

"So how did Bill find my parents?"

"Uh. I guess he looked them up."

"Does Bill know you're here too? Does he know you?"

She nodded and blew her bangs out of her eyes. I noticed that her roots were little-kid blond, like Alan's. She was the opposite of most people who dye their hair, wanting to be blond, with the angry black roots poking out of their scalps in protest. I loved her for this choice, choosing her motor oil hair, rejecting the utterly, conventionally desirable blond girl underneath. But I also had a quick jolt of the hope that someday she'd be able to go as is.

"You changed your hair?"

"No, I haven't dyed it in a few weeks is all."

"Oh. It looks good."

"Thanks. I've been really sad." She paused. "We all miss you."

"I feel like a patronized infant."

"You shouldn't," she said.

"Who's 'we all,' by the way?" I fished.

"Just, I don't know, your mom, Sam, me, Ms. Doman?"

I remembered, suddenly, that Ms. Doman was a real person, not just a character I had invented.

Again, I felt disoriented. "Ms. Doman misses me?" I asked.

"Totally," Sarah said, encouraged for the first time since she'd arrived. "I think seeing me reminds her of you. She calls on me constantly, but then she's super disappointed no matter what I say. It's like being the person she married after her true love died." A little smile played with the corner of her mouth, like she wanted so much for this to be okay, to be able to be friends again, for me not to be gone forever—or to have become someone she didn't know any-more.

And I can't deny that the thing about Ms. Doman made me feel slightly better. But I was too whiny to thank Sarah. So I said, "I can't do anything by myself."

I thought she'd say yes, I could, that I had proven myself, but instead she looked straight at me with her bruised-looking eyes and said, "No one can."

"*You* can."

"Of course I can't."

"Yes, you can. You're always taking care of everyone, especially me—getting me home from school every day, rescuing me from Kyle's that day, getting the—"

I stopped short of saying the word, since my breath ran out as soon as I remembered her stand-ing in the doorway of my room, holding the unmarked DVD. I saw a photorealistic image of Alan moving toward the bed on my laptop screen and felt instantly like I might throw up.

Sarah was watching me closely, her head tilted to the side. "Every single thing you mentioned is because I have a car. And I happen to know, although they were planning to surprise you with it, that they fixed the pedals in your dad's car, which he's about to give you, so from now on you can drive me around. And pick me up at Eliot's next time he dumps me."

"Did Eliot dump you?"

She swallowed, and I could see the outline of a sob, trying to get out of her throat.

"Shit. I'm sorry, Sarah, I had no idea—"

"There's a new Japanese exchange student named Kimiko—"

We looked at each other, and her eyes widened, and her mouth twitched a little, and then she started laughing. And within one second, it was an avalanche of laughs—maybe because she was so nervous, or maybe because she was so relieved to have an excuse to laugh, or I don't know. There were words flying out from in between her gasps: "I mean, Kimiko, really? It was like, he's such a racist—all she had to be was—oh my god, they're like, doing Shinto naked together right now even as we speak."

And suddenly, I was laughing too, even though it wasn't funny, and realizing that it was the first time in weeks that I had heard my own laugh. I was sorry it was at Sarah's expense, and about something so deeply unfunny.

"I'm sorry," I said, as soon as I calmed down. "I'm sorry I wasn't there to pick you up or something. I've been kind of selfish lately, I—"

I expected her to contradict this. But she said, "It's a small thing, obviously. I mean, whatever, teenage love, right?" We watched each other again, both waiting, both knowing this wasn't true, and that it didn't make us feel better. Kyle didn't love me, and Eliot didn't love Sarah. And there was nothing small about either of those facts, really. I thought suddenly of Molly.

"Where's Molly?"

"At school," Sarah said.

The word sent me tumbling back down to the bottom of myself. "What am I going to do?"

"Come back. It hasn't even been two weeks— you can make up the work. Molly and I'll fill you in on everything. There are a million things we've been dying to talk about. Stockard and Greg broke up for one. And well, Chris and Alan got expelled, and . . ." She paused for a moment, as if telling me about them in the same sentence as other people might be insensitive.

"I guess you haven't heard about anything that's happened, right?"

"Not really," I said. "What were you going to say?"

"It was just about Chris and Alan, about Stanford and UCLA?"

"I heard they were expelled," I prompted, "from the paper."

"Stanford and UCLA found out what happened and they're not letting Chris and Alan come."

"They *found out?*" I had an image of the video being screened on campuses across the country. I looked up at the ceiling, got an odd sense of comfort that the same cracks I'd been staring at since I'd gotten to the Motel Manor were still there, right where I'd left them.

"You know, I mean, D'Arts told them." She looked at me strangely, like maybe I hadn't realized something.

"The whole thing was, like, a really big deal at D'Arts, you know, the whole—I mean, it was a huge public relations nightmare." Sarah looked nervous, like she didn't know whether she was allowed to tell me anything, or she thought I'd crumble, that my arms and legs and head would snap off like puppet parts, that I'd literally break down. But I sat still, kept my back straight, focused on my excellent posture.

Sarah slouched down. "D'Arts expelled them to, like, prove they could handle discipline issues or whatever."

I felt a twinge of powerlessness and rage. Goth Sarah was watching me, maybe wanting to see if this news made it better. But what was I supposed to feel, except that it had happened without me there? I wanted to hear about Kyle, but couldn't ask.

"Their lives are totally fucked," Sarah tried again. "And yours isn't."

"Maybe it is, though. I mean, that video is going to last forever. Maybe everyone who meets me from now on—for the rest of my life—will have seen it."

Sarah shook her head. "No," she said. "You're going to apply to college next year and get into Harvard. Or Juilliard. You can go wherever you want and no one will ever have heard of any of this shit. But you have to come back and finish school. We're doing *The Wiz* for the spring show."

"Oh."

"You haven't even missed auditions. And how could Minogue not give you Dorothy?"

"Maybe she'll cast me as a Munchkin."

"No way," Sarah said. "She's definitely all about height-blind casting."

I smiled, and Sarah said, "And anyway, it's just one more year and then you can totally remake yourself once you get to coll—"

"As a seven-foot Amazon?" I asked.

Sarah laughed. "I'll buy the stilts," she said.

"I can't show my face at D'Arts. How can I? I can't."

"Of course you can. Seriously, Judy," she said.

"Think of all the famous people who have, you know—in a way, sex tapes aren't even bad anymore, they're like, normal. More than normal. People do it to get famous! You're a step ahead."

I wanted to believe her so much that I almost did. And she must have seen that she was making progress, because she picked up speed.

"Kyle probably won't even finish high school, or it'll at least take him an extra year at some lame school and then he'll never get into college without them finding out. And Alan and Chris *aren't going to college*. They're about to spend the rest of their lives pumping gas, flipping burgers, pulling old ladies out of the shallow end at Fuller Pool! Alan'll be seventy-nine, with tufts of hair coming out his ears, lifeguarding. Chris'll marry his mom, because she's the only woman who will ever look at him again."

I laughed, in spite of myself.

"Come on, play Dorothy, finish school with Molly and me. Those pricks are gone forever, and D'Arts completely sucks without you."

I was still back on his name, and she knew it. She looked at me. "Do you want to hear about Kyle?" she asked.

I shrugged. "Whatever."

"Apparently he's having some kind of, I don't know, breakdown."

A knot formed in my throat. "What do you mean?"

"During the hearing? He cried until his parents had to take him out."

I swallowed the knot and it rose again, painfully.

"Was he faking?"

Sarah lay back on the bed, grabbed a pillow, and looked up at the ceiling. I wondered what it would be like to be looking at those cracks for the first time. She propped her head up on her hand, and blew her bangs out of her eyes again. They settled right back down and she peered at me through them.

"I heard it happened twice—both days of the hearing. I don't really know. Maybe he was super fucked up about what he did to you, or maybe about his sister or whatever."

I felt something tumble through me, hoped it wasn't guilt. I closed my eyes, rubbed them until pinwheels of light spun under my lids. I had begun to feel that I was sliding back toward something toxic, a pool of bubbling chemicals that would melt my body right off the bones. I began scrambling back up, thinking—which way did *up* mean? Was *up* staying at the Motel Manor forever? Was it never going home? Never asking my parents what had happened in that room?

Sarah had crossed her legs in a kind of yoga position, and had her hands resting on her lap. She lifted them up and looked at them as if she'd never seen them before. "Um, so, Judy? There's something else," she said, not looking up. "About Ginger?"

"Ginger Mews?"

"Yeah, Ginger." I suddenly had an image of Sarah, Ginger, and the entire administration of D'Arts sitting around my kitchen table with my family, informing each other about the sordid, horrible details of my life. Sarah kept her legs folded, and straightened her back even more, preparing herself. Whatever she was about to tell me, I didn't want to know.

"So, it's just, there were others," she said.

"Others."

"Other videos. I mean, of like, other D'Arts girls."

I thought about this for a minute. "D'Arts girls," I repeated, my voice flat.

"With Kyle," she said, "you know."

My mind zoomed back to the stack on his desk. Sarah watched me, probably trying to tell if this was horrible for me. Because she knew that if I still loved him, had ever loved him, then it would be. And it was. I mean, in spite of everything, and even though it wasn't a surprise exactly, it still felt bad to learn that he had had sex with everyone in the world. That my losing it to him had meant nothing. But the idea of those videos also made the one of me seem less uniquely terrible, too, so I could see why she'd decided to tell me. I wondered what made Kyle tape girls. Cruelty? Pathological need? I was thinking, well, maybe after he lost his sister, he needed to memorize everything else that ever happened to him, in case he lost all that, too. Had he made tapes before the thing with his sister? And why was I always trying to excuse him, I mean, even if he had done it out of illness, that didn't explain—I froze mid-thought and turned to Sarah.

"Are they like—all with—?" I couldn't get their names out.

Sarah shook her head. "The other ones are just —Chris and Alan weren't, you know, involved."

I sat there, shrinking into the bed. "So it was just me they—"

"Maybe that's why. I mean, maybe they were the ones who—"

It was the first and only concession she ever made to him. I couldn't tell what I felt, gratitude maybe, relief that she was going to leave that possibility open to me. Maybe that's how I'd make a story I could live with, one where Chris and Alan edited and distributed it, and Kyle was too crazy or helpless or passive to stop it. I considered my A– version, in which he had fought with them about it, tried to keep it from happening. Or the A+ one, where he hadn't even known any of it was happening, the taping or the editing, and had been as surprised as I was at the whole thing. I tried a soft version out on Sarah: "Yeah, I kind of thought maybe Chris was—you know, the one who—"

She cut me off. I didn't know if this was because she knew something I didn't know and couldn't bear to hear me deceive myself, or whether she just didn't care about the details of who had edited what. She was picking at a rip in her stockings, worrying it into the sort of hole that would make her throw them out. "So the thing about Ginger—"

"One of them is of her, right?" I managed to say this as if the weight in my stomach wasn't threatening to sink me into the ground.

"Yeah. I'm sorry," Sarah said. "But that's why everyone found out. I mean, she's the one who told Grames." She got down off the bed and began wandering around the room, picking things up and setting them back down: the TV remote, a crumpled newspaper. She didn't seem to know what to say.

I asked, "Why?"

"I guess people were, you know, kind of saying shit, and Ginger was like, 'There are other ones,' to defend you, so everyone would know."

"Know *what*?"

"That it wasn't, you know, *you*. I mean, that there was no way it was, I don't know, what you wanted." So much for my idea that as long as I didn't try to arrest anyone, people would find me blameless. Sarah said, "Ginger was totally not okay with the one of her, either. And believe me, she didn't want anyone finding out about that video. Or watching it." She paused, while we both considered what horrible things that could mean. She bit her lower lip, appeared to be chewing on it for a minute. "But once she told, it was just so obviously his problem—"

Goth Sarah stopped the aimless pacing suddenly and began collecting clothes and things purposefully. "Do you want this?" she asked, holding up a can of tuna.

"Hell no."

She tossed it across the room into the trash, sank the shot. "Three points!" she said, and then looked over at me as if to apologize. "Come. Get ready and I'll take you home. People are falling apart without you."

"Yeah, right," I said. "Because I'm such a pillar of strength." But I stood up, went to find my shoes.

Sarah said, "I meant Sam."

"Oh."

"The Tappan jazz band is playing at the finish line of some charity run on Saturday, down on Main Street—Sam's apparently drumming."

I had to clear my throat again. "How is he?"

"The science fair was yesterday."

"You're kidding! Our glorious square Earth climate project! My mom really kept you in the loop," I said. I felt joyful for a second and then, before I could even identify the emotion as happiness, was back to careening down a cliff toward my next thought. "Are people torturing Sam about me?"

"I don't know. Maybe. I think he's a pretty confident kid."

I went into the bathroom, pulled the rest of my crispy clothes off the shower curtain rod, where I'd hung them to dry, and shoved the whole pile into my backpack.

"Do you want to call your parents and tell them you're coming?"

"I don't have a phone."

"What does that mean?"

"I drowned it my first night here."

"I wondered if you were getting my messages."

"I wasn't."

"Do you want to use my phone to call them?"

"No," I said, "I'll just see them."

Sarah was standing still now, holding the Whole Foods bags she'd brought in one hand and my copy of *The Bluest Eye* in the other. She looked lost with her black dress, ruined tights, and newly light hair. I was happier to see her than I can express.

She saw me looking at her, tried to guess why. But I felt too tired to tell her I loved her, was grateful, to say any of the things I should have, even just "thank you." We both stood there.

"Can I do anything to help?" she asked.

"Yeah." I put my backpack up onto the bed, clothes still sticking out of it. "Could you jam the rest of this stuff in there while I go say good-bye and thank you to Bill?"

"Of course."

I went out into the spongy, dingy hallway, thinking how it was the last time I'd ever see it, and how Bill might see it five hundred or even a thousand more times. I knocked on his door, two quiet knocks, one loud one. He opened it, in jeans and a plaid flannel shirt.

"Hi," I said.

"Hi."

"I just wanted to stop by to say thank you."

"Thank you," he said.

"No, I mean, I wanted to thank you."

"I thank you, too."

"For listening to my story. That meant a lot to me," I said. "More than I know how to tell you. You're the only person I've told—"

"Thank you for telling me," he said. "That was a good story."

"And I also want to thank you for calling my parents, to tell them I was here."

"That was right," he said. "Your parents are good. They would need to know where you are, so they can find you if you have any trouble. They would need to know that. Or Sarah, your friend Sarah. Sarah would need to know. You have good friends. Sarah is a good friend. And your parents."

"You're right," I said. "Thank you."

I had this contradictory flash, of being unable to believe I might never see Bill again, and, at the same time, unable to imagine seeing him outside of the motel or this particular context, searing and horrific as it was. I felt my eyes heat up.

"You're good, Judy," he said, "very good. You're a good friend, too. I like you very much."

"I like you, too," I said. "I hope it's fishing season again soon."

He turned and went into his room, came out with an ashtray from the motel, green glass with a jagged chip out of it.

"For you," he said, and handed it to me.

As we headed out the front door of the Motel Manor, I heard my name. "Judy Lohden?"

I turned, scared, and the desk clerk was reaching under the check-in counter.

"Ms. Lohden," she said again, gently, "I have something for you." She pulled out an envelope and set it on the counter. Sarah grabbed it and handed it to me.

"Thanks," I said.

"You're welcome," Sarah and the desk clerk both said.

I opened the envelope fast, carelessly, standing there. It tore down the middle and some business cards came spilling out onto the filthy rug. I bent down, saw the logos: *Detroit Free Press*, WPXD TV, M-live.com, ABC, *Ann Arbor Observer*. I stood up without recovering a single card and looked back at the desk clerk.

"These people—they were here?"

She nodded gravely. "I was told to have them call room 214."

I looked down at the cards again.

"Thank you for that," I said.

"Bill Tunner's a real good guy," she said.

I had never heard his last name before.

"Yeah," I said. I turned to leave.

"Well, thank you for staying here, Ms. Lohden."

"Please call me Judy," I said. I turned to go.

"Good-bye, Judy."

Goth Sarah and I walked out into the Motel Manor parking lot, where the light was so bright that I shielded my eyes like a blinded vampire. Sarah threw my backpack in the trunk, and then right before we got in her car, I asked her to take a picture of me, which she did. In front of the sign for the Motel Manor. Then we got in her car and drove away from the place forever. I felt, moving down Washtenaw toward the house I'd lived in my entire life, like I was about to arrive somewhere mysterious and meet myself for the first time.

．．．

Sarah must have called them while I was talking to Bill, because my parents were waiting outside when we pulled up, my mom at the base of the driveway, like she couldn't even bear to wait outside the door or something, and my dad, calm and kind of old-looking, on the front stoop. Sarah stopped the car so I could get out where my mom was, and my mom hugged me so hard I thought she might squeeze the remaining life right out of me. When she held me out to look at me, her entire face was soaked with crying, and the parts weren't even fighting each other. I guess this was a special occasion, or maybe now we'll all do less faking it.

"I made lasagna," was the first thing she said to me. Then she stood up and held my hand, led me into the house, said she had called Chad and told him I was coming home, that he was at swim practice but was going to show up for dinner. I wondered if he'd bring Alice.

My dad kissed me hello and then looked at me as if he'd either forgotten what I looked like and was studying for a test about it, or had been starved for the sight of me. When he was done, he stood up and went to the car and got my backpack, which he and Sarah carried straight downstairs for quarantine in the laundry room. I sat at the table, and when Sarah reappeared from the basement she sat down across from me, and

I thought how normal it was to be sitting there with Sarah. I turned to look at my mom, who had on green plastic oven gloves and was setting a sizzling pan on top of the stove. I could hear my dad puttering around in the laundry room underneath us. I thought how not normal it was that I'd been gone for so many days, how glad I was that Chad was coming. I folded my arms onto the table and rested my face on them. Then I heard Sam's sneakers squeaking through the foyer, and I looked up, straightened my hair a little as he peeped around the corner into the kitchen. I smiled at him and he walked in, wearing orange cargo pants and a white T-shirt nine sizes too big. His hair was very short, and his face was tiny and pink, his neck white. He looked like a delicate lollipop.

"Hey, Judy," he said, his voice all shy. Unlike my dad, he appeared to me to have gotten younger.

"Hi, Sam," I said.

"Look," he said, and he held his hand out. In it was an embossed medal: "Tappan Middle School Science Fair, Third Prize."

"Great! Congratulations, Sam! That's fabulous." I stood up from my chair, and with our third prize as an excuse, squeezed him as hard as my mom had squeezed me.

As soon as I let him go, he went and got a chair, which he pulled up next to mine, unnaturally close. He sat down and put the medal on the table just as my mom arrived with his plate of lasagna.

"It's for you," Sam said to me, pointing to the medal.

"Really? You don't have to do that. You should keep it."

"I want you to have it."

Then he leaned down and began gobbling lasagna so furiously that Sarah and I looked at each other and laughed. I put the medal around my neck.

After Sarah left, Chad arrived, without Alice, and the four of us sat at the table eating salad and more lasagna and garlic bread while Sam talked about the band, Chad about why he was breaking up with Alice (it was almost summer, they would want to see other people), and my parents caught me up on life at the Grill. Halfway through dinner, Chad was suddenly like, "Do you want to tell us what it was like to be away?"

"It was okay," I said. "I really missed you guys."

We all sat there, looking at each other. My mom appeared to me to be holding her breath. "Do you want us to tell you what happened here, sweetie? And at the hearing?"

I thought about it for a minute, shook my head slowly. "Not yet," I said. "Let's just have dinner, and talk about that stuff later. It's okay." I felt very grown up.

Chad smiled at me, nodded as if he understood. Sam reached across the table and spooned another heaping serving of lasagna onto his plate.

The funny thing about that dinner is that even though we didn't talk about the hearing, or the Motel Manor, or even the horrible thing itself, for one of the first times ever, it genuinely didn't feel like we were faking it. It was like we had decided to take the long, inevitable conversation slowly. To put it on hold for a moment while we sat back at the table together. I was grateful.

After Chad kissed me on the head and went back to his dorm, and Sam disappeared into his room, I went upstairs and lay on my bed, thinking about Meghan, looking forward to the conversation I knew we'd have when I called to tell her I was okay, fill her in on the Motel Manor adventure. My mom and dad followed me less than one minute later and sat down on the bed on either side of me. I sat up.

"Thank you for letting me stay there," I said.

"It wasn't up to us. You were very brave," my mom said, deflecting. She looked over at my dad, cueing him.

He cleared his throat. "So, Judy, honey, there were some decisions that we had to make for you while you were—clearing your head." I liked this, clearing my head. I wondered if it had been part of what my mom told him to say, or that was just the part about "decisions," and the clearing-my-head thing was his own way of living with my having run away from them.

I nodded, waited for him to continue. He asked, "Do you want to have that talk now, about what happened, before you go back to school?"

I didn't. Not yet. But I knew they did, and didn't want to make them feel bad. "Can we talk about it after I sleep for a while?" I asked. "I mean, maybe tomorrow or something?"

"Of course," they said in unison.

Then my mom handed me a white envelope. "This came today," she said. "I thought you might want it right away. And as for talking about the last two weeks—everything you've been through, and everything that's happened here—just tell us what you want to know and when, and what you want us to know. Let's all just be as direct as we all can from now on."

"Okay," I said. "First I want to read this letter."

She kissed me and then took my dad's hand. "We'll leave you to it." They walked out, closing the door quietly behind them. Later that night, I would press my ear to the vent and listen to them strategize about when to tell me that they were the ones who had pulled the plug on criminal charges. How were they going to explain that I would have been put through a hellish carnival of a trial, made public, ruined? Whether to tell me that they had, in their hearts, wanted positive endings for all of us, that ruining anyone's life, even the boys', wasn't their goal. They decided to wait until I asked.

But before I even pressed my ear to the vent or heard anything, I read his letter. It was on computer paper, typed. Even in the first moment of ripping that thing open, I wished it were a yellow legal page, anything homemade, with his handwriting on it, a card or something. But there it was, printed:

*Dear Judy, This is not the first time I wanted to go back in time and take back something bad that happened. But there's no way to undo the things that happen. There is also no way for this letter to change things. But I want to apologize to you formally. I am very sorry for what happened, more sorry than I can say in a letter like this. Maybe someday I can try to explain how I could have been part of what happened. I hope I can. I hope you know I cared about you, and I'm sorry for what happened. Yours truly, Kyle.*

Only his name was handwritten, like he was an executive signing a letter his assistant had typed or something. Yours truly? I held the signature up to my face and breathed in, but it smelled like nothing, not even paper or ink. Cared about you, past tense. I folded it back into the envelope and put it in my desk drawer with the lock, where I also had my copy of the DVD.

That's when I went to the vent to listen to my parents strategize. They were so relieved to see me intact and have me home that I'm too embarrassed even to record the maudlin things they said to each other about their love for me. But I was glad to hear all of it, even the long, predictable session about what I could handle knowing and when to tell me everything. Just the feeling of my ear against the floor was so familiar I could have sung and danced for joy.

Instead, I took a long shower, brushed my teeth, put my moon-and-stars pajamas on, and slept for eleven hours in my own bed—without having a single dream.

When I walked in, the place felt different. Maybe because I'd been gone, or didn't remember accurately what it had been like before I left. My parents had wanted to drive me, to come in with me, to take me straight to the office for what I was certain would be an unbearable debriefing with the "administration," one they insisted we would need to have. I told them I wanted to go alone the first time. So the morning after I got home, my dad showed me the raised pedals in the car and sent me to school on my own. It was the first time I had ever parked in the D'Arts parking lot myself.

Inside, a rush of cool air greeted me, and then the smells, both familiar and strange, normal and yet so specific to D'Arts that they seemed rare: Lysol, cafeteria food, chlorine, sawdust from the tech room behind the theater, scent of wood sets being built, paint, sloppy joes, books, other kids, shampoo, lotion, toothpaste, sweat. I thought of Kyle for a minute, his hair and the warm smell of his skin. I walked by the first-floor teachers' lounge; someone had burned microwave popcorn in there, maybe yesterday. I saw Mr. Luther sitting on a couch, grade book in his lap. I kept walking. All the murals were in place: zebras, Greek goddesses, tigers, teenagers.

I climbed the stairs to the second floor and walked to my locker, enduring the heads that turned as I went. My locker was just as I had left it: woven strands of lanyard still twisted and colorful, glass beads in place. It wasn't like one of those movies where a kid gets cancer and when she comes back to school, everyone has shaved their head in solidarity. I mean, no one had put Mylar balloons on my locker or welcome signs or anything. And since I didn't know yet who those other videos were of, I didn't have any specific company for that misery, except Ginger, and that hardly made me feel less lonely.

When I opened my locker, it had the same library book and metal smells, the same pictures of me and Goth Sarah and Molly in our Halloween costumes, one of Sam dancing in our living room, and another of Chad and Alice and me and Sam from the night of the senior voice concert.

I looked down and saw that someone had stuffed some notes in the vertical crack of the locker. I picked up the first one and unfolded it.

*Judy L! You are our favorite hot freak. Stand up, smile at whoever's looking at you, and we'll see you in American lit. If your day totally sucks, we'll skip the afternoon together. Meantime, tell anyone who fucks with you to fuck off or Molly (almost BROWN belt! Yah!) will kick their ass. xoxox, S&M (get it?).*

The second one was a piece of folded notebook paper, which I unfolded and smoothed out. It was my own handwriting, said: "I'm deaf; can't hear you bitches." Underneath that, Sarah had drawn a picture of me, doing fake sign language with one hand and flipping off her and Molly (stick figures) with the other. I was little, with huge hands, especially the one with its middle finger up. She had colored the picture in with crayon, including a brown belt around Molly's stick waist. I laughed, in spite of myself.

Last was a shiny pink envelope with my name on it. I opened it carefully, found a glittery card with hot pink and silver flowers on it. I opened it up:

*Dearest Judy, I have been thinking about you since I heard the news about what happened at school. I am so sorry, and am sending healing energy every day. Love, Mimi Mews (Ginger's mom).*

I could feel eyes prickling across my back, people I knew and didn't know slowing as they walked by. I also heard the regular shuffle of shoes and chattering, giggling, shouting, making out, singing, dancing sounds of another morning at D'Arts. It wasn't all about me, I reminded myself. I wondered what Mimi Mews had thought of Ginger coming forward about the video of herself and Kyle, whether she thought her daughter was a hero. Maybe she was horrified or angry. I doubted it, given the note to me. Maybe she wanted to be friends with my parents now, so they could console each other about their little girls becoming unwitting porn actresses. I hung my jacket, folded Molly and Sarah's note up and put it in the pocket of my jeans. Ginger's mom's note I put in my backpack and left in my locker. I slowly collected my books and turned to walk purposefully down the hall. Elizabeth

Wood and Stockard Blumenthal were coming toward me. I sucked in as much air as I could right as they went by.

"Hey, Judy, welcome back," Stockard said. I didn't hear any sarcasm in it.

"Thanks," I said.

"Yeah, welcome back," said Elizabeth, and then they were on their way, in a conversation about whatever was actually present tense: breaking up, rehearsal, something I knew nothing about. I mean, the thing is, even if you're naked on a video one moment at school, sleeping with three boys, by the next moment everyone is back to thinking and talking about themselves. Sarah wakes up underwater every day about Eliot and the foreign exchange student. And Stockard just broke up with Greg. I bet in her view that's almost as painful as what happened to me. And in a way, she's right. Because suffering isn't always relative. And now she has to have laser surgery to have her OATS tattoo removed, which will probably really hurt. I keep thinking of the weird way Bill said, "That's a good story," like now that it's over, that's all it is.

I walked down the hall, turning to look when I passed Kyle's and Chris's and Alan's lockers. They had been ripped bare, probably by the custodian, Mr. Nicks, but I imagined instead a mob of my loyal friends shredding the stupid movie posters and reel-to-reel tapes that had been on Kyle's, the Lakers crap on Alan's. I didn't remember what had been on Chris's, but now they were all utterly undecorated. I gave myself a minute to dream of the movie version: all my supporters, getting rid of every scrap of evidence that those guys had ever even been at D'Arts. In the movie, there would be no digital copies, no viral version online, just DVDs my friends would be throwing onto a giant bonfire in the backyard of the school, out by the track. They would incinerate every last copy of that wretched thing until it might as well never have existed. We'd all be in it together. I would walk into that scene, head held high, and fling my copy, the final one, onto the flames. Then everyone would cheer and carry me out on their shoulders.

I realized suddenly that I had been standing at Kyle's locker an uncomfortably long time, and that I didn't want anyone to see me there, so I pretended to be preoccupied with my right boot. I bent and fussed with the buckle while secretly looking up at that blank metal door one final time. It makes sense that stripping your locker is the way D'Arts would expel you: erase. In a way, it's the opposite of what happened to me, but also creepy and terrible. I stood up, and Mrs. O'Henry, the counselor, was standing there, her arms hanging at her sides like they hurt, or were really heavy.

"Hi, Judy," she said. I stood up quickly, straightened my sweater.

"Hi, Mrs. O'Henry."

"Your parents called to say you'd be back today. I'm so glad to see you."

I thought I should say thank you, but couldn't. Why had I thought that driving myself to school without my parents would help me prevent this encounter? Somehow I'd assumed that if they weren't with me, I could have a day of people my own age, and not also have to contend with the adult world. One at a time seemed punishment enough.

Mrs. O'Henry said softly, "Can you join me in my office for a talk? Of course, I'll write you a pass if you're in danger of being late to class."

The thought of a hall pass or late pass or any kind of pass had always struck me as ludicrous and patronizing, but now it seemed absolutely comical. I wanted to ask Mrs. O'Henry if she would write me a pass for having been video-taped naked with three guys, and oh, while she was at it, could I have one for running away to a filthy motel and missing two weeks of school? I smiled politely.

"Of course," I said, and followed her down the hallway. She seemed uncomfortably aware that I was behind her, and kept slowing down, parting the hallway crowds, insisting that we walk side by side. I was worried she would take

411

my hand. She was wearing an enormous gray skirt, a white button-down shirt, and a cardigan with pink, black, and yellow flowers on it. She smelled nice, and it occurred to me that she was probably somebody's grandmother. When we got to the main office, I couldn't look up, lest I make eye contact with any teacher who happened to be standing at the mailboxes, or worse, with Mr. Grames, who had probably done nothing but watch the video and field calls from reporters for what must have felt now like his entire tenure at the school. Even the secretaries seemed to be staring. Maybe they had been at the hearing.

Mrs. O'Henry put her hand on my shoulder for a moment to lead me into her small office. She closed the door behind us and gestured for me to sit in a chair facing her desk. I hoisted myself up and looked at her.

"Judy," she said, and I could see that there were pictures of kids all over her desk, and a grown-up who looked a lot like Mrs. O'Henry, and was probably her daughter. There was no guy in any of the pictures, so I thought maybe she didn't have a son. Maybe her daughter was divorced. I looked at Mrs. O'Henry's hand; she wore no wedding ring. Maybe all the women in her family got divorces.

"Let me first say how sorry I am about what happened. This is the sort of occurrence that we, as an institution, never like to see happen at our school. And it is the responsibility of every member of the administration, faculty, and student body, to make sure that nothing of the sort happens again." She paused, maybe realizing how stilted and bizarre she sounded, and slid her half-glasses off of her nose, rubbed her eyes for a minute. "Judy, you're such a bright and promising student, and we're delighted to have you here. We hope you'll finish your education with us, and that you will feel that Darcy is doing everything in our power to make things right."

I tried to nod in a way that looked grateful.

"First of all, do you have any questions? Is there anything you'd like to ask or tell me now? About anything at all."

I shook my head no.

"Well, feel free to interrupt at any time."

We both waited.

"You may know already that there was a hearing held to determine accountability and suitable disciplinary action against Christopher Arpent, Kyle A. Malanack, and Alan Sarft, and that the school has expelled all three young men."

I wondered if it was because her job required her to do a lot of paperwork that she listed them like that, in alphabetical order. She kept talking like a recorded court document.

"You may also know already that there was a thorough investigation into what happened."

I said, "Oh," and looked at her questioningly.

She smiled comfortingly. "In a case like this one, where what happened didn't happen at school—and because force and consent are always murky areas—we, and especially your parents, were unequivocal in our desire to protect you from . . . any further suffering." She gathered herself, sighed. "Everyone, even the prosecutors, frankly, agreed that a trial would be unlikely to lead to a punishment more severe than the school itself was able to dole out—and would benefit no one, least of all you, Judy. Because as unfair as it is, you would have been on trial too. And your parents urged strongly that this be dealt with as privately as possible, by the school community. In fact, they were quite forceful."

I had an image of my dad shoving cops and reporters down onto the lunchroom floor and stepping on their heads.

Mrs. O'Henry had put her glasses back on and been peering down through them, but now she took them off again. A nervous habit, I guessed. Her eyes looked suspiciously red. "I have a daughter," she said, and I glanced helplessly over at the photo of the grown-up on her desk. "I hope it isn't presumptuous for me to say how brave and loving I think your parents have been."

"What about the video?" I asked, partly out of curiosity and partly because I realized suddenly that I could ask Mrs. O'Henry certain questions with an impunity I didn't think I'd ever have around my parents. "I mean, wasn't that—I don't know, was it a—" I couldn't muster whatever was required to articulate the word *crime*.

"Honestly, Judy, two years ago, the state might have leveled pornography charges against the boys for making that video. But these days, this kind of thing is deemed an 'educational issue,' and schools have to assess each case on an individual basis."

"Why?"

"Mainly because of sexting," she said, sighing, and then we both sat there, grossed out that she even knew that word. She waited to see if I would ask why just because these days lots of teenagers send naked pictures of themselves and their friends over cell phones means that making that video wasn't criminal. But I put a blank face on and out-waited her, so she continued. "We did feel it was essential in this case to notify the colleges the young men were planning to attend, of their behavior and expulsion. We have also required that Christopher, Kyle, and Alan issue formal apologies."

At this, I thought I might drown. I forced my mouth open, felt the water rush in against my words: "To me, you mean?"

"Yes, dear. Each will write a—" Kyle's letter had been part of his punishment. Part of his punishment. I thought of this clause several times, imagined saying it into a microphone, popping each *p*. Maybe he had meant some of it. Maybe he was sorry, and glad they'd asked him to write, because it allowed him to say he had cared about me.

Mrs. O'Henry was talking, but I had tuned out entirely until there was a knock on the door. I jolted up in my chair, turned to see Mr. Grames standing there, sweating.

"Good morning, Caroline," Mr. Grames said to Mrs. O'Henry. "Good morning, Judy." He paused, perhaps wanting to acknowledge that "good morning" didn't suffice since I'd been missing for weeks, but unable to think of what else to say.

"Hi, Mr. Grames."

He said, "Well, Judy, I'm so pleased to see that you've returned to school." He seemed to mean it, even cleared his throat once while he was talking. Then we all sat there, dying. I started chewing on my bottom lip like it was a piece of gum. I wished desperately that I had put some in my mouth before this horrific meeting happened.

Mr. Grames, seeing that no one was going to come to his rescue, continued: "I hope you will feel free to ask me any questions you need to in the coming weeks, and that Mrs. O'Henry has helped you understand our response to the events of recent weeks, as well as the options Darcy Arts Academy will continue to make available to you."

"Yes, thank you, Mr. Grames." I was thinking, two more letters on the way. Two more fake letters. What would they say? "Dear Judy, Sorry! From, Alan. P.S. See you at Fuller Pool in our bathing suits this summer"? Maybe Chris would write his as yet another dazzling scene in his screenplay: "Chris: *Sorry, Judy.* Judy: *No prob, Chris, thanks for the great letter!* Blackout."

It was typical that Kyle had already written his and those two other deadbeats couldn't even get their letters done on time—he was always a better student. I was glad for the letters, in a way, though. I mean, at least I would have it in writing that they'd been wrong, and now if I ever wanted to, I could write back. Or call. And say whatever I decide I want to: Fuck you. Or: I forgive you. Or: I'll never forgive you. Or I could not reply for the rest of my life. Because if someone writes to you, even if D'Arts makes them do it, then never responding is a meaningful gesture. It will be up to me forever now whether to give them any relief or forgiveness. Any words.

Mr. Grames was nodding at Mrs. O'Henry and me. He turned to leave, unable, even from behind, to hide his relief at escaping. Mrs. O'Henry and I looked at each other in a moment of odd intimacy at having been interrupted and then left alone again.

She started up. "We would like, if it's agreeable to you, Judy, to have you evaluated. And we will offer as much counseling as you feel you would benefit from, either at school or with a professional of your and your family's choosing. But it's our hope that you will take us up—at least once a week. And if you'd like, you can meet with me once a week as well."

Maybe I looked like I might faint, because she added, "You don't have to decide anything now. You may take your time and come back to me whenever it suits you."

"Evaluated for what?" I asked.

Now Mrs. O'Henry looked at me evenly. "What you've been through would be—well, difficult for anyone, Judy. Darcy—and I—care first and foremost about our students' health and well-being. And we want school to continue to go well for you. All of your teachers are ready to have you back, and prepared to discuss strategies for how you'll make up any work you missed."

Had they had a meeting to talk about me? My life snaked out hideously on the horizon, an endless series of weekly meetings with shrinks and Mrs. O'Henry, forced forever to talk about what had happened, when my plan was to forget about it or file it in the folder in my mind marked, "Consider when you're thirty and can potentially tolerate."

Mrs. O'Henry seemed to be waiting for something, so I said, "Thank you."

"Do you have any questions for us?"

I tried to pause long enough to appear to be thinking it over. "Not right now."

Mrs. O'Henry put her glasses back on. "Are you okay going to class this morning?"

"Yes," I said.

"What do you have next?" she asked. We both looked up at the clock. It was too late to walk into precalc.

"American lit," I said.

"Oh, good," said Mrs. O'Henry. I smiled, thinking, "Oh, good," too. She stood up and I practically leapt to my feet. She kept talking as she came out from behind her desk to open the door for me. "I will check in again tomorrow; perhaps we can schedule your evaluation session for this Friday and your first counseling session for the following Monday? And maybe a sit-down with me to check in either next Wednesday or Friday. In the meantime, please come by my office anytime, even if we have no meeting scheduled. My door is always open."

"Okay, thanks," I said. I was thinking—if Chris and Alan were about to write me letters, then that meant they were alive. This felt oddly surprising. If they were alive, then they would work it out, maybe spend a year sorry, and then be okay, go to college, have lives. We'd all grow up, and this would have happened, but someday it wouldn't even be recent—for any of us, including me. Maybe they'd even have daughters some day and—

"Judy," I could hear Mrs. O'Henry saying as I turned to go, "I hope you'll let us help."

I nodded without looking back, walked out of the office with my eyes pinned to the floor. The hallway felt full of oxygen, and I was breathing thirstily when I looked up and saw that Ginger was standing outside the door, waiting, against the giant rainbow zebra mural. I looked up at her. Her eyes were watering, and she made no move to wipe them. A tear actually dropped on the floor. I imagined it splashing, as if our lives were happening in a slow motion close-up.

"I heard you were—so I—" She was wearing a gray zip-up sweatshirt with a picture of a bridge on it, and black running tights that had a pink band around the waist. Her hair was a mess. Dozens of people were walking by in a colorful blur, but I couldn't make out any of them individually. I was watching Ginger cry, her shoulders folded inward like origami. I wanted to put my arm around her or something, but I couldn't quite bring myself to. "Are you okay?" I asked.

"I'm fine," she said. "I'm glad you're—" she took a breath and put her hands out, palms flat down, as if to steady herself, or maybe break a fall. "I should be asking you—are you okay?"

"I'm fine," I said, emboldened by how not-fine she seemed. Someone had to pull it together; maybe it would be me. "Hey, Ginger, so thank you for, uh, for—" I didn't know where I was going with this. For fucking Kyle too? For getting humiliated a little bit less than I did but still badly enough to have diluted my humiliation? For letting everyone see whatever degrading video there was of you, too? For defending me?

I settled on "Sarah told me."

Ginger nodded and put one of her raggedy, bitten hands on my arm. She had stopped crying. "So, hey, do you and Sarah want to, you know?" she made a little smoking gesture with her index finger and thumb.

I smiled, hoping someday we'd talk about what happened, thinking she had probably loved Kyle too. I could certainly forgive her that. Maybe Ginger and I would keep each other company, long after it no longer felt so incredibly terrible to have loved him.

"We could do it at your house again," she suggested, still holding the imaginary joint, and I thought wow, had she liked coming to my house, eating the dinner my mom made us, watching Sam do his ridiculous dance on the rug? Maybe she wanted to share my family.

I was about to say that would be great when a pack of girls crossed the hall between Ginger and me, and the shape of Rachael Collins emerged from among them. "Judy!" she said, turning and peeling off the circle. Everyone else gave me lingering, interested glances, but kept walking. Except Jessica Lambkin, who hung back with Rachael. I thought immediately of everyone saying Jessica Lambkin had made out with her dad. I wondered how long it had taken her to feel like people weren't thinking of it anymore, and tried to put it out of my mind, so I could be one of the people who didn't imagine it every time I saw her.

"Well, I have to—see you soon, Judy," said Ginger, wandering off.

"Hey, Rachael. Hi, Jessica," I said, even though Jessica Lambkin and I had never talked, and I worried that even saying her name would be evidence that I was thinking about the story of her and her dad, keeping the lie alive. Of course, she could have used my name with impunity even though we'd never talked, just because I'm famous in this school. I mean, everyone, even in the impossible event that they haven't seen the video, knows who I am anyway. Everyone's always known who I am. I guess I'll never have the benefits or drawbacks of being invisible.

"Hey," said Jessica.

"How's Cletus?" I asked Rachael. Jessica looked confused.

"He's good," Rachael said, smiling. "Our fetal cat," she said to Jessica, who nodded vaguely. "More important, how are you?" Rachael asked.

"I'm good, actually," I said, feeling for the moment like it might be true. "Thanks. Hey—listen, I'm really sorry about leaving you in the lur—"

She cut me off. "I totally understand, of course. I saved all my notes. Do you wanna hang out sometime and go over them so you're ready for the AP?"

"That would be great," I said.

"Anytime," she said. "Just text me when you're free."

"I will," I said, and we stood there for an extra second, smiling at each other, maybe because we both knew that I would text her. Or maybe we hoped for even more—that we would end up super close and stay friends for the rest of our lives after we both aced the AP and placed out of college freshman biology. It all seemed possible. I mean, I had been back at school for only half an hour and had already secured a lifetime of free, incredibly awkward counseling with Mrs. O'Henry, a pot date with Ginger, and a nerd date with Rachael. Maybe life would be fabulous from now on.

Upstairs, I peered into Ms. Doman's room. She was sitting at her desk, writing something: grades, maybe, or an idea she wanted to save for later. I had the fully articulated thought "Please let me be like her. I don't even have to be a singer. I can be something quiet, a writer, a teacher, Ms. Doman. Please. Just let me recover from this enough so that someday I can be the one waiting calmly while a girl like me stands in the doorway." But when Ms. Doman looked up and saw me standing there, she didn't seem at all calm. She almost knocked her chair over, getting up and rushing over to me. Then she crouched down in the doorway and did a whole full crazy tall-person-hugging-dwarf hug. She smelled like spring.

When she let go, I thought I heard her sniffle, so I moved away from her and set my books down—on the first desk in the first row.

She noticed this. "Judy," she said. "I'm so—I can't—"

She had never dropped a sentence partway through. I rescued her.

"I have a draft of my college essay," I said. "Would you mind reading it and telling me what you think?"

"Nothing would please me more," she said. "Is it the one about the Hottentot Venus?"

"No, it's a new one, actually," I told her. "About a guy."

Anxiety flashed across her face, naked and painful, and I was excited for the moment when her expression would go back to beautiful and happy, relieved.

I said, "Not that guy. Just a new friend of mine, someone I met called Bill."

She waited, so I added, "When I was out on my own." Ms. Doman was about to say something, but the door opened and Molly came into the classroom. Ms. Doman moved back toward the blackboard.

"Hi," Molly said to her. She bounded the two steps it took to get to where I was sitting, and flung her arms around me before sitting down in the desk next to mine. "Thank god you're back!" she said, smiling with her whole self. "Did you get our note?"

I nodded. "Nice work on the brown belt."

"Thanks!" She lowered her voice, leaned in, "So, you want to skip after this class? I have a new poem I want to show you."

"Yes," I said, nodding vigorously because I wanted to acknowledge the rule-breaking sacrifice she was offering to make. Even though the poem was probably the weirdest thing I'd ever read, I also knew that Molly had never cut class in her entire life. I suddenly desperately wanted to sit outside with her and Goth Sarah, too. Where was Sarah? Other people had begun trickling in, looking over, going silent, turning to each other to confirm it—oh my god, she's back, she came back—then looking again, staring, more and more people, until it felt like the entire class, except Kyle Malanack, quiet, looking, pulsing with my return while Molly and Ms. Doman pretended not to notice. Everyone was noticing or pretending not to notice. Again, I guess.

I looked up from the desk, my face on fire, and saw Goth Sarah standing in the doorway. She took in the fact of me in the front row, then tossed her backpack onto the desk next to mine. She kept standing, though, staring at the gawkers as if she might lunge and attack them. But instead she said, crazy loud in their honor: "Oh my god—Judy Lohden?! Can we like, have your autograph!?"

Half the class looked away fast, caught. There was a scramble to unpack bags, open books, look cool. The other half kept watching, maybe to see what I would do. Would I admit what had happened? Would we all mention it? Would I cry and shatter in front of them? Or pull some wicked hurt-girl magic like in *Carrie* and burn the place down with my furious eyes?

I tilted my jaw toward the ceiling. Maybe everyone would talk later about how proud I'd been, how I'd kept my chin up. And it would be true. Because then I turned from the front row to look right back at that class like a laser. And I grinned. And there it was. You all want to watch me? Take a good long look—I'm right here, beaming: Judy Lohden, Thumbelina, blue dwarf star.

# Acknowledgments

Jill Grinberg, thank you for being a magnificent agent and friend. I can't tell you how much I appreciate your superhuman commitment and your mind. Courtney Hodell, thank you for believing so fiercely in this book from the beginning, and for adding your absolute brilliance at every stage. Robert Pinsky, thank you for being and staying my teacher and mentor, for unfailing encouragement, and for your incredible work.

Researching this, I read dozens of books that were helpful and inspiring. Top among them were Dan Kennedy's profoundly empathetic *Little People: Learning to See the World Through My Daughter's Eyes* and Betty Adelson's triumphant *The Lives of Dwarfs*. Thank you to LPA members Barbara Spiegel and Dan, Barbara, and Becky Kennedy for welcoming me into your community and families, and for being so generous with your time and anecdotes.

Thank you to everyone who commented on drafts: Martha Davis-Merritts, for your trust, stories, and sharp eyes; Cheryl Pientka for your enthusiasm and brainpower; Mark Krotov, for fabulous notes and being on top of everything all the time; Greg Lalas, for the hours at Think, and for freely writing "ugh" so often in my margins; Christine Jones, for so many notes and truths—you are the opposite of loneliness; Lara Phillips, Donna Eis, and Julia Hollinger, for loving me when I was a teenager, showing me *Stranger Than Paradise*, even though I didn't deserve it, and continuing to read; Molly Metzler and Danielle Slavick for your feminista feedback; Tamar Kotz for the truth through the vents; Logan and Stef LaVail, Chesa Boudin, and Malik Dohrn for reading a river-soaked copy; and Thai Jones for the final mile. Thank you to the recent graduates who helped me think about adolescence and voice: Ingrid Bengtsson, Emily Brown, Mollie Ruth, and Kayla Stoler. And thank you, Community High School dean Jen Hein, for the amazingly helpful letter about discipline and nuance.

Thank you to Kathy, for so many talks on this and on the lives of girls; to Harriet Beinfield, for building our nest; to Naomi and Saul Silvermintz, for being such gorgeous role models; to Martina Proctor, for your real-life example of courage and beauty; and to Peggy Sradnick, for a lifetime's worth of parenting guidance.

Thank you, Bill Ayers and Bernardine Dohrn, for your unique genius on love, law, teenagers, and dignity; for reading, parsing, helping with everything all the time; for your supremely generous engagement in the world and in our lives.

And to the real Judith, my mom, and my heroic dad, Ken: for reading this too many times to mention; for utterly unconditional applause and love; for anchoring me to the universe; for all the inspiring, traveling, talking, interrupting, cooking, eating, analyzing, editing, and disco dancing. Mom, Dad, Jake, Aaron, and Melissa, thank you! For your names, stories, lives, and selves—appropriated and rearranged.

Dalin Alexi and Light Ayli: you are the sun we orbit, and I'm delirious with gratitude for your sweet, bossy, inimitable selves. Thank you for showing me *The Wizard of Oz* two thousand times, as well as the fresh truth about everything every day, including bravery and resilience. This "story with a scary part" is for you two.

Zayd, thank you for agreeing to forever when it meant me *and* my manuscripts. And for being unwavering, brilliant, and loving in your readings of both. Thank you for our endless conversation, world, and girls. You are my best and favorite half, co-everything, lucky star.

# A Note About the Author

Rachel DeWoskin is the author of *Foreign Babes in Beijing*, a memoir about her inadvertent notoriety as the star of a Chinese soap opera, and a novel, *Repeat After Me*. She lives in New York City and Beijing and is at work on her fourth book.

**Center Point Publishing**
600 Brooks Road ● PO Box 1
Thorndike ME 04986-0001 USA

**(207) 568-3717**

**US & Canada:**
**1 800 929-9108**
www.centerpointlargeprint.com

SOUTH COUNTRY LIBRARY

3 0614 00239 2134

JUL 2 8 2011